APRIL FOOLS

APRIL FOOLS

An Insider's Account of the Rise and Collapse of
Drexel Burnham

DAN G. STONE

DONALD I. FINE, INC.
NEW YORK

Library of Congress Cataloging-in-Publication Data

Stone, Dan G.
April fools : an insider's account of the rise and collapse of
Drexel Burnham/by Dan G. Stone.
p.   cm.
Includes index.
ISBN 1-55611-228-9
1. Drexel Burnham Lambert Incorporated. 2. Stockbrokers—New York
(N.Y.) 3. Securities fraud—New York (N.Y.) 4. Drexel Burnham Lambert
Incorporated—Employees—Dismissal of. I. Title.
HG4928.5.S76 1990
332.63′2′0973—dc20   90-55339
                                                CIP

Manufactured in the United States of America

Designed by Irving Perkins Associates

ACKNOWLEDGMENTS

My sincere thanks to two great editors, David Gibbons and Don Fine, and to those who were willing to talk about an unhappy subject.

I would also like to acknowledge the wealth of information provided by *The Predators' Ball* by Connie Bruck, *Takeover* by Moira Johnston, *The Wall Street Journal, The New York Times, The Washington Post, New York Magazine,* and *Fortune,* among others.

Finally, I would like to acknowledge the efforts of the thousands of employees who made Drexel Burnham a firm to remember with pride.

*To Drs. Emilita and Thomas Stone
who always offered the best advice
and never sent a bill.*

CONTENTS

CHAPTER ONE   April Fools   1

CHAPTER TWO   On the Street   10

CHAPTER THREE   The World According to Mike   21

CHAPTER FOUR   The New Way   34

CHAPTER FIVE   The Hardest-Working People in America   44

CHAPTER SIX   The Dark Side of the Force   53

CHAPTER SEVEN   Meanwhile, Back at the Stock Exchange . . .   69

CHAPTER EIGHT   The City on the Edge of Forever   88

CHAPTER NINE   The Missiles of October   102

CHAPTER TEN   State of Siege   116

CHAPTER ELEVEN   Mother of Mercy   136

CHAPTER TWELVE   Has the Jury Reached its Verdict?   158

CHAPTER THIRTEEN   The Last Mile   181

CHAPTER FOURTEEN   Fortune and Men's Eyes   208

INDEX   241

DBL GROUP—1989
(HOLDING COMPANY)

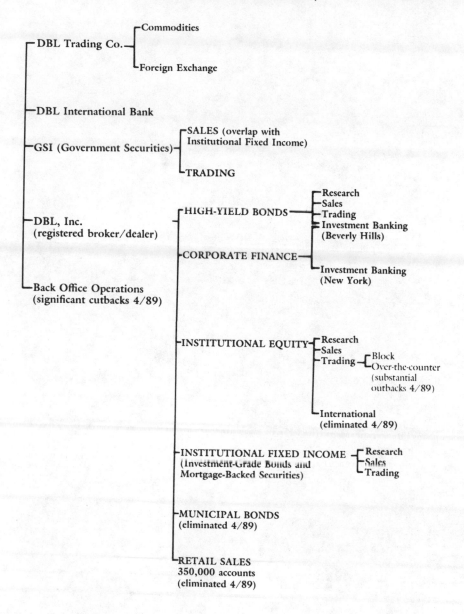

DBL Trading Co.
- Commodities
- Foreign Exchange

DBL International Bank

GSI (Government Securities)
- SALES (overlap with Institutional Fixed Income)
- TRADING

DBL, Inc.
(registered broker/dealer)

HIGH-YIELD BONDS
- Research
- Sales
- Trading
- Investment Banking (Beverly Hills)

CORPORATE FINANCE
- Investment Banking (New York)

Back Office Operations
(significant cutbacks 4/89)

INSTITUTIONAL EQUITY
- Research
- Sales
- Trading
  - Block
  - Over-the-counter (substantial outbacks 4/89)
- International (eliminated 4/89)

INSTITUTIONAL FIXED INCOME
(Investment-Grade Bonds and Mortgage-Backed Securities)
- Research
- Sales
- Trading

MUNICIPAL BONDS
(eliminated 4/89)

RETAIL SALES
350,000 accounts
(eliminated 4/89)

CHRONOLOGY
OF EVENTS

1935
Burnham & Co. is founded by I. W. Burnham.

1970
Michael Milken, a twenty-three-year-old student at the Wharton business school, joins Drexel Firestone, a Philadelphia-based investment banking firm.

1973
Drexel Firestone is acquired; the new company is called Drexel Burnham.

1974
Fred Joseph is hired as a corporate finance officer; a decade later, he will become the chief executive officer of the firm.

1976
Drexel Burnham acquires William D. Witter, which is connected to the Brussels-based Groupe Bruxelles Lambert, the official name of the firm becomes Drexel Burnham Lambert Inc.

1977
Lehman Brothers raises money for three companies through the sale of high-yield bonds; Drexel Burnham will soon dominate the market for original-issue junk bonds, selling $100 billion worth of these bonds by 1990.

1978
Michael Milken moves Drexel's junk-bond operation to Beverly Hills.

1981
Conoco is purchased by du Pont, the first of the mega–acquisitions of the 1980s.

1982
Boone Pickens's Mesa Petroleum attempts a *hostile* takeover of Cities Service, an oil company twenty times its size; Occidental Petroleum steps in as a white knight.

1983
The leveraged buyout of Gibson Greetings provides its new owners, including former Secretary of State William Simon, a 20,000 percent profit in eighteen months; with the help of junk bonds and kind markets, LBOs will become the success story of the decade.

1984
Mesa Petroleum, backed by Drexel, attempts a takeover bid of Gulf Oil; Chevron purchases Gulf for $13.3 billion.

Saul Steinberg's Reliance Group makes a hostile bid for Disney, backed by a $700 million commitment from Drexel's clients; Steinberg accepts greenmail from Disney.

Carl Icahn makes a hostile bid for Phillips Petroleum; Drexel introduces the "highly confident" letter.

1985
April 1; Drexel Burnham celebrates its fiftieth anniversary.
November 1; Delaware Supreme Court rules in favor of Ron Perelman's $1.8 billion hostile takeover of Revlon, financed with $1.1 billion in junk bonds.

1986
April 20; Drexel raises $2.5 billion through high-yield debt for Kohlberg Kravis's $6.2 billion acquisition of Beatrice, the largest leveraged buyout to date.
May 12; Dennis Levine is arrested on insider trading charges.
November 14; Ivan Boesky pleads guilty to one felony count and pays a $100 million fine; within a week, Drexel Burnham is reported to be under "formal order of investigation" by the Securities and Exchange Commission and criminal investigation by the U.S. Attorney's Office; the focus is on Michael Milken and his high-yield bond operation.

December 31; The firm earns $525 million for the year, the highest profits of any Wall Street firm before or since.

1987
February 12; Three arbitrageurs—Robert Freeman of Goldman Sachs, Richard Wigton of Kidder Peabody, and Timothy Tabor of Merrill Lynch—are arrested on insider trading charges, implicated by investment banker Martin Siegel.

February 19; Staley Continental sues Drexel for alleged extortion and manipulation by one of its salesmen; the case is eventually settled out of court.

1988
April 28; Fred Joseph testifies before the House Oversight and Investigations Subcommittee regarding Drexel's employee partnerships.

September 7; The Securities and Exchange Commission files a civil suit against Drexel Burnham, Michael Milken, and four other employees.

December 21; Drexel Burnham, under threat of a RICO indictment, agrees to plead guilty to six felonies and pay $650 million.

1989
March 29; Michael Milken is indicted on ninety-eight counts of securities fraud.

April 13; Drexel settles its civil case with the Securities and Exchange Commission.

April 18; Fred Joseph announces a restructuring that involves the loss of four thousand jobs, Drexel's staff being trimmed from 9,400 to 5,400.

May 12; The firm raises the $5 billion junk-bond portion of the $26.2 billion takeover of RJR Nabisco, the largest leveraged buyout in history.

August 5; Congress passes the savings and loan bailout bill, requiring thrifts to sell all junk bonds within five years.

December 31; The firm loses $40 million for 1989, its first operating loss.

1990
February 13; Drexel Burnham files for bankruptcy.

APRIL FOOLS

CHAPTER ONE

APRIL FOOLS

I couldn't be fonder of you if
you were my own son, but . . .
            —*The Maltese Falcon*

The rumor spread across the trading floor in minutes, and like most negative rumors, it was true. Drexel Burnham, my firm for almost eight years, was about to announce massive layoffs for the first time in more than fifty years—four thousand people would be out of a job. It was April 18, 1989, less than one week after we had finally settled the most extensive and expensive securities fraud investigation in the history of Wall Street.

Fred Joseph, the chairman and chief executive officer of Drexel, came over the "hoot-and-holler" phone system that connected all of the firm's branches together. For two and a half years, Fred, still fighting trim at fifty-two, had done an admirable job of holding up morale—and, in many ways it seemed, of holding together the firm.

When one of Wall Street's most visible figures, Ivan Boesky, was arrested in late 1986 and, in turn, pointed his finger our way, Fred had become the spokesman and chief negotiator for ten thousand employees. Now the negotiations were over, and Fred was here to tell us that, in effect, he was becoming the spokesman for less than six thousand employees. Which, of course, wasn't well received by those who were being fired.

1

The survivors, he told us, would be high-yield (junk) bonds, corporate finance, institutional equity and fixed income, and risk arbitrage. No surprises there. Drexel's junk-bond department dominated its market, doing as much business as all of its competitors. And it was some of the highest-paying business to be done.

The corporate finance department arranged mergers, acquisitions, and the sale of stocks and bonds for corporations. Companies produced goods and services; corporate finance produced deals. These deals were designed to allow a company to become more effective, or in the case of hostile takeovers, to force it along that path. Whether the investment bankers of corporate finance did more good than harm to the economy is still in dispute; what is clear, however, is that they made a great deal of money, and no firm on Wall Street was about to ditch this department.

Tied in with the corporate finance effort was the institutional equity department, which was where I worked. (Officially, we were called the Professional Investor Group, giving us the disconcerting acronym of PIG.) We gave advice to the institutions that invested over a trillion dollars in the stock market. These institutions included banks, mutual funds, insurance companies, and investment advisers; their money came from individuals' savings and, more prominently, from their pension funds. In return for our advice, institutions executed their buy-and-sell orders through our trading desk, and Drexel received commissions on each trade. We didn't make much money; in fact, after deducting all the expenses involved, we lost money. Still, we were important to the firm because we were needed to sell the equity deals that our investment bankers put together.

The institutional fixed-income department was in essentially the same position as my department. The people there traded high-quality bonds for their customers, which was a more competitive and, therefore, less profitable business than selling high-yield bonds. But, like institutional equity, they were useful in placing deals.

The risk arbitrage department took positions in the stocks of companies that were in the process of being bought out by other companies. As long as there were plenty of takeovers being announced, there was usually a nice profit to be made by arbitrageurs.

These were the survivors. Fred Joseph moved on to the departments that were facing the abyss: international research, municipal bonds, and retail sales.

The demise of our effort to research foreign stocks was consistent with Wall Street's general retreat from overseas expansion, a concept that had been in vogue only a few years earlier. Too many costs, too little expertise.

The termination of the municipal bond department was easily understood. In the best of circumstances, it was a highly competitive, low-margin business. But Drexel already had two strikes against it—namely, the felony counts it had agreed to plead guilty to as part of its settlements with the U.S. Attorney's Office and with the Securities and Exchange Commission (SEC). State and local governments don't look kindly on felonies, especially those in which they aren't directly involved. Drexel's chances of getting much business from them were slim to none.

The focus of Fred's comments was on the elimination of the retail system. Eleven hundred salespeople and their entire support staff were out of a job. The mood shifted from grim to ugly. Someone somewhere picked up the phone connecting him with Fred and the rest of the world. "This sucks," he said. And then everyone realized: Their soon-to-be ex-boss was only as far away as that phone in front of them, and they could just reach out and touch him, anonymously.

The professionalism and dignity that had always set the tone in these Drexeline conference calls were gone. In their place was a new bluntness normally reserved for loved ones. If the firm now believed in a brave new world of massive layoffs, then those being pushed out weren't about to leave gracefully.

"Thanks for nothing," said one. "We don't have enough Vaseline," said another. Among the harsh questions, sound effects. It was as if the lions in the circus had looked at the tamer and asked, "Why the hell are we afraid of *him?*

Fred ended the meeting.

The salespeople made the most noise—and they certainly had a right to be angry—but they had less at risk than others. A retail broker is effectively a manager of his own business, relying on the ideas of his firm but selling by force of personality. A retail salesperson can change employers and his clients will follow. Successful salespeople have no trouble finding new jobs because they—actually, their clients—are immediately profitable to their new firm.

The retail salespeople who stayed with Drexel during the twenty-nine-month investigation by and large fell into two camps. Those who were successful would simply move to another firm. Those who were unsuccessful would be in trouble, but until now, many of them had actually benefited from Drexel's ordeal, because the firm was loath to fire anyone while the government was breathing down its neck—bad for morale, bad for its image.

The employees who were really hurt were the back-office personnel, the people who handled the buy-and-sell orders, processed the paperwork, and made sure that everything was done correctly. These unglamorous jobs, which paid the bills for thousands of employees and their families, were already filled at every other firm. New people weren't needed.

Regardless of who you were—back office or line, employed or not—you felt taken advantage of. The firm had always emphasized the importance of its employees; in one advertisement under the heading "10,000 Strong," each employee had been listed by name. Now you had to wonder: How long ago did they decide to fire thousands?

That's not to say that it was the wrong decision at the time. Even though Drexel felt that it had been strong-armed into an unfair settlement with the government, the world would see only that it was an admitted felon. Which would make a retail salesperson's job difficult, at best. The average American, whose view of the business world has been shaped by "Dallas" and "Dynasty," is just not interested in taking investment advice from a firm that he or she considers a den of thieves.

But the question remained: When did management realize that the retail system was marked for extinction? Fred Joseph told us that management had only recently received the recommendations of its strategic consultants, but that answer came across as a lame denial, bordering on evasive. When did management *know*? When did it realize that a retail system reaching every community and a corporate image of paternalism were assets in negotiating with the government, assets that would become liabilities once a settlement was reached?

Fred was not a popular guy that afternoon. If his reputation could be valued like a stock, its price would be in a free-fall, with few buyers and thousands of sellers. His employees were pissed off—most of them felt cheated and many were facing unemployment as well.

But let's be fair. The first responsibility of the managers of a corporation is to maximize the value of the shares that its stockholders own. (In the case of Drexel, a private corporation, most of the shares were owned by employees.) The maximization of shareholders' net worth seems like a cold priority, but it is the basis of our economic system. And to misquote Winston Churchill: "It's the worst system except for all the others."

Assume for a minute that you were the head of Drexel. Your choices were to jettison the retail system while negotiations are under way and risk a public backlash that could wipe out the firm; wait until the settlement is completed before eliminating retail, which would alienate everyone; or keep the retail system (and municipal bonds, for that matter) with the knowledge that it would probably become a significant drain on a firm that was already in financial trouble.

The problem with making this decision was that there were no good options. The best decision was to avoid taking a job in which you have to make a decision such as this.

Perhaps management's choice shouldn't have been such a shock; after all, less than four months earlier, Drexel had agreed to fire Michael Milken—the key figure in the firm's unbelievable success— once he was indicted. But in that decision there was a big fat mitigating circumstance: The government evidently had the weapon, and the willingness, to put us out of business if it didn't get what it wanted. And it wanted Milken out.

The weapon was the Racketeer Influenced Corrupt Organizations (RICO) statute, designed primarily to combat Mafia-controlled businesses. In the hands of Rudolf Giuliani, the politically ambitious U.S. Attorney for the Southern District Court, RICO was held over Drexel's head. The common wisdom, right or wrong, was that an indictment would finish off Drexel long before it ever had its day in court. The firm was in a jam.

At what point was the cost of settling too great, even if it meant the probable liquidation of the firm and the loss of ten thousand jobs? On December 19, 1988, that point had been reached. Two days later, the world turned and a settlement was signed. Drexel agreed to choose six felony counts from a list of allegations that the government had collected.

There was also money involved: $650 million, equal to the earnings of twenty thousand families. As a stockholder in the firm, I took a beating. My share of the settlement with the government amounted to the equivalent of five hundred M-16 rifles with enough firepower to retake Rockefeller Plaza from the Japanese. It seemed like a great deal of money at the time, and it seems like even more now.

As for Mike Milken, he would "remain for the moment." Several months later, he would be indicted by the government and would leave the firm. In addition, his $100 million bonus for 1988 was withheld at the insistence of the prosecutors. He had earned the money and he wasn't accused of any wrongdoing in that year, but still, no dice.

The firing of Milken was treated with mixed emotions on the trading floor. He was the man who had put Drexel in the big leagues, the brilliant workaholic who had sold America on high-yield bonds. He had made his firm the most feared and the most profitable on Wall Street. You had to respect the abilities and the achievements of this guy.

Still, respect didn't mean popularity. Milken and those he had hired weren't exactly the Trapp Family Singers; they fought for every dollar as if it were their first. More important, every accusation against Drexel involved the high-yield bond department. Michael may have been the primary reason for our past successes, but he was also the primary reason for our current troubles.

And then there was the disdain factor. It had come across in a magnificent speech Milken had made to the equity department in October 1986, a time when seemingly nothing could slow him down. In addition to outlining his view of the future, he made some remarks about our lack of effort and intensity, remarks that probably annoyed people more than they would ever admit.

So when Milken was fired, the rest of us could say that the firm had little choice, without feeling too bad. We could say that he had, to some extent, brought it on himself with his take-no-prisoners tactics. We could say that Michael was extraordinary, certainly, but that the firm had exceptional talent, regardless—an argument akin to praising your Lincoln Town Car after the Lamborghini has been recalled.

But when management fired the little people—thousands of them—well, that was different. After all, the government didn't force this decision. And this was close to home. The one-big-family concept at Drexel was history. Whether or not management's decision had merit, few employees now trusted their firm. A new attitude had emerged: No one is going to look after you but you.

By April 1989, I had been with Drexel Burnham for nearly eight years. During that time, Wall Street had changed more rapidly than in any period since the mid-1930s. The unwritten rule that who you knew was perhaps more important than what you knew—that relationships were more important than ideas—had shifted, to the dismay of those with the right connections. Uncivil behavior such as hostile takeovers became fashionable. Wall Street firms took on more and more risk; their profits soared and then collapsed, while their vulnerability to bad times just kept increasing.

Ambitious prosecutors redefined the importance of rules that had sat dormant—and were progressively abused—for fifty years. Parking stock, an infraction that had been treated like parking tickets, became a major felony. Meanwhile, insider trading, a serious crime that deserved serious attention, was never defined in any way that even experts could understand.

The Justice Department unleashed the racketeering laws on the financial community. To many it was a move long overdue, but to others this weapon threatened to negate the most important rule we have: You're innocent until proven guilty. The RICO statute, arguably, is legalized extortion when used to negotiate with financial institutions, which are dependent on public confidence for their survival.

Working on Wall Street in the 1980s provided some unusually good memories and some particularly bad ones. The growth of the junk-bond market, which catapulted Drexel to the top, forced many lousy managers to pay attention to the interests of their stockholders—most of them small investors—or risk losing their coveted positions. My firm, however, also contributed to and benefited from the United States' newfound love affair with debt, as well as with greed.

It was a decade when the stock market tripled, while suffering its worst decline in history along the way; when the average person on the street became more skeptical about most everyone on the Street; and when the financial community created billionaires that ranged in character from a modest midwestern value investor to a New York real estate self-promoter in an age of self-promotion.

It was a time when most people worked hard to make a living, and a few made an absolute killing. Among the many I remember with respect are the vast majority of the employees at Drexel, who gave their jobs their best effort, and the clients with whom I dealt, who cared deeply about the pensions and savings entrusted to them. These people stood out in sharp contrast to the immoral minority of corporate managers who squandered their shareholders' money for their private agenda, of savings and loan owners who gambled with federally insured funds, and of Wall Streeters who worried too much about their commissions and too little about their customers.

Perhaps my best memory of the 1980s was in being a part of a system that worked—and worked well—despite the abuses at every level. Meanwhile, a system that didn't work was collapsing, done in by its bloated goals and false promises. "Russia is a country that is burying their troubles," Will Rogers wrote sixty years ago. "Your criticism is your epitaph. But if a government cheats its people long enough, leaving them in poverty, without hope, their troubles will bury it." At least that's the way it should be. And, finally, that's the way it was.

In April of 1989, however, the impending victory of capitalism didn't mean squat to the employees of Drexel Burnham. Some were trying to figure out what to do with their lives; the rest were trying to figure out what this all meant to them. The top management of my department called a meeting to explain the world to us.

As the salespeople and traders wondered about their future prospects, their mortgage payments, and their kids' tuition bills, one senior manager noted that "a circle exists in a continuous and continuous manner" [sic]. He said that there were "only degrees of difficulty and unhappiness," and he offered some additional drivel about an "unholy alliance."

He spoke of "agony" and "doing our darnedest."

He spoke of Macbeth, of Drexel's need to move quickly. He seemed oblivious to the insult of comparing our firm to a homicidal nut who would end up with his head on a stick.

And yet, ironically, this analogy from hell was prophetic. Within a year, Drexel Burnham Lambert would collapse into bankruptcy. The end, when it came, was swift, unnerving—as if the house you had lived in for years was suddenly swallowed up by a swamp that you didn't even know existed.

The destruction of Drexel raised some unsettling questions. How could the firm disappear less than two weeks after one senior manager assured certain employees that the financial condition was sound—

more than that, strong? How could any firm with $800 *million* in net worth go bankrupt? What good was Drexel's $1 billion in excess regulatory capital (whatever that meant) if it couldn't prevent defaulting on a $100 million loan?

Why didn't the government step in to help the firm and its employees? Was Drexel's crisis that much less important than Hayden, Stone's twenty years earlier, or Lockheed's fifteen years earlier, or Chrysler's ten years earlier, or Continental Illinois's six years before?

Perhaps, and not just for financial reasons. In its prime, the firm had cultivated enemies in high places. "The old Drexel Burnham Lambert that everyone knew and hated for the last ten years is gone," a Bush administration official told *The Wall Street Journal*. Good riddance, many thought.

Did the dislike for Drexel even reflect a certain degree of anti-Semitism? Its leaders, it was said, were "the new breed" of Jews— aggressive and arrogant and effective. They not only didn't belong to the right clubs, they made these clubs less influential in American business.

Would it have made any difference if the firm had kept its retail system? Would the thought of three hundred and fifty thousand investors with accounts at Drexel, all screaming for their money, have made a sufficient impression on the SEC and the Federal Reserve? Would the government have found a way to keep the firm in business, twisting a few well-chosen arms in the banking community?

But this is just speculation. The reality was that approximately five thousand employees came to work on Monday, February 12, 1990, and most were out of a job by Friday. Some exacted a petty revenge by purchasing computers from the firm for twenty cents on the dollar, then canceling the checks once the equipment was out of the building. Morale, already brain dead, was subsequently dealt another blow by the news that management had paid out $260 million in bonuses— over $10 million in one case—only weeks before the end.

"I don't think it's sad for those jerks on Wall Street," takeover expert Theodore Forstmann told the *Journal*. But it was. For every "jerk" whose glorious lifestyle was knocked down a few notches, there were a hundred decent people who found themselves putting their possessions in boxes and leaving their firm for the last time.

And everyone wondered, How could this happen?

CHAPTER TWO

ON THE STREET

It was great when it all began . . .
—*Rocky Horror Picture Show*

The firm I joined in 1981 had been in business for more than forty-five years and had little in common with the firm that it would become in the next five. The underlying culture of Drexel Burnham, however, did lay the groundwork for its almost inconceivable success and collapse, and for its continuing influence on Wall Street.

To understand Drexel, you need to understand its industry. The Street is essentially in the business of selling ideas. It advises corporations on what businesses to buy and sell, and on how to raise money and how to spend it. It advises investors on where to put their money to get the best return without taking on too much risk. It tries to put together the people who have funds with the people who need them; it helps make money flow efficiently. And, as the money flows smoothly from one hand to another, Wall Street keeps a small percentage for its efforts.

This may not sound like a noble cause, but in some ways it is. Certainly, it's an important one. Our economic system is based on the freedom to produce what you want and to purchase what you want.

Supply and demand determine prices, and prices determine what is supplied and demanded in the future. The financial markets allow companies to raise money so they can afford to produce what's wanted; at the same time, the markets give those with excess cash the opportunities to invest it.

Everybody does what is in their own self-interest, and it works out pretty well, in general. The free enterprise system has a great advantage over its competition: It recognizes human nature. From each according to his abilities, to each according to his needs is an admirable sentiment, but it's one that reads better than it plays. An expert in Leninism once noted, according to George Will, that it is a measure of Vladimir Lenin's foresight that none of his predictions have come true yet.

If Wall Street's product is ideas, its raw materials are people and capital. Between a firm's brains and its money, ideas can be created, disseminated, and executed. Thinking up ideas is not easy work, but getting corporations and individuals to believe in them and to put their own money behind them can be harder still.

Drexel Burnham was always a place where employees were given a good deal of freedom to generate ideas or implement them, or both. "People made a very nice living being free in the market, which is what this business is all about," said Allan McCarthy, a salesman who joined in 1976. The firm was organized around profit centers, whereby individual departments were compensated based on their own performance, rather than that of the entire firm. It was, noted one executive, a bunch of businesses under a big tent.

The ringmaster was Isaac Wolfe ("I.W.") Burnham, named after a relative who left his father money. I.W., known by the odd nickname of "Tubby," was—and is—respected by virtually everyone on the Street, and you don't have to work here long to know how rare that is. He founded the firm on April 1, 1935 with mostly borrowed money, and was its chief executive until 1976. "Tubby Burnham was regarded as being there when it counted," according to McCarthy. "If it was a tough time to trade gold, he was trading gold; if it was a tough time to trade treasuries, he was trading treasuries. He was always there."

When an employee was found to have a brain tumor, back before the days of comprehensive health insurance, Burnham saw to it that the firm took care of the bills. When a longtime employee left his wife for a walk on the wild side, he personally interceded. Until 1961 or 1962, he knew everyone by their first name.

Burnham and Co., as the firm was called at that time, had a few hundred employees and a few million dollars in net worth. It had struggled through the Wall Street doldrums of 1959 and 1960, when a busy day in the stock market meant three million shares. The company had only barely avoided a layoff.

Fortunately, the 1960s were great for stocks and better still for brokers. The Nixon administration, however, ushered in an awful era for Wall Street, a time marked by continuing declines in the bond market and two severe declines in the stock market—during 1969 and, brutally, during 1973–1974. Brokerage firms suffered both from their inability to deal with the increased volume of business from the "go-go" years of the 1960s and from the lousy markets that inevitably followed that boom.

One firm that fell on hard times was Drexel Firestone, a Philadelphia investment bank that traced its roots back to the bluest bloods of turn-of-the-century Wall Street—Edward Harriman and J. P. Morgan among them. The firm's problem was simple: A noticeable number of its top investment bankers had left for greener pastures.

The atmosphere there in the early 1970s was somewhat reminiscent of a proper British club twenty years earlier. The Empire was yesterday's news, but nobody was quite up to acknowledging it. According to one Drexel banker, the firm had lost all its significant clients except two local utilities, Philadelphia Electric and Penn Power and Light.

Drexel Firestone did maintain its style, however. One senior partner was described as the perfect model for a life-size FAO Schwarz investment banker doll. One morning, surrounded by the boardroom's beautiful mahaghony walls and under the watchful portraits of the firm's founders, he let loose a brainstorm: Firestone Tire, which had a financial interest in the firm, should acquire Campbell Soup.

Never mind that Campbell was four times larger than Firestone, that there was no strategic reason for them to merge, that Firestone was already on the brink of having the safety rating on its bonds downgraded, or that the Dorrance family, which controlled Campbell could—and would—stop any acquisition attempt. Never mind that this idea was doomed from birth. It was on the table, and some poor MBA would waste a day doing the requisite analysis before this proposal could be politely put to sleep.

In later years, this senior partner would find his niche when he became the chairman of the Finance Committee, a committee that had only one member and which never met.

Drexel did retain one great advantage, nevertheless. In the clubby world of Wall Street, it was still given a prime piece of the syndicates that were formed to sell stocks and bonds. Burnham and Co., meanwhile, wanted to be a major-bracket firm, which was unlikely to happen in anyone's lifetime unless it acquired a major. And so, in 1973, it bought Drexel.

The two firms that joined to form Drexel Burnham (the Drexel name got lead billing to avoid risking its major-bracket status) had about as much in common as the Union and the Confederacy. In the corporate finance department, the predominantly Jewish Burnham group felt that the Drexel people had memories instead of clients, and the predominantly WASP Drexel investment bankers thought the Burnham team would've been better off with memories instead of the clients they had.

This problem was largely resolved by the catastrophic bear markets of the next two years. By the end of 1974, the ranks of corporate finance had been decimated from forty to eleven. "Everyone was thinking M&A [mergers and acquisitions]," recalled a senior Drexel investment banker. "but we were getting nowhere."

In the depths of the 1974 Wall Street death march, Fred Joseph was hired. He had been the head of Shearson's retail system and, before that, had been an assistant to John Shad, the vice-chairman of E. F. Hutton. Shad had hired Joseph out of Harvard Business School, impressed with this young man's background and attitude.

Joseph was the son of a Boston cabdriver; he grew up in a lower-middle-class family, Jewish in an Irish town. Not surprisingly, he became a good amateur boxer. Less predictably, he was accepted into Harvard College; he was the last student from P. T. Campbell High School to make the Ivy League until his brother graduated six years later.

Tony Meyer, a senior investment banker who met Fred after his arrival at Drexel Burnham remembered: "He produced a little handwritten list of companies that he thought he could deliver [as clients]; I could only recognize three of them." Fred rose quickly in the firm to senior vice-president, then to cohead of corporate finance, then to the chief of the department.

Among Fred's strengths was a great charm—he was extremely like-able and articulate and, well, decent. People just disagreed on how sincere his image was.

"He was very, very clever at figuring out what it took to get what he wanted," said Meyer. "He never said anything that I didn't want to hear." According to another former senior officer of the firm who likely bears a grudge, Fred was "a bright, able, attractive investment banker," but cold and aloof on a personal level, a go-getter who "suffered from the Little Man Syndrome." A more generous sentiment was voiced by a young investment banker who joined many years later, "Fred Joseph was a nice guy who set the example, then hired people who had the same point of view."

On a professional level, that point of view was straightforward, one that hadn't changed since the day he walked in the door: Fred wanted to build a highly respected Wall Street powerhouse. And he did, with more than a little help from a friend.

The final piece of the Drexel Burnham structure was the 1976 acquisition of William D. Witter, a small "research boutique," which focused on the analysis of a few industries and their stocks. William D. Witter was controlled by Groupe Bruxelles Lambert, a Brussels-based investment banking firm. As a result of the acquisition of Witter, the Groupe received more than 20 percent of Drexel's stock and the firm officially became Drexel Burnham Lambert Inc.

When I came on board in June 1981, Drexel Burnham was about halfway between the firm that was struggling to meet its bills in the mid-1970s and the firm that would revolutionize American finance in the mid-1980s. It was still a second-tier shop on Wall Street, but the entrepreneurial culture and the people were already in place. To an unusually perceptive business-school student, the hidden potential of Drexel made it the place to go, the opportunity to get in early on what would become the hottest firm on the Street.

I was not that student. Not only didn't I recognize the possibilities for the firm, I didn't even realize what they were interviewing me for:

"Why do you want to work in investment banking?"

"I don't. I want to work in investment *management*."

"Then why are you here?"

"The letter said investment management."

"No, it said investment banking."

"No, it didn't."

"Yes, it did."

I checked the letter. No, it didn't.

The interviewer was pleasant, considering that he was dealing with Wharton's only illiterate grad student.

"Look," he said. "We have a half hour left. I can catch an earlier train, or we can just sit and chat for a while."

"No, why don't you catch the earlier train."

"We'll be in touch."

A few days later, the odds makers took a beating as I got a call from Drexel:

"What positions would you be interested in?"

"What are you hiring for?" I asked. (I certainly could carry a conversation.)

"Everything. What are you interested in?"

I was interviewing for an institutional sales position at Merrill Lynch, so I suggested that.

Again, I was told that they would get back to me, and again they did.

I eventually spent a grueling day of interviews with analysts, salesmen, and officers at Drexel. Because I didn't know quite what the job involved, the early interviews went poorly. By the afternoon, I had a good idea of the drill and, probably for the first time in the process, I sounded like someone that someone would want to hire.

This is not meant as a criticism of the people who decided to give me a job and pay me the exorbitant (in my eyes, at least—at first) salary of $35,000 a year. I did have the Wharton name behind me, and I was finishing up my undergraduate and graduate studies in five years. On paper, I looked pretty strong, which may have encouraged everyone to downplay my occasional confusion in person.

My first assignment of any real importance was to analyze for the sales force a new offering that Drexel was about to sell to the public. It was an odd thing to ask a kid fresh out of school to spend a night reading a one-hundred-page prospectus that explained everything that could go wrong with a company trying to raise $100 million and then expect him to summarize it for a group of pros who genuinely knew what they were doing.

Also, it was the responsibility of corporate finance to explain the strengths and weaknesses of a deal that it had put together and which it wanted the salesmen to sell to their clients. In later years, corporate finance would handle these presentations, providing us with detailed memos and access to the managements of the companies we were trying to finance. But at this stage, the investment bankers just sent the prospectuses to us and expected us to sell whatever it was that these documents told us was for sale.

Churchill once commented in reviewing a book on penguins, "This book tells me more about penguins than I care to know"—a complaint that certainly applied to reading a prospectus. But this first deal that I read at least had the advantage of being in an interesting industry, an industry that Drexel Burnham would raise billions of dollars for in the upcoming years: cable television.

The company itself managed—by mismanagement—to go down the tubes. But it did introduce the firm to a wonderful group of companies that needed to borrow a great deal of money and produced a great deal of cash to pay off that debt. And it did introduce me to a fellow who would become a pseudolegend at Drexel Burnham: The Great Acquisitor.

The Great One was the top investment banker on this cable deal. According to a senior corporate finance officer, "Fred Joseph used to think he was very bright, hardworking, extremely quick at sizing up situations and thinking on his feet." Others had a somewhat different point of view. "I wouldn't hire him to hold my horse," said another senior banker. "My guess is to know him is to hate him." "A big, fat guy with a wimpy, namby-pamby voice" was one salesman's description. "Unless the guy's changed, I always thought he was a moron." One analyst viewed him simply as "a great investment banker and an enormous pig."

I met with The Great Acquisitor once to review some figures that one of the salesmen had requested, and he impressed me with his self-confidence and his apparent thoroughness (unfortunately, I can be a lousy judge of character). He assured me that he had gone over the numbers about twenty times the previous night.

Based on what I learned later about the Acquisitor's analytic ability, his assurance was probably a crock. Someone who had supervised him briefly in an earlier time on an earlier deal mentioned that The Great One's responsibility was to provide the analysis on which to judge that deal. Instead, he assigned it to a junior person, who proceded to botch up the numbers. When his superior on the deal noticed the errors, The Great One did the analysis himself. Wrong again. He redid the numbers. Different results, but still wrong.

My next important assignment was, for me, a several-month walk through the valley of the shadow. Another new salesman and I became the liaisons between our institutional equity department and the convertible bond group. A convert, as you might know, is a hybrid security: a bond (a loan to a company) that entitles you to a fixed rate of interest, which can be exchanged into a certain number of shares of stock (a piece of ownership in that company).

The job was a peach, sort of a Wall Street version of *The Island of Lost Souls,* with its restless natives and House of Pain. It was my first direct contact with any of the boys on the West Coast, and it was the first and last time in my eight years that I would go home most nights with knots in my stomach.

When people at Drexel spoke of the West Coast, they were actually referring to one small office in Beverly Hills. This was the home of the high-yield bond department and, less important, of the convertible bond group. Over the next five years, this so-called branch office, three thousand miles from Wall Street, would become the center of the universe for corporate America.

Of course, I didn't know that. What I did know was that I was a twenty-two-year-old rookie who was out of his league. At first, I had hoped that my new assignment would live up to its billing—a great opportunity, etc. The first phone call my partner and I had with our main contact on the Coast, however, made it clear that we weren't in Kansas anymore. I was obsequious, striving for unctuous. At the end of the conversation, the Gray Prince, a senior vice-president, asked us if we had any questions before he came to New York to meet us.

"No," my partner responded. "But I'm sure we'll think of some by the time you get out here."

Good answer—banal and professional.

"Well," responded the voice on the line. "I don't want to get blindsided."

Huh?

Blindsided by us? Why? Weren't we on the same side?

Maybe, maybe not.

We soon learned that our primary responsibility was to get the salesmen in the equity department to fill out questionaires. These questionaires would tell the boys on the Coast, the portfolio managers with the authority, to buy convertible bonds. Now, no salesman in his right mind is eager to tell anyone else who to call at his accounts to generate business. That's his job; more important, that's his livelihood. If there are stocks or convertible bonds (which are, after all, a form of stock) to be sold to his accounts, he wants to write the tickets. To tell someone three thousand miles away the best contacts is to risk losing those commissions.

Which increasingly seemed like a very likely risk.

Our conversations with the Coast had more in common with the Paris Peace Talks than with two departments of the same firm working toward the greater good. The equity salesmen didn't want to give away their contacts without some ground rules on how commissions on convert trades would be divided, and the Coast preferred vague assurances. They argued that whoever got the order should get the commission, which seemed fair on the surface. The problem was that every transaction would potentially create a battle, and two parts of Drexel would be fighting each other.

The greater problem was that we didn't trust them. Our West Coast contacts were selling machines; what they said always seemed to be geared to moving the merchandise. You didn't get a sense that you were hearing both sides of the story, or perhaps even the correct story.

Every morning, we would be told the list of converts that the Coast had in inventory and wanted to sell. The morning rundown was delivered by our other contact, who we had nicknamed "Bodo," based on the *Lord of the Rings*. Of course, we never called him that on the phone, because we were scared shitless of him—he was the nastiest fuckin' hobbit on Middle Earth.

One morning after he had given us the dozen or so names that we should encourage the equity salesmen to sell to their clients, we asked him for his three favorite converts, the three from the total universe of hundreds of publicly traded convertible bonds that he thought were the best value. He quickly gave us three names from that morning's sell list.

Say it ain't so, Bodo.

The greatest excitement—and tension—was reserved for the deals, when new convertible bonds were offered to the public, and commissions were about ten times higher than those to be earned on converts already trading in the market. The equity salesmen were at a great disadvantage, because the West Coast controlled "the books," deciding which clients would receive these convertible bonds as well as how many they would get. Not surprisingly, on deals where the demand for converts exceeded the number being offered, the lion's share would go to accounts that had ordered the bonds through the convert salesmen on the Coast.

This was frustrating, but this was life. What was unacceptable was the concept of "running ahead," which emerged on one huge and important convertible offering. The Coast tried a popular approach among totalitarian governments: the sham democracy. We were told not to discuss the deal until it was officially filed with the SEC. Fine, that's the rule. As soon as the deal was filed, however, orders started pouring in through the West Coast by the tens of millions. And, by the way, orders would be filled on a first-come, first-served basis.

Somehow, the salesmen out there had managed to educate their clients on the intricacies of the deal and receive orders in a matter of seconds, or for the more sluggish among them, in minutes. It was extraordinary. It was unprecedented. It was bullshit.

We arranged a phone call—my partner, my boss, and I—with the Prince.

"Did any of your salespeople call any of the accounts before the deal was filed?" I asked.

Short pause.

"No."

"Well," I replied like a good/nasty lawyer who never asks a question without knowing the answer, "we were told by two accounts that they were told about the deal a week before it was filed."

Long pause.

Pure venom: "Don't you *ever* ask me a leading question like that again."

And the clouds parted, and the angels hid, and I realized: Welcome to the real world.

A meeting was finally called to hash out our differences, to decide once and for all how to get the two coasts working together in selling converts. I was prepared; I was psyched. In New York, my partner and I joined up with my sales manager, and we filed into his boss's office.

At the other end of the conference line, in Beverly Hills, were the Prince, Bodo, and a mystery guest.

The meeting began.

A voice from the Coast: "Eddie, this is Mike. Can we take care of this another time, you and I?"

"Sure, Mike."

End of meeting.

For me, this was a frustrating nonevent. For the guy at the other end of the line, this was just another of several hundred details he had dealt with that day. At thirty-five, he was already a major force in the financial world and was well on his way to building an empire.

CHAPTER THREE

THE WORLD
ACCORDING TO MIKE

You say you want a revolution,
well, you know, we all want to change the world . . .

—THE BEATLES

Michael Milken did what should be all but impossible: He found a gold mine lying under Wall Street virtually ignored. Our financial markets had been in existence for at least a century, and had been operating under modern regulations for forty years. Any extraordinary opportunities should have been exploited by the tens of thousands of bright, ambitious financiers who had spent their careers looking for the overlooked and the undervalued.

Milken did find such an opportunity—or perhaps more accurately, he created one. As a college student at Berkeley in the late 1960s, Milken read about the systematic undervaluation of low-quality bonds. These were bonds that the rating agencies—Moody's and Standard & Poor's (S&P), in particular—felt were speculations instead of investments. They were assigned a rating of BB ("double-B") or less, well below the top-grade rating of AAA ("triple-A").

These "speculative" bonds had historically offered a high yield that more than offset the risks. Certainly, some high-yield bonds had defaulted, leaving their holders with pieces of paper that no longer

21

paid the interest promised. Still, a well-diversified portfolio provided a better return to investors than they would have received from owning Treasury bonds.

On average, about 3 percent of high-yield bonds had missed an interest payment each year. The prices of these defaulted bonds naturally tumbled, losing some 50 percent of their original value. Therefore, the loss rate on all junk bonds averaged 1.5 percent a year. This loss rate is less than the 3 to 4 percent high-yield premium—the amount by which high-yield interest rates exceed Treasury bond interest rates. The gains from the extra interest are higher than the losses from the occasional disasters.

And it was with this thesis as inspiration that Milken turned corporate America on its head and built a billion-dollar personal fortune from scratch. It is difficult to comprehend the influence he would eventually wield: He became the driving force (some would say the controlling factor) in the most potent market of the 1980s.

Whether he had any idea of the impact he would have when he joined Drexel's nascent high-yield bond department in 1970 is anyone's guess. If anyone could have imagined his future, it was Milken himself. But even he probably couldn't envision what would be accomplished in the next fifteen years, and he certainly wouldn't have believed what could happen in the following five.

What was obvious to him—and to everyone who met him—was that he was no ordinary guy. He was a genius: not in the sense that most people mean when they throw the term around, but in the lights-out, unbelievable category. He was also an extraordinary salesman with a work ethic that would have finished off most motivated young men in six months.

Physically, he was unimposing, about six-feet tall and thin to the point of gaunt, as if food was just an afterthought. In a business known for gray temples and ponderous voices, he had neither. But his youthful appearance didn't matter; his force of intelligence and personality were overwhelming.

At Drexel, Milken was an oddity, a rare Jew among WASPs, trading junk bonds at a firm that still fancied itself among the elite. These junk bonds fell into two camps: "fallen angels," bonds that had once been considered high grade, but whose ratings had been downgraded as the fortunes of the underlying companies had floundered, and "Chinese paper," low-quality bonds that had been issued to pay for some of the wild-and-woolly acquisitions of the 1960s.

He created an active high-yield bond market, and an active market is a necessary condition for a successful market. Buyers want to know that they can sell their holdings at will. Milken was eager to take the role of market maker, because he understood better than his clients and his competitors how much these bonds were worth. The more he traded, the more he would able to earn, buying low and selling high.

He would think up interesting trading ideas and go to his head trader, Charlie Causey, to put them to work. Charlie was one of the only people that Michael ever dealt with who didn't hesitate to criticize him. "Who the hell are you?" someone overheard Causey yell at Milken. "You don't know one side of a bond from another." The two worked together for many years, until Charlie, who had earned all he would need, left for a fishing trip in the late 1970s, and stayed.

Milken earned his first million-dollar bonus before he was thirty. He made his first fortune buying the junk bonds of real estate investment trusts (REITs). These REITs, which invested in income-producing properties and raw land, were the darlings of the market in the late 1960s, but fell out of favor in the 1970s.

The recession of 1974 certainly hurt the value of the bonds, as the underlying properties suffered in a poor economy. But more important, the *price* of REIT bonds was beaten down out of proportion to the decline in their value, as investors' greed was replaced by fear. Milken recognized that at ten or twenty cents on the dollar, these bonds were great buys.

Trading junk bonds was clearly not the extent of Milken's ambition, even early on. According to senior investment banker Tony Meyer, "Michael used to wander into my office in the early to mid-1970s and he'd say, 'Listen, why don't we try to develop some underwriting business peddling bond issues of BB and B companies. I'm very active in this market and we really need a source of business. We're never going to do any business with GM or GE.'

"And I'd say, 'Michael, don't be crazy.' "

In 1977, Milken's idea became a reality: For the first time since the days of J. P. Morgan, bonds of a noninvestment-grade company were sold to the public. The underwriter of these new bonds, however, was not Drexel, it was Lehman Brothers. In fact, Lehman did the first four original-issue junk bonds; after that, it basically abandoned its newly created franchise, a decision that cost it perhaps a billion dollars in potential fees during the subsequent decade.

If Lehman was leery about underwriting high-yield bonds, Drexel was not. For one thing, it didn't need to worry about offending a large number of high-grade corporate clients, because it didn't have many to offend. For another, it had a young trader in-house who knew the junk-bond market and its customers better than anyone on the Street.

And there was a huge pool of possible clients among the approximately 20,000 companies that were large enough to finance in the public markets, but that didn't qualify for an investment-grade rating from Moody's or S&P. These companies, representing 95 percent of the country's total, had been forced to rely primarily on bank debt to finance their growth.

The major problems with borrowing from banks were the restrictive covenants, which told you what you couldn't do in running your business, and the floating interest rate, which allowed the cost of the loan to rise in a recession just when you could least afford it. As Ralph Ingersoll of Ingersoll Publications told *The Wall Street Journal,* "I don't sleep at nights when I have bank debt."

It was a nice fit all around: Drexel needed a franchise of its own, a lot of companies needed financing, a lot of money was looking for high returns, and Michael Milken knew how to bring together the sellers and the buyers. Drexel became the leading firm in high-yield bond financings in 1978 and proceeded to maintain its domination of this market from that time on, doing as many deals as all of its competitors *combined.*

Around this time, Milken moved his operation from New York to Beverly Hills. The senior members of the firm, from Burnham on down, opposed the move, but they couldn't prevent it. Milken, at thirty-one, was already too important; if the firm said no, he could have gotten what he wanted anywhere on Wall Street in just a bit longer than it takes to dial the phone.

He had several reasons for the move to the West Coast. He wanted to return to his hometown, where his parents still lived. He wanted his family to enjoy a better quality of life than they currently had in New Jersey, as inconceivable as that might seem. He wanted his competitors to have as little knowledge of what he was doing as possible. Perhaps he wanted the same for his firm.

(Milken's passion for secrecy was highlighted in confidential depositions taken many years later in conjunction with a lawsuit by Green Tree Acceptance Inc., accusing Drexel of mishandling an offering of bonds and stock. In one of these depositions, obtained by *The Washington Post*, Paul Boyum of Green Tree spoke of his attempt to get the list of those who had bought his company's stock:

> "[Gerald Koerner, a first vice-president in Drexel's corporate finance department] said Milken wouldn't give it to them. The West Coast wouldn't tell the East Coast who they were selling stock to, which to me was unbelievable. I simply didn't believe him."
>
> "Did you say so?" asked an attorney.
> "Yes.
> "What did he say?
> "He said Drexel is a funny institution.")

By 1980, it was obvious that the high-yield bond market was for real. "Every deal that got done made it easier to get the next one done," remembered Keith Hartley, a corporate finance officer who had joined the firm in 1973. "We really felt like we were accomplishing something." Another veteran recalled the mood: "Everybody began to feel very affluent, very good about life, very smart. Guys thought they were really great because they were innovative."

Milken's operation had, by then, branched out to convertible bonds, which would haunt me less than two years later. A new wrinkle on junk bonds emerged as well, which would become the focus of a serious controversy—debt with warrants. The idea was simple: Encourage companies that were selling junk bonds to include warrants, which allow a holder to buy shares of stock at a set price, to make the deals more attractive. These warrants would give bond buyers—who were only lenders to a company—a piece of ownership with its upside potential if the company did well.

The use of warrants, known as "equity kickers," did highlight a basic fact in the junk-bond market: Its growth was more dependent on the buyers than the sellers. There was a virtually unlimited list of companies that would be eager to raise long-term capital at fixed interest rates, which is what these bonds allowed them to do. The hard part was in convincing people, particularly those who made the decisions at institutions such as insurance companies, savings and loans (S&Ls), and advisory firms, to invest billions of dollars in bonds that until recently had been ridiculed or ignored or treated with suspicion.

This was Milken's real challenge, and nobody was better. Even late in his career, when he had become the main man on the Street, he was still willing to make his sales pitch in person. A large insurance company in New Jersey had decided to begin investing in junk bonds; Milken showed up with Jim Dahl, his top salesman. The meeting began a bit after 9:00 A.M. and lasted for five hours. "He would look at a name, and give you the whole history," said a participant. "They just looked at him like he was the Messiah."

A limosine picked him up at 2:15 to drive him to New York for a 3:00 meeting; after that, he had another one at 4:00, and a flight out of La Guardia Airport at 5:15. Someone expressed concern that he would miss his plane. "I'll make it," he replied.

"He was a man who had every fact and figure in order," observed a young investment banker. "He knew the particulars, every covenant, every uptick and downtick. He had the unusual talent of being very technically proficient in a presentation, then being able to step back and talk about the world, the global village."

"He had incredible thoughts, fascinating points of view," a banker from the Coast recalled. "He could sit in a meeting and explain to the chairman of a company why the Germans raising the bundesbank rate would affect snow peas, or why real estate prices in Japan were affecting your mortgage."

Michael Milken had the ability to make the clichéd seem profound because coming from him, it was. When he asked the heads of corporations to tell him their dreams, they knew that here was a man who could make those dreams happen.

Milken almost single-handedly built—and perhaps controlled—a huge financial market. He convinced buyers to abandon their prejudices against junk bonds, and he convinced sellers to pay the price that he said was necessary to place the merchandise. By the beginning of the 1980s, the high-yield bond market, his market, was poised to show the world that it was not only big, it was powerful.

The 1980s on Wall Street was an era of junk-financed takeovers, conjuring up images of anemic dweebs trading inside information and dragging suitcases of cash through lower Manhattan. The reality was a bit different. To begin with, most buyouts were friendly, with both the buyer and the seller agreeing on a fair price without hiring detective firms to dig up dirt on each other.

The times were ripe for a takeover boom. The 1960s' religion of bigger is better had left its followers ill-prepared for the 1970s. The problem was stock prices: They went down when they were supposed to go up. During the good days, big conglomerates could buy high-growth companies and pay for them with shares of their own stock; these holding companies would then look better to investors, because they owned a stable of fast-growing (but unrelated) businesses.

When stock prices headed south, conglomerates could no longer afford to pay up for acquisitions, because their currency—their stock—didn't buy as much anymore. More important, investors began to question the attractiveness of big companies composed of businesses with little or nothing in common. The financial fashion statement of the late 1960s went the way of the Nehru jacket, both for good reason.

Meanwhile, inflation was rising, and the values of corporate assets were increasing, as well. The land that companies owned, the plants that produced their products, and the prices of these products all rose sharply in the 1970s. The investment community, its former optimism rewarded with painful bear markets, preferred to focus instead on the dismal economy and the sorry state of the world, from the U.S. perspective, at least.

The election of Ronald Reagan to the presidency was a turning point. His landslide victory gave him the mandate to get inflation down, and he did. He was willing to accept a price that most politicians would never have: the worst economic downturn since the Great Depression. Following this recession, the economy would grow for almost a decade. Reagan also spearheaded the 1981 Tax Act, which increased the value of corporations by reducing their tax payments.

The stage was set for takeovers. Companies were selling for significantly less than they were worth, and the future was looking brighter. Investors were either unaware of the values, or skeptical that they would ever be realized. All that was needed was the money to pay for the buyouts.

Banks were willing to finance the least-risky part of the acquisitions: the senior debt. They would put up about half the cost of the deal, provided that they had a claim on all the assets in the event that anything went wrong. That way they were fairly certain to get their money back, even if the company went bankrupt.

The people buying the company would contribute a small amount in return for all the equity. Should the acquisition be a successful one, these stockholders would receive the full benefit of the company's increased value; potential profits could be enormous.

The hard part was finding investors who were willing to fill in the middle, to buy the debt that was too risky for the banks but that didn't offer the home-run possibilities of the equity. In order for buyouts to happen easily and efficiently, there had to be a market for this junk debt. And once Milken came around, there was.

In the early years of the takeover boom, the businesses being bought were often the divisions of conglomerates. For example, a small company that didn't have much in common with the other parts of the corporation and whose performance wasn't contributing greatly to the overall results might be divested. The buyers, usually consisting of the small company's management and a group of financiers, would borrow most of the agreed on purchase price.

The success of this leveraged buyout (LBO) would depend in large part on the ability of management, which now had a substantial vested interest in the company's future, to do what it had often been unable to do before: turn the company around. This might involve decisions that it had been prevented from making before by its conglomerate parent, such as entering a new market, or decisions that it had been unwilling to make, such as cutting back on its work force. There was also the question of luck: Would the demand for the company's products exceed expectations, or not?

The potential rewards for a successful LBO were enormous, because the upside went to the stockholders who had put up only a small fraction of the money. Just how great that potential was became apparent to the world in 1983 when Gibson Greetings sold shares of its stock to the public.

Gibson, whose most famous employee was Garfield the Cat, had been purchased from RCA for $80 million, of which $79 million was borrowed. The buyer was Wesray, a buyout firm headed by former Secretary of the Treasury William Simon. When the company went public only eighteen months later, Simon's investment of $330,000 had risen to a market value of $66 million—a gain of 20,000 percent!

Profits like that are not ignored for long, and LBOs became the rage. Acquisitions financed primarily with debt would rise from $11 billion in the 1978–1983 period to $182 billion in the following five years. And at the center of the action was Mike Milken—to some extent helping the process; to some extent feeding it—placing the junk bonds that Wall Street had considered unplaceable.

Takeovers evolved from the unwanted divisions of conglomerates to the conglomerates themselves. Because these companies were selling well below the total value of their subsidiaries—the sum of the parts was worth more than the whole—why not buy the undervalued package, and sell off the pieces?

The leveraged buyout of Beatrice Companies highlighted this strategy. Completed in April 1986, it was the largest LBO to that time; the buyer was Kohlberg Kravis Roberts and Company (KKR), the granddaddy of the leveraged buyout firm. Drexel Burnham financed the junk-bond portion of this $6.2 billion deal, raising $2.5 billion through four different types of securities, from 11% ten-year senior notes (11% interest annually for ten years; strong claim on assets) to fifteen-year floating rate junior subordinate debentures (uncertain interest rate; uncertain claim).

Donald Kelly, a veteran of the food industry and the new chief executive of Beatrice, was able to reduce $100 million in annual costs, according to a July, 1989 *Fortune* article.

As for selling the pieces of this far-flung conglomerate, the new owners were able to find buyers for its Avis car rental, Tropicana juices, Playtex hosiery, Coca-Cola bottling, and international food operations—with total proceeds of approximately $4.4 billion.

The non-food businesses were packaged into a separate company called E-II, in recognition of Kelly's previous company, Esmark. A small percentage of E-II was sold through a 1987 public offering of stock, in which my department played a role; in 1988, American Brands, the tobacco company, purchased all the shares for some $800 million.

The remaining Beatrice businesses—boasting such familiar consumer names as Butterball, Hunt's, La Choy, Peter Pan, and Swiss Miss—were sold to ConAgra on June 7, 1990 for $1.3 billion. In four years, all the bank debt and junk bonds from the Beatrice acquisition was repaid, and KKR more than tripled its $420 million equity investment.

The buy-out of Beatrice, which probably would not have happened if Michael Milken had not made the high-yield market happen, was a friendly transaction—the people running the company were willing to sell. This was not always the case with takeovers in the 1980s. And that is where the real excitement began.

Hostile takeovers are dependent on one basic fact: A company is owned by its shareholders, not its management. When you buy stock in a public corporation, you become a partial owner, entitled to your share of its future profits. You and the other stockholders have the right to choose the board of directors, which then hires the managers. These managers are your employees, responsible for running the company for your benefit, by maximizing the long-term value of your stock.

This system of means and ends works beautifully in theory, but it gets muddled in practice. Managers usually choose their own bosses, the board of directors. The election of the board of directors is, in turn, rubber-stamped by *their* bosses, who are the stockholders. More important, managers tend to run a company as if it were theirs, which can cause conflicts of interest with the real owners.

Most managers want their company to grow—it's only natural. But bigger isn't necessarily better; expanding may just waste money, which will hurt the value of the stock. Or the managers may run the company like a private fiefdom. This too will hurt the shareholders' investments. The managers may also receive a bid to buy the entire company, which is usually bad for them, but good for the stockholders.

Managers are not very flattered when an outside party believes that it can afford to pay significantly more for a company than its stock-market value and still have itself a bargain. A takeover bid tells the world that this company is probably undermanaged, so much so that even at a price 50 percent or more above the current one, better management can make the numbers work.

Not surprisingly, most managers resent the implication that they've been mediocre in doing their job, which is to make the most of a company's assets for the benefit of its owners. They also dislike the thought of losing their jobs. If they reject the takeover bid, however, the story is not over; the final decision rests with the shareholders. And between the first bid and the last tender offer, hostile takeovers can get ugly.

The first large takeover battle of the 1980s didn't involve junk bonds or Drexel Burnham, but it did remind everyone who the owners were. In 1981, Conoco, an oil company, was pursued by both Seagram's, the Canadian liquor company, and du Pont, the Delaware chemical giant. Eventually, du Pont won majority control, Seagram's bought a minority position, and Conoco's shareholders made a very nice profit.

The takeover front was generally quiet as the stock market fell—most people are more comfortable buying when prices are rising, based on the suspect logic that prices will keep rising. The bear market of 1981–1982 created a great deal of concern about the present and the future, which discouraged buyers of both stocks and companies.

In 1982, Boone Pickens and his small exploration company, Mesa Petroleum, made a run at Cities Service, an oil company some *twenty times* Mesa's size. It brought back memories of thirteen years earlier, when Saul Steinberg's leasing company tried to buy Chemical Bank; Steinberg failed, but allegedly not without receiving some insight from President Richard Nixon: "We're not ready for you yet, sonny."

Boone introduced the 1980s to a new character that would take center stage for several years: the raider. At various times, the title would be worn by Steinberg—evidently all grown up—and by men as different in style and skills as Carl Icahn, Ron Perelman, Sir James Goldsmith, Irv "The Liquidator" Jacobs, and Nelson Peltz. Their stories ranged from the almost inevitable success of the brilliant Icahn, whose name would create a healthy dose of fear in corporate America, to the seemingly improbable success of the tenacious Peltz, whose name . . . well, whatever.

Some of these raiders would present themselves as the vanguard of change, the saviors of this country's small stockholders—some forty million of them. They would propose their hostile bids in the language of truth and justice, their motive to free the owners of public corporations from the mediocracy and tyranny of self-interested managers.

Eventually, those who wrapped themselves in lily white would prove more interested in personal profit than in protecting the oppressed. But no one hired them for the role of Sir Galahad, and nothing required them to live up to their rhetoric. More important, their actions didn't negate their argument; some shaking of the status quo wasn't a bad idea.

Boone Pickens was the ideal role model for a raider/crusader, from his folksy name to his sophisticated understanding of takeover strategy. His attempt to buy Cities Service failed, but shareholders, including himself, made a 50 percent profit when Occidental Petroleum acquired the company.

Boone's next target was the mammoth Gulf Oil, and his weapon was the proxy vote. The shareholders were asked to decide whether their company should sell off some of its assets and return the proceeds to them, rather than leave the decision up to the management. In December 1983, the stockholders voted down the proposal, but not by much.

The next step was a hostile bid, and for this, Boone called in Drexel to put the money where his mouth was. Within forty-eight hours, Milken raised $1.7 billion in commitments from various institutions. One point of view that has emerged in later years is that Milken opposed Drexel's move into financing hostile takeovers. As one senior executive noted, "He just flat-out didn't. If Michael had been opposed, it never would have been launched as a major strategy."

Regardless, Pickens's plan to bid for Gulf was shot to hell as the stock price rose sharply before the offer to buy was announced. The reason was simple: Some person(s) started trading on the inside information that a tender offer was in the works.

Boone cut back his takeover plan to a more modest offer for 20 percent of Gulf's shares. In time, the company found a "white knight" in Chevron, another of oil's seven sisters, which purchased Gulf in a friendly transaction for a staggering $13.3 billion. The shareholders reaped a windfall: Their stock had doubled in less than a year.

Drexel, however, was in a pickle. The firm knew it could raise previously unheard of sums to finance takeovers; the problem was in raising the money without alerting the world to the target.

The next major deal raised a different problem: greenmail. Saul Steinberg returned to center stage in 1984, with a hostile bid for Disney. Milken's group raised $700 million in commitments to finance the deal, while a few of us tried to get involved by pressing a trader who did a terrific Donald Duck imitation to call up the Coast, telling them how ticked off he and Mickey were about the whole thing.

No matter. Disney bought out Steinberg's shares—and only his shares—at a premium price, leaving the other shareholders to watch the value of their stock plummet. To many, the repurchase of Steinberg's position suggested the financial equivalent of "Don't go away mad, just go away."

Later that year, Boone Pickens attempted a takeover of Phillips Petroleum that ended on December 23, when he accepted a recapitalization plan. Specifically, Phillips bought back his stock for cash at $53 per share, while the other shareholders were offered a share repurchase that the stock market valued at approximately $46.

On the heels of the Pickens situation, Carl Icahn entered the picture, buying up shares in Phillips. He then made a hostile bid for the whole company, an $8 billion transaction. Shareholders would get half in cash, half in bonds. The cash portion would be raised by Milken from his junk-bond buyers.

An interesting feature of this tender offer was that none of the financing was in place. Drexel simply assured the world that it was "highly confident" it could raise the money; this was the solution to Drexel's problem of financing a takeover without giving anyone advance notice of the target.

Once the offer was on the table, Icahn asked Milken to get immediate commitments for $1.5 billion of the $4 billion that he had said he could raise. It was done in two days.

"His word didn't mean a whole lot until he was able to do it," said Keith Hartley, a Drexel investment banker. But now that Milken had shown he was more than able, his word was gold.

The takeover boom was on. In 1985, acquisitions totaled $180 billion, up sharply from an impressive $122 billion the previous year. Among the deals that Drexel backed were Icahn's $900 million buyout of TWA, Peltz's $1 billion purchases of both National Can and American Can, Perelman's $1.8 billion acquisition of Revlon, Sam Heymann's $5 billion attempt at GAF, and Kohlberg Kravis's $6.2 billion takeover of Beatrice.

Corporate America realized that, for the first time in decades, it was accountable to its owners. Managers recognized that if they didn't improve the value of the shareholders' investment, someone else might. In the summer of 1985 alone, fifty corporations voluntarily restructured, according to Ivan Boesky, an active figure on Wall Street at that time. These corporations had sold off assets and had bought back shares, trying to maximize the stock price. It was nice to see.

Michael Milken didn't introduce takeovers to Wall Street, but more than anyone, he made them an important part of its business. He didn't create an environment where companies were selling for substantially less than they were worth, but he did take advantage of it with a passion—some would say with a vengeance. By the mid-1980s, he was the Street's leading player, with some powerful enemies watching from the wings.

CHAPTER FOUR

THE NEW WAY

The financial community is a loose collection of firms very different in image and approach, from white-shoe genteel to street-tough down and dirty. These firms have little in common beyond a desire to make money by moving money. By 1986, however, they did see eye to eye on at least one point: They all wished Drexel would curl up and die.

The banks, already taking a beating in the back pocket by the late seventies, were hurt further by the rise of the junk-bond market. Their low-cost passbook deposits were leaving for the greener pastures of newly created money market funds, and their blue-chip clients like IBM and AT&T were able to borrow money at lower cost by selling short-term loans, known as commercial paper, directly to the public.

The most attractive business left for the banks was in lending to medium-size companies that needed money to grow, but that were too unproven to sell commercial paper. Unfortunately for the Citibanks and the Mellons, high-yield bonds gave these borrowers another route to take. "We robbed the banks of all their best loans," a Drexel officer boasted.

Investment bankers from the firm approached the chief execs of corporate America's middle class with a compelling sales pitch. They pointed out that these companies were paying a lot more for their bank loans than the stated rate, due to the restrictive covenants attached and the gimmicks such as compensating balances whereby a borrower must leave a certain portion of the loan on deposit with the bank.

Just as important, these bank loans were short term, which left the companies at risk that the loans might be called in the near future. Drexel, on the other hand, could get them long-term loans—by selling their bonds to the public—which would leave them free to focus on building a successful long-term business.

The basic problem that the banks faced was their own shortsightedness; as Milken noted in an interview with *New Perspectives Quarterly:* "The tendency of our financial structure has been to channel loans to industries of the past rather than of the future." Bankers gave their best rates to those who had prospered in the inflationary 1970s, such as oil explorers, real estate developers, and commodity-rich Third World countries.

It was these borrowers, however, who were most at risk—they were already leveraged to the hilt with earlier loans, and the prices of their products had risen to the point where they were killing demand. In effect, the best deals went to the worst borrowers, setting the stage for massive loan losses that the banks are still trying to deal with a decade later.

This country's corporate elite disliked Drexel for a simple reason: The firm was sticking its nose where it didn't belong. Investment bankers were supposed to give advice, gentleman to gentleman, on financing and friendly acquisitions; they were supposed to be charming, well bred, and low handicapped. They weren't supposed to raise money for hostile takeover artists. And they sure as hell weren't supposed to think up hostile takeovers, and then go looking for someone to replace the current managers.

If you were the chief executive of a large corporation, one in which you had spent thirty years climbing the ranks, Michael Milken was your worst nightmare. He couldn't be dismissed as another Ralph Nader or as a peddler of junk; he was a man who had a nasty vision and an ability to see it through. His was the face that you woke up with at two in the morning; his was the name that a fleet of Drexelites used to convince potential acquirers that anything was possible.

And if that wasn't bad enough, these Drexel people were brash and contemptuous, and . . . well, you know. Jews had played an important, if often unwelcomed, role on Wall Street for many decades before Drexel entered the limelight, but most had wanted to become a part of the establishment, not take it apart.

Anti-Semitism is a subtle thing, because prejudice is carefully handled by those intelligent enough to know how disgusting it is. No chief exec whose firm is threatened by a sanctimonious raider backed by an arrogant upstart Jewish firm, as Drexel was perceived to be, is likely to sit down with his therapist and explain, "Well, Doc, the reason I'm ready to kill somebody is fourfold: I've got this bastard out there telling the world what a lousy job he thinks I've been doing—let's give the ego factor . . . say, 20 percent. Meanwhile, he's trying to take over my company and put me on the street—that's a good 50 percent. The shareholders deserve a lot more than he's offering—give that 10 percent. And this whole thing wouldn't have happened in the first place if it wasn't for those pushy Jews—20 percent, easy."

But if anti-Semitism was a factor in Drexel's unpopularity, it certainly wasn't the driving factor. After all, Boone Pickens was a good ole boy, and he was deeply disliked by many oil company executives. What primarily earned Drexel its enemies in high places was its willingness, even eagerness, to aggressively shake up some powerful interests that didn't want to be shaken.

That eagerness was nowhere more apparent than in the firm's relationship with its competitors on Wall Street. Drexel created deals that hurt their businesses, it backed deals that hurt their clients, and whenever possible, it dealt them out of the game. This was a fun place to work: even on the East Coast, there was a certain warm feeling about aggravating people you didn't particularly admire.

Hostile takeovers were an obvious source of confrontation, because the battle lines were usually clear and the stakes involved more than money. Perhaps the costliest from Drexel's point of view was the failed attempt by its client, Boone Pickens, to take over Unocal, which was represented by its investment banker of thirty years, Dillon Read. It was trouble on several levels. For one thing, the Delaware Supreme Court rejected the idea of offering more for the first 50 percent of the shares than for the rest, which it rightly viewed as arm-twisting. For another, it upheld a Unocal plan that could discourage hostile bids in general. But, most important, the Unocal battle created bad blood with Dillon's chairman, Nicholas Brady, who would later become secretary of the treasury.

Drexel's ability to irritate its competition extended far beyond take-overs, and with no apologies. "What really pissed off people," argued an investment banker who came over from First Boston, "was that Drexel could do better deals." At First Boston, he had worked on a huge deal for Navistar—formally International Harvester—to replace high-yield debt with new shares of stock. The lead guy on the transaction, whose last big deal hadn't been a great success, "was just swigging down Pepto-Bismol; he had a little bottle."

When they got to Navistar headquarters in Chicago, the Pepto Man almost had a coronary. The chairman told them that he had been called by Drexel, which had heard about the deal and was suggesting that the company just swap some new debt for the old debt, a transaction known as an exchange offer. First Boston and the comanager on the deal, Shearson, convinced Navistar to stick with the current plan, but as the investment banker recalled, Drexel's recommendation "was, in retrospect, a better idea for the company."

During Wall Street's glory days, First Boston was extremely successful in winning over new clients and generating deals. Their top gun was the brilliant and controversial Bruce Wasserstein, who understood the importance of humility—to him, it had little. His sales approach to potential clients was described by this former investment banker as, "We're First Boston. Do yourself a favor and let us do a deal for you."

Many did themselves a favor, although at least two of the biggest probably wish they hadn't. With Wasserstein as an adviser, Texaco acquired Getty from Pennzoil and Campeau bested Macy's for the rights to Federated. A few years later, Texaco agreed to pay Pennzoil $3 billion for ignoring its agreement with Getty, and Campeau filed for bankruptcy. Of course that is not to suggest that Wasserstein had any foreknowledge that the deals would fall apart.

The investment banker from First Boston told another story of his earlier days with Piper Jaffrey, a Midwest brokerage firm, when he worked on a deal for Apache Petroleum with three other Street firms. One of the investment bankers joined Drexel, which then bid for the whole deal at a lower cost to the company. The upshot was that Drexel didn't get the deal for itself, but it was invited to participate;

the other firms now found themselves sharing a smaller commission five ways instead of four. Apache, however, paid less for the deal than it would have if Drexel had never arrived.

Another example involved the chief executive of a casino company, a down-to-earth guy who described the decor in his hotels as "bordello modern." This exec found himself in the odd situation of having one investment banker too many. He had asked Bear Stearns to raise a chunk of money for him, and was promised an answer by noon. Too nervous to wait quietly, he decides to call Fred Joseph and find out if Drexel might be able to step up if necessary. Fred says fine.

Bear Stearns calls: The answer is yes. The exec tells the investment banker that he spoke with Joseph and asks would Bear Stearns do the deal with Drexel. The response: "Not with those assholes."

The exec calls Fred back to tell him, sorry, but Bear Stearns had first choice, and they sure don't want Drexel on board. Fred's response: "I already told Michael."

All hell breaks loose. For two days, Milken berates this exec, reminding him of the last deal that Drexel had underwritten for him, and that Milken himself had invested in that offering.

"Fred's a pretty persuasive guy," the exec noted. "But if Fred was a three, Michael was a ten." The result was that Bear Stearns kept the deal, but Drexel did the lion's share of future underwriting.

No matter how poorly Drexel got along with most of the Street, nothing matched the relationship between our firm and Salomon Brothers. It was pure—they hated each other on both a professional and personal level.

Salomon was a Wall Street powerhouse. It dominated the markets for treasury bonds, municipal bonds, high-quality corporate bonds, and mortgage-backed securities. Solly was also a major factor in the stock market. It commanded respect; if nothing else, it demanded respect. From Drexel, it got very little.

Salomon particularly resented Milken's unwillingness to share on deals, a process known as syndication. For almost a century, when a firm sold stocks or bonds, it put together a syndicate of other Wall Street firms and everyone got a piece. The biggest pieces went to major bracket firms, then smaller to middle bracket firms, and less to each of the remaining selling group. (The reason that Burnham bought Drexel in 1973, you might remember, was to buy its way into the syndicate big leagues.)

The syndicate system favored Salomon. Its reputation in the high-grade bond market made it a natural to be lead manager on those deals, giving it the biggest piece of the pie and the right to allocate the bonds to whomever it wished. In equity deals, it had a compelling sales pitch to convince companies to choose it as lead manager: It could get wider distribution of the company's stock among both institutions and individuals than could a firm that primarily dealt with individuals. This wider distribution would allow the shares to trade with less volatility once public and would encourage more Wall Street analysts to follow the company on a research basis.

Milken, however, had no interest in the syndicate approach. Simply put, he didn't need any help finding buyers for his high-yield bonds, and he wasn't about to give away commissions just because that's the way things had always been done. Also, junk-bond commissions— averaging 3 to 4 percent of the deal's total size—were the highest on the Street, as much as ten times greater than those in the more competitive, more homogeneous high-grade and government bond markets.

By 1986, Drexel Burnham absolutely dominated the most important financial market and had transformed itself into the most profitable firm on Wall Street. Its net worth had more than doubled in under two years, to the benefit of its employees who owned over 70 percent of the stock. The number of employees had grown from three thousand in 1979 to ten thousand in 1986. The firm held equity positions in 150 of the companies that it had financed, and had created an aura that there was no transaction that it couldn't finance. Drexel was arguably the most influential company in the country.

Milken's operation, with only three hundred people, was obviously the tail that wagged the dog. How much of the firm's profit was generated from the high-yield bond department is open to debate. Management argues that it never exceeded 50 percent of the total, although some people believe the figure was more on the order of 100 percent. One analyst, who thinks the higher number is closer to the truth, half-seriously mentioned to me in 1986 that "Drexel Burnham is a subsidiary of Mike Milken, Inc." The Securities and Exchange

Commission, the most objective of the sources, put the figure for the 1983-1987 period at approximately 50 percent, in line with management's estimate.

If people on Wall Street or Main Street let themselves forget that all roads led to Wilshire Boulevard, there was always the annual High-Yield Bond Conference to remind them. The conference, which came to be known as "The Predators' Ball," brought together thousands of money managers and dozens of company leaders. Held each April, it celebrated the incredible growth of the high-yield bond market, which by the mid-1980s represented 20 percent of all bonds issued by American corporations. It preached the gospel of activist management and served as a catalyst for new deals. At its finale, when all the work was done, it showcased, among others, Diana Ross, Kenny Rogers, and the Chairman of the Board himself.

It was a hot ticket on the East Coast, and those who went returned in awe. The level of professionalism, the cutting-edge thinking, the attention to detail were beyond what anyone had ever seen.

Critics would later charge that among the details attended to involved some young ladies, professionals in their own right. This may have been true, or perhaps not. If it happened, it was wrong—but so what? From the street corners to the occasional honeymoon suite, prostitution is a fact of life, and hardly the worst.

But, of course, this has nothing to do with the reordering of American business, the reason that three thousand people crammed themselves into the ballroom of the Beverly Wilshire at 6:00 A.M. These junk-bond buyers and sellers would have some breakfast, waiting until exactly 6:50 when Michael Milken would take the podium to introduce the first speaker of the day. In his introductions, recalled one listener, he liked to focus on the speakers' rise from humble beginnings and their large personal investments in the companies they managed.

The next twelve to fifteen hours would include company presentations, panel discussions, and guest speakers ranging from raiders to regulators. There were even videos to lighten the mood, including J. R. Ewing advertising a new titanium card for takeovers and Madonna improbably admitting in a dubbed version of her pop hit "Material Girl" that she was a "double-B" girl. And through it all, there was no doubt that Milken was the man in charge, not to be taken lightly.

My department got a small taste of Michael's heavy side in October

1986 at our equity conference, a Friday to Sunday deal at the Vista Hotel in lower Manhattan. It was, in effect, the celebration of our coming of age on Wall Street, even though we recognized that the rites of passage had happened three thousand miles away.

The firm had earned over $600 million between 1982 and 1985, and was well on its way to the most profitable year the Street would ever see. In 1986, Drexel would earn $525 million and be the lead manager on 188 offerings that raised $47.2 billion, more than twice its 1985 record total. Even those of us who didn't know the figures knew the feeling of being part of the most successful firm on Wall Street.

Different speakers, from Fred Joseph to various department heads, outlined where we were heading—namely, further up. Any rational person, and we were very rational about great news, could see that Drexel was unstoppable, with a large backlog of deals just waiting to be processed and an unlimited potential deal flow waiting to be created.

Milken had revolutionized finance or, at least, he had popularized the concept of revolution. His successes were apparent in each morning's *Wall Street Journal,* which carried the announcement of yet another high-yield financing. These announcements, known as tombstones, were the highlight of my morning. Squeezed into a seat on the Long Island Railroad for my daily, dismal commute, I would scan the back pages of the *Journal,* admiring the number of Drexel tombstones and the size of our deals. It even occurred to me that one morning I would go through the paper and find *only* Drexel deals.

And now, Brother Michael was here to explain it all to us, and the room was packed. The first thing that struck me when he arrived that Saturday afternoon was that he looked awfully young to be who he was. (Around the eyes, however, as someone said later, he looked a good deal older.)

Milken didn't have a set speech, referring to notes or speaking from memory. His manner was quiet, serious, and at times even disdainful, as if he were a teacher talking to a few of his lagging students. His comments moved back and forth between investment generalities and company specifics. He told us that we must think in broad, conceptual terms, to take a long-term view.

He gave us his view. Companies, from GM to the local phone system, want change, he said. He touched on one of his favorite themes: Money is not a scarce commodity. You didn't need to read between the lines; you only had to read the lines: The restructuring of American business was going to continue.

The big losers of the future would be the big losers of the past—the people who owned the bonds of investment-grade companies. To him, these bonds had nowhere to go but down, and their holders were saying to the world, "Help me lose as much as possible."

The winners, Milken implied, would be those backing the managers who understood value, and knew how to realize it. "The most important factor in credit and equity analysis is the manager," he argued, not a company's balance sheet or its income statement.

He spoke of individual companies, drawing lessons from their current state of affairs. Macy's, he said, had used the wrong financial structure in their leveraged buyout, a mistake that he predicted would raise the cost to its shareholders by $800 million over a decade. Beatrice, which had recently gone private as well, could boost the value of the company by $1.5 billion just by eliminating $200 million a year in excess expenses. Safeway could improve its profits by cutting back on low-margin private label products, which the customers didn't want anyway.

Warner Communications would benefit from the new technologies created by others, because these meant new markets for its library of recordings. Texas Air was part of an industry that hadn't made money for two decades, but now it was one of five airlines that controlled 75 percent of air traffic. Electric utilities were "changed and changing," with opportunities for stockholders in a deregulated industry.

And so on.

He spoke of market share, pointing out that "the lowest [share] is best in lousy businesses"—for example, in the equity business, the business from which everyone in the audience made their living. We gave advice and put together buyers and sellers, receiving in return a minuscule commission of less than ten cents a share. The opportunity, he said, was in finding ideas that we believed in, stocks that the firm could buy for its own account and that its sales force could resell for a large profit.

Salesmanship: He hit this issue hard. "Getting the idea around is almost as important as getting the idea," he observed. "You must make people make decisions. . . . Your only obligation is to give your best advice, not to eliminate risk. . . . If you can't sell the business, you let down the firm." No equivocating here.

He criticized our efforts: "I get depressed when I go to Sixty Broad," referring to the home office in lower Manhattan where we worked. His comments reflected a general attitude on the West Coast that we couldn't sell insulin to diabetics; our attitude was that, at the right price, his people would sell diabetes. Regardless, he was the man pushing the buttons, and some listeners sensed that he was preparing to take control of the East Coast, as well. It seemed logical, and it probably would've been inevitable if the world didn't collapse on the firm less than a month later.

"What do you want to do with your life?" he asked us, not realizing that his was about to change drastically. What level did we want to attain? He spent some time talking about what it took to be a success on Wall Street. "You must understand value," he advised. "Don't get too caught up in emotion. . . . Don't let ego get in the way. Why not go on making money with our mouths shut? Let the other guy be real big. . . . The rest of the world will come to us eventually if we have the best ideas."

One of his ideas was to restructure the massive Third World debt, known on the Street as "toxic waste." "Our financial establishment bought the mythology that lending to countries was less risky than lending to American business," was how he phrased his viewpoint years later in a magazine interview. Now he was ready to clean up some of the mess that the banks had created, and on a for-profit basis.

Another of his ideas was to introduce Japan's $100 billion a year surplus to U.S. corporations; the American financial revolution could be enhanced and then exported.

The possibilities were staggering. The mood at a corporate finance lunch on November 14, 1986—what would become a fateful day for the firm—was recalled by an investment banker who was in attendance: "We really had the world by the balls."

CHAPTER FIVE

THE HARDEST-WORKING PEOPLE IN AMERICA

Legend tells of the traveler who went into a country store and found the shelves lined with bags of salt.

"You must sell a lot of salt," said the traveler.

"Nah," said the storekeeper. "I can't sell no salt at all. But the feller who sells me salt— boy, can *he* sell salt."

—MARTIN MAYER

To have the world in your hand is no small achievement, especially when you got it there in ten years. Most people wouldn't even dream the possibility, and of those who would, most wouldn't have a prayer. But Mike Milken had done it, at least in his world. By the mid-1980s, he was arguably the most influential financier in the free world.

Over drinks one evening in 1985, a trader and I discussed Milken's rumored income of *$30 million* in the previous year (not realizing at the time that the estimate was low by almost $100 million). The trader pointed out the obvious: If he'd made that kind of money, he'd quit. I pointed out the equally obvious: Anyone satisfied with that kind of money would not be the type of person capable of earning such huge sums in the first place.

Milken wanted a lot more than $30 million or $130 million, raising the question: Why? How could he keep pushing himself, and everyone around him, so relentlessly when he had already earned more than he would need for several lifetimes?

What made Michael tick?

"He loved what he was doing," observed one investment banker. "He got joy from the adrenaline, from the action."

"He was a consummate competitor," noted one of the more astute people I know. "He gave no quarter; he asked no quarter. Eventually, it overcame him, it started to consume him—the need to compete."

There was greed, of course. "Money was his mistress," was one bond trader's colorful phrase, although he would no doubt agree that, for Milken, money was primarily a means of keeping score. "He enjoys winning the game of making money," was a point of view that most observers would agree with.

Milken certainly wasn't materialistic. The yuppie fest of new cars, new houses, new spouses, and self-aggrandizing charity events didn't appeal to him. After he graduated from college, he married his junior-high-school girlfriend. He was the father of three, and his family lived modestly, giving more to charity in a week than it spent on itself in a year. Milken had no interest in the noveau riche hobby of buying a place in high society; more likely, he felt little attraction for the establishment, for the comfortable status quo.

He did have an ego. "He had to in order to convince people," argued one arbitrageur. "He never wavered. You had the sense that he had every answer." One West Coast trader put Milken at the top of the scale for ego, but at the absolute bottom for arrogance.

Fame was unimportant to him—he avoided the press like the plague and remained surprisingly anonymous outside of Wall Street. By his choice, he wasn't on Drexel's board of directors or its executive committee, and he never even received mention in any of the firm's annual reports.

As for power . . . well, that was a different story.

In the final analysis, no one knows what really put the fire in Mike Milken, but Burt Siegel, a senior vice-president at Drexel, was probably closest when he said that Michael's motives "ran the gamut from wanting to do something extraordinarily good to pure greed." Essentially, he had every quality that almost all successful businessmen have—by a factor of ten.

Milken was a bit driven, much as Othello was a bit jealous. It wasn't that he was intense—everybody who's anybody on the Street is intense—it's that he was *so* intense. Maybe when *Webster's* is updated, it'll recognize what the financial community learned a long time ago: in•tense (in-'tens) *adj.* 1. existing or occurring in a high or extreme degree: an *intense* individual. [See M. R. MILKEN.]

His stamina was legendary: He made crucial decisions day after day on less sleep than most people need to figure out what day it is. He created a pressure cooker around himself that he worked in eighteen hours a day; he would've appreciated the comment by Jeffrey Katzenberg of Disney Studios to an employee: "If you're not willing to come in on Saturday, don't even *bother* coming in on Sunday." He never drank caffeine or liquor. He had no intention of burning out.

From the beginning, Milken was able to see the world differently from the crowd, to see opportunity where others saw risk, to keep his emotions in check. He also had an underlying confidence in his own judgment, an ability to believe that his view was not only different, it was right.

That confidence was already apparent by the time he was a college student at Berkeley; he managed money for friends with a fee structure that would've scared most investment managers silly: He got half the profits, but was responsible for *all* the losses.

While other students protested the war, he studied business. Eventually, many of them joined the mainstream, but he stayed on the outside. In retrospect, he did more than most in shaking up the establishment.

He was an inventor, according to Phil Birsch, a Drexel investment banker much as Henry Ford or Thomas Edison. "He invented a new product, and benefited from it." And if, as Chris Ryder, an institutional salesman at Morgan Stanley argues, Henry Ford created this country's middle class, Michael Milken deserves some credit for helping to create a middle class for American business.

It's interesting that Milken began his career with junk bonds as a profitable pursuit and developed in time a fanatical zeal about their possibilities. He was attracted to them in the 1970s because they were underloved and undervalued; in the 1980s, he was able to use them as catalysts for change. This overlooked corner of the bond market gave him the opportunity to achieve what are perhaps his two favorite goals: To make a bundle and to make a difference.

Michael Milken and Fred Joseph shared some characteristics, certainly—after all, they were able to work closely together for almost ten years. They both were ambitious, aggressive, driven; they both wanted to have an impact: Joseph to build a first-rate firm; Milken to build an empire. Neither cared about money in the way that most people do. Both were uncomfortable with the established order—one more for intellectual reasons; the other perhaps more for personal reasons.

Fred was "a multifaceted kind of guy," observed Tony Meyer, who knew Joseph at Drexel for more than a decade. "He loves farming and hunting, and welds metal in his basement. A guy like that can't be all bad." To a young investment banker, Fred was "a nice guy . . . a gloss-over type of guy," and borrowing a line from playwright Arthur Miller: He was "the kind of guy that liked to be liked."

Michael, on the other hand, "didn't give a shit what anyone thought of him," according to one East Coast banker. Sadly for him, Milken would eventually have to start worrying about his image. He would become front-page news for years, and his kids—and their schoolmates—would find themselves reading about him in the same sentence as Boesky, Ponzi, and even Capone. "He and his wife were devastated by the negative publicity," a senior officer remembered.

Both Milken and Joseph were exceptional leaders in their own right. They chose people based on the bottom line, rather than on the right bloodline; in the early 1980s, Fred told *Fortune* magazine half-jokingly that he preferred fat, ugly hirees. "He didn't care what they looked like," said his brother, Steve Joseph, who headed Drexel's mortgage-backed securities department. "He cared an awful lot about how bright they were, how hard they worked, how their ethics were."

An exaggerated example of the Drexel look was offered by Michel Bergerac, the former chairman of Revlon who lost his job to a Milken-financed takeover: "I'll never forget those twenty or thirty guys coming off the elevators," he told Connie Bruck, author of *The Predators' Ball.* "All short, bald, with big cigars! It was incredible! If central casting had had to produce thirty guys like that, they couldn't do it. They looked like they were in a grade-D movie that took place in Mississippi or Louisiana, about guys fixing elections in a back room."

The main man himself didn't spend much energy cultivating the *GQ* look, either, with his "polyester shirts . . . tie too short . . . bad rug" (the toupee was his only concession to vanity). Milken wasn't opposed to dressing well—he didn't wear K-Mart specials to black-tie affairs—but he probably just found the whole thing irrelevant.

Fred was a strong motivator, but as usual, nobody could do it like Michael. He set an example for his personnel that they couldn't beat, but that they tried to join. "He was a one-man factory," said one West

Coast member, who doesn't go in for hyperbole. "He did the work of forty people."

The heart of his operation was on the fourth floor of an office building he owned on Wilshire Boulevard, just off of Rodeo Drive. His key salesmen and traders sat at a long X-shaped desk, more famous on Wall Street than King Arthur's round table. Where the cross hairs met sat Milken.

For the high-yield bond group, the day began with "a traffic jam at five-thirty, six o'clock on Rodeo and Wilshire." By then, Milken was completing an hour or two of meetings with companies that wanted to raise money. As traders, salesmen, and others arrived, they would find a man already deep in work, a man more likely to greet them with a question than with a hello. "He'd ask, 'What about the sixteen and five-eighths Resorts bond? Tell me about that trade.'"

"There were about twenty guys on the floor . . . very tight . . . very familylike . . . very casual in a real tense atmosphere," recalled one trader. From six-thirty to one in the afternoon, West Coast time, the major financial markets were open, and the floor was controlled chaos, salesmen and traders yelling at each other, everyone going on all cylinders.

A client of mine from an insurance company once defined a bond salesman as someone who calls and says, "You need tickets for the game tonight?" Not these guys—they worked hard for the money.

As for Milken, "his eyes were all over that floor. . . . Every decision was second-guessed by him. He knew every position." Meanwhile, he was on the phone constantly, sometimes for only ten seconds a call, and not only to push the merchandise. "He understood the nature of people, relationships, keeping in touch," one person observed. In front of him were folders containing lists on notebooked green accounting sheets—details to be taken care of, thousands of them, written up and down the pages in impeccable handwriting.

Often, the main order of business was to find buyers for a new junk-bond offering. "I want it all sold today," he would say. "He was very good at motivating, pushing a deal over the hump," recalled a West Coast investment banker. "He would call Iowa, if necessary."

After trading hours, there were corporate finance meetings, when company managements explained why they wanted to sell high-yield bonds and why the West Coast's clients should buy them. "You were expected to participate in these meetings," said one trader, and then in summarizing the day: "You had to be on the ball from five to five." There's an old saying: It's not the years, it's the miles; for the guys on the Coast, it wasn't just the hours, it was the pressure.

Following the meetings, Milken might remain to develop new deals with the West Coast investment bankers, who were more likely to work a later schedule, perhaps until ten or eleven at night. When he returned to his home in Encino, a trunkload of documents accompanied him, and, of course, a phone was always waiting.

His employees viewed him with a mixture of admiration, awe, envy, and fear. "When he said do something, you did it," someone said, a comment that was probably a good rule of thumb for all. Milken wanted an atmosphere of confrontation, and that's what he got. He wanted his people to fight, and they did—for a trade, for an order, for a bigger bonus. Joe Garagiola's observation about Billy Martin ("He could get into a fight in an empty elevator") would've felt pretty much at home on the fourth floor of 9560 Wilshire Boulevard.

There were questions about the quality of the people that Milken hired, questions that would figure heavily in Milken's downfall and that of his firm. "Nobody out there was smart enough to do a crossword puzzle, except Michael," said a Drexel East investment banker. "A lot of mediocre people made incredible amounts of money," said a New York–based security analyst, although he had earlier pointed out that "Milken was able to attract . . . phenomenal people." A West Coast trader made a similar argument, saying that he "hired really talented people," while also noting that "Milken surrounded himself with s——s." (Not a compliment, believe me.)

In reality, everyone was right—to a degree. There were those who were extremely bright and those who were better at their jobs than most on the Street. And there were those who weren't. The great ones made more money than they ever thought possible, and the rest made more than they ever thought likely.

Even in an aggressive business such as this, they were unusual. When I spoke with them, there was a familiar defensive/combative intensity at the other end of the line, an unpleasantness, almost as a point of honor. They gave the impression that they were dealing with an idiot, and nothing could possibly annoy them more.

Let's say a client of mine wanted to sell 200 convertible bonds of Batguano Industries, which have a 9 percent yield and mature in 1998:

I am depressed. I pick up the phone and dial 44444, the number for the West Coast when calling internally. The phone rings and rings. How can it ring so long, I wonder—they can't possibly know who's calling.

"Drexel." (Woman's voice, harried)

"Yeah, who trades the Batguanos, nines of '98?

"Hold on."

(Time passes. Treaties are concluded. . . .)

"Drexel." (Woman again, maybe the same one.)

"I'm waiting for the trader on the Batguanos."

(Yelling) "Who does the Batguanos? (Then) "Hold on."

(. . . and ignored.)

"Drexel."

"Are you the trader on the Batguanos?"

"Yeah."

"This is Dan Stone, New York Institutional Equity. Who's this?"

"Archie Rice."

"Hey, Archie, how are you doing?"

(Silence.)

"I've got a client that wants the market on the Batguanos, nines of '98."

"Who's the client?"

(Pause.) "First Guaranty." (Wish I hadn't told him.)

"How many bonds?"

"Two hundred."

"Buying or selling?"

"He wants both sides." (I know that answer will piss him off, but it makes certain my client gets a reasonable bid for the bonds.)

"One oh two, one oh three." (He's pissed.)

"Thanks, Archie. I'll get right back to you if he wants to do 'em."

(Click.)

(Well, my guy can sell at least one hundred bonds at 102, or $1,020 per bond. If I'd only asked for the bid, it might've been only 101. Or for that matter, if I'd only asked for the offer, it might've been 104 instead of 103. By asking for both sides of the market—by not saying whether my client is a seller or a buyer—Archie has to give me a reasonable number at either end.)

I couldn't blame the West Coast for trying to make the most profit possible, even on an insignificant chump-change trade like this, but

I'd bet that they'd blame me for putting my client's interests ahead of theirs. Or, as they might put it, ahead of *our* firm—our firm, their pocket.

"The culture was to keep all the money on the West Coast," according to a trader. There was a vindictive sense of fairness involved: This was Mike's franchise, no one else's. There was also Mike himself, with his photographic memory, his attention to just about every detail, and his "piercing, laserlike eyes," wondering why one of his traders or salesmen or investment bankers let some of their money slip away. It's hard to imagine anyone looking forward to finessing an explanation.

The common wisdom was that Milken wanted 100 percent market share. Closer to the truth was Milken's comment to a company president in the late 1970s, as recalled by an investment banker who sat in on the conversation: "Mike said he didn't want to do one hundred percent of the business; he wanted to do seventy-five percent of the business with a hundred percent of the profit." Someone suggested that his two favorite words were *more* and *next,* two words that went a long way in defining the man. Regardless, his competitors didn't stand a chance, and those that put up a good fight sometimes became employees.

Milken controlled the high-yield market, from the data on a decade of bond trading to the location of every junk bond in public and private hands to the pricing of new offerings. And everybody who serviced him got a piece of the largest pie in captivity. Some committed their lives to getting an obscenely large and wonderful slice; others were content to be overfed for a reasonable effort.

Drexel's investment bankers were in heaven. "You could do whatever you wanted," said one from the Coast. "A company would say, 'Can you do this, this, this?' Yeah, we can do anything."

"It was one of the most fun places to work since it was so unstructured," recalled one from New York. "You could work on different types of projects. . . . There was a sense of freedom, of creativity."

"There was a remarkable pulse to the place," said another. He spoke of "Drexel-speak shorthand," putting together deals rapid-fire: "I've got a private company, seventy-five million dollars; you've got a public company, bleeding, can't get its act together."

"All right, we'll put 'em together. I'll get this guy to do the mezzanine [buy the junk bonds]."

"I've got the senior debt done."

Slam, bam—a new company, probably a better one. According to this officer, "Every other investment bank I've ever witnessed would masturbate on the subject for two weeks."

And for obvious reasons. They didn't have Drexel's entrepreneurial nature, they didn't have its personnel, and let's face it, they didn't have Milken. "He had the relationships," noted an East Coast manager, "and the others in corporate finance were more in the processing role." "He was heavily relied on to think up deals," said a corporate finance officer. "He created them, then stepped aside." "Toward the end, many of the deals came in through Milken," said Tony Meyer. "If you are with a firm that has an edge, and you're assigned to process a deal, you look good."

The Great Acquisitor "was a classic example among Drexel people," one officer said of the firm's heyday. "He's dragging a hundred megaton bomb in a cart, with a device in a box to set it off, and he can't figure out why he's so important. Then he begins to believe it."

By late 1986, the rainmakers at the firm found it easy to believe anything, and those who weren't here found it easier to justify joining. At the top business schools in the country, the best and brightest were eager to climb aboard, as well; one graduate of Harvard Business School described Drexel as "the absolutely, one hundred percent shop to get into."

Those who got the call, the rookies and the elite, found themselves in the middle of the action, with unlimited opportunities and occasional temptations. "There was a tremendous free flow of information," said one officer, "because there was a strong feeling that everyone knew what the rules were." In case people forgot—or tried to forget—Fred Joseph would remind his investment bankers every four to six weeks, according to this person, with a speech to the effect of: "I know I'm a broken record, but we have a lot of sensitive information; if anyone violates the law, you're not only out of the company, you're out of the industry, and we'll do whatever we can to see that you don't work again in this business."

Unfortunately, not everyone in the firm heard the message—or chose to listen. Some crossed the line into the unethical, a few into the illegal. It was wrong, it was unnecessary, and finally, it was fatal.

CHAPTER SIX

THE DARK SIDE OF THE FORCE

Just win, baby

—LOS ANGELES RAIDERS' MOTTO

"Without exception, everything that he wanted to do was with a view toward either screwing the client . . . or was illegal," recalled a senior East Coast investment banker of a young West Coast trader. "He never had a single honest thought in the whole three-week period—not a one. Everything was: 'Here's the way we make the most money for Drexel,' and every time I would say, 'But we can't do that, it's against the law; it's against the spirit of the underwriting contract,' this, that, and the other thing. He'd say, 'Who the *fuck* are you working for anyway; are you working for Drexel or the SEC?'

"They were all trying to please Michael, and they knew that the way to please Michael was to make a lot of money. . . . If at the end of the day, they could say, 'Michael, we made twenty-three thousand dollars on ABC, seventy-eight thousand on DEF, one hundred and two thousand on XYZ,' he'd be pleased with them, pat them on the head, maybe give them a Mercedes."

There were those who were so eager for approval or money that they stepped into the gray, and a few that stepped over the line. They

53

made a lot more for themselves, a little more for their firm, and they hurt the reputations—and futures—of ten thousand other people who didn't have any interest in being associated with the unethical or the illegal.

These buccaneers on the coast were a minority, but one to steer clear of. There was, of course, the Gray Prince, who had helped to make my first several months at the firm such fun. "There wasn't anything that he wouldn't have done to sell a deal," a New York–based salesman commented. "No holds barred—anything it took to sell it he would use, whether it was accurate or inaccurate." This salesman also remembers telling the Prince that some customers were interested in selling stock, when the West Coast wanted buyers. "They'll carry them out in a stretcher," was his absurd, but otherwise charming, message for the clients.

In negotiating a $25 million deal, the differential between what the client company wanted to pay and what the West Coast wanted it to pay had been narrowed to only $15,000. "You've gotten ninety-five percent of what you wanted," an investment banker argued. "Let him leave with a good taste in his mouth." When the Prince refused, the banker offered to pay the difference out of his own pocket, rather than try to twist the last 5 percent out of his client.

There was also Cadillac Man, a supersalesman who landed in a lawsuit for selling, allegedly with the help of a selective memory, a half-interest in a company destined for bankruptcy. The buyer, a nearby savings and loan, purchased a phenomenal $300 million of junk bonds in less than a year and eventually went bankrupt, as well. (But there's a happy side to the story: It was their real estate, not their bonds, that was primarily responsible for the bailout from taxpayers.)

There was the Young Turk, who would later turn state's evidence to protect himself, and Bruce Newberg, who would refuse even though it meant an indictment. And there were the lesser players who would rather face their maker than face their boss—Mr. One Hundred Percent—the man they deeply admired and feared.

"I had great trouble with their techniques and tactics and ethics," a top institutional equity salesman said. He recalled a trade that he had suggested to a client: Sell shares of Occidental Petroleum (Oxy), and buy Oxy's preferred, which had a 17 percent yield and was convertible into Oxy common stock. The Coast had the Oxy preferreds for sale, and the client bought 250,000 shares during the day from a trader out there.

"At the end of the day, the trader says, 'Okay, what's this account number?'

" 'Well, you'll find out tomorrow when you see the ticket.'

" 'Oh, no, no, no. We're gonna write the ticket out here.'

" 'Oh, no, no, no. We're writing the buy side here. You may want to write the sell side out there.'

"Back and forth. So I put him on hold, and I called Billy who was handling the trade for me. And I said, 'Bill, take those Oxy trades and get them key punched right now. So he went over there and put them in. A minute or so, he signaled me, so I called back [the trader on the Coast] and said, 'So, what did you say?'

" 'We're gonna write the ticket out here.'

" 'You're not writing the ticket out there.' (They would've taken all the commission).

" 'You want me to get Michael involved in this?'"

"I did tense just a bit, but I said, 'Put him on the phone.'

"Never put him on.

"If I had explained to Milken what had happened, he would've said, 'Fine, you deserve that side of it; we'll take this side of it.' But this trader was so worried that the next day—and it happened—Milken would say, 'Where's the other side of this Oxy trade?'

"That was his mentality. They didn't want to let it get away. He set that tone, but the underlings took it to an even further degree."

"There were an awful lot of people who spent an awful lot of time saying, 'Michael says,' " remembered Steve Joseph. "They would try to please Michael and anticipate what he wanted." They would also stand a much better chance of winning any battle if they could use Milken's name in their behalf—how could anyone outside of that office know whether or not he had actually said whatever he was supposed to have said.

Which raises the big question: Were the ethics of the buccaneers the ethics of their boss? They didn't have his strengths so they had to rely more on their swords. Still they weren't renegades—they were on his ship, at his side by his choice.

It's difficult to believe that Milken was unaware of conversations a few feet from him, when by his own admission he had trained himself to listen in on almost every conversation on the floor. Perhaps, as one Milken supporter argued, those who crossed the line made a point of doing it when he wasn't around to hear. But if he did hear, then he condoned it, for reasons both obvious and obscure.

"Michael had major blind spots that developed as things went along," argued an East Coast investment banker. "He very much had a trader's mentality, as far as rules and laws and regulations were concerned. He viewed them as impediments to the free flow of trading activity that should be regarded with contempt; I don't think he took securities regulations seriously.

"I think we've been trained as a nation to admire guys who say, 'Don't sit there talking about obstacles all day—just get 'em the fuck out of the way so we can move forward.' At the same time, some things are not mindless laws; some things deserve your attention, like the law against rolling your mother-in-law down the stairs. That really isn't something that you have to figure out a way around; that's something that you really have to observe."

Some would argue that Milken observed all the regulations and laws, and that even his eventual admissions of guilt were only made with a loaded, although entirely legal, gun at his head.

Others might agree with one East Coast salesman's description of Milken as "a benevolent king sitting on his throne, giving out munificent benefits. And yet, lo and behold, there's the tax collector and the executioner and the judge advocate and the inquisitor—there are all these folks running around" in the king's name, with the king's blessing.

And there are others who would argue that the king didn't mind knocking around a few peasants himself or getting his own hands dirty.

One thing is certain: Milken played to win—with his competitors, with his clients, with his employees, with the East Coast, and with the market.

"You didn't do business with a Drexel competitor unless Drexel said okay," a former executive of Columbia Savings and Loan told *Institutional Investor Magazine*. "Mike was an animal in terms of the other Wall Street houses." The complaints that surfaced from competitors over the years focused on the usual suspects of bad manners and bad ethics—primarily, misleading and mistreating them on the increasingly rare deals where Drexel and other firms were supposed to work together.

There was also the issue of last-minute adjustments to a deal, which hurt both the competitors and the clients. In this case, the terms of a deal are changed almost at the end, too late for the company to hire a different firm. One East Coast investment banker mentioned Milken's willingness to tell a company that he had "bought the deal," committing him to completing the deal on the terms discussed; one variable was left undecided, however, leaving a loophole to make later changes.

Companies selling junk bonds were asked to pay huge fees—three times greater, proportionally, than on high-grade bond deals—to compensate for the difficulty in selling these deals, even if that difficulty was not always apparent. In 1983, MCI Communications, the long-distance telephone company that was Drexel's most celebrated high-yield bond client, filed a $500 million offering. The company was asked to pay a commission of 2 percent or $10 million, the reason being that such a large deal would be hard to sell. On the day of the deal, Milken asked the company if they want to *double* the size to $1 billion—but he still wanted that 2 percent fee.

When Rupert Murdoch's Newscorp hired Drexel to sell $1.1 billion in bonds to finance its acquisition of television stations from Metromedia, it agreed to an unusual compensation schedule. The commission on bonds that were sold to the former holders of Metromedia would be 2 percent; that on bonds sold to new buyers would be 4 percent. Milken and the Great Acquisitor gave Newscorp their estimate: The breakdown of buyers would be half old, half new. After the bonds were placed, however, the company was informed that more than 90 percent of the buyers were new bondholders, implying a much higher commission. Not surprisingly, the company asked for the list of buyers, and it's still waiting for the names.

As part of a junk bond offering, a company might be asked to provide warrants which would give the holder a potentially lucrative piece of the company's stock. These warrants might be used to "sweeten the deal," making it more attractive to possible junk-bond buyers—no problem with that. Or these warrants might be used as partial payment to the Wall Street firm underwriting the deal—again, no problem. The potential for abuse occurs when a client is asked to provide a package of warrants to be used as sweetner *and* payment. In this case, the warrants might not find their way to the buyers—they might not be necessary to sell the bonds. But the client might not know that.

To clear up any misunderstanding, Fred Joseph told the high-yield department in 1985 that all clients must be told explicitly which warrants were intended for the buyers and which for the firm. How well this rule worked in practice is open to some question. The $6.2 billion Beatrice deal, discussed in Chapter 3, included $33.4 million warrants at a bargain price of $.25 each. A proxy statement provided to Beatrice shareholders, and quoted by Abraham Briloff in *Barron's* (December 5, 1988), indicated that these warrants were to be sold "in connection with the sale of debt securities other than senior notes"—presumably, as sweeteners to the $1.9 billion worth of subordinated bonds.

Ninety-nine percent of these warrants, however, showed up in the hands of BCP Partners some fourteen months later, according to a public document review by Briloff. The partners of BCP were Drexel and certain of its employees.

Drexel contends that the warrants were meant to be sold *only* to the buyers of the most speculative bond issue—the $150 million floating rate subordinated debentures. More than that, this bond issue was offered *first* to Drexel; in effect, it was an additional payment—above and beyond the $86 million cash fee—to the firm for its investment banking efforts, allegedly with the approval of the client, Kohlberg Kravis. (Kohlberg Kravis, through a public relations representative, declined to comment.)

But that is not the end of the story. The firm chose to buy some 10 percent of the junior bonds with the accompanying warrants. The balance of the warrants—which were destined to produce a 5,000 percent profit—and the bonds apparently were bought by private partnerships put together by Milken, and available only by invitation.

The invites went to employees on the West Coast, selected investment bankers on the East Coast, and even some executives from client companies. These partnerships, eventually numbering in the hundreds, gave Milken leverage over those people that he relied on most. In effect, these desirable partnerships allowed him to dole out favors to a selected group, favors that could only be collected far in the future when the partnerships cashed out.

The result was the creation of a superclass within Drexel, without the knowledge of most of us in the firm. Lucrative merchandise, such as warrants, which should have gone to all the employees, went instead to the ruling class. (I'm talking about the stuff that was *earned*; anything that was obtained by deception wasn't needed or wanted.) Allegations would later surface in congressional hearings that these partnerships engaged in self-dealing on junk bond offerings and trades that were possibly illegal, and unquestionably unethical.

If Milken was generous with those in the firm who helped his business, he could be intimidating to those who occasionally hurt it. Once when a research analyst prepared a report on a corporate client with a neutral conclusion on its stock, his boss received a phone call from Michael. The analyst recalls Milken's message, as relayed by the research director: "There is no such thing as an unhappy corporate finance client. There is such a thing as an unemployed analyst."

Actually, the neutral opinion on the stock turned out to be optimistic, as its price fell by 60 percent in subsequent years. Bear in mind, however, that Milken's attitude on this one may have been influenced by personal factors: The chief exec of this company had helped a member of Michael's family in a time of crisis—this may not be a valid excuse, but it certainly qualifies as a damn good reason.

One investment banker remembered a "very direct experience that had a lot to do with becoming at least partially disenchanted with Michael, and it also had a lot to do with my decision that as soon as I saved enough pennies in the jar, I was getting my ass out of Drexel. . . . My phone rang one afternoon." It was the treasurer of an important client company. "He said, 'I'm on the phone with Michael,' and Michael said, 'Hi, ———, how are you?'

"[The exec] went on to say, 'There's something that we've been kicking around that we want to talk to you about.' I said, 'Shoot,' and he said, 'We've be talking about the possibility of making a tender offer for the warrants [that had been sold to the public]. They're trading for around one and one-quarter bid; Michael is of the opinion that we can bring in the whole issue for a dollar fifty. [These warrants were given to buyers of the high-yield bonds in an offering several years earlier. They gave the holders the right to buy stock in the company at a set price; accordingly, if the stock price rose above this price, these warrants would be profitable to holders. The price of the stock, however, had declined sharply—the warrants would remain out of the money unless the stock quadrupled in the two years before they would expire. Because of this, the warrants were selling for about $1.25 each; Milken felt that the company could purchase all of them for $1.50 per warrant.] That way we would get rid of the overhang on the common stock. What do you think?'

"And I said, 'This is kind of a hip-shoot since I haven't been thinking about this, but if you want a quick reaction: Why bother?' [He went on to explain the business and tax reasons that argued against using the company's cash to repurchase the warrants.]

"And [the exec] said, 'Yeah, I was sort of coming to the same conclusion myself, but we'll keep thinking about it and I wish you would, too'—and bye, bye, bye, and everyone hung up.

"Thirty seconds later, the phone rings, and it was Michael. He said, 'I don't think that was very polite'—those were his first words.

" 'What?'

" 'Pissing all over my idea.'

" 'How was I supposed to know it was your idea? He called up—I had no way of knowing whose idea it was. I feel compelled to honestly respond to a client if he asks me a question. If you had wanted to set the stage for maybe trying to persuade the company that they should do it, why the hell didn't you call me up?'

"He said, 'I just wanted you to know that I don't think it was very polite, and that's my message for today.'

"And with that he hung up."

"Mike's whole pattern was to push the wall," said another corporate finance officer. The days of stodgy investment bankers waiting for their clients to call when they needed financing were over—for better and worse. This banker spoke of the pressure to get clients to maintain the junk-bond momentum. Such pressure inevitably led to questionable practices.

One allegation against the firm involved coercing companies to become clients. "People did business because they had to," said an East Coast investment banker. But this was a two-edged sword.

The most notorious allegation of coercion involved some conversations between employees of A.E. Staley, a food processing concern, and Jim Dahl. Staley was told that Drexel owned 1.5 million shares—over 5 percent of the total—and that it "wanted to be Staley's investment banker." Dahl allegedly told Robert Hoffman, Staley's chief financial officer, "It is very important for us to sit down and talk before you do something that hurts me and before I do something that hurts you." The company had other plans: It sued Drexel. Turnabout being fair play, the suit, which included the allegations just mentioned and was widely reported in the media, including *The Wall*

Street Journal, was eventually dropped after Drexel agreed to buy a division from Staley for $35 million, which one competitor valued at $10 million.

The other side of the sword was that some companies were willing, even eager, to hire Drexel as their investment banker to protect themselves from the possibility that a corporate raider might want Drexel to help them finance a takeover bid. In effect, they were buying insurance against Milken showing up on the other side of the table.

One of America's premier companies, a rumored takeover candidate, tried to co-opt the firm, according to a corporate finance officer. Fred Joseph refused, telling the company that Drexel "wasn't in the business of raider protection. Joseph's behavior was absolutely exemplary," he added.

Certainly, Drexel was interested in advising blue-chip companies on how to defend themselves against hostile takeovers—the best defense being to raise the perceived value, and therefore, the stock price, so that no one could afford to pay up for the shares. In this officer's view, however, the firm wanted to be hired for its talents in helping a company, not as a payoff to keep it from helping a company's potential enemy.

Along this line, Drexel scored a coup when Marty Siegel of white-shoed Kidder Peabody agreed to join the firm in 1986. He brought enormous respectability and a long list of corporate clients—and as it would turn out, a few skeletons in his closet.

The firm's interest in representing, and defending, blue-chip companies was good business—steady fees, powerful clients, improved image. It did not reflect, however, a change of heart regarding the merits of hostile takeovers. These takeovers were shaking up the status quo to the benefit of the actual owners of American business: some forty million stockholders.

But takeovers also had negative consequences that received less publicity from Drexel. Companies were leveraged to the hilt: If they pulled through, the greatest benefits accrued to the buyers who put up a small investment; if they failed, the greatest harm fell on the employees and the bondholders. In addition, the old stockholders, who received a premium price for their shares, often learned that they still had been bought out on the cheap. And managers, afraid to plan for a future that they might never survive long enough to see, allowed their companies to become less competitive. (Whether a short-term focus made their companies more vulnerable to takeovers, rather than less, is an issue worth considering.)

Serious questions arose as well from friendly takeovers. Consider management-led leveraged buyouts, in which Drexel played the lead financing role on the Street. The buyers here are the folks who are supposed to make money for their stockholders, not for themselves. If their companies are undervalued, their management skills are often the primary reason. Regardless, they are morally—and legally—responsible to do something about it, and that something doesn't involve hiring an investment banker to help them lock in the profit for themselves. And yet they did.

Drexel had no obligation to appoint itself the conscience of the free market, but it could have done a better job in choosing its champions. The concept of the entrepreneurial owner-manager, dedicated to the interests of the stockholders, often read better than it played. Perhaps the most extreme case involved a fellow who would eventually be convicted of tax evasion in overvaluing a gift to a church; as one investment banker asked, "Why would anyone want to do business with him?"

In the high-yield market, everyone wanted to do business with Milken—or, more accurately, they needed to. He was the market. He developed it and he sustained it. His competition in the 1970s and early 1980s was weak. "First Boston had had a bad experience," said a corporate finance officer. "Salomon didn't want to touch it. . . . Morgan Stanley was not interested. . . . Bache was doing the deals we turned down."

Milken and his department were, in effect, responsible for controlling an increasingly important market. To their credit, according to an investment banker, "They took such good care of their constituents—Milken always seemed to make them whole." But there was a flip side: "A lot of deals were made on the trading side," said a West Coast banker. "You scratch my back; I'll scratch yours."

The idea of trading favors is an integral part of business and personal life. On Wall Street, it was a part of every market. For example, a client might want to get rid of some stocks or bonds that a firm doesn't want to buy, but the firm does and takes a loss. The client is told of the loss and is expected to make it up with additional commissions on other trades or on new deals.

The quid pro quo concept, in some cases, carries with it a sour smell. Most people on the Street are small players and, if they wish, can steer clear of these cases without affecting the markets in which they work. Milken, however, was the lead player in his market, which like all markets, relied on confidence; this sense of confidence, in turn, was dependent at any given time on a perception of health.

Perhaps this point of view justifies an attitude that, as long as the favors are balanced out over the long haul, it doesn't matter whether every trade is a fair one. Perhaps not. It certainly doesn't justify an inner circle of favored clients who bought the hard-to-place deals and who enjoyed a place in the partnerships.

Another concern involved the issue of overfunding. "A lot of companies were overfinanced to create additional currency for high-yield bonds," noted a young East Coast officer. In these cases, client companies were encouraged to raise more money than they needed, and to put the excess cash in junk bonds. "Some of these companies were so small and naive, they relied on Drexel . . . they needed Drexel . . . Drexel was totally in control."

There is, however, a simple argument in favor of overfunding. Because a small company, unlike an IBM or AT&T, can never be certain that it will be able to raise money in the future, and because raising that money is a time-consuming and even expensive process for the company, there is a great deal to say for financing as much debt as possible. Eventually, the additional funds will be needed, and the company won't have to try raising more cash at that time.

Be that as it may, there was criticism of this practice, and from no less a source than I. W. Burnham. "It's wrong for an underwriter to say to a company that needs fifty million dollars, 'We can get you a hundred million,'" he told Connie Bruck. "I am always telling my guys, it's wrong."

By the mid-1980s, however, Burnham's influence on his firm's policies was insignificant. He was in his seventies and had not been Drexel's chief exec for almost a decade, having been eased aside by those senior officers more in agreement with Milken's aggressive philosophy—"He gave an inch at a time," according to a Drexel veteran. "Had I. W. been in charge, things would've been different," argued one research analyst. "He asked too many questions," said a longtime trader, after noting that "the old man loved Michael, too."

Regardless of how any of us in the firm felt about Milken, not too many questioned his success or his tactics. There were reasons, some better than others. One salesman pointed out that Drexel Burnham's stock, owned primarily by its employees, rose about 1,000 percent between 1982 and 1986. "That's why everyone turned their heads," he argued.

In fairness, the employees on the East Coast were in the dark about what was happening in the high-yield department three thousand miles away. (The same point can be made as well about the majority of employees in that office.) The guys on the Coast were a tough group, but there was no law against that.

Wall Street prides itself on playing hardball—even though the high-yield bond department was more likely than most to steal second base, spikes flying, or put a fastball in someone's ear, their tactics seemed more a matter of degree than of good versus evil. If being an occasional asshole was illegal, the Street might start resembling Love Canal; for that matter, if greed alone bought you a ticket to jail, every state would probably have more people making license plates than using them.

Rationalizations? Maybe. One thing's for sure, senior management should have had a clearer picture of what was happening in its most important department, which represented anywhere from half to all of the firm's income. So why didn't it? There's the obvious argument: "They didn't care what Milken was doing since he was making them rich," said a trader.

Another argument is that Milken didn't want to be watched more closely, and that by the mid-1980s, what he didn't want didn't happen. As one executive noted, Milken had moved to the West Coast but management hadn't.

There's also a different point of view: Why would Milken cheat, especially in the most regulated business in the world? He didn't need to. His brilliance and foresight, and even ambition, should have been the best defense against him breaking the law. Why would he do anything that stupid?

"My feeling was, with that department sailing as close to the wind as it was, that sooner or later, something was likely to happen," said a senior investment banker, "something that would blow them into the water." The first explosion occurred on May 12, 1986, at Drexel's New York headquarters. Dennis Levine, a thirty-three-year-old investment banker, was charged with insider trading. His arrest was easily dismissed as isolated and unimportant, which it was and wasn't.

As Levine explained in a May 1990 *Fortune* article, he had joined Drexel in early 1985 after his former firm, the investment banking powerhouse Lehman Brothers, merged with Shearson—a retail brokerage house and, since 1981, a subsidiary of American Express. "Levine was considered a great get at the time," recalled a former Drexel exec, who added, "Wall Street is very famous for not checking out its people very well."

Dennis Levine was a role model for ambitious B-school graduates: young, personable, rich. After years of power breakfasts, working lunches, and four-star dinners, he wasn't likely to win any race that relied on more than gravity, but then again, who cared? He was an important investment banker, a man in the action, involved in several of the most exciting battles of the 1980s: Carl Icahn against Phillips, Oscar Wyatt (of Coastal) against American Natural Resources, Sir James Goldsmith against Crown Zellerbach, and Ron Perelman against Revlon.

His 1985 bonus was more than $1 million, a healthy increase from his 1978 salary of $19,000 as a Citibank trainee. He was also well on his way to making over $11 million in illegal profits from trading on inside information. He traded by making collect calls from a pay phone to a secret Swiss account at Pictet & Cie and, later, to the Bahamian subsidiary of Geneva-based Bank Leu.

Levine's unraveling was a bit convoluted. Executives at his bank, more than impressed by his unerring stock picking, were copying his decisions for their own accounts and placing the bulk of the buy-and-sell orders through a Merrill Lynch office in Venezuela. One or more employees there jumped on the insider trading bandwagon, as well. In mid-1985, an anonymous letter was sent to Merrill, accusing two of them. Merrill called the SEC, which began investigating Bank Leu.

After ten months, the bank decided that immunity was more important than confidentiality, and Levine's name was turned over to U.S. authorities. To make matters worse for him, he found out that his partner, Robert Wilkis of Lazard Freres, had ignored a number of agreed-on precautions. Levine decided to settle with the government, pleading guilty to four felonies and disgorging his $11.5 million in illegal gains; he also implicated his friend, Wilkis, and his more recent partner, Ivan Boesky.

Boesky was a very big fish, the most successful of Wall Street's arbitrageurs. In earlier days, these arbs had searched for inefficiencies in the financial markets, where they could buy one security and simultaneously sell an identical, or nearly identical, security. This would lock in a profit at no risk.

Takeovers had created a new twist: "risk arbitrage." Risk arbs made bets on mergers. If a deal was announced, the shares of the target company would rise toward the price being offered. The stock price would rarely reach the offer price, however, because there was always a chance that the deal would fall through, particularly a hostile takeover. Risk arbs made their living by deciding what price to pay for a stock following the announcement of a deal.

For example, if IBM receives a bid of $150 per share from The Pep Boys (Manny, Moe & Jack), its price might only rise from 100 to 140. If an arb bought the shares at 140 and the deal went through three months later, his or her profit would be $10 per share; on a percentage basis, the return would be about 7 percent ($10 divided by the $140 investment) for three months. If you annualize this figure, the return is four times greater, or some 30 percent.

Of course, the deal might fall through. These three boys might have trouble raising the $90 billion purchase price. If this happened, the arb would lose $40 per share when the price of IBM fell back to 100. On the other hand, another bidder might enter the fray, offering more than $150 per share and giving the arb an even greater profit.

The final result is dependent on a number of factors, from a bidder's ability to pay to a target's willingness to sell to the personalities of the players to the opinions of various courts. The stock and bond markets, meanwhile, might influence a deal by rising or falling. Also, management might decide to hold out for a higher price, or raise the price itself, or fight to stay independent, no matter what it did to the price.

A risk arb tries to determine the odds that an announced takeover attempt will succeed, or even to determine which deals will be announced. He relies on information from public statements, court decisions, past history, proxy filings, company analyses, educated guesses, and contacts on Wall Street. The occasional arbitrageur takes this process a step too far, steering a shortcut through the law by seeking out the most accurate information out there: inside information.

Risk arbitrage in general is neither well understood nor well liked. It is viewed by the public as the financial community's equivalent of white slavery, selling corporations to the tender mercies of the highest bidder. In fact, arbs serve a valid role, giving shareholders an opportunity to sell their shares before a deal might fall through. Still, arbitrageurs are usually viewed as the heavies; Carl Icahn, himself a former arbitrageur, captured the popular view with a comment to author Moira Johnston, author of *Takeover:* "I've told my wife, if I need surgery, get me the heart of an arb. It's never been used."

Boesky rode the takeover wave of the 1980s, which produced deals—and risk arbitrage profits—of unprecedented size. As he became a great success and a minor celebrity, he tried to make risk arbitrage respectable, even enviable. "I think greed is healthy," he told students at Columbia Business School. "You can be greedy and still feel good about yourself."

He also wrote a book, *Merger Mania,* with the intriguing subtitle: *Arbitrage: Wall Street's Best Kept Money-Making Secret.* Not surprisingly, he neglected to mention that the secret ingredient of the best kept secret was inside information.

The book is interesting on several levels. There's the following line at the end of the foreword: "This book is dedicated to ending the tall tales about risk arbitrage." Or the admission in chapter four: "A great deal of information is available from Wall Street research firms." It just may not be legal.

Or the Cheshire Cat smile, chiseled features, and intense eyes facing you on the front cover. You have to wonder: What was going on in this guy's head? He knew he was a fraud. Were fame and fortune more important than self-respect or were they his basis for self-respect?

During the glory days of 1985 and 1986, Boesky appeared to relish his role among the rich and famous—the king of the arbs. He certainly seemed right for the part. He worked too hard, slept three to four hours a night, dressed in dark suits, owned a pink Rolls Royce, lunched at Lutece, spoke with a deep, formal voice, and produced extraordinary results.

"I can't predict my demise," he told *The Washington Post* in 1985, "but I suspect it will occur abruptly."

For most employees at Drexel Burnham, Ivan Boesky's past successes and future prospects were, well, irrelevant. He was a distant figure, operating in a world far removed. That is, until the news of his settlement with the government was released—one sentence on the Quotron machine after the market closed on Friday, November 14, 1986: Boesky had pleaded guilty to one felony and agreed to pay $100 million in fines and restitutions.

For my firm, it was the beginning of the end.

CHAPTER SEVEN

MEANWHILE, BACK AT THE STOCK EXCHANGE...

Life is pain. Anyone who tells you different
is trying to sell you something.

—*The Princess Bride*

While Drexel's high-yield bond department and its investment bankers were restructuring corporate America in the first half of the 1980s, the firm's equity business was prospering as well, existing almost in a parallel universe. We contributed modestly to the firm's spectacular rise, although we never produced the kind of impact and money that Milken's troops made. Still, outside of monarchs and dictators, nobody else did either.

Compared to the real world, we were pretty lucky. We worked hard and smart, we were overpaid, and we had a great boss: the stock market. When most people think of Wall Street, they think of the market—not bonds or commodities, but the market: stocks. Even junk bonds, which put a torch under the financial community, were never more interesting than when they affected the stock market. They made page one when they financed takeovers that drove up the stock prices of target companies, putting the fear of Mike into the managers of undervalued companies.

The high-yield bond department was certainly involved in the market, but the equity department lived it, and that was fine with me. The stock market is a fascinating challenge, one designed to make most people miserable, where the experts gravitate toward the obvious, and the obvious is obviously wrong.

The most bizarre aspect of Wall Street is that it has managed to attract the best and brightest to the challenge and then forced them to play under a set of conditions that almost guarantees lousy results. You couldn't have thought up this system if you tried.

The problem begins with the priority: To make money. No problem yet; certainly, no surprise. The folks who give the advice and manage the money, however, have created the problem by adding one requirement: They want to make money *quickly*. This little addition to the priority has managed to muck up the process.

But what a process, especially during the rising markets and rising profits of the 1980s. It began each day with the morning meeting, a thirty- to sixty-minute drill that occurred simultaneously throughout Wall Street. When I joined Drexel Burnham, the meeting started at eight-thirty; by the time I left, it was starting almost an hour earlier.

For most of that time, the institutional equity sales force would walk down from their desks on the ninth floor of 60 Broad Street to the conference room on the eighth, where the research department was based. (A senior exec once described the department to a veteran analyst as a bunch of prima donnas linked up by an air-conditioning system.) Joining us at the morning meeting were the research analysts who would be speaking, other analysts who were just sitting in, research support staff, and those retail salesmen who, to their credit, weren't content to rely on the ideas fed to them by their sales managers.

The conference room, modestly furnished by anyone's standards, seated about a hundred, and was equipped with microphones. When the conference call system was hooked up, all the branch offices could listen in on the meeting. The system had been with the firm longer than most people in the room, and seemed to have a mind of its own, sometimes abandoning our branch offices from Boston to Century City.

The morning meeting was normally run by the director of research, who had the primary responsibility of deciding which analysts should speak and in which order. A change in the firm's rating on a stock, particularly from hold to buy, was a top priority. An important event at a company—a large new order or a downbeat forecast from management, for example—was another priority. Lower down the list was a minor change in an earnings estimate or the reemphasis of an existing recommendation.

For eight years, people complained about the morning meeting, particularly its length. In time, the meetings ran more efficiently, with analysts hitting the key points quickly and comprehensibly. This was offset, however, by the growth of the equity research department, which probably doubled in size while I was at the firm. The result was that the presentations became tighter, but there were more analysts vying for the mike. The killer weeks were those following the end of each quarter, when companies reported their earnings for the previous three months, and fifteen to twenty analysts would show up each morning.

I certainly couldn't blame them. The success of a "sell-side" analyst was, in large part, dependent on being heard and listened to by our clients. The best way to leverage a message, whatever that message might be on a given day, was to get the sales force involved. When thirty salesmen are making calls on a particular stock, the analyst gets exposure and, sometimes, immediate impact. If thirty salesmen each convince a few clients to buy shares in a new recommendation, the price of that stock will rise with its opening price.

For example, in January 1985, David Healy, our respected copper analyst, added Phelps Dodge to the buy list, his first recommendation in the group since 1979. The outlook for copper prices, by his calculations, was favorable—the inventory-to-consumption ratio, a measure of supply and demand, was approaching shortage conditions. If prices rose as expected, Phelps Dodge would be a prime beneficiary. The salesmen, and the clients, recognized the importance of this call, and the shares rose more than a point on the opening. Phelps would triple before Dave would pull his recommendation.

The impact of a major call can be felt on the downside as well. In April 1985, Arthur Kirsch removed Philip Morris from the buy list, after strongly—and successfully—recommending it for years. The concern, highlighted in the previous day's *Wall Street Journal,* was that tobacco litigation would become a major cloud over the stock for the first time since the early 1960s. Arthur's rating change became everyone's first call, and not surprisingly, Morris's share price plummeted, dropping 7 percent on the first trade that morning.

Naturally, the analysts who had the greatest impact were those who had earned the respect of the salesmen and the clients. Regardless, every analyst stood to benefit from the sales force's support. If I'd been a research analyst, I would've found a reason to speak at the morning meeting three days a week.

But as a salesman, I was a listener, and time moves slowly when other people get to do the talking. Occasionally, time would seem to stop in its tracks. The morning meetings, however, were for information not entertainment, although there were some lively moments every so often. In one 1983 meeting, an analyst spoke about Paradyne's new computer-related something or other and was asked to explain how it worked (a good question because salesmen, and investors, have a tendency to get caught up in a story even if they don't completely understand it). Following the Paradyne analyst was the Tampax analyst, who began his presentation with: "I hope nobody is going to ask me how this works."

The best comment at a meeting was made during the wild 1980 run-up in gold prices. When asked how high the price might reach, the analyst quoted Adam's first words to Eve: "Stand back, honey, I don't know how big this is gonna get."

Enjoyable or not, the morning meeting was crucial: It provided the sales force with ammunition for the day, the ideas and names to discuss—the new recommendation, the stock that was removed from our buy list, a notable increase in an earnings estimate, a significant new development in an industry. For the balance of the day, we would be on the phone, as would salesmen from all the brokerage houses, with the clients—the institutions that invested people's savings and pensions in the stock market.

We would provide these professional investors with an edited version of what our analysts had said—what had happened at a company, what we expected to happen in the market, what our best stocks were, what our favorite analysts liked, whatever. We also discussed the stocks they were buying and selling and asked them their favorite ideas.

The tone and content of the sales presentation depended on the individual salesperson and, of course, on the individual client. Some were interested in ways to make money that day, most focused on a three- to six-month horizon, and some even thought in terms of several years.

There were the gunslingers trading in and out of large blocks of stock based on the latest piece of news or rumor; these were the funds that fire the imaginations of small investors when they think of the pros. A rumor that the Federal Reserve will provide more money to the economy? They buy stocks. An announcement from the chief financial officer of a company that earnings in the quarter will rise by less than expected? They sell shares in that company.

My clients didn't include the gunslingers, and I didn't mind. Investing is done best by investors, not speculators, gifted or not. More important, as a salesman, I wasn't particularly interested in being a well-paid rumormonger, trading bits of the latest and the hottest. Bear in mind, good information can sometimes be too good, and the dividing line isn't always clear.

Other salesmen were better at dealing with this issue, and several others were just better at this job. I may never have asked to cover a gunslinger account, but then again, no sales manager ever offered me one either.

The gunslingers were usually a part of a larger group known as "hedge funds." A hedge fund, by definition, simply has the right to "short stocks": selling shares that they don't own, with the intention of repurchasing those shares at a lower price, and pocketing the difference. This permits them to hedge their exposure to the stock market. Some stocks are bought, hoping for a rise in their prices; others are shorted, hoping for a decline in their prices. A portfolio of "long" winners and "short" losers allows a great stock picker to make money no matter which direction the stock market heads.

Not all hedge funds are gunslingers—far from it. In fact, one of the best investors I know runs a hedge fund focused on long-term performance. He recognizes that even if you buy the cheap ones and short the expensive ones, you may have to wait a while for the market to come to its senses.

Most institutional investors can't short stocks and are considered more conservative. These institutions include bank trust departments, insurance companies, mutual funds, and most investment advisers. These were my clients, from Rochester to Baltimore and New York to Cedar Rapids.

Because my accounts were not among the big boys like Citibank and IDS and Alliance Capital, they primarily relied on me to tell them what Drexel was saying and what was worth paying attention to. The larger buy-side players could count on phone calls from our research analysts directly, in addition to the sales calls. Our analysts spoke with their analysts and their portfolio managers, as did all the analysts from all the other Wall Street firms.

Sell-side analysts also had to stay in touch with the companies they followed, usually ten to twenty of them in one or two industries. They had to be on top of everything that was happening, and they had to have an expert opinion on what was about to happen. They had to understand industry trends, and recognize or anticipate new ones.

They had to write morning meeting notes, and weekly research abstracts, and stand-alone company/industry reports. They had to translate all this information into conclusions about whether each stock should be bought and sold, and then convince the sales force and the clients that they were right. And then they had to be right.

Analysts essentially had to work their butts off if they wanted to be well respected and not just well paid.

They also faced pressure of a different sort: the possibility that a negative analysis of a company would invite retaliation. The retaliation that most analysts face is the loss of access to one of the companies they're covering. Because their best source for information about what's going on at a company is management, no analyst is eager to be critical. The world of an analyst is a lonely place when nobody returns his or her phone calls.

Accordingly, sell recommendations are like black holes: They exist in theory, but try finding one. Analysts prefer to rate the lemons as "neutral," "long-term hold," "okay to hold," or in rare cases, "okay to sell." If a brokerage firm is covering seven hundred stocks as we were in 1986, half of them might be buy rated, or some variation of *buy,* and the overwhelming majority of the rest might be various types of *hold.* The remaining four names are *sells.*

These pressures on analysts might raise a question in your mind: Why not be a salesman instead? For one thing, salesmen—the good ones—work pretty damn hard, as well. They spend their days on the phone, and their nights and weekends reading material about the companies their firms follow and about the economy and the market in general. As with analysts, their jobs require repetitive, often boring sales calls, ongoing administrative tasks, and the patient development of relationships; their success is based on the football principle of four yards and a cloud of dust.

In one respect, analysts have a great advantage over salesmen: they know more about what they're talking about than the clients. Don't underestimate the psychic benefit of being the most knowledgeable one on the phone or at a meeting. A salesperson spends a good part of his day speaking with portfolio managers and buy-side analysts about companies they own or follow, companies that they have reason to know inside and out.

Most important, salesmen generally understand the stock market more thoroughly than analysts. They have a clearer view of the so-called big picture and are less likely to lose the forest for the trees. They are in a better position to recognize that the best company is often not the best stock, that a great story is not always a great value. And this kind of understanding is rarer than you might think.

In fact, just the ability to identify an intelligent idea and get it across coherently is a rare talent. Especially when you're sitting at a long desk with about twenty square feet of your own, with people talking and yelling around you. In this environment, you tend to develop tunnel thinking, somewhat oblivious to the noise and even to the people around you. One time, I accidently lit my wastebasket on fire and had to drown it with my tea. The guy sitting next to me didn't even notice the flames and the smoke. (Unfortunately, the smoke started to spread, creating a minipanic; I took the diplomatic route of acting ignorant. The "source" of the smoke was finally located, an air vent about twelve feet away from me. While the experts fixed this imaginary problem, I just went about my business wearing my best "nobody here but us chickens" look.)

But even with the noise, distractions, and other disadvantages of the trading floor, it did have some good points, the biggest being the traders themselves.

On the equity side, there are several types of trader. The "block traders" execute orders to buy and sell those stocks that are traded on the stock exchanges around the country, the largest by far being the New York Stock Exchange (NYSE). The orders for these "listed" stocks are transmitted from the clients to our trading desk at 60 Broad to the floor of the stock exchange, and each is executed by the specialist for that particular stock. Specialists are responsible for maintaining "orderly markets" in their stocks, putting together buyers and sellers, or stepping in as the buyer or seller of last resort.

Once the orders are filled, they are communicated back to the trading floor, and the clients are told what was done and at what prices. Often, the client is the firm itself, buying or selling stocks with its own money for its own account. These decisions are handled by the "position traders."

Unfortunately, position trading is generally a losing proposition for Wall Street. Position traders are usually in the business of helping clients and losing money. For example, if a large institutional investor wants to sell 300,000 shares of General Motors, and there are only buyers in the market for 200,000 shares, the client might ask the firm to buy the remaining 100,000 shares for its own account.

This is normally an unwelcomed request, for a simple reason. The firm ends up with 100,000 shares that it now wants to get rid of, but there are no buyers left. Supply and demand being what they are, the price is likely to go down, unless someone new steps up to buy in size or some unexpected good news comes to the rescue.

To make matters worse, the firm doesn't make much on the two hundred thousand GM shares that it was able to find a buyer for, known as "agency trading." Let's say that the equity desk negotiated a commission of eight cents per share; the firm gets $16,000 for the two hundred thousand shares it sold to others and $8,000 for the one hundred thousand shares it was stuck with. If the price declines by one-half—less than 1 percent—the loss on that one hundred thousand-share position is $50,000, or twice what it received in total commissions.

Grim business.

The "over-the-counter traders" are similar to the position traders; they buy and sell shares for their own account, in their case, shares of companies not listed on any exchange. A stock traded over the counter (OTC) is usually assigned two or three "market makers" at different firms; these traders are responsible, as you might guess, for making markets in the OTC names. This involves giving bids to customers who want to sell and making offers to those who want to buy. Their business is generally profitable, more like specialists than position traders.

Drexel traders prided themselves on being regular guys—most had worked their way onto the desk from clerical jobs in the back office. College degrees were rare, MBAs were distrusted, and bullshit was held to a minimum.

There was also an underlying machismo that had survived the 1970s and 1980s. Alan Alda would've felt uncomfortable on the desk, and Richard Simmons would've been pummeled. In fact, Wall Street at all levels liked the tough-guy image; even Fred Joseph, a polite, refined man, hunted deer with bow and arrow, and was once overheard telling his investment bankers at a high-yield bond conference: "If you can't write a ton of business in this place, it's like not being able to get laid in a whorehouse."

On the trading floor, bad taste was always in style. A salesman recalled one of I. W. Burnham's visits to the ninth floor: "[An OTC trader] yelled, 'Hey, Stubby!' Mr. Burnham, being the aristocratic gentleman that he is, replied, 'I beg your pardon.' The trader yelled back, 'Hey, Stubby, you run this joint? I got to tell you a few things I don't like about this place.' "

Once, a stripper showed up for a trader's birthday, paralyzing the whole floor and costing the firm thousands of dollars in lost business. (The guys on the Coast tried the same routine for Milken's fortieth birthday—Michael never left his phone, and his eyes never left his desk. And the stripper never returned.)

The trading floor was always in motion, to use a tired cliché. But it was also on the move, literally. During the 1980s, to accommodate the increase in trading personnel, the various departments moved from the east side of the ninth floor to the west side and then back again. With each move, miles of wiring connected beneath the elevated floor had to be reconfigured and rerouted.

In later years, my desk was located near the absolute corner of the trading floor, which occupied a space about the size of a football field. To my left and in front were the other institutional salespeople of my department, occupying three rows. Beyond them were the block and position traders spread out around the semblance of a large, X-shaped desk—it was the East Coast's version of Milken's layout. Next to them, in one long row, were the "options traders." Farther down were the OTC traders and those who traded international stocks (until they were fired in April 1989).

If you looked across the floor, you could see a tremendous diversity of people: WASPs, Jews, Catholics, Italians, Irishmen, you name it. Blacks were certainly underrepresented, particularly in positions of authority. Whether this reflected direct prejudice—and I'm speaking of all brokerage firms now—or some perception that clients would be uncomfortable is unknown and, in the final analysis, irrelevant. The same walls that Jewish bankers faced a century ago are facing blacks now, and they've got their work cut out for them.

Women traders had it tough—they just weren't entirely accepted. But saleswomen and female analysts faced a mixed bag. Some were the victims of male chauvinism; others benefited from a form of reverse discrimination. Those who played up to the egos and the insecurities of male managers and clients often received favored treatment. It wasn't that either party acted or reacted consciously. It wasn't that Wall Street was necessarily any different from anywhere else. It just was.

Another fact of life for salesmen, analysts, and traders was T&E: travel and entertainment. Fortunately, most of my clients were in the northeast, so few trips lasted more than a day. They normally involved escorting an analyst to various meetings with various clients.

The overwhelming majority of these business trips were very much as you would guess: routine, productive, and dull. Occasionally, with bad planning and bad luck—missed trains, delayed flights, late clients—even a day trip could last a lifetime.

Once on a trip to Pennsylvania, the analyst and I got so lost we had to ask for directions at a gas station. Off we went, and promptly got lost again. After another thirty minutes of driving around, we stopped again for directions, only to find ourselves back at the same gas station as before.

My favorite fiasco was a 1987 visit to New Jersey with our chemical analysts. These two analysts had just joined the firm from Dean Witter and were considered heavy hitters. I had invited along a friend of mine to drive, to reduce the chances that we'd end up wrapped around a tree. At breakfast, we realized that the handouts were still in the car, but we didn't know where the car and its driver were.

Once I had found the handouts, we faced the next problem: the handouts themselves. Some of the figures were so small that they were virtually impossible to read, especially at eight in the morning. Then the check arrived, and my credit card was rejected, although fortunately, not in front of the analysts. (The clients were friends and wouldn't have been surprised.)

We began the next appointment by locking the keys—and of course, the handouts—in the car with the engine running. I sat through the meeting, picturing my friend trying to break into the car with a coat hanger on the other side of the conference room wall some forty feet away.

Our one o'clock lunch meeting in Newark didn't involve lunch, so by the time we arrived at our three o'clock meeting we were desperate. I only had enough change for two candy bars, which the analysts didn't think to share. And to round things out, my sales manager gave me grief for taking this high-priced talent to New Jersey before they had even met with the major New York accounts. He even threatened to fire me if it happened again, a strangely hollow ultimatum that added the perfect finishing touch to the trip.

At times like this, it was absurd to tell myself that I had a great job, but even such mixups didn't change the basic fact that I was fortunate to be where I was. As an institutional salesman, I was given a desk, a phone, analysts to tap for ideas and information, accounts to cover, and a good deal of freedom to say what I wanted when I wanted. I didn't have to risk my own money, and I was paid more than the average guy working as hard, or harder.

There were also fancy lunches to remind us all how lucky we were to be a part of the Street. At these lunches, analysts or invited guests would speak, and there would often be a sense in the room that we all belonged to a special club. Occasionally, these lunches were worth the three hours out of your day; more often, they were a waste of time and money.

If nothing else, Wall Street did more than its share to support the witty and the wise, the expert speakers who shot up on the Metroliner from the nation's capital, entertained and enlightened for about an hour (for about $10,000), and returned home a little better off for the experience.

The most impressive was Barber Conable, currently the president of the World Bank, articulate and humorous, who told us in 1984 not to underestimate Walter Mondale because "his choice of vice-president was certainly better than Jimmy Carter's." The most irritating if witty speaker was Mark Shields, political pundit and raconteur, who predicted in 1988 that Dukakis would win, took his fee, and returned to his happy place on a weekly TV show, from which he could righteously criticize Drexel.

In addition to lunches, there were shows and other events to enjoy with clients. And there were boondoggles in places like Puerto Rico and Captiva Island and Vail, opportunities for clients to spend time with managers, and salesmen with clients. Which raised a difficult question: At what point does the valid process of entertaining clients—after all, people prefer to do business with people they know and trust—slip into the invalid?

For one of our lesser competitors, the question was easily answered: it—or more precisely, its salesman—had long ago blitzkrieged through the invalid into the embarrassing and illegal. As one Drexel salesman recalled, "I met with the director of research from this midwestern account, a distinguished-looking guy puffing on his pipe, and he said to me, 'I think you do an excellent job, and I like your research, but what I really like is ———. With them, I get into the back of a limo, and there's a girl in there, and she takes down my pants, and pulls my pud.' "

In comparison to those guys, my department was in Mr. Rogers's neighborhood. Money was spent ethically, if sometimes extravagantly. Perhaps the greatest waste was an annual ritual known as the megaclub, in which the salespeople who had reached a certain level of commissions would get a free long weekend at some resort. If the question earlier was where to draw the line, the question here was practical: Why do it at all?

The motivation argument was a weak one, because these people were paid a percentage of their commissions and, therefore, already had a reason to maximize business. The argument that it was important to develop relationships with clients didn't even exist, because no clients were invited.

Perhaps the biggest drawback was that this freebie went to those whose success may have been as much a reflection of their accounts as of their abilities. Total commissions are not always the best measure of a salesperson's success. Because institutional accounts split up their commission business among the various Wall Street firms, market share is often the better guide. Ask yourself: Who's the better salesman, the one with $150,000 in commissions—15 percent of the business from an account that pays Wall Street $1 million a year in total commissions—or the one with $200,000—2 percent market share from an account that generates $10 million in annual commissions?

The major reason for the megaclub was probably the worst one: It allowed the managers and the major producers of the department to enjoy a free one on the house. It was a ritual repeated throughout Wall Street, a tradition that preceded and continued through the glory days of rising markets and rising profits.

These glory days, the bull markets in stocks and bonds, fattened the profit margins of the brokerage houses in three ways: gains on the securities held by the firms, more trading by the clients, and a greater volume of new offerings of stocks and bonds.

New offerings are usually a bull market phenomenon, especially in the stock market. Rising prices encourage companies to sell stock, because they get more money for each share—this is common sense. Rising prices also encourage investors to buy shares, since people have a dangerous habit of assuming that the good times will continue—this is greed.

The first wave of new issues in the 1980s was in 1983, when speculators developed a seemingly insatiable appetite for small companies, particularly small technology names. These types of stock had been rising sharply since the bear market of 1974, and almost a decade later, had become the darlings of the market.

The wave peaked out in the second half of 1983. One expert argued that the actual turning point was a new issue called Muhammed Ali Arcades, an unusual concept whose original investors evidently didn't include the champ himself. This particular deal defined that moment in time when a crowd stops and subconsciously asks itself: What's wrong with this picture?

Plenty, as it turned out. The shares of these small new issues plummeted in price, as the reality of poorly conceived business plans intruded on the blind hopes of speculators. Sadly, and predictably, the players who were hurt the worst were small retail customers, people unfamiliar with investing and reliant on sometimes unscrupulous outside advice.

Drexel Burnham had little participation in the 1983 boom, because it didn't have a strong reputation in small technology stocks. Companies prefer to sell their shares through a firm that is well known in their industries. Drexel's relative absence from the boom, and subsequent bust, was a blessing. The firm didn't accumulate the bad will that accrued to those who underwrote these small-cap tragedies.

In the 1984–1986 period, by contrast, Drexel was a major player in stock offerings, in large part because of Michael Milken. He had established the firm's reputation among middle-size companies, and in some cases, had already sold bonds for them. He had made it possible for managers and raiders to "take companies private," buying up all the public stock with monies raised from junk bonds; later, these same companies were going public again, seeking buyers for their shares. Milken had also contributed mightily to the environment of success that had attracted a corps of aggressive and talented investment bankers.

These bankers arranged stock offerings for some of the more famous companies of the 1980s. This underwriting process included presentations to potential investors, known as "road shows," at 60 Broad Street and throughout the Drexel system. As an institutional equity salesman for the firm, I had the opportunity to meet several of the decade's top financial celebrities.

There was Carl Lindner, the billionaire investor/raider/Baptist who leaned over and politely introduced himself in a quiet, gentle voice, evidently unaware that I, and everyone else in the room, knew exactly who he was.

There was Saul Steinberg, the enfant terrible of the 1960s, who had prospered after his takeover attempt of Chemical Bank had been crushed; when his private insurance company, Reliance, went public, he asked potential investors to be his partners, although his squeeky voice and not-so-squeeky reputation didn't help his case. Almost four years later, the shares of his company have fallen by 50 percent from the offering price, while the stock market has risen by 50 percent.

There was Bill Farley, the corporate builder who was considering a bid for public office (the presidency, no less) and who already had a politician's talent for giving me the willies. His company, Fruit of the Loom, took three years to earn what it was supposed to earn in one, but it eventually became a success story, benefiting from the popularity of its new products and the skills of its managers.

There was Frank Lorenzo, with a quiet, some say ruthless, intensity, who structured a huge airline, and made his name synonymous with union busting. His wife once described him as "just a simple guy who likes to buy companies," while organized labor viewed him as evil incarnate. As a newscaster might say, he reaped the wind when he voluntarily put Continental into bankruptcy to cut wages, and sowed the whirlwind when he was forced to put Eastern into bankruptcy to pay creditors.

There was Rupert Murdoch, the urbane, impressive media baron from Australia, who was building a newspaper and television empire on three continents. His $1.1 billion purchase of six Metromedia TV stations formed the basis for an increasingly viable fourth network.

There was Ted Turner, the folksy, less impressive media baron from Atlanta, who had tried to buy CBS and had once suggested that if Drexel would raise the money, he'd buy Russia. But if Turner himself seemed offbeat, his track record was clearly on the money. "He's inately a genius," commented media analyst John Reidy. "He's worth a billion-five, and he's the major factor in cable."

There was Richard Bernstein, the recent owner of Golden Books and its stable of titles like *The Poky Little Puppy;* he smoked cigarettes with such ferocity that it seemed he would suck out the filter. After the price of his company's shares plummeted due to disappointing results soon after the offering, Bernstein returned to speak to the Drexel sales force with a claim of naïveté that came across as contrived and cynical.

There was Bob Pittman, only twenty-seven at that time, who had created Music Television (MTV) and could have easily sold shares of stock in himself. There was the management team of McCaw Cellular Communications, which raised billions of dollars from stock and bond offerings, even though they were so young that a man sitting near me commented, "They seem like nice boys."

There were great Drexel deals, such as an offering of Telex stock in 1981 to skeptical investors at less than $5 per share, which would rise almost twentyfold at its peak. There were awful deals, none worse than the sale of stock with warrants for Flight Transportation, a company that was accused of fraud and whose chief exec unwittingly taught me a memorable lesson: Never invest with anyone who wears sunglasses indoors. (Drexel reimbursed its clients for almost all losses caused by this fiasco, at a cost of $7 million.)

There were public partnerships, primarily sold by other firms, that were designed for small unsophisticated investors, to their regret. "Wall Street in general has done a lousy job of selecting and selling limited partnerships," acknowledged Howard L. Clark to *The Wall Street Journal.* (Clark had replaced Peter Cohen in January 1990 as the chief executive officer of brokerage giant Shearson Lehman Hutton.) Some $85 billion of these public limited partnerships were sold in the 1980s—this figure does not include the totals for *private* investment partnerships that were sold to supposedly sophisticated individuals during the decade.

All in all, there was no aspect of this business that put salesmen in a more difficult position than the selling of deals. New offerings are approximately *ten times* more profitable to Wall Street firms and their salesmen than normal trades. Managers want the deals done, and "selling the calendar" is always a top priority; salespeople want the commissions, and the praise that leads to new accounts and to greater commissions in the future.

But a salesman must not only look after the interests of his firm; he must also look after those of his clients. In theory, there isn't any conflict: Wall Street wants to give the best advice possible, and clients want to get the best advice. With deals, however, theory can take a beating because new issues are usually not great buys. The shares of new issues are rarely underloved and undervalued and, historically, they are below-average performers in the market.

Should a salesman sell a deal that the firm wants sold, even if there are better ideas available? There is a case to be made that a salesman's first priority is to his firm, and that new offerings are the lifeblood of an otherwise unprofitable business. There is a better case to be made, however, that the clients' interests should be paramount and that good advice is in the firm's best long-term interest—credibility is a hard-won asset that can pay off handsomely, even if it never seems to.

Warren Buffett, the chairman of Berkshire Hathaway and this country's premier investor, recently wrote about one of his companies, the *Buffalo News,* and the trade-offs between profits now and profits later. His discussion could have easily applied to Wall Street itself. Both the *News* and the Street provide a valuable service that relies on the unique expertise of its people. And both face a balancing act between short-run and long-run profits.

In the case of the *News,* the emphasis has been on long-term profits, focusing on more news and less advertising. This has hurt its immediate profitability, but has created a better product that will benefit future profitability.

In the case of the Street, the emphasis has been on short-term profits, focusing on ideas that produce the greatest commissions and fees, but not necessarily the best results. This has helped its profitability in any given year, but has hurt its reputation with its customers. The selling of deals, in short, creates a problem.

Different institutional salesmen dealt with this problem in different ways. A few avoided deals, although this approach didn't do wonders for their current or future incomes. Many tried to focus on the occasional pearls; the problem here was that everyone wanted these likely winners, and the demand for them dwarfed the supply—in these "hot" deals, a client might request 50,000 shares, and receive 1,000.

Many salespeople sold the deals as best they could, out of loyalty to their firm and to themselves. They weren't being malicious; almost certainly, they cared about their clients. They just let themselves believe in the deals they sold, because they wanted to believe and because it was easy to believe.

The investment bankers, whose loyalties were to the companies they represented, would come to them with enticing stories of the future prospects for a growing industry, for a great new product, for a dramatic earnings turnaround. They provided projections that justified the prices that were being asked, forecasts that were detailed and well reasoned.

And when those forecasts proved optimistic, and the reality fell short of the projections, there were always good explanations. The salespeople could point fingers of blame at the investment bankers who had misled them, and be righteously indignant.

But, over time, this line of reasoning becomes a weak excuse. Good salespeople recognize that an investment banker is under great pressure to get his deal done; more than that, he wants the deal done at close to the lofty price he had predicted when he was bidding for the company's business. Good salespeople recognize that the optimistic forecasts may be more a best-case scenario than a most-likely one. And they treat these great forecasts with great skepticism.

Skepticism was not only the stock in trade of good salesmen, it was also a part of any successful money manager's portfolio. Our clients knew—or should have known—that new issues were more likely to perform poorly and that the projections for the future should be taken with a huge grain of salt.

Those institutional investors who bought deals were smart enough to know the odds. Some of them tried to shift these odds in their favor, by selling their positions in the new issues on the offering day. They took advantage of a fact of life in new offerings: A brokerage firm that underwrites a deal has a responsibility to support the price of the shares for several days.

Therefore, a client can play a "heads I win, tails I break even" game. If the stock price rises after an offering, the client can "flip" his shares for a quick profit; if demand in the aftermarket is weak and the broker has to support the price, the client can usually sell his shares back at no loss.

From the viewpoint of the broker, however, a flipper is a pain in the ass, a client who isn't interested in owning the shares he buys. There were two ways to deal with this problem. One was to use the miracle of computerized trading, and track down which accounts were selling shares after the offering. Then the firm could take back the large commissions that flowed to the salesmen on these accounts; after all, a salesman shouldn't profit at the expense of his firm, and it's reasonable to assume that most salesmen knew which of their accounts were legitimate buyers and which were flippers.

Another approach was pioneered, it seems, by none other than Milken, although no one ever owned up to it. This approach was simple and effective: Support the price of a new issue at a level below the offering price. That way, if clients wanted to flip their shares, they took a loss.

Although flipping was an unpleasant reality, the blame here lies primarily with the salesmen, not the clients. Institutional investors couldn't be expected to pass up the opportunity for an easy profit, faced as they were by tremendous, and unfair, pressures to outperform the market. Their performance was measured every three months, a time frame that precludes investing in any real sense of the word.

In any three-month period, stocks will rise or fall for many reasons, only one of which involves valuation. In that short time period, stocks will sell for what the crowd is willing to pay for them, and the driving factors may be fear and greed, not logic. As the great author and investor Benjamin Graham once noted: In the short run, the stock market is a voting machine, a reflection of popularity; in the long run, it is a weighing machine, a reflection of reality.

Some of the best minds in the country, therefore, were forced to become speculators, trying to make educated guesses on which stocks would rise or fall in the near future. Rather than buying cheap and selling dear, they were under pressure to outguess what everyone else would be buying or selling. It's as if they found themselves in a car race in which all the drivers watched each other instead of the track.

Naturally, institutional investors have wills of their own, and there was no law that required a short-term mentality. But those who ignored the focus on quarterly performance were at risk of losing their clients, primarily pension funds. The treasurers of pension funds are not experts on the market and are susceptible to the foolish hope of great results every quarter of every year.

This problem is exacerbated by the advisers to pension funds, who would look fairly useless if they simply counseled patience, even though this is often the best advice. In addition, the impressive qualities of money managers in general—knowledgeable, articulate, persuasive—encourage pension funds to believe that beating the market in the short term is less of a challenge than it actually is.

The result was a strange but carefully balanced world of misplaced priorities, in which both Wall Street and its clients found themselves trying to make money quickly and letting the long term take care of itself. Which, unfortunately, it did.

The Street's priorities led to a boom in profitability when the deals—with their enticing commissions and not-so-enticing fundamentals—were plentiful. These same priorities led to a decline, even disappearance of profits, as the deals soured, leaving clients with a bitter taste not easily forgotten.

These priorities contributed to the rise and fall of Wall Street in the eyes of its customers, a loss of esteem that will take years and years to recover.

CHAPTER EIGHT

THE CITY ON THE EDGE OF FOREVER

"Jim, do you realize what you've done?"
—DR. McCOY, CHIEF MEDICAL OFFICER,
STARSHIP *Enterprise*

The last chapter was description; this one is dialogue: a fictional conversation with a favorite client, a portfolio manager with some $60 million in stocks. The events are based on facts—some past, some future—telescoped into one morning's call . . .

—This is Walt.
  Hi, Walt. Dan.

—How are you?
  Fine, how you doing?

—Okay, I guess.
  Where were you yesterday?

—I had a board meeting. Took the whole morning.
  How'd it go?

—It's the same old b.s. I try to explain what we're doing, but they don't understand.
  Well, I don't envy you trying.

88

—Yeah, it's pretty frustrating.

How was your weekend?

—Good. The boys are starting baseball now that the basketball season is over.

You still playing basketball on Sundays?

—No, that ended last week. How was your weekend?

I went to some black-tie function the other night, Friday, a big thing for the Air/Space Museum. You'd think of all the charities to support—of course, they got to use the ship, which probably wasn't a coincidence.

—What ship is that?

Oh, it's a World War Two aircraft carrier that's been put to bed, turned into a museum.

—How was the party?

All right, I guess. Kind of, I don't know—all those yuppies crammed together. Can you imagine what one U-boat could've done.

—I think it could have done a lot of good.

Yeah, maybe. You ever notice how the preppy types have such . . . great hair?

—Isn't that your group?

No, but I'm jealous. That must be some gene pool up in Connecticut. Anyway, what are you buying?

—Nothing. The main fund is seventeen percent in cash, and we may go up to twenty percent. I don't like the market here. But it's not easy [sitting on cash when the market's rising]. We underperformed the averages by two point two percent in the first quarter, and we're trailing by another one point eight percent for the first six weeks of this quarter.

Ignore all that short-term stuff—just worry about investing.

—I wish I could. But I had to explain to the board why I'm lagging this year, and it's not a lot of fun.

If you're thinking about raising cash, what would you sell?

—I'm not sure. We may lighten up on the cyclicals, since I think the economy is heading for trouble.

Any names in particular?

—Some of the steels, and maybe a little GM.

Well, Rand is negative on GM, and he's a great stock picker. You know, I was going through an old article from 1975, and it talked about some bright young analyst who had been right on the auto stocks, and it was him—over a decade ago.

—Yeah, he's one of the best.

What price were you looking to sell the GM?

—I'm not sure, maybe seventy-two.

Do you want me to put in a seventy-two limit [sell at a price of $72 per share, or better] for you?

—No, I'll have Leonard [his trader] call Joe [our trader].

I'll let Joey know.

—Okay.

Anyway, you didn't miss much yesterday. Our economist talked again about the unemployment numbers that came out on Friday—said the same basic things: payroll numbers weaker than expected . . . still looking for the strong bond market near term, then heading down as the economy picks up in the second half. Nothing new there. He was in again this morning to talk about the updated numbers on the first quarter's GNP [gross national product]; they came out about a half hour ago. Did you see them?

—Sure. They seemed to be in line.

Yeah, they were. Consumption a little stronger than expected. Inventories a bit weaker than he thought, which is a good sign for a second half pickup in the economy [as companies rebuild their supplies]. The bond market just opened a little weaker on the news, down about twenty ticks [twenty–thirty-seconds or about two-thirds of 1 percent].

There was some stuff on investment strategy as well. We're still positive on the market, no change there. Did you read the last strategy piece?

—I glanced at it. Did you get Salvigsen's latest piece? [Stan Salvigsen is a top-notch investment strategist, who writes about the economy and the markets with his partner, Mike Aronstein.]

No, I don't get his stuff until you send it to me.

—I'll send you a copy. It was a good one; it's called "The Briar Patch Effect."

What did it say?

—He still thinks we're in big trouble with the debt.

Is he as negative as before?

—More than ever. He thinks we're facing possible deflation [and depression] at some point. He talks about the dangers from all the government guarantees—like the S&Ls—that have only made things worse [by encouraging bad lending and, accordingly, bad debts].

So he's still buying T-bonds [treasury bonds]?

—Sure.

Send it along. Anyway, we've got a few interesting ideas today. No new recommendations, which is kind of surprising for a Tuesday. Jerry talked about the Cippalone [tobacco liability] trial, which should be decided any time now—it's gone to jury. I think Philip Morris [the number one tobacco company] is a good buy. I mean, I wouldn't want these guys as friends, but the company does throw off a ton of cash.

They've never lost a [product liability] case, but that's not the real issue. Jerry [our tobacco analyst] was saying that they could afford to lose one case a week at one million dollars a shot, and still pay all their legal costs for the year by January third.

The important thing is that a class action suit against them isn't going to happen, and without that, the litigation question isn't really a factor. Plus, think about it, if you sue tobacco companies for selling cigarettes, why not sue liquor companies? What's the difference? Or why not sue cereal companies for selling sugar to kids? Where do you draw the line?

Anyway, the numbers are great. The company earned almost eight dollars [per share] last year, and it should earn over nine dollars this year. And the free cash flow [the money earned over and above the company's needs] should be an additional eight or nine a share. That's pretty damn impressive for a stock selling close to eighty.

One of my smarter clients made the point that if you looked at [Philip] Morris's financials and covered up the name, it would look like a screaming buy. Also, Peter Lynch [the former manager of the top-rated Magellan Fund] has pointed out that, over time, the stock price of a company tends to track its earnings, and earnings here should grow fifteen to twenty percent for the foreseeable future.

—But you guys aren't recommending it, are you? I thought you took it off the buy list about three weeks ago.

Yeah, Jerry's concerned that the stock will drop if they lose the Cippalone case, but he's a good analyst and he recognizes that it's cheap long term. Of course, they could go out and overpay for another acquisition like they did in '85 with General Foods. They probably will at some point: Buying General Foods was not too bright, but once they did that, it makes some sense to buy another food company and get the economies of scale with distribution and SG&A [selling, general, and administrative costs]. The shareholders would be a lot better off if they just took all that cash and bought back stock, but even if they don't, the second acquisition wouldn't be as bad as the first.

So it's a good idea: great business—you know how many Marlboro cigarettes alone are sold every year?

—I don't have the slightest idea.

One hundred and twenty *billion*. Twenty percent of all the cigarettes smoked are Marlboros.

And if Congress bans advertising, it would help Philip Morris since they're already the best known. Remember the ban on TV advertising back in the seventies? That helped the tobacco companies. They're all better off if nobody advertises.

Anyway, they have the business, the numbers are powerful, and you have an issue with the trials that is scaring investors, but which isn't really a big long-term negative.

—We already have a pretty full position. We're not going to sell any. Maybe we'll buy more, at some point.

I'll let you know what happens with the trial when the decision comes through.

Scott [our airline analyst] reemphasized his recommendation on UAL and AMR [United and American Airlines]. He puts the breakup value on UAL at a hundred and fifty or more, stock's around a hundred; American's worth about seventy. He makes a good case for them: no new airports, value of the gate slots, a few airlines controlling most of the air traffic. Now that the wars are about over, the survivors can start raising prices. You have any interest in these?

—Not really.

Yeah, I don't like 'em either. I've been so wrong on the airlines for so long, but I can't see changing now. It just seems like a lousy business, needing to spend all that money on new planes. Not much left over for the shareholders.

As someone was saying, it's been a tough group for stockholders to make money in for a helluva long time. Maybe it's going to change now, but if it does, it'll do it without me. [Which is exactly what happened, for a while.]

He also likes Texas Air as a speculative trade—he puts the value of Eastern, net of debt, at sixteen dollars per share or more, and the stock's about twelve. So you're getting Continental Airlines for less than nothing. You ever fly Continental?

—A few times. They don't fly much out of here, and if I go from Chicago, I usually take someone else.

One of our aerospace analysts was in Denver once. He's afraid of flying to begin with, will only go in a [Boeing] seven sixty-seven, and only a new one—he even checks the serial numbers on the plane. Well, his airline—American, I think—canceled the flight because a storm was heading in. So he asks the agent what to do, and she says that she can put him on a Continental flight leaving in a few minutes. So he says, "But I thought you said there was a storm coming." "Yeah," she says, "but they think they can make it."

Harlan was in this morning pushing Penn Central. He's a great analyst, as you know—one of the few that I'd give my money to manage, if I had any.

—Oh, come on. You guys on Wall Street make a fortune.

Mine's pretty well tied up—I still live like a college student.

—I have no sympathy for you guys. None at all.

It *can* get kind of crazy sometimes. We had one analyst who was making maybe thirty thousand a year as a professor. Then he joins us for about a hundred grand. Then he gets hired away for something like three hundred grand. His income went up ten-fold in a year.

But someone who's been around for a while made an interesting point. He basically said that people may look like they're getting overpaid now, but this is a feast or famine business, and when things get bad, they get really bad. You and I have seen mostly good times, but there were fifteen lousy years before the party started.

—I still have no sympathy for you guys.

Fair enough, I don't have much either. Hell, a friend of mine in Drexel's training program told me that some guy there expects to be making half a million two years from now—and this clown doesn't even have a job yet.

—I'd like to know where that fellow ends up.

[At another firm.]

Fair enough. Anyway, Harlan's case on Penn Central is simple: the stock's selling for twenty-two, the company has about twenty dollars per share in cash or cash equivalents, and the rest of the businesses are worth maybe fifteen dollars. [Carl] Lindner's one of the smarter guys out there, and he was trying to buy shares at twenty-four. This idea isn't a home run, but there's not much risk, and it makes sense.

Stimpson was in this morning, also. You missed a beauty. He said, "Here's an opportunity for us to do some business," and he suggested swapping out of Federated [Department Stores] and into May [Department Stores]. I have a client that owns a lot of Federated, but I told him that he probably shouldn't listen. There's a bid on the table for Federated [from Campeau Corporation], and in this day and age, deals usually get done. Plus, I didn't like that attitude of trying to get people to do things just to do things. He's a nice guy, and maybe that's not what he meant, but still . . .

—What was the name of your last retail analyst?

You mean Edith Kessler?

—Yeah, where did she end up?

She went over to ——— about a year ago—I'm pretty sure she's still there. You should've seen her at the morning meeting, waving those red fingernails around. Even James, who's the best salesman I know, was mesmerized. I think most of us in this business had a tough adolescence. You were lucky, Walt, getting married when you were, what, sixteen?

—No, I was twenty-two. I'm from Indiana, not India.

Oh, sorry.

—Hey, it's better than New York.

I don't know about that. If you ignore the danger and the dirt . . . and the expense . . . and the generally crummy lifestyle, this a nice place to live.

—Why don't you move out to the real country?

I'm what my friend calls a classic New Yorker: unhappy in the city and miserable everywhere else. So when are you coming to visit?

—I might be there for a conference in July.

That's a good time of year—no humidity. Let me know once you have it set up. We'll see a show or something.

—Fine, I'll know soon.

I'll take you to a Crazy Eddie store—you can tell everyone you meet how you were smart enough to avoid that gem.

—I'm sure glad I did.

What a fiasco. The analyst, you remember him, came in the morning after the company announced that it was getting into home shopping, a big thing back then. He said, and I remember his words, "We should be putting our clients into the stock right here." It opened at twenty-one and something, a new high, and then went down to just about zero. He recommended it all the way down until it hit about five, and then dropped coverage. It's not often that you see a stock lose almost a hundred percent of its value.

If you're interested, Walt, Carrigan's on the hoot-and-holler talking about the insurance stocks. I can get the details and call you back.

—No, the group doesn't show up too well on our momentum work [a type of analysis that focuses on past stock movements to predict future ones].

Well, if the bond market does well these guys should benefit, but as for pricing in the industry, I don't think we're going to tell you first when it improves. By the way, do you remember the insurance analyst we had when you and I first started talking?

—No, I don't think I do.

Once, a long way back—I was pretty new here—this guy was boasting to me about being right on some earnings projection, and I asked him if he wanted to speak on the system. He turned to me and said, "Who the fuck do you think you are, telling me what to do?"

—He sounds like a fun guy to work with.

He was a wild man. I heard that one of the salesmen almost got into a fist fight with him. He was a bright, bright guy, but man, was he arrogant—made some remark about his seven-figure income once. He took in a ton doing corporate finance work [acting as an investment banker advising companies on restructurings, mergers, and acquisitions].

—What's he doing now?

I heard he quit Wall Street for spiritual reasons—he's running a used car dealership in Tibet.

—I sure don't doubt it.

Anyway, on the deal front, it's pretty quiet. The one you should look at is Circus Circus. They're doing a secondary [offering]; the two head guys are selling some of their holdings. That's usually a bad sign [if management is selling, why should you be buying?], but these guys have been selling some of their shares every so often ever since they went public at seven and a half in 1983, and the stock is at thirty-eight now. And, even after the offering, the two of them will still own some sixty percent of the stock.

The casino business is a license to steal, and nobody runs their business better than this company. They're breaking ground on a new casino in Las Vegas, the largest in the world. It's unlikely that they'll be going into Atlantic City any time soon. They don't like the politics and the economics. It's funny: When they came public back in '83, part of the attraction was that they would probably enter Atlantic City; now, part of the attraction is that they won't.

My biggest concern is that we get a nasty recession, especially on the consumer side, and discretionary spending goes down the tubes. But even this might not hurt them as bad as others, since they focus on the small spender. Plus, people might shift their vacations from real places to Vegas.

I've liked this stock since we did the first offering, and the management has treated its shareholders right.

—I'll take a look.

I'll have Sherry send you the red herring [the prospectus].

We also filed one million three hundred and fifty thousand shares of Metcalf & Eddy, involved in water supply and waste-water treatment . . . also handles hazardous and solid waste. It's a great industry, given the mess out there. It's an IPO [initial public offering] and the price range puts the shares at about sixteen times latest twelve months' earnings. Allen [& Company] has the books [they're the lead manager on the deal], and Kidder [Peabody] is a comanager. Corporate finance will be in to talk to us this afternoon, and I'll let you know if it sounds interesting.

—Okay.

As for the others, we've already talked about them.

—Is that it?

Yeah, that's about all. You've been quiet.

—Yeah, I guess so.

Something bothering you?

—It's just the same old stuff.

Like what?

—The other day, we had a problem with one of our holdings: Abbott Labs. This is a classic, just an absolute classic. The stock is down from 48 to 44 in about a week. Nestlè announced that they were entering the baby formula market, and five or six analysts pulled their recommendations. They're afraid that Nestlè's advertising is going to take business from Abbott. But it's not going to happen. I've got two kids and I'll tell you: You feed your baby what your doctor tells you to. And that's where Abbott is strong—with the doctors. We own a position in the stock, and we're probably going to add to it. Down four points in a week and now people pull the recommendations—it really makes me mad. We're just going to have to do our own work, that's all.

Well, you know, we've talked about this before—why don't you just rely on the three or four really great stock pickers at each firm you deal with, the few who consistently outperform the market? If you do that with five or six shops, you'll have about twenty analysts you can rely on.

—It's just the whole business that annoys me. You guys recommend a stock, and then when something goes wrong, you pull it off the list and we get stuck.

First of all, it wasn't us. Second, you're a big boy, and you know by now that these things happen, so you should expect them and avoid them. Analysts are under pressure to be on the winners and off the losers. And clients want ideas that are going to outperform in the next quarter or two, which is ludicrous, but that's what they want.

—I'm just tired of all the whores on Wall Street.

Oh, hell, we have this "whores" discussion every three months, Walter. But like I said, you know the way things are, so why don't you deal with—You know what annoys me? I've talked with you just about every morning for over six years, and some other salesman can call up every now and then, and push the deals and make as much or more.

—Yeah, I know, but we've been cutting back on deals.

If I were a portfolio manager, I doubt I'd do any deals. As a salesman, I'll show them to you, but I don't try to get you to buy the ones I don't like.

And then some guy from some firm pushes some deal and sends you the internal sales memo [a confidential memo from a firm's investment bankers to its sales force]—which he isn't allowed to do if you haven't noticed—and you do fifty thousand shares on the offering, and you give that firm twenty five thousand dollars, and you put five grand in his pocket.

And you do fifty thousand shares with us, on some regular stock that seems to make sense, and we make a fraction of that. So do me a favor and don't stick us with everyone else. We've given you some pretty lousy ideas, for sure: that American you-know-what deal in '81 was a lemon, and I really screwed up with the Alloy [Computer offering]—I let myself get caught up in a story I didn't really understand, but you did get out whole. Be angry if you want, but be fair. You've done all right by us.

—No, I'm just fed up with the whole thing. If the deal is hot, we get zip; if it's a dog, we get all the stock we ask for.

Then don't ask for any. Just worry about putting your own kids through college.

—Don't remind me.

Listen, I'll be out till next Tuesday. I'll be finishing up in Omaha for the Berkshire Hathaway annual meeting.

—How much stock do you own?

One share.

—That's it?

Hell, the shares are about forty-five hundred dollars each.

—Yeah, I know.

I just own one share so I can go to the annual meeting and hear Warren Buffett.

—Well, when you see Buffett, ask him about that deal he did with Salomon Brothers.

[The deal was one of the most interesting I saw during eight years on Wall Street, with lessons that went beyond the particulars of this story. As for those particulars: In the middle of 1987, Minerals & Resources, a company controlled by South Africa's Harry Oppenheimer, decided to sell its 14 percent position in Salomon Inc., the parent company of Salomon Brothers. There was little interest in its twenty-one million share stake, but eventually, a potential buyer emerged. That buyer was none other than Ron Perelman, the corporate raider who had built a huge conglomerate through acquisition, the crown jewel being Revlon. The cosmetics company had been taken over, with Drexel's financing and advice, following a bruising battle with the company's management, which was attempting a leveraged takeover of its own.

[The possibility that Perelman would become Solly's largest shareholder had to be a nightmare for Salomon chief exec John Gutfreund. Here was Perelman, a guy who had spent the last decade accumulating companies, and it wasn't likely that he'd be happy with an ownership stake of only 14 percent, regardless of his assurances. And if Perelman decided to bid for control of Salomon, the firm that would probably raise the money for him would be Drexel, Gutfreund's least favorite company on the planet.

[Also, if Perelman went after Salomon, Gutfreund almost certainly couldn't count on the shareholders to support him against Perelman. The stock price of Salomon had already collapsed from over $55 per share to $35 per share in just over a year, a casualty both of a poor market for brokerage stocks and of poor decisions by Solly's management. Stockholders were unlikely to reject a bid of perhaps $50 per share for their shares.

[Gutfreund had a problem. The solution, as he saw it, was for Salomon to repurchase the Minerals & Resources stake at $38 per share and sell a special issue of convertible preferred stock to Buffett. By placing a large issue of preferred stock with Buffet, an issue that could be converted into a significant piece of the common stock, Gutfreund would make a takeover considerably more difficult. There was no agreement from Buffett that he would support Gutfreund in the face of a takeover bid from Perelman, but frankly, there didn't need to be. Buffett's reputation was of a man who stood firmly behind the managements of the companies in which he invested—he would not vote his shares in favor of a takeover.

[But now there was another problem: the numbers didn't make sense. The cost to Salomon would be $809 million to buy back 14 percent of its stock. Then the company would turn around and sell a 12 percent ownership stake to Buffett for $700 million. So far, so good. Solly was buying twenty one million shares at $38, and selling eighteen million at $38—same price at both ends.

[The problem was that the company's costs would increase by about $50 million a year! Buffett would own preferred shares paying $63 million a year in dividends, rather than common shares paying $12 million in annual dividends.

[It was a fiasco. Perelman offered to buy a convertible preferred on more favorable terms to Salomon than it was giving Buffett, but of course, his kind offer was refused. He walked away, and within two months, was probably thanking his lucky stars, as the price of Solly's shares plummeted to seventeen; almost three years later, the stock languishes at twenty-five.]

What would you like me to ask Buffett about the Solly deal, Walter?

—Ask him if the deal was his idea originally, or was it John Gutfreund's.

He's not going to answer that. In fact, I doubt he's going
to answer much of anything about that deal. He was offered a
great bargain, and he took it; he did right by his shareholders.

—Do you think Michael Milken had anything to do with Perelman's interest in Salomon Brothers?

It's a damn good question, and I don't know. It's no secret
that Solly and Drexel hate each other. Maybe this was going to
be the Milkman's ultimate "in your face" shot. It also would've
been a smart move to finance a takeover of Solly—new management, new relationship. A good investment. And when it comes
to investing, there are very few people in his league.

He's actually got a lot in common with Buffett—disciplined,
motivated. Both are geniuses, which sure as hell doesn't hurt.
Common sense. Confidence. Not much interest in following the
crowd. Not much interest in this conversation, either.

—What do you mean?

I can tell I'm boring you.

—Not really. When is the Buffett meeting?

Next Monday. I'm just going for the day.

—But you're out for the week.

Taking some vacation.

—You can't do that. Remember what happened the last time you
did?

CHAPTER NINE

THE MISSILES
OF OCTOBER

This is the end of capitalism as we know it.

—A STOCK TRADER, OCTOBER 20, 1987

W alking off the plane, I was in for a rude awakening: The headline read: "Stock Prices Fall on a Broad Front; Volume is Record." It was Saturday, October 17, 1987, and I was returning from a vacation in Ireland, a week during which I had been oblivious to the growing chaos on Wall Street. *The New York Times* brought me back to reality in a hurry. "Dow Drops 108.36." In five trading days, the Dow Jones Industrial Average had fallen by 235 points, almost 5 percent of its total value.

The scary part of the equation was not how far the market had fallen in a day or a week, but rather how far it might fall when it opened again on Monday. Friday's big loss was the first 100-point decline, and more than half of it came in the last hour and a half. This was a recipe for national fear, the kind of fear that puts institutions and individuals on the phone with their brokers, each giving a variation on the same theme: "Just get me out!"

This kind of fear had been absent during the market's 17.5 percent tumble from its August 25 peak, and seemed to be missing in the decline of Friday, October 16. Saturday's *Times* reflected this lack of serious concern, at least among the pros. "Several experts predicted that the market's recent drop was just a pause before a healthy climb," noted one article.

The question on that Saturday was whether the sentiment of individual stockholders and institutional investors would now be jarred into panic, with everyone heading for the exit at the same time. Was the great bull market of the 1980s over and a bear market now in its place? Within three days, a new question would emerge: Was the financial system itself facing a meltdown?

The bull market in stocks, which had celebrated its fifth anniversary only two months earlier, had been peculiarly unsatisfying for many investors. The market had more than tripled, certainly, but it only seemed easy to make money in retrospect. The "logical" decisions at each point in time had a nasty habit of leading investors down the wrong paths.

Consider August 1982. The country was deep in the worst economic decline since the Great Depression; interest rates were in double digits; and Mexico was on the brink of defaulting on its loans, a default that might trigger a chain reaction of bankruptcies among Third World countries. Meanwhile, the stock market had fallen by 20 percent in a year and languished not far above the level of two decades earlier.

The mood among investors and experts varied between pessimism and catatonia. Those in the market were hurting, and those on the sidelines had little interest in joining the massacre. There didn't seem to be any good reasons to buy stocks, but in fact, there were a few great ones.

The Federal Reserve, which controls the supply of money, began leaning on the spigot in a big way, flooding the financial markets with dollars. The battle against inflation, which it had been fighting since October 1979, had turned in its favor. The economy was in the tank, and the potential catastrophe in Mexico provided yet another reason to get money into the system. Accordingly, the cost of money—interest rates—went down, and bond prices went up.

This lay the foundation for the glorious bull market. Stocks were cheap and the outlook was improving. The market rose by 50 percent within a year, and the pessimism of 1982 was replaced by the optimism of 1983. This optimism approached euphoria when it came to small technology names, and as discussed earlier, the demand was more than satisfied with a crop of new issues.

In the same way that the pessimists of 1982 missed the rally, the optimists of 1983 rode the decline. Stock prices fell by some 20 percent by mid-1984, as interest rates rose sharply in response to our supercharged economy. These high rates succeeded in slowing the country's growth, and rates began falling again in May. In late July, the consensus of pessimism was once again disappointed, as stocks rose quickly and sharply.

Both the stock market and the bond market rose fitfully into April 1986. At that point, bonds peaked (and interest rates bottomed). Stocks went into a yo-yo pattern, rising in June, falling in July, rising in August, falling in September. Those investors who tried to jump in and out of the market once a "trend" was established were whipsawed; everyone else was just knocked off balance.

A sharp two-day decline in September, followed by the Republicans' loss of the Senate and the Boesky scandal, contributed to a level of pessimism not seen since 1982. But instead of fulfilling expectations, the market once again fooled the crowd. Stocks rose by 50 percent between November 1986 and August 1987.

They rose in spite of rising interest rates, which had climbed by two percentage points since the spring. Because bonds compete with stocks as investments, the higher rates made stocks an increasingly unattractive place to invest. But no matter—the market was riding the wave of the Greater Fool Theory, the expectation that someone somewhere would have the cash and the desire to pay more for stocks in the future. The most likely prospects, Wall Street prophesized, were the Japanese, with their yen to spend and their yen to spend it here.

On August 24 and 25, the market rose sharply to new all-time highs, and then quietly worked lower over the next six weeks. Investors were unconcerned. Even a ninety-point decline in the Dow on October 6 was treated with apathy by the vast majority of experts. After all, hadn't every decline in the last five years proven a buying opportunity?

But this time was different. Investors, having spent years reluctantly absorbing one lesson, were about to learn another: Overvalued stocks decline, and often with a vengeance. Valuation may take a while to assert itself, but it always does.

The catalyst for the decline might be invisible as it was in August, or apparent for all to see as it was in October. The week preceding Monday, October 19 provided two such catalysts that were body blows to the market. Both originated from Washington. Congressman Dan Rostenkowski, the head of the powerful House Ways and Means Committee, proposed an idea designed to raise the cost of takeovers. Because takeovers were the bread and butter of the market's spectacular and speculative recent runup—"Every stock was in play," recalled a NYSE floor trader—any measure to slow them down was flirting with disaster.

The other blow was delivered on Sunday as *The New York Times* headlined "an abrupt policy shift" from the Reagan administration, which would now allow the dollar to fall in value. Normally, a falling dollar is beneficial for stocks to the extent it's inflationary, and stocks rise with inflation.

The concern, however, was that our economic relationship with a major trading partner, West Germany, was moving from cooperative to confrontational. Treasury Secretary James Baker in particular was upset with the actions of the West German central bank, which on Wednesday had raised its benchmark interest rate for the fourth time in several months.

How instrumental either of these events was in creating the crash is unknown and perhaps irrelevant. What mattered was that stocks were selling for more than they were worth, and the greed that had sustained their prices for a time had now been displaced by fear. And because fear is the stronger emotion, the decline would likely be swifter than the advance.

"By the end of the week, everybody was long and wrong," according to a trader, meaning that investors owned stocks and were better off if they hadn't. Arriving at 60 Broad early on the morning of Monday the nineteenth, I was expecting bad news, and the early reports were certainly grim. The foreign markets, which had opened before ours, were getting battered. "Everybody in Europe and Japan was trying to unload American stocks," the trader remembered. This heavy selling overseas assured that the U.S. market's opening was going to be ugly.

More than that, it was a nightmare. The first indication of just how bad things might be came within a minute of the opening bell, when the futures market opened in Chicago. The S&P futures market is a proxy for the stock market, and its opening price implied an *immediate* decline of over 4 percent! Already, the market was down by the same amount as it had fallen on Friday.

One institutional fixed income salesman recalled walking over to our OTC trading desk around 10:00 A.M. "Look over here," an OTC trader said, showing him a stack of tickets a foot and a half thick, three to four hundred orders waiting to be executed. Individual investors, which own the bulk of OTC stocks, wanted out.

While the stock market was in panic, the bond market was in disarray. In the government bond market, a trade of treasury bonds is easily done: A bid for the bonds is made by a bond trader, and if the client accepts it, the trade is over. But that is on a normal day, and October 19 was not a normal day.

A major client called up his Drexel fixed income salesman that morning, and asked for a bid on $13 million T-bonds, not a large order for this market. The salesman called up the trading desk and was told, "We can't give you a bid—we don't know where the market is. We can take an order (to sell the bonds once we find out a fair price]."

The salesman relayed the news to the client. "You know I never give an order in the government bond market," replied the client. "I can get (these trades) executed anywhere."

"Not today."

Soon afterward, the client called back: "Take an order."

Back at the stock market, the situation had slipped from hopeless to impossible. By 11:00 A.M., only one and a half hours into the trading day, the average stock was 8 percent below its Friday closing price. A powerful rally followed, cutting the decline in half. At this point, Drexel's head trader made a fateful decision.

Believing that the worst was behind the market, he announced that the trading desk was going to make a big bet on an upside move—the desk bought stock index futures. His gamble would cost the firm $25 million.

"There was a sense on the floor that (the rally) was bullshit," recalled one of the NYSE traders, who didn't share the optimism of Drexel's head trader. "Right or wrong, you had to get some liquidity. The momentary lift was just a gift from the gods. The first rally always fails; the only ones who didn't sell were morons."

Around 1:00, Richard Phelan, the president of the NYSE, suggested that the exchange might close before the end of normal trading hours, creating a feeling of panic that the exits, however narrow, might be shut entirely. The market fell another 4 percent in an hour. At 2:15, it was down by 13 percent on the day. Already the scapegoats were being lined up; according to *Time,* a man climbed on a car, yelling, "Down with Reagan. Down with MBA's. Down with yuppies."

The last hour was bizarre—the market just sank, minute by minute. "It wasn't as wild as people would think," remembered a senior trader on our desk. "It was busy, very busy. Everyone was thinking, 'It'll stop here . . . it'll bounce here . . . can you believe this?' "

In the institutional sales department, I sat quietly like many others, and watched as the prices on my Quotron machine fell, and then fell further. People didn't call and people didn't seem to make calls. What was there to say? History might have been happening, but at the time, there was a sense of unreality, as if those numbers on the Quotron screen had become unhinged from the actual world. As if we were all watching a plane suddenly lose its ability to fly and slowly, unbelievably but inevitably, tumble out of the sky.

On the floor of the exchange, there were no buyers—none. As for the sellers, their orders reflected an edge of desperation: "Sell one hundred thousand McDonalds . . . if you can't, sell one hundred thousand Reynolds . . . if you can't, sell one hundred thousand Coke."

The big names got mauled, not because they were inferior stocks, but because at least they could get sold at some price. In the over-the-counter market, some trading desks refused to answer their phones. Because a market maker in an OTC stock is required to make a bid, many simply hid from their clients. To the credit of Drexel's OTC traders, they answered the phones, even though it meant losses.

Black Monday suffered from a series of factors that fed on the decline and contributed to it, that forced investors and speculators to sell stocks regardless of their underlying values.

The biggest factor was the feeding frenzy of portfolio insurance and program trading. Portfolio insurance was designed to protect an institution against a significant decline in the market. The idea was simple: If the market fell by a certain amount, a computer would automatically sell stock index futures, thereby protecting the current value of the portfolio.

Unfortunately, portfolio insurance, some $60 billion of it at the time of the crash, had a difficult time dealing with the real world. The initial declines in the market triggered the selling of futures, which quickly made the futures cheaper than the actual stocks they represented. The program traders then stepped in to take advantage of this discrepancy. They bought the cheap futures and sold the relatively more expensive stocks, locking in a risk-free profit.

But the decline in stock prices that resulted from this program trading triggered additional selling of futures by portfolio insurers. Unless investors step in at some point, the computers can create something of a downward spiral. But average investors—individual and professional—were unwilling to buy stocks until they stopped falling; if anything, they wanted to get whatever they had in the market out.

Some of them had to get out, like it or not. Individuals who had bought stocks with borrowed money received "margin calls," forcing them to sell unless they put up more money.

Mutual funds needed to raise cash to pay their clients—individual investors who had decided that the market wasn't for them, after all. Also, these funds needed liquidity to meet the anticipated, if unpredictable, redemptions of investors who would be calling once they heard of Monday's massacre on the evening news.

Some specialists on the floor of the New York Stock Exchange and the American Stock Exchange were facing the possibility of bankruptcy. The stocks they had accumulated as part of their obligation as buyer of last resort were in a near free-fall that Monday afternoon, and their capital was being rapidly depleted. They were forced to sell what they could when they could.

By the time the bell rang at four o'clock, the market was down 22.8 percent. This was almost twice the decline in the Crash of 1929. In dollar terms, the stock market had lost $500 billion in one day, and $1 trillion in two months.

President Reagan reacted to the debacle by trying to reassure the public. "I don't think anyone should panic, because all the economic indicators are solid," he said, which perhaps was true if you ignored the budget deficit, the trade deficit, and the debt situation. More to the point, his choice of words sounded vaguely similar to Herbert Hoover's six decades earlier, a similarity that wasn't going to reassure anyone.

The chairman of the Federal Reserve, Alan Greenspan, received the news that the Dow Jones Industrial Average had closed down 508 points when he stepped off a plane in Houston. He had left Washington around noon, when the market was rallying sharply. His reaction to the number was relief: He thought the decline was 5.08 points.

Only one week earlier, he had been on the cover of *Fortune* magazine, his picture below the heading, "Why Greenspan is Bullish." Although the article focused on his positive view of the economy, the implication from the title was that he was favorable on the stock market, as well. The reporter, Sylvia Nasar, noted that "the stock market's speculative fever, a longtime Greenspan worry, has cooled a bit." That is, until it plummeted 30 percent in one week.

If the *Fortune* article raised some doubts about the new Fed chairman, his actions following the crash earned him nothing but respect. He had already commissioned a report from his staffers on how to deal with a financial crisis, although it's unlikely that he had any idea of just how bad things could get in one day.

That evening I watched "Adam Smith's Money World," which, of course, focused on the crash. Among the guests were Tom Wolfe, author of the then best-selling *Bonfire of the Vanities,* and Jimmy Rogers, a successful private investor and a well-known bear on the market. Wolfe observed that once the dust had settled, you would find it impossible to find anyone who would admit to having owned stocks on Monday morning. Somehow, everyone would've been smart enough, by their own admission, to have sold before the debacle. It was a good comment, astute and funny.

Less humorous was Rogers's comparison of Black Monday, not with the Crash of 1929, but with the Panic of 1907. Rogers was still negative on the market, and his comparison was clever for two reasons. First, it talked about an event that almost nobody knew anything about and, second, it introduced a terrifying word to millions of nervous investors: *Panic*—with a capital *P*.

Greenspan of the Fed was determined not to let this happen. Financial panics are based on fear, he knew, and the best way to stop them was to restore some confidence—specifically, some confidence that there would be money available for those who needed it. In the 1907 panic, there was none. In the Depression, there wasn't enough. In October 1987, there would be plenty.

Monetary policy was turned on a dime. The tight policy of the summer, designed to slow an overheating economy, was immediately replaced by one of ease. On Tuesday morning, banks were called and told that they shouldn't hesitate to lend, because the Fed's window would be open if they needed funds. Greenspan also approved the following announcement, released before the market's opening: "The Federal Reserve, consistent with its responsibility as the nation's central bank, affirmed today its readiness to serve as a source of liquidity to support the economic and financial system."

The world seemed a much friendlier place early that Tuesday. Overnight, the bond market had enjoyed its sharpest rally in history; the interest rate on government bonds had fallen by more than one percentage point. Stocks were still overvalued relative to bonds, but the gap had narrowed significantly in twenty-four hours.

There were some comments at the morning meeting that we were still positive on the market—just white noise as far as I was concerned. The real issue was that bond market rally and its favorable implications for the stock market—for the short term, at least. I left the meeting in high spirits.

The market responded as hoped, rising over 10 percent in the first hour of trading! Then it began to sink. As *The Wall Street Journal* later reported, the specialists on the NYSE had already lost two-thirds of their $3 billion in capital, and were in danger of losing the rest. They owned stocks that were dropping in value, and they weren't interested in buying more.

The brokerage firms were hurting, as well. They were long stocks and were having difficulty getting credit from their banks. As for individuals and institutional investors, once the market started falling, their interest in buying disappeared.

The shares of the most famous names in American business stopped trading: Sears at 11:12 . . . Kodak at 11:28 . . . Philip Morris at 11:30 . . . 3M at 11:31 . . . Dow Chemical at 11:43. Hundreds, perhaps thousands, of smaller stocks were frozen. The financial markets began to shut down.

A little after noon, the Chicago Mercantile Exchange closed down its stock index futures market. Leo Malamed, chairman of the Merc, had been told that the NYSE was considering a halt in trading, and he was afraid that his market, already battered by Monday's losses, would be overwhelmed with sell orders. Other futures and options markets soon followed.

By 12:30 P.M., the stock market had given back all its gain and more, and the NYSE, the most important stock exchange in the world, was

I.W. Burnham

Fred Joseph

Fred Joseph

U.S. Attorney Rudolf Guiliani.

Gary Lynch, chief of enforcement
for the Securities Exchange
Commission.

Michael Milken with his wife, Lori.

Martin Siegel, an investment banker
at Drexel who was implicated by
Ivan Boesky for insider trading for
transactions executed while he was at
Kidder Peabody.

Ivan Boesky

Saul Steinberg

Timothy Tabor, an arbitrageur at Kidder Peabody, pleaded not guilty to insider trading; the charges were later dropped.

Dennis Levine, after he was sentenced for insider trading in February, 1987.

Robert Freeman, formerly of Goldman Sachs, outside U.S. District Court in Manhattan after pleading guilty to insider trading, August 17, 1989.

Richard Wigton of Kidder Peabody leaves court after pleading not guilty to insider trading charges, April 16, 1987; as in the case of his associate, Timothy Tabor, the charges were dropped.

Carl Icahn

Ivan Boesky arrives at Federal Court for sentencing, December 18, 1987.

Michael Milken (left) with his attorney, Edward Bennett Williams, April 27, 1988, before the House Oversight and Investigations Subcommittee.

Milken and his attorney, Arthur Liman, arrive at New York State Supreme Court, April 7, 1989, for Milken's arraignment.

Rudolf Giuliani announces Drexel Burnham's settlement, December 22, 1988; he is flanked by Assistant U.S. Attorney John Carroll.

John Shad, chairman of Drexel, leaves the offices at 60 Broad Street on February 14, 1990, the day after the firm filed for Chapter 11 protection.

A Drexel employee carries personal belongings from the headquarters after the firm went bankrupt.

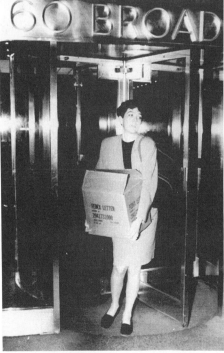

debating whether to close its doors. Several brokerage firms, including Salomon Brothers and Goldman Sachs, reportedly told government officials that they were in favor of a shutdown.

There was an eerie feeling, on our trading floor and throughout Wall Street, a feeling described by a trader on the NYSE as, "Holy shit, the system's not working." At this point, anything could've happened, and something unbelievable did. A small futures contract on the Chicago Board of Trade, the only stock market–related contract still trading, started rising rapidly. In a matter of minutes, it was up by 20 percent!

This extraordinary rally gave a boost of confidence to shell-shocked specialists and investors. It was just what the market needed, and not a moment too soon. An interesting question would later surface: Had at least one brokerage firm manipulated this futures contract? The matter was never really pursued and for good reason: When the cavalry comes to the rescue, you thank it, you don't investigate it.

Another positive came into the picture around the same time: Various companies, with the encouragement of the government, began announcing share repurchases—General Motors, Citicorp, GAF, Shearson Lehman, and U.S. Steel among them. These buy-back proposals told investors that someone—and someone knowledgeable—was willing and able to buy stocks. Although these announcements didn't require companies to buy anything immediately or at current prices, they did remind investors that maybe the world wasn't ending, after all.

Meanwhile, back at 60 Broad, I was trying to get clients to buy Kellogg, on the macabre but simple concept that, even if the economy did go into a depression, people weren't going to cut back on cornflakes. At $38 a share, investors were paying less than ten times earnings for one of the strongest companies in America.

If I'd been smarter, I would've also pushed another idea that was just about a sure thing. One salesman, who I'd run into that morning outside the men's room, had mentioned that Dreyfus was selling for $16 per share, even though it was sitting on $13 per share in cash. Their whole business, net of cash, was being offered for almost nothing. Unfortunately for my clients, I was less struck by his idea than by him: this salesman, a long-time veteran and one of the best, was confused and flustered, the first and last time I ever saw him that way.

By noon on Tuesday, the entire Street was feeling pretty much the same. An hour later, everyone started feeling a whole lot better. The market was rising. Stock prices climbed from their lows of the day, and never returned. "Institutions, in classic fashion, put in bids at the old lows, thereby confirming the lows," a trader said, referring to investors' natural inclination to hope for prices that wouldn't be seen again.

By the 4:00 P.M. bell, the Dow Jones Industrial Average was up over 100 points to 1,850. The next day, it rose almost 200 points more. The crisis was over, at least for now. The market would remain volatile for weeks, and the volume of trading would remain heavy, but the sense of panic was gone.

On Wall Street, the results were bad but not fatal. The specialists lost a reported $750 million on Friday and Monday, but still managed to earn a terrific profit for the year. The brokerage firms, which might have gone under if the market had continued to tank and the banks had cut off their credit, survived.

At Drexel, the biggest loss was on the equity trading desk, which cost the firm $25 million and the head trader his job. "He was out of his element," one trader commented. "He was an intelligent guy; he knew the business, but he didn't handle pressure. When those [phones] start to ring, you've got to perform." Later in our conversation, this trader noted, "A smart guy plays the percentages. You can't just throw caution to the wind."

Almost every investor was hurt by the crash, and a few were hurt badly. The one hurt worst was actually one of the smartest and most successful investors in history: George Soros. He had bet that the overvalued market would continue to rise, feeding on its own optimism and speculation.

After Black Monday, he decided that the Greater Fool Theory was no longer valid, and sold his stock index futures contracts. Unfortunately for him, the execution of his trades was disastrously handled, adding to his problems. The net result was an $800 million loss in two weeks (although he still showed a significant profit for the year). If there was a lesson to be learned, it was that even the greatest investors can get massacred trying to trade the market.

The most tragic result of the crash was the killing of a Merrill Lynch branch manager by an irate and deranged investor named Arthur Kane. In response, according to *Time,* several Merrill employees in Queens starting wearing buttons that said, "I am not the branch manager."

If the sense of panic among investors was gone, the sense of fear was not. Some investors dealt with this fear by walking away from the market, for good—or at least, for now. The market is just a casino, they thought, a place to gamble and eventually lose.

As logical as this might have seemed, and still seems, to many, it's simply not true. The market was and is a place to invest in the future of companies, and all its dramatic ups and downs don't change a thing. If anything, a volatile market helps investors, giving them that many more chances to buy low and sell high.

While some investors left the market, most stayed. For many of them, however, the lesson learned was not to look harder for good ideas, but rather to look for new experts to give them easy answers. This is too much to expect of anyone, and dangerous to rely on. One top guru to emerge from the crash, a strategist for a major Wall Street firm, almost immediately tripped up by incorrectly trying to predict the market's direction in the week following the crash.

Investors in general did share a common concern: Did the stock market debacle of 1987, so similar to that of 1929, mean that another savage bear market was on its way? The 1920s pattern of declining inflation, continuing economic growth, rising stock prices, growing speculation, and eventual collapse had been repeated in the 1980s. Would the 1929–1932 decline, a fall of almost 90 percent from top to bottom, be repeated as well?

More important, people wondered if the crash of 1987 would be followed by a depression. Nobody knew, of course, but it sure as hell was worth wondering about (and, considering the debt crisis, it still is). Part of the problem was that almost nobody understood exactly what had happened in the twenties and thirties, but everybody knew that they didn't want it to happen again.

The 1920s were good years for the general public, especially for the investing public—much like the 1980s. But the economy and the stock market were fundamentally different back then, and direct comparisons between the two eras could be misleading.

The stock exchange wasn't regulated by the government, and the public had little protection. The NYSE was run like a private club for the benefit of its members—brokers, floor traders, and specialists. Its higher purpose, that of allowing corporations to raise money and people to invest in the future of these corporations, was easily lost in the shuffle.

The biggest problem was that companies weren't required to tell their owners much about what was going on, and their managers were free to trade on inside information. The average investor was flying blind.

Pools were formed to manipulate stocks, buying and selling the shares among themselves and creating a rising price. Eventually, small investors would jump on the bandwagon of this "winner," allowing the pools to unload their own positions.

In other schemes, operators, sometimes illegally in league with the specialists on the floor, relentlessly knocked down the prices of stocks, short selling the shares until small investors wanted out or were forced out by margin calls. Then the boys in the game could then buy back their shares at bargain-basement prices.

"There were no short selling rules," recalled one veteran who began as an $8-a-week runner on the NYSE in 1927. "They would bang the bids, and stocks kept coming in—they made a lot of money. It was legitimate in those days."

Things were a mess. Still, the public didn't really understand what was being done to them, and the bull market obscured the thievery under a wave of easy profits.

But business as usual was about to be replaced with business by regulation. The Crash of 1929 and the horrible, grinding bear market of June 1930 to July 1932 transformed the huge gains of the 1920s into devastating losses. Then, in early 1933, the Senate Banking and Currency Committee, with its young counsel, Ferdinand Pecora, exposed Wall Street's shady practices.

The public rightfully felt raped, and the Great Depression only fueled the anger. The crash didn't cause the Depression—the buildup of debt, the shaky structure of the banking system, and the Smoot-Hawley Tariff Bill get primary blame for that—but the Street's greed and the economy's collapse were easily associated.

The result was the Securities and Exchange Acts of 1933 and 1934, which created the SEC and laid down laws to prevent fraud in the markets. The laws were vague, certainly. At the time, their vagueness was seen as a minor victory for Wall Street, which had opposed any regulation at all.

But there was an irony to it. "The law as it stands forbids and requires so little that we may truthfully say there is no body of laws as yet governing the securities markets until the commission considers, adopts and promulgates them," was journalist John T. Flynn's reaction, as noted in John Brooks's *Once in Golconda*. Brooks then comments: "But the point—and for Wall Street's whole future, a crucial point—was that the commission existed, and had broad powers to do just that. An historic moment had passed almost unrecognized. The cops were on Wall Street's corner, and they were well armed."

More than fifty years later, Drexel Burnham would find out just how well armed they were.

CHAPTER TEN

STATE OF SIEGE

The future ain't what it used to be.
—POGO

The laws that were written in the distant wake of the Crash of 1929 became the basis for the government's investigation of Drexel Burnham, the most intensive in the history of the Street. By the time of the second crash, in October 1987, the firm had been the focus of prosecutors from the Securities and Exchange Commission and the U.S. attorney's office for almost a year. During that time, the outlook for both Drexel and Wall Street had changed significantly, and for the worse.

In a sentence, what a difference a year makes. In November 1986, Wall Street was riding a wave of prosperity, and no firm more successfully than Drexel. The most profitable end of the business—mergers and acquisitions—was on a tear, junk bonds were the catalyst, and my firm dominated that market. For the year, it would earn $545 million.

By November 1987, the end of Wall Street's glory days was in sight. Although the brokerage firms had averted a crisis—a possible collapse of the industry, in fact—brought on by October's crash, the high profitability they had enjoyed was a thing of the past. The stock

116

market would eventually recover to new highs, but Wall Street's bottom line would not.

The bond market, which had been declining since April 1986, was marginally profitable in most of its segments. Municipal and government bonds had become too competitive, as banks and foreign firms vied for the business. The mortgage-backed securities (MBS) market, where thousands of home mortgages were pooled together and sold as bonds, had produced huge profits for a few firms in the early 1980s; by 1987, however, the MBS market had become a low-margin business as well, under the onslaught of new competition. For Merrill Lynch, it became an intensely negative-margin business in April 1987, when one trader lost $400 million on one security.

High-grade corporate bonds, never very profitable, stayed that way. In addition to low margins, the firms that traded these bonds faced "event risk." This was the risk that something bad would happen to the underlying company—a leveraged takeover, for example—that would cause a downgrading of the bond's safety rating and, accordingly, a fall in its price. As Steve Joseph noted—and thousands on Wall Street and Main Street had learned—"One long and wrong would kill you."

The high-yield market had held together during 1987, producing generous profits for brokerage firms and modest profits for bondholders. An ominous trend was developing, however, as deals fell in quality and buyers showed less appetite for junk bonds in general—this gathering storm would have devasting consequences to Wall Street, especially to the firm that had pioneered this market.

The stock market had obviously been the one most impacted in the year. Ten months of rising prices were wiped out in two months; more important to the Street's future profits, the public's enthusiasm for stocks, particularly new issues, was shot to hell in twenty-four hours. And potential buyers of companies no longer envisioned a future in which anything they bought could eventually be sold for more. Takeover fever was cooling.

By late 1987, Wall Street was a very different place to work from just a year earlier. And no firm faced challenges greater than those at Drexel Burnham. It had suffered the changing fortunes of Wall Street along with its competitors. Unlike other firms, however, Drexel was deep in the midst of an investigation that threatened its future, even its survival.

If the crash of October 1987 was a watershed event for my department—and for every equity department on Wall Street—the revelations of November 1986 had been a cataclysm for my firm. While the Street had seen the world change, Drexel had seen the world turned on its head.

There was no warning—it had just happened. On Friday, November 14, 1986 at 4:40 P.M., Ivan Boesky's guilty plea was announced—one felony and a fine of $100 million. On Monday the seventeenth, the unbelievable became a reality for ten thousand employees: Their firm was under investigation by the SEC.

Subpoenas had been delivered at the time of the Boesky announcement, requesting information on transactions that involved Drexel Burnham and its star, Michael Milken; Carl Icahn, the raider and Drexel client; Victor Posner, whose takeover of Fischbach would later emerge as the subject of Boesky's guilty plea; and Boyd Jeffries, the head of a Los Angeles–based brokerage firm that specialized in buying and selling shares in the "third market"—the legal but uncommon practice of trading shares when the stock exchanges are closed.

The mood that Monday morning at 60 Broad was one of shock, as if the tests from a routine checkup had just come back, and there was something . . . something, well, seriously not right. We wanted answers, but at this stage, there were none. Someone told me that the West Coast operation wasn't taking calls. There was a sense of dread on the trading floor that day, a fear that people pushed just to the side.

Meanwhile, the stock market was heading south on the rumors that the major force behind the takeover boom might be in deep trouble. The Dow Jones sold off fifteen points that first day, a relatively big move at that time; the following day, it plummeted an additional 43 to a level of 1,817.21. The hardest hit was Gillette, which had been considered vulnerable to a Drexel-financed takeover—its shares fell by 11 percent in one day.

In corporate finance, one investment banker described the impact of Boesky's allegations as "an immediate barometric change. We went from invulnerable to vulnerable . . . from a powerful group of investment bankers to villians." Said another, "There was a certain amount of distrust"—after all, no one knew what the government wanted, or how many were under suspicion.

In the high-yield department, one executive recalled: "When it hit, it was pretty devastating to everyone." According to a West Coast investment banker, "There was a definite, anxious feeling . . . an air of impending doom," although not a sense of certainty.

"All the people who worked for Michael Milken believed him to be honest," he said, adding that "they may think that the laws are wrong." His comments reveal two important factors in understanding the actions and attitudes of many employees during the investigation: A strong faith in Milken and an underlying belief in his integrity, if not necessarily in the rules that are supposed to define that integrity.

The initial word from management was a memo on that first Monday to all officers from Robert Linton, the chairman of Drexel's board, and Fred Joseph, our chief executive officer, stating, "We have been cooperating. And we intend to continue cooperating." These comments could be interpreted either positively or negatively.

On Tuesday, *The Wall Street Journal* reported that "the Securities and Exchange Commission has issued a formal order of investigation targeting Drexel Burnham Lambert Inc. in an intensifying probe focusing on Drexel's high-yield 'junk bond' operations and its ties to Ivan F. Boesky." The paper also identified eleven transactions that were under investigation; the companies involved in these transactions were Fischbach, Occidental Petroleum, Diamond Shamrock, Harris Graphics, Pacific Lumber, Lorimar, Telepictures, Unocal, Wickes, Phillips Petroleum, and MGM/UA. Most of these names would remain the focus of the investigation for over two years.

The following day, Wednesday the nineteenth, the *Journal* noted that Drexel was also under investigation by the U.S. attorney's office: ". . . a grand jury has issued subpoenas as part of a related criminal probe." That same day, Fred spoke to employees in the first of many conference calls; his tone was encouraging. He told us that the firm hadn't "uncovered any wrongdoing internally," that "we have absolutely no indication that any individual at DBL has done anything to violate securities laws," that a grand jury had been in place since May and Drexel was *not* a target of that investigation, that "the U.S. attorney may make a statement saying that no firm is the target," and that "there is no reason to believe that the firm will be faced with criminal proceedings."

He also noted that Drexel's 1986 revenues would exceed $4 billion, and that the firm had $700–800 million in excess net capital—cash above and beyond what the regulators required—which sounded reassuring even if we didn't exactly know what that meant.

The investigation provided a bitter irony with the *Journal*'s revelation on Thursday, November 20 that Boesky had been allowed to sell at least $440 million in stocks prior to the announcement of his plea bargain. In effect, he was permitted to trade on a significant piece of inside information—that Wall Street's major arbitrageur was about to accuse the most influential force on the Street of massive fraud. In doing so, he saved his investors and himself tens of millions of dollars.

Around this time, the head of my department spoke to us, first to the senior salesmen, then to the juniors—as with most managers, he loved a hierarchy. He predicted, based on what he had been told by his superiors, that we were in for a two-year process, which turned out to be one hell of a prediction. There was a sense in that small office, or at least in my imagination, that we were ready for anything that was thrown at us—already, there was an us-vs.-them attitude that would both help and hurt our cause.

On November 26, Fred was back on the system, telling us that he didn't have much to report, but he wanted to keep open the lines of communication. "The firm is going to be tough as nails on any violators of securities laws," he said. There was "no firm grip on where they think they're going . . . the direction seems to be on aggressive hostile takeovers." If so, fine—he felt good about this area.

He added that no senior officers were at risk, in management's view, which was very good news if that applied to Milken, as well. He later commented that the firm "will become more aggressive with the press," which had the impression that we were stonewalling, an impression that it had almost certainly gotten from the government.

Drexel's relations with the press were never warm. The firm was the target of a massive investigation, which put it in a difficult position. Drexel didn't know which transactions to focus on beyond what it read in the press, and it didn't know what Boesky had told the government.

Regardless, the firm's own investigation, conducted primarily by its in-house legal staff and lawyers from Cahill Gordon, was hamstrung—unknown to most, the principal target of the allegations, Mike Milken, would only deal with Drexel's investigation through his attorneys. Whatever the truth, the shortest path to it was unlikely to be between two sets of lawyers.

And even if the firm had all the facts, the best place to defend itself was in the courts, not in the press. For those making the accusations

and investigating them, the priorities were different. Those in Boesky's camp and in the government wanted the allegations to seem as
overwhelming as possible; perhaps others would step forward to cut
a deal with the prosecutors, reducing their possible sentences by
pleading guilty to lesser charges and implicating others. The more
individuals who came forward, the stronger would be the case against
those that didn't, and their firm.

If there were those who were willing to illegally leak confidential
information, the press was willing to print it (which is its right and,
to some extent, its responsibility). Reporters and their editors were
obviously not interested in sitting by, waiting until the financial story
of the decade reached the public record.

For the first several weeks of the investigation, the morning papers
were the low point of my day. I would grab them early when I arrived
at the train station and quickly glance at the *Journal*'s headlines in the
near dark as I walked to the 6:38 Valhalla Express. Inevitably, there
would be an ominous article to help get the blood flowing.

On December 5, the *Journal* carried a front-page article: "Deals in
Boesky Probe Show Increasing Links With Drexel Burnham." There
was no doubt: We were the focus of the government's investigation,
and were likely to stay that way.

The article outlined the main transactions under suspicion, most of
which had been identified on November 18. There were nine deals,
each involving an actual or attempted takeover, each involving purchases of stock by Boesky in advance of public knowledge of these
deals, and each involving Drexel as an adviser to one or both companies in every transaction:

• Pennsylvania Engineering's takeover of Fischbach Corporation.
• AM International's acquisition of Harris Graphics.
• Lorimar's merger with Telepictures.
• Occidental's aborted takeover of Diamond Shamrock.
• Maxxam's acquisition of Pacific Lumber.
• Carl Icahn's attempted takeover of Phillips Petroleum.
• Trans World's purchase of shares from Golden Nuggett.
• Mesa Petroleum's attempted takeover of Unocal.
• Wickes's purchase of a division from Gulf + Western.

The principal allegation against the firm, not surprisingly, was
insider trading, a serious crime that had evolved from the Securities

and Exchange Act of 1934. The core of the act was Section 10-b, which made it unlawful to buy or sell any security using "any manipulative or deceptive device or contrivance in contravention of such rules and regulations as the Commission may prescribe as necessary or appropriate in the public interest or for the protection of investors."

Which is to say, the SEC was given the authority to prohibit whatever it felt needed to be prohibited. Insider trading was high on that list. The commission believed it unfair for a company's managers and advisers, who have access to information that its shareholders and potential shareholders do not, to be allowed to profit by trading on this information. Certainly, in the 1920s, these insiders had lined their pockets by doing just that.

In time, the SEC expanded Section 10-b to include 10-b-5: "Anyone in possession of material inside information must disclose it to the investing public or abstain from trading." And, as William Hancock noted in *Executive's Guide to Business Law,* "The category of persons owing a duty under rule 10(b)(5) is virtually unlimited." Investment bankers and other advisers are, according to the courts, clearly within that category.

As for what constitutes *material* information: "The courts hold that . . . insider trading activity itself is highly pertinent evidence of materiality." This means that by simply trading on the basis of any information, you are implying that the information is material, whether or not you thought it was. So there.

The December 5 article also raised the possibility that another law had been broken in at least one of the nine deals under suspicion. This was the law, also created by Section 10-b, that prohibited one party from buying a stock for the benefit of another, thereby disguising who actually owns the shares. This type of deception can be as insignificant as holding shares for someone until they raise the necessary cash, or as significant as assisting the takeover of a company by allowing someone to control a large position in violation of rules requiring disclosure of that fact.

The common term is "parking," and apparently, it was not uncommon on Wall Street. People on the Street viewed this crime more like parking on a sidewalk than parking on a pedestrian, but until the takeover boom of the 1980s, the violations had probably involved the insignificant situations of one person doing a favor for another. Regardless, it was against the law, and Drexel was under suspicion for playing a role in breaking that law.

The firm's official reaction, delivered through someone identified only as "a spokesman," to the allegations—trial by media, actually— was included in the article: "It is hardly news that Drexel Burnham had an investment banking relationship with the particular companies you have chosen to focus on. It's all well understood that Mr. Boesky took positions in most large merger transactions, and that some of these were Drexel clients would not be surprising. Apart from Dennis Levine, who stole information and sold it to Mr. Boesky, we know of no one at Drexel Burnham who provided inside information to Mr. Boesky. We in no way would condone any violation of the securities laws."

The position that the firm staked out in the first weeks was the position it would hold to for the next two years: It knew of no wrongdoing by anyone, and the accusations were made by a convicted felon hoping to reduce his sentence by implicating others.

After the initial shock and the subsequent wave of bad publicity, the trading floor fell back to normal, a different kind of normal, but a routine, nevertheless. Life in the trenches wasn't dramatically changed; people did what they had always done—their jobs. Our product was the same, and our clients were almost entirely supportive. The cloud hanging over the firm's head was a major concern, but not a daily one.

In the high-yield department—the focus of the investigation—the concerns were more immediate. The government wanted information from the employees of the department and from their boss. Junk bonds would continue being sold—$1 billion was raised for Safeway Stores in mid-December, an extraordinary accomplishment considering the environment—but the key person behind this department and this market would progressively fade from the scene during the next eighteen months.

The firm as a whole found itself on a long road to oblivion, a step-by-step process that would last over three years. Jesse Livermore, the legendary stock trader, argued six decades earlier that all surprises follow the direction of the major trend, and for Drexel, that trend was down.

The year 1986 ended with a letter from Fred Joseph announcing that we had hired our ten thousandth employee in December, up from some fifteen hundred in 1974, when he had joined the firm. The number of employees who owned stock in the firm was about two thousand and our excess capital was more than $800 million. Business was strong: Since the Boesky announcement only six weeks earlier, $6.6 billion in high-yield debt had been raised in fifty different issues. What didn't need to be said was that the firm was completing the most successful year since it opened its doors in 1935; at the same time, its future was never as uncertain.

If misery loves company, and it does, Drexel got some in February 1987. The heads of risk arbitrage at Goldman Sachs and Kidder Peabody, Robert Freeman and Richard Wigton, were arrested, along with a former Kidder associate, Timothy Tabor. The charge was insider trading.

The accusator was Martin Siegel, a "bright, articulate, charming" investment banker, who had left a $2.5 million a year job at Kidder to join Drexel in 1986. Although his office was next to Dennis Levine's, and both had dealt illegally with Ivan Boesky during their careers, neither knew of the other's crimes. The circle was completed when Levine fingered Boesky, who then fingered Siegel. During 1983 and 1984, Siegel had received $700,000 in cash, some of it in a suitcase, in exchange for passing along inside information.

Dennis Levine and Marty Siegel had another distant connection, in spirit only. Levine's picture had appeared in Drexel's 1985 annual report, published in the spring of '86. Following his arrest on May 12, I was told at the time, Levine's picture was replaced—with Siegel's. For the firm, it was a bizarre reminder that everything that could go wrong would go wrong.

As for Siegel, once implicated, he cooperated with the government, pleading guilty to one count of insider fraud and accusing in turn Freeman, Wigton, and Tabor, among others. Interestingly, Siegel had not engaged in any insider crimes since joining Drexel, indicating as one senior exec noted, "He wanted to go to DBL as a whole new person." Regardless, he was caught, and now he was trying to cut his losses.

On a human level, the arrests of the three arbs was sad, especially in the case of Wigton, who was handcuffed and led off his trading floor. As for the outcomes of these highly publicized arrests . . . well, they were more than sad, they were disturbing. It's a story for a later chapter.

However unfortunate on a personal level, it was a relief to see other brokerage houses dragged into the unhappy family of government suspects. In the *Journal*'s article of two months earlier, there had been some foreshadowing: "The SEC is also known to be investigating other transactions that haven't yet been identified and could involve firms other than Drexel." Now the possibility was a reality.

The two firms involved dealt with the crisis in very different ways. Goldman Sachs, the last of the great Wall Street partnerships, stood behind its partner, Freeman. He was innocent until proven guilty, the firm believed, and he would be treated accordingly. On the Street, whatever opinion each person had of Goldman, their opinion was now that much higher.

Kidder Peabody, a prestigious investment bank with a roster of blue-chip clients, took a different tack. It suspended Wigton until the resolution of his indictment and negotiated a $25.3 million settlement with the government within four months. Kidder was a subsidiary of General Electric, recently acquired. The boss of GE, Jack Welch, was said to have been infuriated by the accusations, believing that he had been misled by the former partners of Kidder who had sold him the firm.

In advance of its settlement with the government, General Electric replaced Kidder's senior management. The top spot went to Silas Cathcart, formerly the chairman of Illinois Tool Works Inc., prompting one officer to tell *The Journal*: "I was thinking just the other day that what we need in here is a good tool and die man."

Kidder's settlement had some encouraging implications for Drexel. There were multiple allegations involved, as with the investigation of my firm, and the cost of the settlement was not significant by Wall Street standards. Because the core of the government's case against Drexel was a $5.3 million payment by Boesky to the high-yield department, hardly a big-ticket item, perhaps a reasonable fine could be agreed on.

Even Boesky's payment of $100 million as part of his guilty plea, the highest in history, would be affordable. After all, the firm had over $1 billion in equity, it had earned over $500 million in the previous year alone, and it had already begun putting aside money for a settlement. Drexel also had a diverse portfolio of "merchant banking" positions—ownership stakes in various companies that it had financed over the years. These equity holdings were worth a great deal more than their stated values, we thought, further boosting the true value of the firm.

What this line of reasoning ignored, however, was that the government was almost certainly not interested in letting Drexel off the hook for less than its punishment against Boesky. He had been given a favorable deal *because* he had implicated the top guns on Wall Street—Milken and his firm. Drexel couldn't expect better treatment.

Also, that $5.3 million payment did not involve a single transaction. According to Boesky, the payment was the net result of many illegal transactions, some for which he owed Drexel, and others for which he was owed. The firm's position, from beginning to end, was that the $5.3 million was a payment for legitimate investment banking services, specifically research that the Coast had done for Boesky's arbitrage company. The government, not surprisingly, was more comfortable with Boesky's explanation than with Drexel's.

By mid-1987, the investigation had been expanded. In addition to the demand for documents from Drexel, the government had subpoenaed information, reported *The New York Times,* "from more than a dozen financial institutions that were among the largest 'junk bond' clients of Drexel Burnham Lambert, Inc., a number of sources with knowledge of the investigation said yesterday." According to that same late-February article, the SEC was also investigating the activities of Carl Icahn, who had been involved in several takeover battles, in most cases with Drexel's support.

Meanwhile, the firm went on a public relations offensive, hoping to shore up morale, and to counteract the image that the allegations were creating with the public and with potential corporate clients. In February, Drexel took out huge advertisements in major publications with the slogan: "Ten Thousand Strong." Beneath the heading was a list of all the employees by name.

There was also an effective ad headed "It's Time to Fight Back," listing "seven myths about Drexel Burnham and our business that are frequently heard these days. They appear with something you rarely hear at all—the facts."

Another advertisement stated that "95% of the Companies in America are Considered Junk," pointing out "that of the 23,000 corporations in the United States with sales greater than $25 million, fewer than 800 are considered investment grade." In a similar vein, another ad was headlined, "Junk Bonds. Who Needs Them?" with subheadings that included, "Workers Need Them" and "Rising Stars Need Them." The ad also included a list of ninety-three companies, drawn from a pool of over one thousand, that had raised money in the high-yield market.

Television spots, created by Chiat/Day, appeared presenting specific cases in which Drexel's high-yield financings had helped out communities, and highlighting its new slogan, "Helping People Manage Change." The TV ads, according to one well-placed officer, generated a strong and favorable response on Main Street.

Personally, I found the ads dull and downbeat. Someone recently made an interesting point about these spots—he said that they reminded him of political advertising. They certainly did have an unsettling, even eerie quality to them, with their stark landscapes and threatening themes. There was, for example, a spot that showed an empty playground with a ghostly swing rocking back and forth. We learn of a municipal insurance crisis that might have closed playgrounds such as this, and that thanks to Drexel Burnham, the necessary money was raised—children fade into the scene. Unfortunately for the firm, one ad actually caused negative publicity with reports that it hadn't been filmed in the town it was referring to, a somewhat irrelevant if correct criticism.

While trying to win the hearts and minds of the general public, Drexel was also trying to influence the generals. A strong lobbying effort was focused on Washington, which had to be the least enviable job at the firm. For one thing, it's smart politics to steer clear of potential scandal, unless you're on the offensive. For another, politicians weren't terribly fond of takeovers, and of the folks who financed those takeovers. Although hostile takeovers represented less than 5 percent of junk-bond financings, it was these that made the front pages and brought pressure from the target companies, and their employees.

The word from Washington was rarely good, but on April 1 of 1987, it was just annoying. One of our senior executives in the capital was quoted talking of the youngsters on Wall Street who didn't have the experience to "absorb the ethical standards of the industry." Scapegoating the so-called greedy kids of the Street might play well on Capitol Hill, but it didn't say much for the man.

Later that month, the news from Washington was bad—predictable but still bad. Senator William Proxmire, chairman of the banking committee, was told by Gary Lynch, director of enforcement at the SEC, that "major cases" were upcoming. Lynch had joined the SEC out of Duke Law School and had succeeded John Fedders as head of the Enforcement Division in 1985, at age thirty-five. Low-key but intense, extremely knowledgeable, terse in speech, Lynch was clearly the type that you would rather have on your side of the table. Drexel, of course, never had that choice.

Back in New York, Fred Joseph was on the system a few days later, on Friday, April 24, predicting that "most likely, investigations will go on for quite some time." He reassured the rank and file that there was "nothing in the subpoenaed documents that we're concerned with," emphasized that the firm still hadn't found anything wrong, and noted that the first quarter had been "spectacular." It was difficult not to come away from his talks feeling better about things.

The following Tuesday, he was on the system again. Charles Thurnher, a senior vice-president in charge of administrative matters on the West Coast, had been advised by his lawyer to cooperate with the government, according to Fred. Whether he would or not was unknown (the previous day's *New York Times* had indicated that Thurnher had already agreed to cooperate). Regardless, it had an ominous ring to it, suggesting that he had something to hide and something to tell. Fred pointed out that immunity from prosecution didn't necessarily imply guilt—on Thurnher's part or anyone else's.

Still, it raised questions of why the government would offer him immunity, and why his lawyer would want him to take it. There was certainly a logical explanation: The investigators wanted more information so why not give immunity to a small but centrally located player; from Thurnher's point of view, why shouldn't anyone accept immunity if offered, regardless of what they knew?

But, then again, maybe he knew a great deal that would hurt Milken and the firm. He certainly knew a great deal more than all but a handful of the employees, and if there was incriminating evidence, it seemed likely he would be aware of it.

There was also the feeling, however simplistic that it was wrong for one member of Drexel to incriminate another. (What's the highest paying job at Drexel?—was a question asked at the time. Answer: Charlie Thurnher's food taster.) If this was a firm known for its intensity, it was also known for its intense loyalty, whether to I. W. Burnham, Michael Milken, fellow employees, or to the concept of the firm itself.

Fred tried to put the various concerns to rest, arguing again that Drexel knew of "no wrongdoing by anyone at the firm," and that if anything illegal was found, the guilty party would be gone. He also noted that the government now seemed more interested in the behavior of individuals than of the firm as a whole, which was comforting because it implied that the risk to Drexel, and its stockholders, was diminishing.

A similar point was made to me about a week later by a senior analyst with excellent connections within the firm. During our out-of-town trip to meet with clients, he predicted that the firm wouldn't be indicted, although he thought that Milken and others would be. "They've been hoping for us to fess up," he said, "but we're not going to, because there's nothing to fess up to." Now, *that* was encouraging to hear.

More good news came with a mid-May review of business for 1987's first half. Revenues were well over $1.5 billion in less than five months, down from 1986's extraordinary pace, but still excellent by any other measure. Profits after deducting taxes (and reserves for a potential settlement) were $122 million, excess capital now exceeded $1.1 billion, our market share was holding, and the backlog of investment banking business waiting to be done was described happily as "almost too strong."

Meanwhile, all was relatively quiet on the legal front with the U.S. attorney's office. At the SEC, interviews with various members of the firm had been scheduled for the next several months, and it was suggested that the investigators were "sort of flopping around," with one senior officer noting that he was "not overwhelmed by their preparation or knowledge."

Life was definitely looking brighter, especially if you were young, ignorant, and on the East Coast. I worried too little about the future of my firm, and too much about most everything else. The stock market was booming, of course, offering everyone on the ninth floor, and on trading floors throughout Wall Street, an unusual opportunity to make a good deal of money—an opportunity that was soon to end. Stocks were rising, volume was heavy, and new issues were popular.

By late September, the market was within 10 percent of its all-time high, and the crash was still a month away. Business at the firm was very strong, as Fred Joseph explained on Monday the twenty-first. Revenues were estimated at $3.6 billion for the year, the firm had been profitable in every month, and the value of the stock—which, as mentioned before, was primarily owned by two thousand of the employees—was comfortably above $1 billion.

The SEC, Fred told us that Monday, was conducting an "active, major investigation into . . . anything." The U.S. attorney's office was much less active, waiting, he thought, for the SEC to conclude. "Very important from our point of view," Fred noted, "we have not found any evidence of wrongdoing by anyone at the firm."

The upcoming major case against Drexel that had been implied in April had not arrived yet; if anything, its resolution seemed a distant problem. Perhaps there wasn't really a case against the firm at all; no charges had been brought after ten months of intensive investigation, and management continued to argue our innocence. Wishful thinking, perhaps, but there were reasons to be hopeful.

The attack against the firm faded further into the background as 1987 wound down, and remained there until the following April. "The first year, we all felt we lived in a police state," recalled a senior officer from the high-yield department. There was hope that 1988 would bring better news but, of course, it didn't.

If the focus in Washington during April 1987 was on the investigation, in April 1988 it was on the limited partnerships at Drexel. These limited partnerships, as you might remember, were available to selected members of the high-yield and corporate finance departments. The implied promise was that the participants could invest alongside Mike Milken. "I asked Fred Joseph how these partnerships would be screened," recalled one senior investment banker. "He said, 'Basically, Michael will be making the decisions.'"

By 1988, there was a mind-boggling assortment of different partnerships—only sixty-eight known to the public at the time—primarily involving Drexel officers, but with a few well-known outsiders: in one group, RWLC Partners, three of the eight partners were Lionel Richie; Steve Wynn, chairman of Golden Nuggett; and Kenny Rogers, whose most popular song offered some good advice about knowing when to hold 'em and when to fold 'em.

On April 28, the House of Representatives' Subcommittee on Oversight and Investigations, chaired by John Dingell of Michigan, considered a set of disturbing allegations: that the partnerships engaged in self-dealing, allocating themselves portions of junk-bond deals, at the expense of clients. Another question raised was whether the high-yield department treated these partnerships more favorably than clients in the *after market,* where these newly issued bonds traded publicly.

The hearings began a little after 10:00 A.M., with an introductory speech by Representative Dingell, who one Wall Street executive described as "the most powerful man in the country," referring to Dingell's authority over the SEC and the financial community. Following the chairman's introduction were initial comments from Representatives Ron Wyden of Oregon, Norman Lent of New York, Jim Slattery of Kansas, Michael Bilirakis of Florida, and Gerry Sikorski of Minnesota. The overture had a definitely congressional tone: "I want to commend you, Mr. Chairman, for undertaking this inquiry and say that I believe you've shown great concern for procedural fairness in this matter and I think that is something that this member very much appreciates. . . . Mr. Chairman, I too, commend you for holding this follow-up hearing. I quite often ask at the outset that we be open-minded and objective, and since these are information-gathering sessions, the only way we can actually gather information in an objective manner, is to be open-minded. . . . Mr. Chairman, thank you. I too, add my midwestern and flat tenor or bass voice to the chorus of commendations to you and the staff for this ongoing effort to examine our securities markets."

Fred Joseph received his first surprise of the day when, contrary to what he thought was an understanding with committee staffers, his lawyer, Irwin Schneiderman of Cahill, Gordon & Reindel, was not permitted to testify without waiving attorney-client privilege. Because Schneiderman obviously wasn't willing to reveal confidential discussions with his client, he chose not to be sworn in as a witness. He retained his role as a counsel to Joseph, which meant that Fred would have to provide answers for the record on all questions, including those of securities law.

The major law in question was Section 10-b-6 of the Securities and Exchange Act of 1934. You might recall that 10-b-5 dealt with insider trading; this one focused on fraud in the distribution of new issues. As Representative Dennis Eckart explained at the hearing: " 'The overall purpose,' the SEC says, 'is to assure a public distribution of securities for which there is a public demand, to make certain that NASD members do not restrict the supply of the offering by withholding shares, thereby forcing [your customers] who want to purchase the securities to acquire them in the market at a higher price.' "

Simply put, until every client's order is filled, nobody connected with the firm is entitled to any portion of a deal.

The committee focused on two high-yield offerings: Texstryene and Beatrice. In the Texstryene deal, 25 percent of the bonds went to the limited partnerships, even though at least two clients didn't receive their requested allotments. Lutheran Life ordered $2 million worth of bonds and received $500,000; Vanguard Mutual Fund asked for $5 million and was allocated $750,000, fully 85 percent less than its request.

As for the Beatrice deal, to quote Representative Slattery: "BCI Holdings Co., Inc., of course, is the corporation that was set up to acquire the Beatrice Companies in a leveraged buyout in 1986. The Beatrice leveraged buyout was the largest, up to that time, at least, involving $2.5 billion in high yield bonds issued by Drexel.

"The bonds were sold on April 10, 1986 and divided into four issues. One issue was for $950 million at 12.75 percent, and there were other issues adding up to the total of $2.5 billion.

"Now, the subcommittee's investigation has identified at least twenty-four insider accounts which purchased over $235 million of BCI notes. Now, the insider transactions ranged from a $40 million purchase by Western Capital, which was owned by Lowell and Michael Milken, to a $170,000 purchase by Lowell Milken IRA [individual retirement account].

"The BCI bonds went up in value almost immediately, and by June 30, the insider accounts had resold $61,385,000 of the notes to Drexel for a $2,804,000 profit.

"The subcommittee staff has also learned that while Drexel insider accounts were purchasing over $115 million of the 12.75 percent notes, Drexel's public clients were denied BCI notes they wished to purchase."

Fred Joseph responded that the rule against selling new issues to insiders applied to the offerings of stocks, not of high-yield bonds. He pointed out that the use of the word *shares* indicated that the intention was to regulate equity deals. Fred also argued that, unlike stocks, the junk bonds of one company are essentially the same as the junk bonds of another company with the same rating; therefore, one is interchangeable with the other, and "there is no opportunity to harm someone by holding a bond out of the market by not allowing them to participate in the issue."

Legally, this argument has not been settled, even to this date. A 1983 SEC ruling suggests that high-yield securities are covered by Section 10-b-6, contrary to Drexel's point of view. The ruling allowed two new exceptions, neither of which were junk bonds, the logical implication being that they were still under its umbrella. But as a senior Drexel official noted, the SEC doesn't seem eager to settle this question in the courts.

As a practical matter, however, junk bonds are very similar to stocks. And there were times when junk-bond deals generated more demand than supply, and the price of those bonds did rise in value immediately. Clients who weren't allowed to participate did get hurt by being denied the profits from this increase.

More important, basic fairness dictates that professional responsibility supercedes personal greed, that insiders stand behind their clients, not ahead of them. And unless I have completely misread Fred Joseph for the past nine years, he believes exactly the same.

The second set of allegations against the high-yield department and the partnerships involved self-dealing in the after market. Specifically, the subcommittee examined the Texstryene deal again. The debt was offered on February 11, 1986 at $987.50 per bond. Between February 12 and February 19, the department repurchased 6,950 bonds from clients at no more than $1,000 per bond.

On Friday, February twentieth, 200 bonds were purchased from two clients, in both cases for $1,005 per bond. On the same day, 3,400 of the same bonds were bought from a limited partnership for $1,040 per bond. On Thursday the twenty-seventh, 1,000 Texstryene bonds were bought from a client for $1,030 per bond. The following day, three partnerships sold 9,000 bonds for $1,065 per bond.

Something was wrong, something that couldn't be explained away by market fluctuations. The partnerships were given better prices than clients—sweetheart deals—and the decisions were made by those who personally benefited from them. The congressmen may have been concerned that clients were being mistreated, but in reality, it was Drexel Burnham's employees that were being cheated by a few of their peers. The bonds in the partnerships were bought back at unfairly high prices, effectively taking some $400,000 from the stockholders of the firm on this one deal alone.

Fred Joseph's performance at this hearing was generally criticized, but let's be realistic. He testified for seven hours in lousy health, under oath to a committee that hadn't convened to congratulate his firm for its contributions to society. He was forced to address questions of securities law that he had expected his lawyer to handle. Ask yourself how carefully you'd choose your answers if you were constantly under threat of perjury, and how you'd feel on the receiving end of a discussion such as the following:

MR. DINGELL: You believe, or you know?

MR. JOSEPH: I believe so.

MR. DINGELL: See, I believe in the Almighty—

MR. JOSEPH: I think so, if that's helpful.

MR. DINGELL: —but I never met him and I never shook his hand, and I've never seen him, but I've got a strong belief. So, you are functioning on belief, as opposed to knowledge?

MR. JOSEPH: I'm saying I think so. I'm not absolutely positive.

Or consider his widely ridiculed statement: "I think I'm confused." It was one sentence in response to a legal question, one comment at a hearing that generated one hundred pages of questions and answers. If anything, it shows clearly why you can lead a full life without ever testifying before a congressional committee.

The most important problem Fred Joseph had was that he sat down at the table with a very weak hand. The allegations that the limited partnerships had taken advantage of clients and fellow employees were very serious and almost certainly true. Fred was forced to bob and weave in defense of an indefensible situation, one that was a minuscule part of Drexel Burnham, but one that had hurt its stockholders and its customers.

As the chief exec of the firm, he was nominally responsible for these partnerships, even though his own participation in them was insignificant (he invested in two partnerships during the 1987–88 period.) In fact, only three members of the firm's executive committee, less than one in five, chose to join up for the easy profits.

The reports of these questionable profits for the chosen few, carried in the following morning's papers, were bad for morale at Drexel and bad for the image of the firm. The partnerships told a story of greed— but more than that, of abuse.

Perhaps there was a lesson to be drawn from these surprising and depressing revelations, a lesson that what had happened on a small scale probably happened on a larger one as well. Or perhaps these abuses were isolated mistakes made by a few without Milken's knowledge.

An answer here would have gone a long way in addressing the real question: Was Mike Milken guilty? This had been the focus of the battle between the government and the firm; in the following year, the two sides would finally resolve the battle, if not the doubts.

CHAPTER ELEVEN

MOTHER OF MERCY

"You threaten like a dockyard bully."

"How should I threaten?"

"Like a minister of state, with justice."

—A MAN FOR ALL SEASONS

Charges were filed on September 7, 1988. The Securities and Exchange Commission alleged that "Drexel Burnham Lambert, Michael Milken, and others devised and carried out a fraudulent scheme involving insider trading, stock manipulation, fraud on Drexel's own clients, failure to disclose beneficial ownership of securities as required, and numerous other violations of the securities laws."

The transactions, and the alleged crimes, as cited in the SEC civil complaint were

- Pennsylvania Engineering's 1984 purchase of Fischbach (stock parking)
- AM International's 1986 acquisition of Harris Graphics (stock parking)
- Lorimar's 1985 merger with Telepictures (insider trading)
- Boesky's 1986 short sales of Lorimar shares (stock parking)
- Maxxam Group's 1985 takeover of Pacific Lumber (fraud)
- Golden Nugget's sale of MCA shares (stock parking)

- Turner Broadcasting's 1985 acquisition of MGM/UA (stock parking)
- Occidental Petroleum's proposed 1985 merger with Diamond Shamrock (insider trading)
- Drexel's 1985 purchase of Phillips Petroleum shares (stock parking)
- Stone Container's 1986 convertible bond offering (stock manipulation)
- Kohlberg Kravis's 1985 takeover of Storer Communications (insider trading)
- Trades between Boesky and Drexel in 1985 to create tax losses (tax evasion)
- Viacom's 1986 leveraged buyout (insider trading)
- Wickes's 1986 takeover of National Gypsum (fraud)
- Wickes's 1985 convertible preferred offering (stock manipulation)
- Boesky's 1985 short sales of Wickes shares (stock parking)
- Boesky's 1986 payment of $5.3 million to Drexel (repayment of illegal profits)

Representative Edward Markey (D–Mass.) commented on these charges by stating, "Wall Street con artists like Ivan Boesky were mere puppets controlled by one of the most successful Wall Street firms of the 1980s." What he forgot, or forgot to mention, was that these were *alleged* crimes; nothing had been proven. This may seem a technicality to many, but, of course, it's not—it's the basis of our legal system.

If the firm was unhappy that it was facing these charges, it certainly wasn't surprised. In February 1988, the SEC staff had recommended taking action against Drexel. In May, the staff had prepared a confidential memo to the commissioners of the SEC. This memo, which was leaked to *The Washington Post* in August of the following year and quoted in part there, outlined the staff's case; among the allegations:

- In 1985, Milken directed a Boesky employee to buy and sell bonds, some at nonmarket prices, which provided Boesky with quick profits at Drexel's expense.
- In 1986, Milken indirectly encouraged the destruction of documents involving transactions with Boesky

- Also in 1986, Milken and Boesky discussed a cover-up of the allegedly fraudulent $5.3 million payment.

The SEC commissioners voted unanimously in June to give their go-ahead for the staff to file civil charges against Drexel.

The firm had made its case before the vote—"We stated that we were convinced that they were wrong," Fred Joseph explained in a memo to employees—but its point of view didn't carry the day. Fred's memo also raised for the first time "the possibility of a settlement to put this behind us."

That same month, management considered another possibility: slashing the size of the firm from almost ten thousand employees to only two thousand. The idea was rejected as impractical, and as you might guess, was never mentioned to the rank and file.

For three months, we waited for this shoe to drop and, when it came, the sense of the employees was an acceptance of the inevitable. As for the clients, there was little backlash. We had informed every one of them of the likelihood of civil charges at the time of the SEC green light, and almost none of them deserted us when these charges became a reality.

If the SEC filing wasn't a surprise, somewhat puzzling was its delay until September. As a *Wall Street Journal* editorial noted in July, "There's a heavy air of expectation in the canyons of Wall Street and along the palm drives of Beverly Hills that someone is finally going to officially charge Drexel Burnham Lambert with something. Leaks and innuendo have kept the investment bank in the headlines for two years, but now Drexel is girding for a full-scale legal fight."

Well, now the fight was on. Twenty-one SEC attorneys, after twenty months of investigation, had produced the official complaint, 184 pages in length, dealing with eighteen transactions. Seventeen of those involved the firm—four of its employees, actually: Mike Milken, his brother Lowell, and two traders, Cary Maultasch and Pamela Monzert. All but two of these transactions involved Ivan Boesky as cohort and principle witness.

"The evidence was overwhelming," argued Gary Lynch, the SEC enforcement chief at the time, currently a partner at Davis, Polk & Wardwell. "There were always multiple witnesses on every allegation. There was substantial corroboration for all allegations from inside and outside the Boesky organization."

Needless to say, Drexel's view of the case was different. In a letter to clients on the day of the filing, the firm said, in part:

A thorough examination of the SEC complaint shows that the charges rely almost entirely on accusations by convicted felon Ivan Boesky. The most telling aspect of this action is that, after an almost two-year investigation which we understand to be the most exhaustive in SEC history, the SEC essentially has charged nothing beyond what Boesky alleged in 1986 when he was bargaining for leniency.

To be exact, eight of the nine allegations raised in the *Journal* article of December 1986, almost two years earlier, were included in the SEC complaint; the remaining nine hadn't been mentioned at the time, and two of the transactions—the 1985 Lorimar/Telepictures merger and the 1986 Viacom leveraged buyout—didn't involve Boesky.

The following day, September 8, I. W. Burnham sent a memo to the members of his firm:

I am writing to you now as one of the many thousands of employees of the firm that I founded on April 1, 1935. I am obviously the employee with the longest length of service, but not yet the oldest employee. I have been Honorary Chairman of the Board of Directors since May 1984.

The waiting period for the charges by the SEC is now over and I would like to tell you that I think we should all support completely the leadership the firm has had from our Chief Executive Officer, Fred Joseph, and from our Chairman of the Board, Robert Linton. They and many others of our Executive Staff and, in addition, all kinds of specialists and advisors have done a wonderful job in leading this firm through the past two years of accusations, innuendo and false rumors. From the very beginning we have been told by our attorneys that they felt that our firm and its employees are innocent of the charges that might eventually be unleashed against us and them. We have to believe that.

Burnham had always thought the world of his employees, and by September 1988, his opinion had been justified in one important respect: their loyalty. The accusations and rumors that he referred to had been lousy for current business and threatening to future prospects. And still, almost nobody had left.

In my department, not one person had chosen to leave since the Boesky scandal broke. On the entire trading floor, I only knew of one trader who had left because of the threat to the firm, and he returned before the SEC charges were filed. In the research department, I can remember only one analyst who left for another firm, and he went over as part of a team with a group of investment bankers. In corporate finance, "virtually everybody stayed," as well, recalled a New York–based investment banker. And if loyalty to the firm was strong on the East Coast, loyalty to Milken was fierce on the West Coast.

"It was almost an obsession," remembered a senior equity trader in New York. "I wouldn't even talk to people [regarding other jobs]. There was no way I could move out and leave those people behind." He said it best not because that was the feeling in everyone, or even in most people, but because that was the feeling in the best people. And Drexel had more than its share.

His comments reminded me of those in *Goodbye, Darkness,* an autobiographical account of the Pacific War by William Manchester. Although slightly wounded, Manchester had left the field hospital to rejoin his Marine company rather than return to the States, and to safety, alone. Whatever was going to happen, he wanted to share it with them. And he was very nearly killed.

For Drexel, the SEC charges were just the first part of the shooting war. The SEC is permitted to file only a civil complaint; criminal charges are the province of the U.S. attorney's office. This would be the real battle, and a nasty one. But it was a mismatch—the prosecutors had a new and awesome weapon and a willingness to use it. Drexel's best defense was an appeal to fairness, which as history has repeatedly shown, is one poor excuse for a defense.

The key figure on the other side of the table was Rudolf Giuliani, the U.S. attorney for the Southern District of New York. To one former assistant U.S. attorney, he was "fair, energetic, problem oriented, funny . . . [with] a can-do, creative approach." To the folks at Drexel Burnham, he was the anti-Christ.

In a 1987 *Vanity Fair* article, Gail Sheehy provided a vivid description of Giuliani, that of a "bloodless white face with dark steady eyes"—"Just look at his eyes," said a senior Drexel official—"and goofy haircomb . . . [with] his monk's face and his altar-boy lisp."

His upbringing, in fact, was strongly Catholic; he even considered entering the priesthood. Instead, he attended New York University Law School, graduating with honors in 1968. After serving as a law clerk for two years, he became an assistant U.S. attorney for the Southern District. The high point of his five years as a prosecutor there was reached during the 1974 bribery trial of Brooklyn congressman Bertram Podell. His cross-examination was reportedly so intimidating and effective that the defendant asked for a recess, and pleaded guilty.

In 1975, Giuliani went to Washington, becoming an assistant to the deputy attorney general in the Ford administration. "Previously a liberal Democrat," *Current Biography* noted, "Giuliani switched to the Republican party during that period after concluding that the Democratic party's view of global politics was, in his words, 'dangerous.'"

When Carter came in, he went out. After four years in private practice as a partner at New York–based Patterson, Belknap, he returned to Washington in the wake of Reagan's victory, to take the number three position at the Justice Department—associate attorney general. Interestingly, he downplayed the previous administration's focus on white-collar crime, concentrating instead on the fight against drugs.

In 1983, Giuliani returned to the Southern District of New York, this time as the boss. In his first full year as U.S. attorney, the number of indictments rose by more than 20 percent. His office secured convictions in several major organized crime cases, and he personally prosecuted Stanley Friedman, the head of the Bronx Democratic party, who received a twelve-year sentence for bribery.

The focus shifted to the securities business when Ivan Boesky, realizing his days were numbered following Dennis Levine's decision to cooperate with prosecutors, chose to cut a deal with the government in the second half of 1986. The primary responsibility for the ensuing criminal investigation fell to the securities fraud unit, headed initially by Charles Carberry; in August 1987, he was succeeded by Bruce Baird.

Baird, who projects a sense of calm that you wouldn't expect in a high-level prosecutor and who possesses a sense of purpose that you would, was a seven-year veteran of the Southern District by that time. He had been the head of the narcotics unit, and before that, had served in the organized crime unit. Working under him were two young assistant U.S. attorneys, John Carroll and Jeff Fridella, formerly of the narcotics unit.

But the main man was Rudy Giuliani. His style was hands-on, and those with problems found that the best way to resolve them was to speak with him directly. "You could always go in and talk," recalled a former assistant U.S. attorney. On Giuliani's door was a sign that read "This is an open door," although it was said to be always closed. Behind it was a scene described as similar to "a floating crap game," with Rudy usually surrounded by his prosecutors, in wide-ranging discussions.

The tone of the office was set by the boss, and in the case of white-collar crimes, that tone was, in Giuliani's own words in a 1987 *Washington Post* interview, "If you can present people with the distinct possibility, even if not the probability, that they could be caught and that they can be held up to public shame, ridicule and possible prison sentences, you're going to be able to affect their behavior."

He also had the weapon that would certainly affect their behavior once caught, a law that made it much riskier to face trial and possible conviction, a law that for better or worse encouraged defendants to plea-bargain rather than to fight in court. This law had sat on the books for more than a decade, a sleeping giant, until Giuliani pioneered its use. It was one part, Title IX, of the Organized Crime Control Act of 1970. Officially, it was called the Racketeer Influenced Corrupt Organizations Act, better known as RICO. (The common wisdom is that this acronym was inspired by the gangster Rico, portrayed by Edward G. Robinson in the 1930 film "Little Ceasar.")

RICO is perhaps the most powerful and least understood statute in this country, an extraordinary law with extraordinary possibilities. To get a handle on RICO, consider first the state of mind when the act was written. Two decades ago, the Republicans had recaptured the White House, partly on a law-and-order pledge. In particular, people were fed up with the government's inability to deal with mobsters, and with their success both in expanding illegal ventures—drugs in particular—and in infiltrating and corrupting legitimate businesses.

Congress met fire with fire, approving the act in 1970. An excerpt from the introduction explains what the government had in mind:

> The Congress finds that (1) organized crime in the United States is a
> highly sophisticated, diversified, and widespread activity that annually

drains billions of dollars from America's economy by unlawful conduct and the illegal use of force, fraud, and corruption; (2) organized crime derives a major portion of its power through money obtained from such illegal endeavors as syndicated gambling, loan sharking, the theft and fencing of property, the importation and distribution of narcotics and other dangerous drugs, and other forms of social exploitation; (3) this money and power are increasingly used to infiltrate and corrupt legitimate business.

That explanation is fairly straightforward; certainly, it is broad enough to cast its net around virtually every member of organized crime. In the case of Title IX, RICO, the net potentially covers the entire sea. Its definition of what constitutes a racketeer is someone who commits at least *two* listed crimes within a ten-year period. The list of crimes ranges from murder, kidnapping, arson, extortion, and the sexual exploitation of children to mail fraud and wire fraud, which means that a law was broken using a letter or a telephone.

The potential penalties under RICO are severe: up to twenty years in prison for each violation and damages amounting to three times the ill-gotten gains. It was a prosecutor's dream, and Giuliani made that dream a reality. RICO paved the way for stiff sentences in the Southern District's successful prosecutions in the mid-1980s of organized crime and of politician Stanley Friedman.

In September 1988, the employees of Drexel didn't know much about RICO, but we sure knew that we didn't want it anywhere near our firm. At that time, the outlook was cloudy. "Based on recent actions, it is obvious that the Government will consider racketeering charges in any case involving a series of actions," a memo from Corporate Communications noted. "We know that the normal meaning of racketeering is not applicable to the firm or its people."

Soon after, Fred Joseph, in a meeting with my department, announced the encouraging news that our lawyers believed that the firm wouldn't be "RICO'd"—the odds were less than one in five. He mentioned, however, the story of a friend of his in the firm who had suffered a heart attack, but was given an excellent chance of survival; when your life is on the line, Fred pointed out, even a one in ten chance seems awfully high.

But who were we kidding? The number was a hell of a lot higher than 10 or 20 percent; if we had thought about it realistically, rather than hiding in the comfort of a lawyer's blind guess, we would have realized that the chances of being RICO'd were closer to 100 percent. Giuliani had already extended RICO into the area of securities law, to the case of Princeton/Newport, an arbitrage firm that had been fingered by Boesky.

On December 17, 1987, the government had raided the offices of Princeton/Newport, confiscating 336 tapes in search of incriminating conversations. At the time, the raid was reminiscent of the Feds crashing a numbers racket or busting up a speakeasy in prohibition Chicago. The raid produced evidence of tax evasion, which led to the August 1988 indictments of five people, four from Princeton/Newport.

The fifth, Bruce Newberg, was a trader in Drexel's junk-bond department. Bright and high-strung, Bruce had spent most of his career working for Michael Milken, who regarded him highly. It would have been a coup for the prosecutors, who had indicated that Newberg would also be indicted in the cases against Drexel and Milken, to secure him as a cooperating witness against his former boss. Even facing the possibility of more than twenty years in jail, however, the young trader refused.

The prosecutors' ultimate target was becoming increasingly obvious. "We have no real interest in Princeton," attorney Jack Arseneault recalls being told by Bruce Baird. "We have no real interest in Berkman [his client]. However, we believe that Berkman can help us with Regan [another defendant], and Regan can help us with Drexel Burnham and others. If you cooperate with us, fine. If you don't, we'll roll right over you." Baird claims that these comments were "not accurate."

Two things seemed clear: Drexel was the target, and the prosecutors had no problem with playing hardball. In an August 4 memo responding to a *Wall Street Journal* article, we were told, "Our lawyers concur with the observations in the story that prosecutorial pressure tactics have been a driving force in many aspects of the Princeton/Newport case."

In the words of Paul Grand, the attorney for Charles Zarzecki, "it was a prosecution that was, I think, carefully and specifically designed to destroy Princeton/Newport as an ongoing business because the people refused to give up their right to a trial and to give evidence against others."

However justified or unjustified the tactics were, the result was that

Princeton/Newport went out of business in December 1988. Structured as an investment partnership rather than as a corporation, its limited partners were allowed to withdraw some or all of their money once a year. For Princeton/Newport, that date was November 19.

The partnership was told that additional charges would be filed against it. As Diane Parker, who worked with one of the attorneys on the case, explained to *Barron's* magazine: "Well, the government missed one deadline and then another, and then changed it to December 5. So Princeton/Newport changed the redemption date to December 10" to allow its partners an opportunity to see the new indictment before deciding what to do with their money.

"But the prosecutors kept putting it off and putting it off, and then finally they said that they weren't going to do anything until January." According to Bruce Baird, "The superseding indictment was delayed in the normal course of business."

Realizing that the limited partners would withdraw their money in the face of threatened but unknown charges, Princeton/Newport ended its partnership and closed its doors on December 8, 1988.

There was another aspect of the Princeton/Newport case that was ominous for Drexel. RICO provided for the pretrial freezing of assets. Freezing assets in advance of a trial simply assures the government that if it wins its case, there is something left to win. (Organized crime has a nasty habit of bleeding dry the assets of indicted companies under their control—cash disappears, inventories of products vanish. By the time the trial is over, the corporation is just a shell, with no assets to pay any settlement to the government.)

Princeton/Newport had been required to post a bond of $24 million, later reduced to $14 million, even though the alleged illegal profits were only $446,000. The questions that Drexel faced were: If indicted under RICO, how much would it be required to put up before trial? More serious, how much more would it be required to post in the future when the government returned with superseding charges? And the real question: Would the firm survive to see its day in court?

A financial institution is held together by confidence—the confidence of its employees, its clients, and its lenders. The company must have a reputation for integrity and the potential for a bright future to attract and retain the type of people who can ensure that integrity and future. The two-year investigation against Drexel had certainly questioned its integrity—in several specific instances, at least—and clouded its future. Still, the firm itself remarkably had held together.

As for the clients, their confidence is crucial. They must believe in the quality of a firm's products, which in Wall Street's case, are ideas. When the products are as amorphous as this, credibility is an important part of the equation. The seller must have an image of integrity to maintain the confidence of the buyers.

On another level, there must be an aura of respectability about the firm that *allows* the clients, who have a fiduciary responsibility to protect the savings and pensions that they invest, to listen to its ideas. This responsibility, broad and ill-defined, might involve avoiding a firm that is under indictment, even if nothing has been proven. The clients don't know for sure, and often, the easiest approach is to steer clear of any potential trouble.

The risk to Drexel's relationships with its clients if indicted was unknown, but there would be damage. Especially if there was a RICO indictment. Aside from the possible penalties in the future, there was the certain and immediate stigma that this particular law created. RICO accuses its victims of being racketeers, members of criminal organizations.

The bizarre thing about it is that, if you are in fact a member of organized crime, the stigma doesn't matter. Your friends won't mind if they read that you are a suspected racketeer; in fact, they probably don't even read. And being called a racketeer won't hurt your reputation among business partners that have nicknames like "Slippery Nick" and "The Weasel."

As for clients, they are not likely to turn their backs on you, since your relationship with them is based on a different kind of trust—the understanding that, for a generous fee, you won't burn their companies to the ground. Essentially, the racketeering label does its real damage to those who don't consider themselves racketeers, but who will be tried and convicted in the court of public opinion long before they ever hear a verdict.

If the confidence of employees is important and that of clients is crucial, the confidence of lenders is mandatory. Almost all of a financial institution's money comes from lenders, not stockholders. In Drexel's case, more than $28 billion of its $30 billion in assets were borrowed—fully 96 percent of its capital was in loans of one form or another. This type of leverage is common in banks, savings and loans, and brokerage firms.

Most of the assets that these firms hold are fairly liquid; they can be converted into cash quickly. The great danger is that some of the current lenders might decide that they want their money back just when no other lenders are willing to step in with new money. This can cause a sense of panic among the remaining lenders, who might also try to take out their money, and immediately. The result is a variation on the Depression-era nightmare: a run on the bank. Money is withdrawn faster than the assets can be liquidated at fair value, and the financial institution collapses.

A run-on-the-bank scenario can affect institutions as diverse as the dubious Vernon Savings & Loan and the extraordinary Bedford Falls Building & Loan. All you need is a loss of confidence, valid or not. To maintain this confidence, the government decided in the 1930s (after the Crash) to guarantee people's deposits.

And because confidence is such a fragile commodity, Congress even made it illegal "to defame a financial institution," according to one Drexel officer. And yet, he argued, the prosecutors had spent two years casting a dark shadow of doubt over Drexel, a financial institution whose survival depended on the confidence of its lenders.

To this point, the confidence had been maintained—when loans had come due, there had always been lenders willing to roll those loans over, to provide the firm with a steady flow of cash to run its business. The big question was: Would the cash flow dry up and the lenders disappear if Drexel were indicted, particularly under RICO? The management believed that the firm could survive if indicted under the Securities and Exchange Act of 1934, but not if the racketeering statute was used.

The reasoning was simple: Under RICO, Drexel would have to post a bond in advance of trial, to avoid a freezing of its assets. The bond, it was believed, could amount to as much as $1 *billion*. This potential debt to the government would take precedence over all debts that the firm incurred subsequently. Because most of a brokerage firm's loans are short term in nature, it wouldn't take long before all of its lenders would be forced to take junior positions—similar to a second mortgage on your home—to the government's claim.

To make matters worse, this claim would approach the total value of the shareholders' equity. If the claim ever had to be paid, the stockholders would lose most of their money; if there were other legal or operating losses as well, the firm's equity might be more than wiped out, and the firm's debts would then exceed its assets. For those who like equations, $D > A = B^2$ (D, debt; A, assets; B, bye).

Lenders like equations—their lives are ruled by them. What they don't like is lending their money to companies that have equations like the one above. And if that didn't scare them off, the likelihood of a superseding indictment, and an additional unknown bond, might.

What was known in December 1988 was that an indictment was coming, and soon. After twenty-five months of investigation, during which Drexel had spent $140 million in legal and other fees, during which the firm had lost untold hundreds of millions of dollars in potential profits on deals that didn't get done or that wary clients took elsewhere, during which one and a half million documents were examined . . . after twenty-five months during which Drexel stuck to its original claim that it was innocent, Giuliani decided that the firm would be prosecuted under the RICO statute.

"Peter Fleming [one of Drexel's top attorneys] said of Rudy that he's a reasonable man," recalled Burt Siegel, the head of the equity operation and a member of the board of directors. "He can be reasoned with, even if the people who work for him are tough." This was a miscalculation, he noted later.

Siegel, who one salesman praised as a "smooth-elbowed man in a sharp-elbowed world," pointed out another miscalculation: the hope that, even if Giuliani wouldn't listen to reason on the use of RICO, the Justice Department itself would. The hope was that the department, which was required to approve each RICO case, wouldn't give the go-ahead regardless of Giuliani's wishes. This was a naive hope, however, given both the strength of his relationship with Washington—he had worked in prominent positions at the Justice Department for almost five years—and the generally poor perception of Drexel throughout the government.

If Giuliani's choice of weapon was considered unfair at 60 Broad Street, it was viewed as entirely appropriate at One St. Andrews Plaza, the home of the U.S. attorney's office. "The high-yield bond department was a criminal organization," said Bruce Baird, later noting that "the basic Justice Department rule is that you bring the most serious charge that fits the facts."

The evidence behind those facts, in Drexel's view, was primarily based on the testimony of Ivan Boesky. Unknown to the firm at that time, the government claimed that "at least six former employees of the Boesky organization have corroborated pieces of the Boesky story." The government's hand was further strengthened in the late fall when three important employees of the high-yield bond department became witnesses.

Jim Dahl, Milken's top salesman (other than himself), was required to testify under an arrangement used in Mafia cases in which the witness is given immunity, like it or not. Accordingly, Dahl couldn't refuse to answer questions under the Fifth Amendment, because he was now guaranteed against incriminating himself with his specific responses. He could, however, be indicted for perjury if he answered those questions untruthfully. Following his grand jury testimony, Dahl evidently became a cooperating witness in exchange for complete immunity.

Cary Maultasch, a second witness, worked out of New York, about a hundred feet from me on the trading floor, handling equity transactions for Milken's department and clients. Like Jim Dahl, Maultasch had been told by prosecutors in September that he would likely be indicted along with Drexel and Milken. Unlike Dahl, he wasn't offered immunity; eventually, he agreed to cooperate with the government in return for a deferral of its decision on whether or not to prosecute him.

Terren Peizer, an aggressive and successful young trader who had been hired from First Boston, also agreed to cooperate. Given that he was offered immunity and that he sat next to Milken at the X-shaped desk, the implication was that he had something interesting to say. Neither Peizer nor Dahl found themselves very welcome back in the high-yield department. "They were not allowed on the floor," recalled a trader in this intense and close-knit department. "No one would talk to them."

"The whole thing changed with Dahl and Peizer and Maultasch," said Burt Siegel, adding that the board of directors "had no idea what they said."

There was also a lingering doubt regarding the Princeton/Newport allegations. That indictment concerned the parking of stock to generate tax losses, an accusation that had also been raised against Drexel and Boesky in the SEC complaint. Among the tapes that had been confiscated was a conversation in which Drexel's Bruce Newberg called his counterpart at Princeton/Newport, Charles Zarzecki, "a sleaze bag." Zarzecki responded, "You taught me, man." Newberg: "Welcome to the world of sleaze."

The picture painted was one of crummy morals, if not criminality.

One question raised was whether Milken knew of Newberg's actions, and whether the firm was liable for those actions. Another obvious question was the familiar one of whether Newberg's attitude was unusual, or whether it reflected a general way of doing business in that department.

The government's most compelling piece of written evidence was a collection of notes by Boesky's accountant, Setrag Mooradian. These notes allegedly dealt with the much-discussed $5.3 million payment from Boesky to Drexel. Lowell Milken had contended in a 1986 letter that the payment was for perfectly legal research, and the firm, after its own investigation, had agreed that it was for "legitimate investment banking services." The government, on the other hand, believed that the $5.3 million was the amount that Boesky owed Milken's department for its share of illegal profits.

The Mooradian notes purportedly showed, on a several-page ledger, the profits and losses from various transactions that influenced the $5.3 million figure. Among these transactions were the Maxxam/ Pacific Lumber, Turner Broadcasting/MGM/UA, AM International/Harris Graphics, and Kohlberg Kravis/Storer Broadcasting deals.

One possible problem with Mooradian's notes, however, was that they might have been reconstructed by the accountant from memory or from fantasy. At the time of Dennis Levine's arrest, certain documents at the Boesky organization were said to have been destroyed. The original notes, if they existed at all, might have been part of that group—after all, if they were what they were supposed to be, they were certainly incriminating.

Fred Joseph faced two difficult questions: did Mooradian ever take notes regarding an allegedly illegal payment to the firm and, if so, were these the actual notes, or were they reconstructed? More specifically, were these profits and losses recorded at the time of the actual deals during 1985, at the time of the $5.3 million payment in March 1986, or after Boesky's decision to cooperate with the government in late summer 1986?

One lawyer representing Drexel believed that the Mooradian notes were reconstructed in the late summer; another agreed with the prosecutors that they were "contemporaneous," written in March 1986. There was no way to know for Drexel to know for sure. One senior official familiar with the negotiations pointed out that Fred

Joseph was permitted to view the notes for only about a minute. According to this official, Fred's best guess was that the Mooradian notes were originals.

More important to the board of directors than Drexel's chances in court were Drexel's chances of getting to court. Senior management thought that in the event of a RICO indictment the firm could not avoid bankruptcy. Even with a settlement, Drexel's survival was far from certain, but a critical wound has great advantages over death.

In negotiations with Giuliani, Fred's greatest leverage, oddly enough, was that threat of death. Many in the firm were willing to take a RICO indictment, whatever the consequences, rather than accede to what they considered was a grossly unfair settlement. Rudy wanted a settlement—no rational man is eager to put nine thousand people out of work for the alleged crimes of a handful. It was also common knowledge at the time that Giuliani would likely run for mayor of New York. The thought of putting thousands of people out of work, people with family and friends, would have been political suicide.

And even if Drexel did survive a RICO indictment—which the prosecutors believed it could—the case against the firm would be a challenge for the U.S. attorney's office, dealing with technical issues and relying heavily on circumstantial evidence. A settlement was the best of either world for Rudy.

It was a classic case of brinksmanship. Giuliani was holding most of the cards, but if he insisted on anything too unreasonable, he would end up holding a corpse. And a corpse that big is difficult to bury, if it can be buried at all. Joseph, on the other hand, wanted to protect his firm and his employees. Cutting off Drexel's future to spite its prosecutor might provide a great psychic dividend, but that sense of moral superiority would likely wear off long before thousands of good people found new jobs.

Joseph proposed a settlement offer of $100 million; Giuliani asked for $750 million. On Monday, December 19, negotiations fell through for reasons that had to do with much more than money. The government insisted on a number of points that the board of directors found "objectionable on every ground," according to a board member. Among the provisions was one that was extraordinary, perhaps even unprecedented: The firm must waive its attorney-client privilege, allowing the government to examine discussions between Drexel personnel and its lawyers, conversations that had been conducted in confidence.

Another of the unacceptable points allowed the government, at any time in the future, to "arbitrarily decide that we had abrogated the agreement," according to a senior executive familiar with the negotiations. Because, in his opinion, "the prosecutors had lied to us in many ways," giving them carte blanche to terminate the settlement at their discretion would keep the firm and its employees at the mercy of people he didn't trust.

The board voted twenty-two to zero against the government's proposal.

That afternoon, Fred told the employees, "At the present time, discussions may be winding down. We could be indicted at any time, beginning tomorrow. . . . It's very clear that the firm didn't do anything wrong, and couldn't really know." This was the first time in memory that Fred had spoken of the firm's innocence and not of the individual employees.

At the time, I was glad to hear that we would fight, rather than settle. I was aware that there was a real chance of bankruptcy, but it took another eighteen months to realize how disastrous that might have been. Besides, I felt that if we believed what we were saying then fighting the charges according to the law was the right thing to do. Pleading guilty as an accommodation, as the lesser of two evils, arranged and signed by a few people behind closed doors, was not what this system was all about.

If my reaction to the breakdown of negotiations was one of grim satisfaction, that of the investment bankers was of outright joy. When Fred made an appearance that evening at the corporate finance department's annual Christmas party, he was cheered. The battle was on.

Within forty-eight hours, the battle was off. The U.S. attorney's office responded to Drexel's defiance by dropping all but two of the conditions that the board had objected to. The remaining two applied directly to Milken: He must be fired and his bonus for 1988 must be withheld. "They were really paranoid about Michael running the company," recalled Burt Siegel. He noted that the main prosecutors on the case all had worked in the narcotics unit, the implication being that these men were used to drug kingpins who held onto control of their operations in fact if not in appearance.

The board considered the new terms. There were three other important factors—two old, one new. The prosecutors still refused to indicate how large a bond Drexel would be requested to post when it was indicted. Clearly, uncertainty worked in their favor; better to let the firm imagine the worst. They weren't eager to make it any easier for Drexel to decide in favor of fighting the charges.

Another logical consideration for the firm was that its relationship with the judge on its case, Milton Pollack, couldn't be much worse. The blame for that was squarely on Drexel. The firm had asked Judge Pollack, who was presiding on all Boesky-related matters, to remove himself from the case based on a supposed conflict of interest. The conflict was a stretch at best: A company owned by Pollack's wife was being bought out, and Drexel was involved in the financing.

The firm's argument was insignificant, bordering on insulting. The more likely reason that Drexel wanted a different judge was that, if its case should come to trial, Pollack had a reputation for being tough on white-collar defendants. In the St. Joe Mineral case, his threat of a $50,000 per day fine encouraged an Italian bank in Switzerland to "persuade" the defendant, Guisseppe Tome, to face a U.S. court. Instead, Tome pleaded guilty. This novel approach to the problem of extradition came to be known as "Pollack's Law."

Not surprisingly, Pollack, an eighty-one-year-old judge who had served on the bench since his appointment by LBJ, refused to excuse himself from the Drexel case. The firm appealed his decision to a higher court, but lost. The firm's strategy on this one was the public relations equivalent of the Little Big Horn or Gallipoli.

The problem with Pollack was small potatoes compared with one that had materialized in recent months. After more than two years of investigations, the firm had discovered a partnership that it had never been told about: the MacPherson Partners. To make matters worse, this partnership had benefited from some shenanigans on an offering of high-yield bonds for Storer Broadcasting.

The bonds included equity warrants; these sweetners were stripped from the bonds and sold to clients, the bulk of them, it seems, to one client in particular. This client allegedly resold the warrants back to Milken's group, which in turn sold them to the MacPherson Partnership. Among the beneficiaries were individual money managers, raising the question of whether this hidden scheme was a payoff to favored individuals for doing business with the department.

This mystery partnership, which the firm reported to the U.S.

attorney's office, seriously hurt Mike Milken's credibility with the board. According to Steve Joseph, management had heard allegations that "individuals were receiving warrants directly" and had questioned Milken. "Michael had said that it never had happened."

On Wednesday, December 21, assistant U.S. Attorney John Carroll called Tom Curnin, Drexel's lead outside counsel, to say that, unless the firm settled the case, a RICO indictment would be filed that evening. The firm's lawyers were said to have checked their sources in Washington and confirmed that all the necessary papers had been filed with the Justice Department. It was decision time.

"There was not a lot of acrimony in the discussions," remembered Siegel, even though the board was highly politicized. "The Belgian investors very much wanted to settle," he added, referring to the six seats controlled by Groupe Bruxelles Lambert, which had owned over 20 percent of Drexel since 1976.

"The biggest block, the Frogs, was into the firm for nothing," was one West Coast officer's view of the Belgians. His comment, an insult to the wrong country, did make one interesting point: Groupe Lambert's stake in the firm, although worth a great deal on paper, was mostly profit; its initial investment was only a small fraction. As for the others on the board, "the older people had a high percentage of their net worth in the firm," this officer noted—they didn't want to risk bankruptcy. "So they voted their pocketbooks," he concluded. "That was a business decision, and that was done."

The settlement terms were six felonies and $650 million. Take it or leave it. The board had been told to decide by 4:00 P.M., when the grand jury was scheduled to leave. As the deadline neared, one of the senior executives went "bat shit," according to a participant. Fred Joseph assured him that the grand jury would wait. Around 4:05, the final vote was taken. The result: sixteen to six in favor.

"There was a school of thought among those who voted against, that the firm couldn't survive that kind of settlement, and if the firm goes down, let it be the fault of the government," was Siegel's analysis of the decision. "The majority opinion, and I was among them, was that we absolutely could not survive a RICO indictment. But there was a chance that we could settle, and run the business."

Another Drexel director who voted in favor also argued that the firm needed a settlement. According to him, the firm knew from the banks that a RICO indictment would cost it its credit rating and, accordingly, its lenders. Although, in his opinion, there had been "no real improvement in the settlement terms" from those that had been unanimously rejected only two days earlier, he had accepted the proposal.

The six directors who found the terms unacceptable, regardless of the risks, were Leon Black, cohead of mergers and acquisitions; Herb Bachelor, overall head of corporate finance; John Kissick, in charge of the West Coast's corporate finance department; Alan Sher, head of the retail system; Howard Brenner, a senior vice-president of trading; and Fred Joseph.

Fred made a tactical error by voting against the settlement that he had negotiated. He had hoped that his protest vote would be a signal to the employees, especially those loyal to Milken, that he opposed the settlement in principle. Instead, he just invited criticism.

"I didn't think we were guilty," explained Howard Brenner, one of the remaining five who voted against the proposal, later noting: "I didn't like the fact that we hadn't settled with the SEC." That settlement would still have to be negotiated and approved before the firm could try to put the scandal behind it.

In his opinion, the prosecutors made "criminal law out of administrative offenses." And, repeating the most common objection, he argued that "RICO was being used unjustly."

He also argued an uncommon point: "I don't think they would have RICO'd the firm if it had refused to settle." In this high-stakes poker game, he believed that Giuliani was bluffing. Drexel had three hundred and fifty thousand retail accounts throughout the country; although these accounts were insured by the Securities Investor Protection Corporation (SIPC), there is never any foolproof insurance against fear. If the firm went bankrupt, its individual clients might have panicked at the thought of losing their savings, instigating a loss of confidence in all brokerage firms, healthy or not.

The director who explained these various reasons for opposing the settlement also raised a pragmatic objection: Even if the firm was guilty, a $650 million penalty was unfair. "The fine was a hideous amount of money," was one salesman's description. "It had no relation to anything in reality."

According to Siegel the firm had added up the actual damages, assuming it was guilty of every charge—the total was $150 to 200 million. Analyzing each count in the SEC complaint, I estimated a number closer to $73 million:

Fischbach/Boesky financings	$33,000,000
Harris Graphics	7,000,000
Lorimar	2,000,000
Lorimar short sales	—
Maxxam/Pacific Lumber	3,000,000
MCA	—
MGM/UA	3,000,000
Occidental Petroleum/Diamond Shamrock	—
Phillips Petroleum	—
Stone Container	8,000,000
Storer Communications	1,000,000
Tax loss trades	1,000,000
Viacom	2,000,000
Wickes/National Gypsum	7,000,000
Wickes convertible preferred stock	2,300,000
Wickes short sales	4,000,000
TOTAL	$73,300,000

Note that the total includes $30 million in fees for three financings of Boesky-controlled companies. The $73 million total doesn't include the $66 million fee Drexel received for arranging the MGM deal with Turner Broadcasting, which almost certainly would've happened without the alleged insider trading; if you disagree, add in the fee to the total.

Regardless, the settlement as approved called for a payment of $650 million over three years, $500 million upon approval by Judge Pollack. Of the total, $300 million was assessed as a fine; the remaining $350 million was to be set aside to pay civil claims against the firm. If all those claims ended up costing more than $350 million, the additional amount would come out of Drexel's pocket; if the claims came in at less than $350 million, whatever was left over went to the government.

The financial impact on the firm was "not horrible," according to Fred Joseph, who was naturally trying to make the best of a difficult situation that day, Wednesday the twenty-first. Based on his explanation to us, it seemed that Drexel had already set aside about $400 million for the possibility of a settlement, now a certainty.

If the financial part of the agreement appeared manageable, the legal side was unknown. We were accepting six felony counts. Although the firm wasn't actually pleading guilty—the wording was that we "can't dispute the allegations"—almost no one would note the difference. To the world, Drexel was now an admitted felon.

The firm was allowed to choose its crimes from among Boesky's allegations, with the exception of the Fischbach deal—the government insisted on that one. Boesky had pleaded guilty to one felony—conspiring to file a false statement—regarding Fischbach, and with Drexel's plea to stock parking, the prosecutors' case against Milken on this transaction would be considerably strengthened.

The firm's remaining five choices reflected a desire to minimize its potential liability to the inevitable civil lawsuits. It effectively pleaded guilty to two transactions involving stock manipulation—Stone Container and C.O.M.B. (not part of the SEC complaint)—and three transactions involving stock parking—Phillips Petroleum, Harris Graphics, and MCA.

The reaction to the settlement was mixed, as expected. Representative John Dingell said in a statement: "Pickpockets get several years in the slammer for stealing small amounts of money, and deservedly so. Now we have executives apparently admitting to receiving hundreds of millions which they may have stolen." In response to a question from *The Wall Street Journal* on the settlement's deterrence value, he quoted from Gilbert and Sullivan's "The Mikado": "My object all sublime / I shall achieve in time— / To make the punishment fit the crime."

The *Journal* itself had a somewhat different point of view:

> After much waiting, the government's extraordinary case against Drexel Burnham Lambert has ended in a rather ordinary way. Drexel pleaded guilty to six felony counts and agreed to a $650 million fine. There will now be no trial, and while the guilty plea sends a message, it must be said that the rest of the securities market is left to wonder what precisely the message is.

CHAPTER TWELVE

HAS THE JURY REACHED ITS VERDICT?

Son, you're on your own.
—*Blazing Saddles*

If the settlement with the government took the employees of Drexel from the fire into the frying pan, it put its most famous employee on a skillet of his own. Michael Milken, as required in the settlement, would be fired once he was formally indicted. His fate would be separated from that of his firm's.

More than that, his firm would cooperate with the prosecutors in the continuing investigation of his activities in the mid-1980s. Although Drexel had officially been cooperating since Boesky's initial allegations more than two years earlier, there is cooperation and then there is cooperation. According to both Gary Lynch of the SEC and Bruce Baird of the U.S. attorney's office, Drexel hadn't exactly set the standard.

"There was a pattern of delay in response to document requests," said Lynch. "They certainly weren't cooperative," was Baird's comment, who noted that if you feel you have "a decent chance" of winning the case, this isn't a bad strategy. And Drexel did feel that it had a strong case.

Now the firm had a settlement, one that required its cooperation. And it no longer had the threat of prosecution hanging over its head.

For Milken, that threat was a certainty—it was only a matter of time. On March 29, 1989, a grand jury handed down a ninety-eight-count indictment against him, with seventeen counts against his brother and twenty-two counts against Bruce Newberg. The indictment dealt with twenty transactions, most of which were familiar from the SEC complaint six months earlier. (Almost every transaction involved multiple counts against the defendants, the most common being mail fraud and wire fraud.)

Milken potentially faced up to 520 years in jail, but realistically, no more than 300. He was also liable for the vast majority of a potential forfeiture that, according to government calculations was $1,845,404,494—an almost inconceivable amount of money. The lion's share of this, some 60 percent, comprised the *entire* amount in salaries and bonuses that the three men had received between 1984 and 1987—even though the transactions identified by the prosecutors provided only a small fraction of that income.

The indictment contained several trades in which, according to the 1988 SEC complaint, Cary Maultasch was involved. Maultasch was not actually named in the government's indictment. He would probably have been called as a corroborating witness. Jim Dahl and Terren Peizer, the other two junk-bond employees who had received immunity in late 1988, did not appear to figure in these charges; their testimony would probably be used in a superseding indictment.

"The three-year investigation has uncovered substantial fraud in a very significant segment of the American financial community," announced Benito Romano, the acting U.S. attorney since Giuliani's retirement on January 31. "A serious criminal problem has infected Wall Street." Milken's statement offered a different perspective: "In America, an indictment marks the beginning of the legal process, not the end. After almost two and a half years of leaks and distortions, I am now eager to present all the facts in an open and unbiased forum."

Well, this forum is hardly open or unbiased, but nevertheless, let's consider the indictment as a jury might, because to tell you what you might already know, a jury never did. To keep you reading, you've been chosen as the foreman. In fact, yours is the only vote that matters—everyone else in the Southern District of New York was able to find a valid reason to be excused from jury duty.

So the verdict is in your hands. I'll try to give you both sides of the case as best I can—no hidden agenda. You make your own decision here; I'll give you mine in the last chapter.

Now let's review the charges against Michael Milken in the 110-page indictment, in the order in which they're presented. This indictment, along with the SEC May 1988 memo and September 1988 complaint—and with some educated guesses—are most of the evidence we have. You have your work cut out for you: no witnesses; no give and take between the prosecution and the defense; no chance of your verdict holding up on appeal. But what the hell.

The first two counts of the indictment are the big ones: RICO charges. Specifically, Milken was accused of racketeering conspiracy and participation in a racketeering enterprise. That is, he arranged and took part in a pattern of illegal activities.

The following fifty-four counts involved mail fraud and wire fraud. Whenever a trade is completed, a written confirmation of that trade is generated and sent to both parties; in an illegal trade, the sending of the "confirm" is mail fraud. Similarly, if a telephone is used to place an illegal order, wire fraud is committed.

Counts fifty-eight through ninety-one dealt with securities fraud; ninety-two through ninety-seven concerned false filings of who owned what; count ninety-eight involved assisting in the preparation of a false tax return. Ninety-eight counts in all—an overwhelming number of charges against anyone. And if only one of them were found to be true, Milken would face up to five years in prison. If two or more were found to be true, then he could be convicted of racketeering and could face an additional twenty years for each of the two RICO charges.

The average person, at some level, must wonder: How can this guy not be guilty? If not, why would the government bring a huge and frivolous case and why would a grand jury approve an indictment based on these charges? And not just two charges or even three, but ninety-eight!

The guilt or innocence of an individual, however, is not determined by the sheer force of numbers, or even by a grand jury. The decision belongs to a group of people who get to hear both sides of the argument and who are decent enough to give the defendant the benefit of the doubt. Here, the burden of fairness is on you, the reader-jury.

The Takeover of Fischbach (main allegation: stock parking). This one is a bit convoluted. According to the prosecutors, Milken and Boesky "commenced a secret arrangement involving a series of unlawful securities transactions" by mid-1984. (All quotes in this chapter are from the indictment unless otherwise noted.) This alleged arrangement was central to fourteen of the twenty transactions under suspicion.

The first on the list was the takeover of Fischbach Corporation, a construction company. In the government's view, Milken and Boesky illegally assisted Pennsylvania Engineering (PenEn), controlled by Victor Posner, in taking control of Fischbach.

PenEn had agreed in 1980 that it wouldn't attempt to acquire Fischbach unless another company purchased more than 10 percent of Fischbach's stock. Allegedly, Milken had Boesky, who was promised indemnification against loss, purchase more than 10 percent of Fischbach, and the standstill agreement was off. PenEn raised $56 million through high-yield bonds in February 1985 and used the proceeds to buy a majority position in Fischbach.

One disturbing piece of evidence found among the Boesky files was a May 1984 memorandum regarding Fischbach, written by Boesky employee Nancy Hollander. The memo concludes with: "I will communicate the situation to Mike Milken. He just wanted to let the situation stand as it was today." Which raises the question: Why should Milken have any say in this "situation?"

If the allegations are true, Milken, by promising to indemnify Boesky, would have been guilty of stock parking. True or not, Milken earned some $3 million in commissions for his department and about a third of that for himself. Bear in mind, though, if he indemnified Boesky, he stood to give back some or all of the profits in the event that Boesky lost money, which in fact, Boesky did.

Another consideration: If Boesky (or anyone else) had bought the 10 percent position by his own choice or on Milken's recommendation—provided that Milken didn't promise to pay any of Boesky's losses and wasn't acting on inside information of PenEn's intentions—then there were no laws broken. Assuming this were the case, what then would have been Boesky's motive to buy 10 percent of Fischbach? Perhaps he hoped that by freeing PenEn from its standstill agreement his shares would rise in value if and when PenEn came into the market.

After reading the details of this first transaction, you probably now realize that any review of alleged financial fraud ranges between the dull and the confusing. Transactions such as these are difficult to understand—it is a problem faced by lawyers, prosecutors, judges, and juries. But it is important to look at the details and the allegations for yourself and to draw your own conclusions.

Golden Nugget's Sale of MCA Stock (stock parking). By July 27, 1984, Golden Nugget (GNG), a gaming company, had bought 2.4 million shares of MCA, with the thought of possibly acquiring the whole company. Deciding against a tender offer, GNG sold 1.1 million shares to Milken's department. These shares were then sold to Boesky, supposedly with the understanding that Drexel would cover his losses—if true, Drexel would remain the real owner of the shares, and the "sale" to Boesky would constitute illegal parking of stock.

The question here is, what purpose did Boesky serve in this alleged scheme? What difference did it make if Drexel sold to Boesky who then sold the shares in the market, or if Drexel just sold the shares directly? Either way, the market was going to have to absorb the shares, and the price of those shares was likely to go down.

(A GNG representative evidently tried to cushion this blow, according to the indictment, by stating publicly in October that GNG held just under 5 percent of MCA and that "for now" it planned to maintain its current position. Meanwhile, GNG was in the process of selling almost half its position, which it *didn't* state publicly. Isn't something wrong here?)

The sale of the MCA stock to Boesky raises another question: Why would Milken accept responsibility for any losses? Unless he was interested in doing GNG a multimillion-dollar favor, the motive behind this one is weak. And if he did want to do this favor, why not just sell the shares himself and take the loss directly? Why break the law by secretly arranging to reimburse Boesky's company for this same loss? It doesn't make much sense.

The Diamond Shamrock (DIA)/Occidental Petroleum (OXY) Merger Talks (insider trading). On January 4, 1985, Drexel was hired as an adviser to Occidental Petroleum, which had agreed on the previous day to merge with Diamond Shamrock. That same day, the two companies publicly announced that a merger was possible. Also on the fourth, Boesky bought 3.6 million shares of DIA, allegedly "with the understanding that the Drexel Enterprise and the Boesky Organization would split profits and losses."

On January 7, DIA and OXY publicly announced the details of the proposed deal, and Boesky bought an additional 180,000 DIA shares. He also sold short 327,000 OXY shares, in the hope that they would decline in value. After the close of the market on the seventh, the two companies announced that the merger had fallen through, causing sizable losses for Boesky.

This allegation accuses Milken of directly or indirectly passing along inside information to Boesky, which is a serious crime. The facts, however, aren't conclusive. There is some question as to whether Boesky began purchasing Diamond stock *before* the public announcement on January 4, when the whole world was told that a merger was in the works. The indictment doesn't clarify this point. The September 1988 SEC complaint implies that he did trade before the 1:23 P.M. announcement: it alleges that Boesky made his initial purchases at a price of $18.50, a price that was only available earlier in the day.

In fairness, however, even if this were true, it doesn't necessarily mean that he was trading on inside information. Perhaps Boesky did what risk arbitrageurs do, buying shares in a possible deal in the hope of making a small but quick profit if the deal went through.

Taking things one step further, even if he *were* trading on inside information, it doesn't necessarily mean that he had received that information from Michael Milken or from one of Milken's associates. Although Drexel would be a prime suspect, there were several other companies who had access to the same inside information, and a number of people within those companies who could have passed it along.

The most damaging piece of circumstantial evidence is an entry on a three-page ledger allegedly found in Boesky's files, an entry which strongly suggests that Boesky was splitting his losses on the Diamond/Occidental deal with someone—that someone almost certainly was Drexel, if the ledger is to be believed. This ledger is an integral part of another allegation—concerning the $5.3 million payment—and is explained in more detail below.

Repayment Trades (reimbursement for illegal transactions). In late November 1984, Boesky allegedly sent ledger sheets to Milken, detailing $10 million in losses from the Fischbach and MCA transactions and additional losses from other trades. From January to mid-March, "the defendants Michael R. Milken and Lowell J. Milken conducted a series of sham and bogus trades at artificial prices . . . to repay the Boesky Organization for its losses on trades made on behalf of the Drexel Enterprise."

According to a letter from Boesky to Milken dated November 28, 1984 and released by Assistant U.S. Attorney John Carroll, Boesky told Milken that "it will be appropriate to resolve all of the enclosed." The enclosed was evidently a three-page ledger, which listed the profits and losses from ten stocks and one bond, but which in no place refers to Milken or Drexel.

The ledger, said to have come from Boesky's files, includes the two names mentioned above: Fischbach and MCA. But it also mentions eight other stocks, none of which figures in the indictment. The question here is, if this ledger is in fact evidence of an illegal arrangement between Milken and Boesky, why wasn't Milken charged on all ten names? Perhaps the prosecution wanted to focus on those transactions that it felt had the best chance in court. Perhaps the other eight figured in the repayment trades. Or perhaps none of these transactions were illegal.

As for the alleged repayment trades, if they took place, they must exist on some computer—it would be important to see whether or not Boesky was in fact given unfair prices.

A reference to these trades was included in the SEC's May 1988 internal memo, which alleged that Milken himself suggested bond trades for the Boesky organization, resulting in quick profits for it. "Some of these trades were at prices significantly different from market prices," says the memo, "but many were at or near prevailing market prices."

The person who claims to have taken these orders from Milken is Michael Davidoff, Boesky's top trader, who pleaded guilty to one count of securities fraud and is cooperating with the government. Accordingly, Davidoff would be likely to testify about these trades. If he confirmed Milken's direct participation in unfair trades, that's pretty strong circumstantial evidence. (But keep in mind that there is always a possibility, however slight, that any cooperating witness might tell prosecutors what he thought they wanted to hear, thereby increasing the value of his testimony and reducing the severity of his sentence.)

Another factor in your decision here must be whether or not you believe that the underlying transactions—Fischbach and MCA—were illegal. If not, then there were no illegal profits and losses to reconcile. From the other perspective, if in your opinion there is enough evidence to determine whether the reconciling trades were bogus, then you'd have a much clearer idea on the legality or illegality of the underlying transactions.

Tax Loss Trades (tax evasion). In late February and early March 1985, according to the indictment, a Boesky employee asked Milken and others to help Boesky's company evade taxes. To do this, Drexel sold Cigna and OXY stock to Boesky in early March. Both stocks were about to pay a dividend; after the record date, the shares fell in price as expected. (The record date is the day that determines who is entitled to a dividend payment. If you are the owner of record on that day, you will receive the dividends on your shares; if you are the owner on the following day, you won't. Therefore, a stock will fall in price by the amount of its dividend.)

After the record date, Boesky then repurchased the shares from Milken's department at a lower price, establishing a loss for tax purposes. The dividends that he was entitled to were not actually paid until April, after the end of his March tax year.

Accordingly, he was able to take a write-off in one year and not have to pay taxes on the dividend until the following year. He still had to pay the same amount of taxes, but not for a year; in effect, he finagled an interest-free loan from the government.

This type of tax loss trade is not illegal. The allegation is that Milken's group had an understanding with Boesky that it would reimburse him if the stocks fell by more than the amount of the dividend. In the case of the three trades, that difference was about $3 million.

Why would Milken or anyone else guarantee Boesky's losses on these trades? Even if you assume away ethics, there was no possible profit on this deal for the person offering the guarantee. The best explanation, if you believe the allegation here is true, would be that these trades were just one part of an ongoing illegal relationship.

Purchase of Phillips Petroleum Stock (stock parking). On March 5, 1985, Phillips announced a recapitalization plan that involved a buyback of 55 percent of its stock. Boesky owned over four million shares, but his capital was less than required by the SEC. The allegation is that Boesky sold his shares to Drexel, with the understanding that he would be responsible for any losses and would be entitled to half of any profits. In effect, Milken's group would park the stock for him, in return for 50 percent of any profits.

In a complicated series of transactions, Boesky's company sold 4.1 million shares on March 7 and 11 to Drexel, which then resold the shares to three clients and six employee partnerships. After the Phillips recap was completed, and 55 percent of its shares had been repurchased, the three sold their remaining shares to Drexel, which then resold them to seven partnerships.

Between April 12 and 19, Boesky bought 1.75 million shares—this figure is almost 45 percent of what it had sold Drexel only a month before, which coincidentally or not, is about the number of shares it would have been left with if it had tendered its 4.1 million shares of Phillips. Between April 19 and June 3, Boesky sold the 1.75 million shares he had just repurchased from Drexel.

The circumstantial evidence here is fairly compelling. Boesky had a capital problem, and the series of transactions that followed fit the pattern you would expect if Milken's group was in fact parking stock for Boesky until his capital position improved.

The fact that ten different employee partnerships controlled by Milken bought and sold two million shares in one month doesn't add to the credibility of these transactions. On the other hand, the partnerships took a loss on the trades, which would seem unusual if there was a sweetheart deal between Boesky and Milken. As I indicated earlier, analyzing financial transactions can be frustrating.

Reconciling the Books (repayment of illegal profits). By May 1985, according to the indictment, ". . . the Drexel Enterprise owed the Boesky Organization for profits on the unlawful Phillips Petroleum trading. In or about mid-May 1985, a Drexel Enterprise member and a Boesky Organization employee attempted to reconcile the outstanding balance on the Boesky Arrangement." It is unclear whether or not the balance was reconciled, or if so, whether anything was done about it.

The Takeover of Storer Communications (insider trading). This one is confusing. In early April 1985, Drexel was hired by Kohlberg Kravis Roberts & Co. (KKR), the best known of the firms that arrange buyouts. On May 3, KKR announced an agreement to buy Storer.

By July 1, Comcast Corp., another media company, was considering a competing bid for Storer. KKR considered raising its bid if Comcast made an offer.

On July 8, Milken allegedly "caused" Boesky to buy 124,300 shares of Storer, with the understanding that all profits and losses were Drexel's.

On July 16, Comcast did make a higher bid for Storer.

On July 22 and 23, Boesky sold thirty-eight thousand shares, allegedly on Drexel's behalf.

On July 29, Comcast increased its first offer. Eventually, KKR—Milken's client—increased its bid and won the company. Drexel's fee was $49,550,000. Drexel's alleged profit from Boesky was $1,066,000.

The allegations here are very serious: The abuse of inside information. Among the questions that should be asked: Why did Milken, who was involved with KKR since early April, wait until July—two months after KKR's public announcement—before having Boesky illegally buy shares for Drexel's benefit? Why did he have Boesky sell thirty-eight thousand shares two weeks later? He certainly knew that KKR was considering a higher bid, and in fact, it did raise its proposed price.

Why would Milken do something so illegal and dangerous? His personal share of the "illegal profit" was no more than $150,000; his share of the entirely legal fee from KKR was more than $6 million. From another angle, why would he be involved in a corrupt scheme that produced $150,000 in income over five months, at a time when his legitimate income exceeded $500,000 a day?

Perhaps he thought that KKR would lose to Comcast, and he wanted to make an easy profit, legal or not. Perhaps both his sense of ethics and perspective were absolutely shot. Perhaps he didn't do anything wrong.

The Takeover of Pacific Lumber (insider trading). Since the spring of 1984, Drexel had been an adviser to Maxxam, a real estate company, regarding a possible acquisition. On September 30, 1985, Maxxam made an offer to buy the shares of Pacific Lumber at $36 per share. Two days later, the company raised its bid to $38.50 per share.

From on or about October 1, 1985, to on or about November 8, 1985, the defendant Michael R. Milken and another Drexel Enterprise member caused the Boesky Organization to buy approximately 1,843,000 shares of Pacific Lumber common stock, at prices that were often above Maxxam's then publicly announced offering price, and to sell approximately 769,000 of those shares. . . . The defendant Michael R. Milken secretly agreed with the Boesky Organization that any profits or losses on these shares would belong to the Drexel Enterprise.

On October 28, 1985, Maxxam raised its offer to $40 per share, and completed the takeover in December. Drexel's fee was $20.5 million and two hundred and fifty thousand Maxxam warrants. The alleged illegal profits from trading on inside information was $1,025,000, less than $1 per share.

This allegation is similar to the previous one, and the questions raised there would apply here as well.

Interestingly, the SEC's allegation that Milken wanted to drive up Maxxam's acquisition price because of a disagreement over Drexel's fee—a very serious and bizarre charge—is not included in the U.S. attorney's indictment.

The Acquisition of Harris Graphics (stock parking). In April 1983, Harris did a financing through Drexel; as part of that financing, 3.2 million shares were sold at $1 per share. The firm purchased 300,000 of these shares. By October 1984, partnerships composed of both selected Drexel employees and selected clients had purchased 1.2 million shares (11.8 percent). At that time, an initial public offering of 3,000,000 Harris shares was completed.

From May to September 1985, Boesky bought 853,800 shares of Harris, allegedly with the understanding that Drexel would cover all losses and divide any profits. Also as part of the understanding, Boesky was to speak with Harris's management privately and offer to buy the company at $17 per share, a 10 to 20 percent premium to the stock's price at the time. In September 1985, Boesky filed a Schedule 13-D form with the SEC; this form is required of anyone who purchases more than 5 percent of a company.

Since May 1985, members of Milken's department had been trying to find a buyer for the company. On May 9, 1986, AM International agreed to buy Harris for $22 per share. Drexel raised $100 million for AM to assist in its acquisition; the fee was $4 million. In addition, Drexel earned a $6.3 million profit on its three hundred thousand shares.

Boesky's profit was $5.6 million and Milken's was $6.5 million. The partnerships made an additional $19.4 million.

The allegation here is that Milken and Boesky had an arrangement in which Boesky bought stock for Drexel's benefit. The logic is that Milken wanted to put Harris "in play," creating the impression in its management and in potential acquirors that a buyout was inevitable. The activity in Harris's stock, the public filing of a Schedule 13-D, and the various overtures to management by Boesky and others regarding a takeover would all be consistent with such a strategy.

There is also a question that is not raised because it doesn't involve the law: How did individual employees, through the partnerships, end up with four times as many shares—bought at the bargain price of $1 each—as did their firm?

The Harris Graphics offering of October 1984, incidentally, was the first occasion that many of us in Drexel's equity area became aware of the partnerships. In the prospectus for this deal, the names and holdings of all the limited partners were listed (as time went on, other prospectuses would only include each partnership's name and that of its one general partner). This offering gave us a peek at the potential profitability of these partnerships, although the actual figures were beyond our imaginations. (One partner, a senior West Coast officer, allegedly made $161 million in profits—and it wasn't Michael Milken or his brother, Lowell.)

The MGM/UA/Turner Broadcasting Deal (insider trading). In early July 1985, MGM/UA told Drexel that Turner Broadcasting (TBS) was interested in buying the MGM Film Library. On the sixteenth, MGM/UA publicly announced that it had approached Drexel regarding the sale of the film library. On August 7, MGM/UA and TBS publicly announced an agreement in which TBS would buy MGM/UA, and then resell UA—United Artists—back to Kirk Kekorian, MGM/UA's largest shareholder and one of the more astute financiers in the country.

On the same day as the announcement, Boesky began buying shares of MGM/UA, allegedly with the understanding that all profits and losses were to be split between his company and Drexel. From August 7 through November 8, 1985, Boesky purchased 2.7 million shares and 169,000 warrants.

Drexel eventually raised $1.4 billion for TBS and received a fee of $67 million. Boesky's profit was $3.6 million.

Based on what we know, this aspect of the case against Milken seems to be weak. If Milken was willing to pass along inside information to Boesky for personal profit, why didn't he do it in July, when the world hadn't already been told about the deal? Boesky didn't begin buying shares until the day of the announcement, along with every legitimate risk arbitrageur in America.

And again, there is that mismatch between Milken's legitimate income from this deal—over $7 million—and his share of the alleged profit from Boesky—about $220,000. If Milken cheated on this one, he is every psychiatrist's dream patient.

The $5.3 Million Check (repayment of illegal profits). Maybe he is that patient. If there is a smoking gun, this would be it. According to the September 1988 SEC complaint:

> During 1985 and the first three months of 1986, [Charles] Thurnher, at Milken's direction, systematically kept track of the profits and losses on securities transactions that were part of the Arrangement. Thurnher kept Milken apprised of the results of these tracking activities. [Cary] Maultasch provided Thurnher with information about securities that were subject to the Arrangement [with Boesky] and instructed him not to store the trading information in a computer.

The May 1988 SEC memorandum adds an ironic twist to the story. According to the memo: "Thurnher did not trust Mooradian, believing that he sometimes claimed Boesky had purchased amounts of Fischbach stock in excess of reported daily volume or at prices beyond reported daily high and low prices. Thurnher thought Mooradian's calculations of Boesky's losses from Fischbach to be inflated. He has admitted that he, in turn, fabricated a loss figure for a position in Unocal common stock that Boesky had asked Milken to take for him."

As for the allegation in the indictment: Boesky's company owed

Milken's department for its share of illegal profits, and on March 21, 1986, the two conducted a series of trades at artificial prices to reduce Boesky's debt; the remainder, $5.3 million, was paid by check to Drexel.

At this time, Boesky was in the process of raising money for a new limited partnership. His auditors insisted on an explanation, in writing, for the payment. After some debate, the following explanation was drafted:

> There was an oral understanding with Ivan F. Boesky of The Ivan F. Boesky Corporation that Drexel Burnham Lambert Incorporated would provide consulting services. There were no formal records maintained for the time devoted to such consulting services. There were no prior agreements as to the specific value of such consulting services to be performed. There was no prior determination of the specific value for such consulting services until March 21, 1986, which amounted to $5,300,000.00 due to Drexel Burnham Lambert Incorporated. Such amount was mutually agreed upon.

The agreement was signed by Ivan Boesky and Lowell Milken.

Drexel raised $660 million in high-yield debt for Boesky's new arbitrage partnership; the financing fee was $26.6 million.

The potential smoking gun in this allegation is the set of notes—a several-page ledger, actually—that was said to be kept by Boesky's bookkeeper, Setrag Mooradian. As mentioned in the last chapter, there was a good deal of uncertainty as to whether the Mooradian notes were the real McCoy.

It appears that they were. The original notes allegedly kept track of numerous transactions by Boesky in 1985 and 1986, and were destroyed after Dennis Levine's arrest in May 1986 but prior to Boesky's decision to plead guilty and cooperate some four months later.

Copies of these notes were found, again allegedly by the government, in Boesky's files about a year later, and were publicly released by Assistant U.S. Attorney Carroll in June 1989. In his words, the notes were "one of the contemporaneously created 'scoresheets' comparing the Boesky Organization's tallying of the arrangement with the defendants' tallying of the arrangement."

The notes from early 1986 begin with the following comments, written by hand on ledger paper:

"Ivan,

the new items on Page 2 haven't been analyzed yet. Charlie is calling me Tuesday with details on these trades & other questions such as Phillips & Unocal. On Page 1, I've made some comments on some of our differences.

Set"

Logically, the three people referred to in this memo are Ivan Boesky, Charles Thurnher from Milken's department, and Setrag Mooradian.

The notes list forty-nine different securities—stocks, bonds, and warrants. On page 1, there is a comparison between "Seemala P&L & Interest" [profits and losses, with interest, for one of Boesky's companies] and "Their P&L & Interest" for twenty-eight securities, including those of MCA, Fischbach, Diamond Shamrock and Occidental Petroleum. (Diamond and Occidental, which were not included on the ledgers mentioned earlier, are listed as "DIA 50%" and "OXY 50%" which would be consistent with Boesky's allegation that any profits or losses on these two transactions were meant to be split evenly.)

Page 2 of the ledger lists sixteen securities, valued as of December 31, 1985. Each listing ends with the comment "we owe" or "they owe us" and an amount under the heading "Drexel." Page 3 records five securities, their "Cost or Proceeds with interest," their market value as of January 31, 1986, and what is evidently their profits or losses at that time. Among the five is MGM, which is part of the indictment; the MGM entry, however, doesn't indicate a 50-50 split, as alleged by Boesky.

The evidence in the Mooradian notes is compelling, but not conclusive. For example, if the figures in these notes are a record of an illegal arrangement, why are only eleven of forty-nine transactions discussed in the indictment? And why is MGM listed as a $3.2 million *loss* to Boesky in the ledger, but as $3.6 million *profit* in the indictment? More generally, could Boesky have felt that he was entitled to reimbursement for ideas that didn't work out, while Milken felt differently?

If the Mooradian notes were thought to be a smoking gun lying in Boesky's files, there were no such gun in Drexel's files; in fact, there was no gun at all. Charles Thurnher told prosecutors that he had discarded Boesky-related documents in April 1986, after Milken had said that he didn't want to be kept informed of transactions with Boesky. According to Thurnher, as quoted in the May 1988 SEC memo: "He told me to forget it—that it was all a bunch of [expletive] anyway and he didn't care."

According to the SEC enforcement division: "The staff doubts that Thurnher spontaneously destroyed documents based on such a casual remark and without direction from Milken. . . . The staff believes it more likely that the records were destroyed after the commission's case against Dennis Levine was filed on May 12, 1986."

The difference of opinion and timing is significant. Thurnher's statement indicates that Milken didn't ask for documents to be destroyed, and that he had lost interest in his department's transactions with Boesky *before* Levine's arrest, which was the first public announcement of an insider trading investigation. In short, no cover-up. The SEC staff, by contrast, implied that Milken probably took a more direct role in the destruction of the documents, and that these documents may have been destroyed after the possibility of investigation and prosecution had become public.

The SEC memo also includes a related allegation that wasn't part of the indictment, but would likely become part of the trial: that Milken and Boesky discussed a cover-up of the $5.3 million check. "Boesky and Milken met in July 1986 to discuss how they could substantiate the 'consulting services' gloss which they had used to conceal the true nature of the $5.3 million payment," said the SEC staff. "In this meeting, Milken cautioned Boesky that they needed to be more careful because of the 'new environment,' which Boesky understood to be a reference to the Levine case and its progeny."

The allegations in the memo provide some additional considerations in your decision, but bear in mind, they present the SEC's point of view, not Milken's.

Purchase of Wickes Shares (stock manipulation). In April 1985, Wickes Companies, a low-tech conglomerate, sold eight million shares of convertible preferred stock through Drexel. One of the terms of the deal allowed Wickes to redeem—repurchase the shares at a stated price—the preferred if the underlying common stock traded above $6.08 per share for twenty of thirty days.

By April 23 of the following year, Wickes common had sold above $6.08 per share for nineteen of twenty-seven days.

On or about April 23, 1986, the defendant Michael R. Milken and other Drexel Enterprise members caused the Boesky Organization to purchase approximately 1,900,000 shares of Wickes common stock in order to manipulate the price above $6.08 per share. On that day, Wickes common stock closed at $6.125. As a result, Wickes was able to force the redemption of the $2.50 Preferred.

Drexel's fee for handling the redemption was $2.3 million.

The logic behind this allegation is compelling. Milken's client wanted to redeem the preferred; the common shares were near but below the required price; Boesky stepped in at a crucial moment, buying 1.9 million shares in a single afternoon; the stock closed above the required price.

In Milken's defense, the standard of proof is "beyond a reasonable doubt." Circumstantial evidence, supported by the potential testimony of both Boesky and others, might not establish that a manipulative scheme was concocted, and equally important, that Milken himself was aware of it.

Purchase of Stone Container Shares (stock manipulation). On March 27, 1986, Stone Container, a packaging company, filed an offering to sell $100 million of convertible bonds and $100 million of convertible preferred stock. Both issues were to be underwritten by Drexel.

The company allegedly told the high-yield bond department that it didn't want the deal done unless its stock price was higher. (This is perfectly legal—a company has every right to decide on a minimum price at which it's willing to sell, just as any investor does.)

On April 14, Boesky bought 29,100 shares—37 percent of the total number of shares traded that day—and the stock rose above $46 per share, closing at 46¾, up 1¾ points. Seventy-eight thousand shares traded that day, two to three times the stock's normal volume.

On April 15, Boesky bought an additional eighty-five hundred shares, and Stone closed at $46.375 per share. That same day, the high-yield bond department completed the $200 million offering of debt and preferred stock; Drexel's fee was $5.9 million.

On May 1, Boesky sold his shares to Drexel at a loss, less than three weeks after buying them.

The allegation here is that Boesky bought Stone's shares for the benefit of Drexel, with the understanding that he would be reimbursed for any losses. All the arguments from the previous transaction apply to this case as well.

Sale of C.O.M.B. Shares (stock manipulation). C.O.M.B., a discount retailer, filed an offering to sell $25 million of convertible bonds through Drexel. Bruce Newburg of Drexel's high-yield group allegedly conspired with Charles Zarzecki of Princeton/Newport to reduce C.O.M.B.'s stock price in advance of the offering: "On or about April 11, 1985, the defendant Bruce L. Newberg, in a recorded telephone conversation with coconspirator Zarzecki, told Zarzecki of the impending public offering of the convertible debt and instructed him to sell C.O.M.B. common stock. The defendant Bruce L. Newberg agreed with Zarzecki that Drexel would cover any loss Princeton/Newport suffered on such sales. In that recorded conversation, Bruce L. Newberg told Zarzecki:

The stock is sixteen bid, up from fifteen and three eighths.

I don't want this thing to be sixteen bid.

I want, y——, y——, you know, to get rid of it, y——, ah, you know. I want, I want it down to at least fifteen and three quarters and hopefully lower. Umm . . . , I wouldn't mind you selling a little bit first. And um . . . , you're indemnified, uh, you know, my—, it's, y——, you know what I'm saying."

On that day, according to the indictment, Princeton/Newport sold short forty thousand shares of C.O.M.B., and the stock closed at fifteen and seven-eighths. That same day, April 11, C.O.M.B. decided to postpone its offering until April 16.

On April 15, Princeton/Newport allegedly sold short seventy-five hundred shares of C.O.M.B., and the share price again ended the day at fifteen and seven-eighths.

The evidence in this case is more compelling than in the previous one because of the tape. Bear in mind, however, that the person on that tape is Newberg, not Milken. And Newberg isn't testifying against Milken; in fact, he is pleading not guilty himself. Where, then, is the evidence that implicates Milken?

Sale of U.S. Home Shares (stock manipulation). U.S. Home, a home builder, filed an offering on March 28, 1985 to sell bonds and warrants. On April 10, two days before the expected offering date, Newberg allegedly told Princeton/Newport to sell short fifty thousand or more U.S. Home shares. "Thereafter, in a recorded telephone conversation, a Princeton/Newport co-conspirator said to Zarzecki, 'Okay it's bad for Drexel to be doing this shit because . . . they're stepping on the stock basically, right?' "

On April 11, Princeton/Newport sold short nine thousand shares.

The allegation here is similar to that in the C.O.M.B. transactions, that Newberg arranged for Princeton/Newport to knock down the price of a corporate client's stock. The indictment, however, doesn't include any conversations between Newberg and Princeton/Newport regarding the U.S. Home deal. And what is the case against Milken?

Games with Mattel (stock parking). This one is a bit convoluted (for a change). According to the government, on April 24, 1984, Drexel agreed to purchase, with the option to resell, $172 million of debt and equity securities as part of Mattel's recapitalization. On June 4, Mattel filed a proxy seeking approval from its shareholders for this recap; the proxy failed to disclose, as required, that Drexel owned 6.9 percent of Mattel's convertible preferred stock because Lowell Milken and another high-yield employee hadn't told the company of this position.

In July, Drexel's ownership of the preferred had risen to 7.8 percent, and this position was hedged by a short position in the common stock—that is, when the short position in the common was netted out against the long position in the convertible preferred, Drexel had no stake in the company. On July 12, Bruce Newberg allegedly "caused the Drexel Enterprise to transfer its hedged Series A Preferred position to Princeton/Newport with the secret understanding that the Drexel Enterprise retained ownership of and the economic risk on these securities."

Between August 23 and September 6, Princeton/Newport bought an additional 55,000 shares of the preferred and shorted additional shares of the common, again as part of an alleged parking scheme.

From January to March 1985, Princeton/Newport sold a chunk of the preferred shares that it had bought, and on April 8, sold what it still owned to Drexel.

These allegations are difficult to get a handle on. First of all, there doesn't seem to be any possible illegality with Drexel's purchase of the $172 million position, unless you believe that the failure to disclose Drexel's preferred ownership on the proxy taints the whole transaction.

As for that preferred stake, it seemed to be hedged by a short position, implying that Drexel's actual ownership stake in the company was somewhere between little and nothing. More important, why would Lowell Milken and his associate want to hide Drexel's hedged position from Mattel? What is the motive, and where is the criminal intent?

The parking allegation is an unusual one. Logically, a person parks stock with others to retain his equity stake in a company without the public's knowledge. Why would anyone want to park a hedged position, which has no equity stake? What did Newberg expect to gain from such a scheme, and why was it necessary to begin with? And if Princeton/Newport was parking this hedged position, why did it sell "a substantial portion" in the open market, and not to the firm for which it was supposedly holding the shares?

And again, where is the evidence against Michael Milken?

Tax Loss Trades (tax evasion). From November 1984 to February 1986, Princeton/Newport sold and repurchased securities to create short-term capital losses and long-term capital gains, a legal strategy to reduce taxes. Allegedly, these transactions were done with the understanding that Princeton/Newport would be responsible for any gains or losses in the security prices between the sale date and the repurchase date—such an understanding would have made these trades illegal.

Two specific 1985 trades are cited, and one tape is referred to: "The defendant Bruce L. Newberg and an employee of Princeton/Newport, in a recorded telephone conversation, discussed the repurchase price of the Lear Petroleum securities and a sham transaction in Trinity convertible bonds."

Unless that tape is incriminating—and if so, why wasn't the specific dialogue quoted as in earlier cases?—these allegations against Newberg aren't nearly as strong.

And what is the case against Milken? That he conspired with Newberg, who isn't testifying against him? There must be more than that.

The Merger of Lorimar and Telepictures (insider trading). On September 10, 1985, Lorimar and Telepictures, both involved in movie/television production, met to discuss a possible merger of the two entertainment companies. That same day, both companies contacted Milken for his advice.

On September 30, according to the earlier SEC complaint, Cary Maultasch, who worked for Milken, purchased 106,900 Lorimar shares for the high-yield convertible bond account at the firm—this purchase accounted for 85 percent of Lorimar's total volume that day. On October 2, Maultasch placed an order with Drexel's trading desk to purchase an additional 110,000 shares at a price of $30 per share or less; 53,000 shares were purchased, almost half of that day's volume.

Negotiations continued on the merger until October 3, and the final agreement was announced on October 7.

The trading profit on the 159,900 shares purchased for the high-yield convert account is estimated at $1.2 million (I don't know how the prosecutors arrived at the $4.3 million figure stated in the indictment). Drexel's fee for advising on the merger was $2.1 million.

The circumstantial evidence here is devastating. Because of Maultasch's alleged involvement, a real jury would likely have the opportunity to hear his view of events. The SEC complaint stated: "During this period, Milken communicated this [merger] information either directly or indirectly to Maultasch for the purpose, among others, of purchasing Lorimar common stock for Drexel's benefit." It would be interesting to hear what exactly that meant.

If Maultasch were to testify that he received instructions to buy Lorimar stock directly from Milken, the evidence of insider trading would seem overwhelming. As it is, it's disturbing.

(Note: According to the September 1988 SEC civil complaint, Cary Maultasch was also involved in several of the transactions described earlier: Storer, Pacific Lumber, MGM, Wickes, and the $5.3 million payment. His alleged involvement, however, does not mean that he was aware of any illegalities, if in fact any laws were broken.)

The Viacom Leveraged Buyout (insider trading). On September 10, 1986, Viacom, an entertainment company, contacted Milken regarding a proposed buyout of the company by its management. Viacom's managers wanted Drexel to finance the deal for them.

On that same day, the high-yield bond department bought 296,576 shares of Viacom stock, accounting for 21 percent of the volume. Also on the tenth, the department sold $10,500,000 of Viacom convertible bonds and purchased $500,000 of a different Viacom convert.

The Viacom leveraged buyout proposal was publicly announced on September 16; on completion of the deal, Drexel received a fee of $8.4 million. According to the government, the trading profits from the September 10 transactions was $1.8 million.

Here again, the circumstantial evidence seems devastating—certainly, there is the appearance of insider trading for large profits. But the facts of this case are more bizarre than conclusive.

The reason is that the prosecutors made an unlikely mistake. They thought that the $10,500,000 convertible bond sold on September 10 represented the equivalent of 26,355 shares—not a very significant sale in the face of a 296,576-share purchase that same day. In reality, however, that convertible bond sale represented the equivalent of 263,550 shares; they were off by a factor of ten.

Accordingly, the trading done on the tenth increased the department's ownership of Viacom shares by 51,000, not 272,000. This is still a lot of stock, especially when it is bought on the same day that Milken was told of an impending acquisition of the company. But why would someone trading on this inside information sell this huge convertible bond position? It is a puzzlement.

Another factor to consider is the date. This allegation is the only one of the twenty that occurred after Dennis Levine's arrest in May 1986. Once it became apparent that Levine was cooperating with the government, Milken might have suspected that Boesky was in trouble, since Levine couldn't cut a deal unless he had something to offer in return. If Milken thought that Boesky's days were numbered, he would have realized the risk to himself, the fact that his name might pop up in conversation when Boesky was hauled in by the prosecutors.

Therefore, if Milken was cheating with Boesky, he might have realized that every transaction he had done, *or would do,* could fall under intense scrutiny. (On the other hand, if Milken *didn't* have an illegal arrangement with Boesky, the date of this allegation doesn't matter. But under that assumption, all the Boesky-related allegations against Milken, fourteen in all, are out the window.)

Assuming that Milken *was* part of a scheme with Boesky, trading on inside information in September 1986 for a $500,000 illegal profit on a deal that would generate a legitimate $8.4 million fee doesn't seem like a smart bet for a smart man. Perhaps this ignores ego and greed, but that's for you to determine—you're still the foreman.

And now it's time for your verdict.

CHAPTER THIRTEEN
THE LAST MILE

"How, from where we started, did we
ever reach this Christmas?"

"Step by step."

— *The Lion in Winter*

The indictment of Milken was followed, two weeks later, by a settlement between Drexel and the SEC. With this settlement, in April 1989, the firm found itself at a crossroads. Within a year, the firm would find itself in bankruptcy.

The SEC settlement had been expected soon after the firm's agreement with the U.S. attorney in December; instead, negotiations had dragged on for more than three months. "If you want to put us out of business, let us know," Fred Joseph told Gary Lynch. The SEC did not want the firm closed down; it did, however, insist that careful safeguards be set in place to monitor Drexel's activities. Perhaps, as one officer suggested, it was also under pressure from Congress, pressure to further punish a firm that hadn't developed much goodwill on Capitol Hill even in the best of times.

The provisions of the SEC agreement tightened up the firm's oversight procedures and seemed reasonable, at least from my perspective. The major sticking point—whether the high-yield department should remain in Beverly Hills—was resolved in Drexel's favor. Concurrent

181

with the agreement, the firm announced that John Shad would join us as our new chairman. He replaced the somewhat invisible Bobby Linton, whose resignation, we were told, "was not required or requested by the SEC." Shad had been the chairman of the SEC during the 1981–1987 period, before becoming the U.S. ambassador to the Netherlands. At sixty-six, Shad was returning to the private sector, where more than two decades earlier, as an executive for E. F. Hutton, he had hired a young Harvard graduate named Fred Joseph.

Given the past relationship between the two, it was logical to assume that Shad was chosen primarily for appearances. He certainly looked and sounded the part of the Wall Street executive: tall and heavy jowled, with a deep voice and a sterling résumé to match. Shad was now the nominal head of Drexel Burnham, but the power was expected to remain with his former protégé.

I doubt many employees viewed Shad's appointment as anything more than necessary. Having suffered for twenty-nine months under seige, the employees couldn't be expected to welcome an outsider to the top ranks of the firm. It didn't help that this outsider was rumored to be receiving a multimillion-dollar salary for showing up. What most people didn't realize was that Shad didn't care about the money—he added it to an earlier $20 million donation to Harvard Business School; he took the job out of a sense of obligation, a sense that he *was* necessary.

Along with Shad, the firm hired two others to serve on its board of directors: Roderick Hills, a former chairman of the SEC as well, and Ralph Saul, a former president of the American Stock Exchange. These three "outside directors" also served as the Oversight Committee, with primary responsibility to catch anyone, who in spite of everything that had happened, might still be interested in playing the dark keys.

Drexel also brought in a new lawyer, Saul Cohen, who was promised more than $2 million a year. In Cohen's case, the money wasn't donated to anyone, and with no apologies. His philosophy on the subject was simple, as explained to *The Wall Street Journal:* "You're not taken seriously [among investment bankers] unless you make lots of money. I was the most expensive . . . general counsel in the universe, and they knew it." To his credit, he earned his income. He faced a difficult challenge, one that touched on a more significant issue at the firm, and he did one hell of a job.

His challenge was to negotiate an "appropriate" fine with each of the fifty states—after all, Drexel had admitted guilt to six felonies, and every state would feel obligated to mete out some punishment before it would allow business as usual. Negotiating these fines would be particularly important if the firm wanted to remain a retail brokerage firm, dealing with individual investors.

And that was part of the larger question: Did Drexel want to stay in retail? Did it want to remain a full-service broker or, now that it had settled both the criminal and civil investigations, did it want to become a smaller, more focused firm?

The top officers of the firm met on the weekend immediately following the April 13 settlement to analyze Drexel's strengths and weaknesses and to consider its future. Under pressure from representatives of the high-yield bond department, the decision was made to jettison the retail sales department and to cut back in several other East Coast operations. Total layoffs: four thousand employees.

It was a fateful choice, more than anyone likely realized at the time. The numbers supported the decision. Retail had been unprofitable in fourteen of the previous fifteen years, losing, by one executive's measure, about $50 million a year. (Determining how much a retail system actually loses is difficult, because it helps to move the merchandise that makes other departments more profitable. For example, corporate finance's success is dependent in part on retail's ability to sell the deals. The actual losses from Drexel's retail system are in dispute as well—according to one former executive, Smith Barney was solidly profitable with the sixteen retail branches that it picked up as a result of Drexel's decision to exit the business.)

More than the retail system's unprofitability was the fact that its sales force had been shrinking, implying that the best people were heading in the wrong direction. "The good ones were being picked off; the poor ones stayed," argued one observer in the firm.

But there were other factors involved. Loyalty was one. "Hang in there, hang in there, then you cut them," was how an equity trader described the April announcement, although he did feel it was the correct business decision. He added, "They stressed for two years through all the bullshit, 'Be loyal, be loyal,' then they dropped the hatchet."

Another consideration was insurance—specifically, insurance against the collapse of the firm. "Retail was the face of the firm in forty cities," said a former exec—Drexel was the broker for three hundred and fifty thousand individual accounts, representing perhaps a million Americans who sure as hell wouldn't want to see their broker go bankrupt. And because of that, the government would have a strong vested interest in helping the firm in a crisis. Once retail was gone, Drexel had, in the words of a senior investment banker, "no widows and orphans."

"They underestimated the impact of retail," another banker argued. "I asked them, 'How do you propose to sell equity deals?' They said, 'Oh, we'll go back to the way it was ten years ago; we'll syndicate deals.'" The problem with this, he pointed out, was that things had changed, and Drexel was the major reason. We had led the way in outdating the old style of placing a deal and in angering our competitors. The West Coast had opposed the idea of sharing commissions by syndicating pieces of its bond deals to other Wall Street firms; for years in the highly profitable junk-bond market, a Drexel syndicate was a contradiction in terms. At this point, the Street wasn't likely to help us out.

Of course, there was the institutional equity group—my department—which could try to place the stock deals that our corporate finance department put together. But the chances that we could sell everything on the deal calendar were slim. For one thing, the new offerings that had been sold in recent years had, on balance, done poorly, and portfolio managers were understandably skeptical. Once burned, twice shy—just like everyone else.

The larger problem was that deals throughout the Street are generally overpriced, as mentioned earlier, and institutional investors are smart enough to be selective. Sadly, the overvalued is more easily sold to the relatively unsophisticated retail investor.

If the environment for "working the calendar" was poor, the environment for working in general was worse. Morale on the trading floor had bumped along the bottom since the December settlement four months earlier. The letdown was similar to running a marathon, and being forced to quit with a mile to go. This letdown wasn't discussed or even consciously felt, it was just there.

The circled wagons were gone, the logic that we're innocent until proven guilty was now irrelevant. We could look anyone in the eye and say that we had been forced into a settlement, but still, we had pleaded guilty. It was an odd and uncomfortable position to be in.

There was also a sense that we had played into Giuliani's hand that day in late December, that we had given the mayor-aspirant a big, fat gift, one that he had received as a result, as the British would say, of bad sportsmanship. He was now a hero, a latter-day Thomas Dewey, having taught those crooks on Wall Street—us—a well-deserved lesson.

It hardly seemed fair. Fairness dictated that if the firm had broken the law, let that fact be proven in court. And if, because of RICO, the firm never saw its day in court, let there be no doubt as to why.

But this didn't happen, and life went on. We explained the settlement to our clients and friends; we told them again of RICO and coercion. And we did our jobs as best we could.

In early February, the equity department spent a Friday evening and Saturday at the Vista Hotel in lower Manhattan to consider the outlook. "The one message I want everyone to walk away with tomorrow is that we are going to achieve growth with profitability in 1989," said the senior vice-president at the podium. "And the only way we are going to achieve this is contained in a paraphrase of the old Gillette jingle from the boxing matches. We've got to 'look smart, act smart, and be smart.' "

The smart bet, as you might guess, was to take all the money spent by the department on this lost weekend and apply that money against our losses. Large group meetings are the classic example of the reach exceeding the grasp—very little gets accomplished. It is a familiar pattern. The group tries to address its major grievances, inevitably locking in on some irritating but essentially irrelevant problem. Everyone instinctively feels safe attacking this paper tiger, and discussion flares. Of course, little if anything is ever subsequently done, but then again, who cares?

On Saturday, the various equity departments—sales, trading, and research—were grouped in separate rooms, and each department head spent the morning talking with each group. In one meeting, the head of the international equity effort was asked if the firm was planning to expand its coverage of international stocks. The question was perfectly valid because we were only following about ten foreign stocks. In response, the head man proceeded to list most of these stocks, effectively avoiding the real issue. His answer, however, did highlight another basic fact of meetings: People easily become defensive.

The upshot of the 1989 equity conference was not a surge in

motivation. What did wake up the equity group was the decision, ten weeks later, to drop the retail system, eliminate the international equity department, and severely cut back on the trading of over-the-counter stocks. Now, people had something more fundamental to worry about: their jobs. Was there another shoe to drop? Further cutbacks? Further layoffs? A jolt of fear cleared away the malaise that had settled in during the previous four months.

As management steered away from its "weaknesses," it continued to focus on its strengths—or more specifically, on those areas that had been its strengths in the past. Obviously, the core of our profitability for years had been the high-yield bond department. Tied in with this department was the investment banking effort on both coasts, which generated the deals that the junk-bond group sold to its clients.

But there was trouble in paradise. The high-yield bond department was particularly angry at the treatment of Milken, who was essentially fired by his firm. More important, the main man was gone and the market that he had pioneered was about to go to hell in a handbasket.

The collapse of junk bonds was far from apparent at the beginning of 1989. Fred Joseph was more concerned about the consequences if his high-yield employees and investment bankers left for greener pastures following the settlement than about the consequences if they stayed.

In corporate finance, "there were a bunch of people putting tremendous pressure on Fred for compensation," recalled one investment banker. "We can go anywhere," was the attitude, according to another. Fred guaranteed the bankers that the bonus pool for 1989 would be at least three-quarters of the 1988 pool—this wasn't an exorbitant offer because Drexel's corporate finance income in the first few months of the year was likely to be enormous.

In the high-yield bond department, individual agreements were negotiated with the top employees, fixing minimum and maximum levels. Ironically, the firm was forced by the government to make multimillion-dollar deals with both Jim Dahl and Terren Peizer, two employees who had agreed to testify against Milken and the firm, and who weren't welcome in their own department.

In that department, there was an "underdog mentality," according to one West Coast officer, a desire to show the world that the junk-bond group could still sell the deals. The first half of 1989 was notable for one deal that had been negotiated in the previous year: the $25 billion takeover of RJR Nabisco by the leveraged buyout firm of Kohlberg Kravis Roberts & Co. The deal was a boon for Drexel— $227 million in fees—and the financing was a masterpiece. There would be almost $13 billion in senior debt lent by banks. At the other end of the financial structure, KKR would invest $1.5 billion for the stock in the new company and purchase $500 million in debt that for several years would pay interest in the form of more bonds rather than in cash, known as payment in kind (PIK).

Drexel had already sold $5 billion in high-yield bonds. The $5 billion in bonds were divided into two debt issues: $1.25 billion of first subordinated increasing rate notes and $3.75 billion of second subordinated increasing rate notes—the interest rate on these issues would rise every three months. In the event of bankruptcy, these bonds would only have a claim on RJR assets after the banks had been paid in full; on the brighter side, their claim would come ahead of the new stockholders. And not surprisingly, the "first" notes would get paid before the "second" notes.

In the spring of 1989, Drexel was the lead manager on the sale of $4 billion in bonds, the proceeds of which were to redeem most of the increasing-rate notes described above. Drexel sold $3 billion of 12-year subordinated bonds—$1 billion of PIK; $2 billion sold at a significant discount from face value. With Merrill Lynch as co-manager, Drexel also placed $525 million of 12-year subordinated bonds (interest paid in cash), $225 million of bonds with a reset feature (the interest rate could be raised in the future), and $250 million of 10-year floating rates notes (interest rate would rise and fall with market rates).

The old stockholders of RJR received a terrific price for their shares, more than a double in less than a year, but only three-quarters of that price was paid in cash. The other quarter was in the form of two esoteric securities: a senior converting debenture—a zero-coupon bond that in four years could be converted into shares of stock if the holder chose (but then they wouldn't receive any interest payments)—and a cumulative exchangeable preferred stock—a preferred that pays its dividends in cash *or* in additional stock and is exchangeable into debt.

The purpose of this incredible collection was to allow the new company to take on a tremendous amount of debt and still have a reasonable chance of paying it; that's why several of the securities don't pay out cash for several years. All this debt made the equity extremely risky, but the new stockholders, KKR, were willing to take on that risk for the opportunity to make an enormous profit.

From the other side of the coin, these securities had to be designed to attract investors with different risk/reward profiles to a company with more debt than most countries. Making this deal work for both borrower and lender was quite an achievement, whether or not you believe deals like this should be done in the first place.

The RJR Nabisco deal, an unqualified success for the firm, also highlighted a concern. When Fred Joseph had thanked Henry Kravis of KKR for hiring Drexel as its adviser and financier, Kravis replied, "Fred, don't thank me. I'm using Drexel because you're the only ones that can get it done. As long as you are, I'm going to use you." The problem was how to maintain that top ranking, and at what cost?

The top deal makers remained with the firm, comforted by compensation guarantees and probably secure in the knowledge that they couldn't do any better anywhere else. Unfortunately, two crucial ingredients for continued success were missing. Milken was gone and the market was changing for the worse.

Without Milken, the high-yield bond group was a shadow of its former self. He ran a department of nearly three hundred people without relying on a chain of command; he was the difference between the ultimate entrepreneurial organization and organized chaos. As he slowly disappeared from the scene to focus on his defense, there was no one willing or able to replace him.

Eventually, John Kissick, the head of West Coast corporate finance, was given responsibility for the entire high-yield group. "The reins were thrust upon Kissick," said a West Coast bond trader, who viewed him as much better suited for his previous job: "He was not a people person . . . he didn't want to be in the public eye." With Kissick often off the trading floor and the head trader, Warren Trepp, "doing his own thing," according to the same source, the decision-making process appears to have taken a beating.

How badly the junk-bond market suffered from the loss of Milken is unclear, but one thing is certain: It did suffer. He had given the market a sense of confidence in its ability to price these new securities correctly and to trade them efficiently. One investment banker recalled a comment from a colleague in April 1989: " 'This place is in trouble. Nobody knows how to make a market in this shit.' " "In the last year," the banker argued, "no one wanted to admit that without Milken, the high-yield market wasn't mature enough to survive the bumps."

The problems that would emerge ranged from the subtle to the obvious. By 1989, the junk-bond market was a victim of its own success and that of the stock market. Stock prices had tripled during the 1980s, creating two significant dangers. First, takeovers were more expensive and the bonds sold to finance them were, therefore, more likely to fail. In 1984, takeover prices were six times a company's cash flow, on average; in 1989, the ratio was up to nine. Looked at from a different perspective, whereas cash flow had averaged one and a half times interest payments in 1984, the coverage ratio had declined to only one in 1989. In a nutshell, the chances of bankruptcy had risen dramatically.

Second, the buyouts of the past seemed brilliant in retrospect because rising prices had allowed the buyers to sell off part or all of their acquisitions at higher and higher prices. But rising prices in the future were hardly guaranteed—logically, the more prices have risen in the recent past, the *less* likely they'll rise in the near future.

More important to the high-yield market than the raising of money to pay for takeovers was the raising of money to finance the ongoing operations of existing companies. Unfortunately, companies in general had a good deal more debt on their books than a decade earlier—taking on more debt would naturally create more risk for both the sellers and the buyers.

Meanwhile, the enthusiasm of these buyers was fading fast. By April 1989, Milken was officially gone. That same month, a study was released by Professor Paul Asquith of Harvard that sent a shudder through the financial community. The study analyzed the frequency of high-yield bond defaults; the media interpreted the results to mean that junk bonds missed interest payments significantly more often than had previously been thought. This conclusion was inaccurate, but it did raise a valid question: Just how risky are these bonds?

Over the next year, Drexel would find out the hard way. The firm was determined to focus on its previous strength: selling lucrative junk-bond offerings to its vast network of buyers. But looking forward, this strategy involved underwriting high-risk deals in a market that was facing a crisis of confidence. What made these deals particularly high risk was that they put the firm in the dangerous position of buyer of last resort. In a solid market, it's a calculated bet; in an uncertain market, it's an invitation to disaster.

A brokerage firm borrows most of the money it uses, and most of that debt is borrowed short term. It must be very careful about picking up assets that can't be easily sold, because its liabilities must be paid every few weeks or months. Normally, these debts can be paid by selling new short-term loans; if not, they must be paid out of the firm's cash. And, as you probably know from dealing with debts of your own, the less cash you have, the less likely your lenders will accept new loans. In fact, if you have trouble paying one lender, they'll all want cash.

For a broker, business is a balancing act. It must maintain a strong financial position to keep its lenders happy, but it must also be active in the markets it serves. It must be willing to buy the securities that its clients want to sell; otherwise, these clients won't want to deal with the firm in the future. This applies to new offerings as well. The corporate client wants its bonds sold to the public; if the brokerage firm can't find buyers for all these new bonds, it will find itself under pressure to buy the remainder for itself—in the hope that it will scare up, perhaps literally, some more buyers in the future.

If the broker places all the bonds, it banks a nice fee from a happy seller; if a chunk of these bonds ends up in its inventory, it takes in a nice fee and a potential time bomb. Can the bonds be sold? At what price? When will the firm need the cash that's tied up in those bonds?

Drexel's management realized the potential dangers, although it certainly underestimated them. There were other considerations as well. It wanted to retain its number one ranking in the junk-bond market: "To maintain our position, the firm is prepared to commit whatever resources are necessary, whether it is capital or personnel," Fred Joseph reportedly told those attending the 1989 high-yield bond conference on April 5.

Drexel also wanted to prove to its present and future corporate clients that it could still do the deals, and it wanted to maintain the flow of fees that these offerings provided. "The firm needed to show it could close deals with Milken gone in the face of bad markets," argued an East Coast investment banker.

There was perhaps no single deal that highlighted these motives, and their consequences, more clearly than the West Point-Pepperel financing. Bill Farley, a health and leverage fanatic, had been a corpo-

---

rate finance client since July 1984, when Drexel raised $75 million toward his purchase of Condec, a defense contractor. The following month, the high-yield department sold $150 million more in bonds for the parent company, Farley Metals.

In 1985, Drexel raised $500 million for Farley's $1.4 billion buyout of Northwest Industries, a collection of companies, the crown jewel being Fruit of the Loom. Next was West Point-Pepperell, a Georgia textile company. After a bitter battle, Farley's $1.6 billion bid was accepted in February 1989. And that's when the story really begins.

The West Point financing involved a relatively new approach for Drexel: a bridge loan. This is a loan made directly from a brokerage firm to a borrower, one who needs cash in a hurry to pay for a takeover. Ironically, the bridge loan had been designed by other Wall Street firms to compete with Drexel, specifically with Milken's "highly confident" letter—his promise to raise whatever money was necessary, and quickly. Because they couldn't match his ability, they chose the high-risk approach of lending their own money. In theory, once the takeover was completed, they could sell junk bonds for the new company, which would repay their loan with the proceeds.

The great danger, of course, is that the brokers won't be able to sell those junk bonds, and the temporary bridge loan becomes a permanent nightmare—in this case, Drexel's nightmare.

A key factor in the successful completion of the West Point-Pepperell acquisition, and the repayment of the bridge loan to Drexel, was the sale of a major West Point subsidiary, Cluett Peabody. Cluett boasted a collection of well-known apparel companies, and was originally expected to sell for $800 to 900 million. A buyer was located—Bidermann Industries U.S.A., a subsidiary of Paris-based Bidermann Group; the price, however, had fallen by almost 20 percent.

The "due diligence" was set in motion, with Bidermann's investment banker, the Lodestar Group, preparing estimates for Cluett's profits, and comparing these estimates with the projections prepared by Farley's investment banker, Drexel. Unfortunately, Lodestar's estimates for the second half of 1989 were some 40 percent *below* those of Drexel, the primary reason being the worsening climate for retail companies. Further complicating the negotiation process for Farley Industries was that its desire to sell Cluett Peabody was a great deal stronger than Bidermann's desire to buy Cluett.

As you can imagine, the selling price took a beating. When the smoke finally cleared months later, substantially all of Cluett—Arrow shirts, Gold Toe socks, and Schoeneman menswear—was sold for $410 million—$350 million in cash and $60 million in debt of discounted value—effectively one half of the original expectations for these three divisions.

There was also a human side to this fiasco. Milken had always argued that the prime consideration in the financing decision should be the qualities of the managers. "In the long run, people are what determine the credit-worthiness of a company," he told interviewers at *New Perspectives Quarterly* in the fall of 1989. Decades earlier, J. P. Morgan had offered much the same point of view. The West Point deal raised some serious doubt on this score.

From Drexel's perspective, "it was a deal that was done without much of an eye on the consequences," according to an East Coast investment banker, who noted how unusual such an attitude was— normally, he argued, investment bankers are able to convince themselves that their deals will turn out favorably.

When all was said and done, Drexel apparently ended up with some $180 million of its cash tied up in a bridge loan to West Point-Pepperell.

The West Point deal was not the only bridge disaster of 1989. The firm also sank $43 million into a loan to Paramount Petroleum, a refinery that slid into bankruptcy within six months of cashing the firm's check.

The man who brought this deal to the firm was Peter Ackerman, the mastermind behind the RJR Nabisco financing. A brilliant, creative strategist, he had worked with Milken for years, arranging how deals should be structured. It was challenging work and the pay was pretty good: Ackerman would earn more than $100 million in the 1988–1989 period, in large part due to RJR.

Unfortunately, the RJR deal was one of the few bright spots for the firm in 1989. Two others were deals in which Drexel benefited by refusing to participate: the proposed acquisition of Prime Computer by longtime Drexel client Ben LeBow and the takeover of Ohio Mattress, known on Wall Street as "The Burning Bed," which left First Boston holding a $450 million bridge loan.

But if Drexel dodged a few bullets, it caught several others. One was the refinancing of JPS Textile's debt. JPS was created in May 1988 with the acquisition of J. P. Stevens, a South Carolina textile company, by Odyssey Partners, a leveraged buyout firm. The new company was now selling almost $400 million in junk bonds to repay the original debt, which required interest payments that rose over time. Incredibly, Drexel was unable to sell more than half of the offering and ended up buying some $200 million of this unwanted debt for itself.

There were also the Edgcomb Metals and Memorex deals, which saddled the firm with $100 million in bonds that were essentially wallflowers; and the Resorts International debt, which only made a single interest payment.

Integrated Resources, a long-time client, found itself on the road to bankruptcy, which proved costly to Drexel. A former packager of tax shelters, Integrated's "costs were just out of sight," according to one investment banker. "You can defer a lot of costs," he added, "but sooner or later. . . ."

In June, the company, which was rechristened "Disintegrated Resources" by one high-yield bond analyst, was unable to meet a payment on its short-term paper. Drexel, following the precedent set by Goldman Sachs in the Penn Central bankruptcy, decided to guarantee its customers' investments in the company—the price tag of Drexel's guarantee could eventually reach $100 million.

Far more disturbing than this was the subsequent decision by Drexel's board of directors to indemnify against loss the private partnerships that involved selected members of the firm. These secretive partnerships, once so attractive, which had operated in a separate but unequal status, were now in danger of being used for possible illegalities in the purchase and sale of junk bonds. And the partners were concerned. The partners were also senior investment bankers and important high-yield personnel.

But not to worry. If the partnerships, which had benefited at the expense of the firm and perhaps at the expense of the law, end up devastated by lawsuits, the firm will pay the losses. Or more specifically, the stockholders of the firm will pay. It's reminiscent of the scene in the film *Brazil,* where a fellow is brutally arrested in his living room, while his wife, stupid with shock, is politely asked to sign the necessary forms requiring her to pay for his interrogation.

The expected price tag for guaranteeing the partnerships is unknown.

If Drexel's financing choices were within its control, there were several crucial events in the second half of 1989 that were not and that soon haunted the firm's earlier decisions. The first of these events was the savings and loan bailout bill passed in August. This long-overdue legislation, Congress's first attempt to resolve a several-hundred-billion-dollar crisis at least partly of its own making, included a body blow to the junk-bond market: savings and loans were required to sell their high-yield bonds by 1994.

This provision was significant for two reasons. First, the market was told that $14 billion of junk bonds, 7 percent of the total, were going to be sold. Second, these bonds would probably be dumped sooner rather than later, because there was no reason to wait. S&Ls were no longer permitted to carry these bonds on their books at face value; if they had been, they probably would have held onto the bonds for a few more years to avoid recognizing any losses in their values.

(This quirk of accounting—carrying bonds at par—was still permitted for other types of bonds. In fact, to go back a few years, if all financial institutions had been forced to account for bonds at market value instead of face value during the 1980s, a large chunk of the insurance industry would have gone bankrupt, because their bond holdings were worth significantly less than their stated value. The losses incurred in "marking to market" these bonds would have wiped out their equity.)

Not only was the high-yield market faced with the near-term prospect of $14 billion in bonds coming down the pike, it also had to deal with the reality that S&Ls would not be buyers of these bonds in the future. Supply up, demand down—a bad combination.

That's not to say it was a bad move on Congress's part. The whole concept of allowing S&L's to invest in any risky asset with taxpayer-guaranteed money is a bizarre experiment in "free-market" socialism. And although high-yield bonds were an excellent investment up until the time of the bail-out bill, their future performance would have been suspect, for reasons outlined later.

In addition, the concentration of junk-bond holdings in the thrift industry—half of *all* holdings among 3,000 thrifts were in the hands of only five of them—was a danger sign, a signal that a few players were making some enormous bets with federally insured deposits. In fact, each of the top five owners of junk bonds is now insolvent, and four of these thrifts have been seized by the government.

All in all, junk bonds didn't cause the savings & loan crisis, but they will add to its eventual cost. Still, to keep things in perspective, the junk-bond holdings of thrifts will add less than one percent to the total losses that taxpayers face.

The month following the S&L bill was the calm before the storm. A minor reorganization of senior management was announced on August 30—the main winner seemed to be Arthur Kirsch, the director of our equity research department, who would now become the head of sales and trading as well, reporting directly to Fred Joseph. Fred also reassured employees that the firm wasn't planning any further eliminations of stock market–related departments. "We must be in equities, however difficult," he said. Our institutional equity department was highly regarded on the Street and was needed to sell new offerings of stock.

As for business, August had been a lousy month, we were told. Still, the firm had earned some money for the year, the backlog of investment banking deals yet to come was described as strong, and our fixed costs had been reduced to $750 million from $1.1 billion. To the average employee, who had no idea of the bridge loans and bonds accumulating dust in our basement, the outlook for the firm seemed encouraging.

Fred also mentioned that the settlement with the government, signed eight months earlier, was nearing its final stage. Two weeks later, the agreement was finalized following the prosecutors' decision to drop their insistence that Drexel withold Milken's bonus for 1988—a year in which no crimes were alleged to have been committed (this bonus, estimated at no more than $50 million by Drexel, was never paid). On September 11, the settlement was approved by Judge Milton Pollack and the firm's carefully worded guilty plea was formally entered: "Based on the information available to us, we are not in a position to dispute the allegations."

In addition, as part of the settlement, $500 million was given to the government. "How do you replace $500 million in cash," asked Burt Siegel. "Nobody was willing to put new money in." His conclusion: "You pray for a good market. When the market runs against you, there's no place to hide."

Unfortunately, that would be the story for October, as the stock and bond markets went down with a passion. On Friday the thirteenth, stocks fell more than 7 percent, suffering their worst decline since the crash two years earlier. The financing for the proposed $6.8

billion acquisition of United Airlines fell through, creating a crisis of confidence that spread through the stock market. The hardest hit was United itself, which fell 57 points to $223 per share. Drexel lost $25 million on its large position in these shares alone.

In the junk-bond market, the only way things could have been worse was if it rained. The refinancing of Ohio Mattress fell through, turning First Boston's temporary bridge loan into something considerably more permanent. More significant, Campeau Corporation, the Canadian retail giant that had paid $6.6 billion for Federated Department Stores in 1988, defaulted on its bonds. According to a First Boston officer familiar with the negotiations, Chairman Robert Campeau was offered a deal by its lead banker, Citibank, which would have allowed him to meet his interest payments. Evidently, Campeau refused the offer; by the time he was forced to reconsider, it had been pulled.

Drexel had no part in the Campeau and Ohio Mattress fiascoes, but as the largest player in the junk-bond market, it also suffered the consequences. Although the firm's inventory of high-yield bonds was only half what it had been in 1986, its holdings still approached $2 billion. And those positions were all affected by the weakness in the market.

The month of October 1989 ended with an $86 million loss for Drexel. To add insult to injury, someone among the small group of executives who were aware of these losses leaked this information to *The Boston Globe*. The public disclosure of these private problems undoubtedly caught the attention of the bond rating agencies, as well as of the firm's lenders.

In late November, Drexel was dealt a serious blow: The safety rating on its short-term debt was reduced. "We didn't expect the downgrade," said an accounting officer. "For once, the rating agencies were proactive." Still, the agencies must have been aware of the front-page problems in the junk-bond market, and they had been clued into the firm's miserable October results.

Drexel's commercial paper rating was cut from A-2 to A-3. This may not seem like a big deal, but as one Wall Street exec told *The New York Times*, "There is no A-3 market to speak of—it trades by appointment only. When you go from A-2 to A-3, you're essentially out of the market."

Specifically, the problem was with the firm's commercial paper, its short-term IOUs that aren't backed by any specific assets. Drexel had $700 million in commercial paper outstanding, which had to be continuously reborrowed, usually every thirty to sixty days. And if it couldn't be reborrowed, it had to be repaid.

The firm was now in danger of being squeezed out of business—it was losing money, and cash, and there was the ongoing risk that its lenders would take their money and run. During December alone, $420 million of Drexel's commercial paper was redeemed by lenders, according to the SEC.

Unlike most of the other major firms on the Street, which were subsidiaries of huge corporate parents, the firm didn't have a Big Daddy to bail it out if worst came to worst. As for Groupe Bruxelles Lambert, which owned 26 percent of Drexel's stock, "relations were pretty poor," according to Drexel's Burt Siegel—during the glory days, Lambert had been treated less like a rich uncle than an unwanted aunt.

The Lambert Group did lend the firm some cash at year-end, backed by specific assets, but it declined to make an equity investment. On that subject, the bottom line given to Fred Joseph was to improve the bottom line: start showing profits, and Lambert would consider making a further investment after the end of the first quarter, in April 1990.

Drexel ended 1989 with a $40 million loss and decidedly mixed prospects for the new year. "I really believed we had a good chance of getting there," recalled Fred Joseph at a meeting for Drexel debt holders. "Every department expected to break even at worst."

One officer on the West Coast who was involved with Drexel's efforts to maintain its borrowings from the banks, however, was a great deal less optimistic. Given his position, he had access to excellent information from both the auditors and the rumor mill. "I knew it was going badly," he said. "The banks could pull their lines [of credit] at any time." Many in his department took their cash and securities out of their personal accounts at the firm, to avoid the risk that these assets might be frozen if Drexel went bankrupt.

This officer also mentioned the bonus payments. The bonuses, many of which had been guaranteed in early 1989, amounted to $150 million in December and an additional $110 million in January 1990. What concerned him was that Drexel paid $64 million of these bonuses, not in cash, but in a PIK preferred stock. "We all know why people issue PIK preferreds," he noted. "And it's not because you're healthy."

By the end of January 1990, the firm's health was considerably worse. In addition to the nearly $200 million cash outflow from the bonuses, Drexel lost $52 million from its operations. Fees from investment banking transactions were less than $10 million in the month, although these fees were expected to reach $120 million in the subsequent two months.

These large investment banking fees, as well as the operating improvements from the firm's other departments, never had the opportunity to be realized, however. In February, Drexel's financial structure collapsed. For months, more cash had been going out the door than coming in, and the firm finally ran out of sources to replace it.

Drexel's best source toward the end, interestingly, was itself. As loans came due and lenders demanded their money, Drexel Burnham Lambert *Group,* a holding company that was responsible for the debts, borrowed cash from its subsidiary, Drexel Burnham Lambert *Inc.,* which was the brokerage firm that you think of when you hear the name Drexel.

This holding company structure, which is common on Wall Street, became a nightmare for the firm and its regulators. DBL Group was borrowing the money from DBL Inc., because it was desperately short of cash, and DBL Inc. had more than it needed. DBL Inc.'s excess cash was the amount of money that it held above and beyond the amount that the regulators required. This extra cash was the famous "excess net capital" that Fred Joseph had been referring to for three years, which had reassured employees that the firm was in terrific financial shape even if we didn't really know what the term meant.

Now Drexel, specifically the Group, needed that money to pay its debts. It borrowed $220 million from DBL Inc. over several months, reducing the broker's excess capital to $330 million. The firm didn't inform the SEC, which is responsible for regulating DBL Inc., because it was only borrowing *excess* cash, which by definition, was money that wasn't required in the first place.

The SEC found out on February 7. The following day, it told Drexel to stop upstreaming cash from DBL Inc. to DBL Group. This cash might be excess capital, but the regulators had the right to keep it where it was, and that's exactly what they did. Their concern was that DBL Group would borrow too much from DBL Inc., thereby threatening the broker's survival by replacing its cash with IOUs from the Group.

The SEC's job was to keep the broker solvent, and they were taking no chances. Its actions made it likely that the Group would default on its loans, which in turn, would probably create a chain of circumstances that would throw the broker into bankruptcy as well. But its concern at this point was that DBL Inc. maintain as strong a financial position as possible.

In the SEC's mind, allowing DBL Group to borrow the remaining $300 million in excess capital from DBL Inc. would only have postponed the firm's default by one or two days. Although the commercial paper outstanding had been reduced to $150 million by early February, Drexel had other short-term loans that were maturing in that month and next, in total about $700 million according to the SEC.

The firm believed, however, that these lenders would roll over their loans when they came due rather than demanding repayment. It proposed a plan to the SEC, the NYSE, and the New York Federal Reserve Bank on Friday, February 9 that involved reducing its operations and selling major portions of its bond and stock holdings. The result, it hoped, would be a leaner firm with enough cash to run its businesses effectively. But the SEC didn't buy this argument.

Another source of cash for DBL Group had been a different subsidiary, DBL Trading Corp., which specialized in commodity and foreign-exchange transactions. Allegedly, Trading Corp. had leased gold from various foreign governments, then sold the gold and purchased future contracts for an equivalent amount. Since futures contracts require only a small up-front payment, usually less than 10 percent of the total value, Trading Corp. was left with the vast majority in cash, some of which it lent to DBL Group. (Whether or not Trading Corp. had the right, legally or ethically, to lend this money is in dispute.)

On Monday February 5, according to one senior executive, a major bank pulled DBL Trading Corp.'s line of credit, and $200 million was transferred from DBL Group to Trading Corp. on Wednesday evening. Evidently, this left Trading Corp. with approximately $600 million in loans, many of them the result of gold-leasing agreements. Among the lenders were several Eastern European countries, which were soon to receive a painful introduction to capitalism.

By Monday the twelfth, Drexel was running out of room fast. On the trading floor, one salesman described the scene as "eery, complete quiet, no phones ringing, no nothing." Another salesman advised him, "Don't talk to anyone. Don't call your wife, don't call clients and don't tell anybody anything. Everything is being taped." (Which was not true, according to an official at Drexel.)

The rating on its remaining commercial paper was reduced further that day; although only $150 million were left, this downgrade would certainly send an ominous message to the firm's other lenders.

Drexel turned to its bankers, hoping for a temporary $350 million loan. As collateral, the firm offered a package of assets, most of which were its remaining junk bonds. The market value of this package was estimated at $800 million, more than twice the requested loan, but the banks refused. "The banks were petrified," said a senior Drexel officer. "They had already lent us $1.05 billion" from an ongoing credit line and were unwilling to take on more risk.

Among foreign companies, there was evidently no interest in acquiring the firm. No Japanese or European broker was eager to take on the responsibility of Drexel's contingent liabilities—the unknown sums that the firm might owe in the future if lawsuit settlements exceeded the amounts already set aside.

At 1:00 on the morning of Tuesday, February 13, Fred Joseph spoke with Richard Breeden, chairman of the SEC, and Gerald Corrigan, president of the New York Federal Reserve Bank. Their advice: Put yourself in bankruptcy. At 11:00 A.M., the firm announced that it had defaulted on $100 million in loans. Before the end of the day, the news was official: After fifty-five years on Wall Street, Drexel Burnham was finished.

The end for Michael Milken came two months later. A bit after noon on April 24, 1990, he entered Room 110 at the Southern District Courthouse to plead guilty to six felonies. He looked composed—not relaxed, but in control of himself. His wife and his mother sat in the front. Around them in the standing-room-only crowd were reporters from, as best as I could tell, every newspaper with a circulation of more than ten.

Judge Kimba Wood, the most recent—and, at forty-six, the youngest—appointee to this federal district court, entered soon after Milken, and the proceedings began. It was a ritual of questions asked and answered, almost by script. If you go to trial, do you understand that you will have a presumption of innocence? Yes, your honor. Do you understand your right to change your plea? I do. Do you understand that you have to acknowledge guilt? Yes. Are you seeing a doctor or psychiatrist? No. Is your mind clear? (Pause) Yes, your honor.

And so on.

Arthur Liman, Milken's principal attorney, clarified that the prosecutors had agreed not to recommend a specific sentence; John Carroll, the assistant U.S. attorney on the case since its inception, concurred, pointing out that this was consistent with general practice. Judge Wood noted that the settlement of the criminal case included a $200 million fine to the government, and that the settlement of the SEC's civil case required an additional $400 million payment to a fund for shareholders who had been hurt by the crimes that Milken was now acknowledging.

Those crimes carried a maximum penalty of twenty-eight years in jail. The judge told Milken that she might order that he serve his sentence consecutively or concurrently—if concurrently, the maximum penalty would be five years. She also warned against attempting to predict her final decision, which would be announced some five months later.

Interestingly, by agreement, Milken's cooperation in the government's ongoing investigation would not begin until after that final decision. Liman argued that his client had an obligation to cooperate "fully, accurately, and truthfully," but clearly, the prosecutor's leverage over Milken would drop significantly once sentenced. Carroll acknowledged as much: When asked by Judge Wood if the defendant's cooperation would be as complete after her decision, the prosecutor replied, "We certainly hope so."

As part of the plea process, Milken read an intriguing statement, known as an allocution, admitting his crimes. It's lengthy, but because of the carefully chosen wording of his admissions, it's worth seeing in full.

I was the founder and head of the High Yield and Convertible Securities Department at Drexel. In pioneering the creation of new instruments for the financing of companies, most of which did not have access to the capital markets because they did not have investment-grade ratings, and in making markets in such securities, we operated under unique, highly demanding, and intensely competitive conditions.

But I do not cite these conditions as an excuse for not conforming to all of the laws that governed our highly regulated business. I am here today because in connection with some transactions, I transgressed certain of the laws and regulations that govern our industry. I was wrong in doing so and knew that at the time and I am pleading guilty to these offenses.

One of the accounts we did business with was the Boesky organization, which also did business with many other firms. Drexel did some financings for and trading with the Boesky firm, but Drexel's business with the Boesky organization never approached 1 percent of the business of our department.

He traded in stocks; I traded primarily in bonds, or their equivalent. But because he was a major factor in the securities markets, he had the potential to become a more significant account. We were not social friends and had little in common. His philosophy of business was different from mine.

The relationship started as an arm's length and correct one. Unfortunately, however, certain of our transactions involved reciprocal accommodations, some of which violated the law, including those that are referred to in this allocution.

In 1984, our department had purchased some securities of Fischbach, a company in which Victor Posner had an interest. Drexel had provided financing to several other companies which Mr. Posner had an interest in.

In early 1984, Mr. Posner publicly announced that he intended to acquire Fischbach. Boesky was familiar with the Fischbach situation and wanted to purchase Fischbach securities. I encouraged him to do so. I do not remember exactly what I told him almost six years ago, but I indicated to him that he would not lose money.

The Boesky organization began buying Fischbach securities and eventually bought over 10 percent of Fischbach including securities that had been owned by Drexel. Over the next months, he called me incessantly to complain that the price of the stock was dropping, that Drexel was responsible for his losses, that my comments to him were guarantees against loss and that he expected us to make good.

I assured him that Drexel would make good on his losses. These assurances were not recorded on the books of Drexel and I did not expect that they would be reflected in any Schedule 13-D's filed by the Boesky organization, and, in fact they were not. Thus, I assisted in the failure to file an accurate 13-D. This was wrong and I accept responsibility for it. This is the basis for Count 2 and is one of the overt acts in Count 1 [conspiracy].

As for Count 3 and the second overt act of the conspiracy count, in the fall of 1984, a client of Drexel, Golden Nugget, wanted to sell a substantial amount of MCA stock. I wanted the shares to hit the market in a way that would not identify our client as the seller and adversely affect the price that it might receive.

So I turned to Boesky, whose business it was to buy and sell large amounts of stock and who I knew had an interest in entertainment company stocks, including MCA. I told a Drexel employee to ask him to buy the blocks of MCA shares as they became available from Drexel's client.

I did not tell the client how I was disposing of the stock. Drexel crossed the blocks between its client and the Boesky organization which subsequently resold most of these shares into the market. When Boesky complained that he had lost money on his initial purchases of MCA, I promised that we would make up any losses the Boesky organization suffered on its purchases and sales and thereafter it bought more MCA stock from Drexel acting on behalf of our client.

This promise was not recorded on Drexel's books nor made public, and it was wrong not to do so. It was my intent that the block sales would enable our client to receive a better price than it might have obtained if I had not agreed that Drexel would make up the Boesky organization's losses on the MCA stock.

In July 1985, the Boesky organization asked Drexel to purchase approximately one million shares of stock in Helmerich & Payne. The Boesky organization agreed that it would repurchase this stock in the future and promised that it would make up any losses Drexel incurred while holding this stock.

Although I was not involved in the purchase of these securities, I later learned of this understanding. I approved this understanding. I also gave instructions to sell the stock back.

The understanding that the Boesky organization would make up any losses was an oral one and the stock while held by Drexel was not, therefore, charged to the Boesky organization's net capital as required by the securities laws and rules. This is the basis for Count 4 and the third overt act.

As I stated earlier, there were other accommodations of a similar nature between the Boesky organization and Drexel, some of which were wrong. After Boesky complained about his losses and insisted that we make them up, I asked a Drexel employee in early 1985 to check the amount of the losses that the Boesky organization had incurred.

In order to make up these losses, I caused Drexel to execute certain bond trades which resulted in profits to the Boesky organization. Thereafter, a Drexel employee tried to keep track of how the Boesky organization stood, in terms of profits and losses, on these and certain other transactions, though so far as I know this score-keeping was never exact.

Counts 5 and 6 and the remaining overt acts relate to transactions between Drexel and David Solomon. Mr. Solomon was a portfolio manager who specialized in high-yield securities. His company, Solomon Asset Management Company Inc., was a large customer of Drexel, as well as of other firms.

Among the institutions for which Mr. Solomon managed a high-yield portfolio was the Finsbury Fund, an offshore fund that had been underwritten by a Drexel affiliate. Drexel paid an annual 1 percent commission to its salesmen for selling this fund abroad and charged this commission to the High Yield Department because the Finsbury Fund traded in high-yield securities.

Sometime in 1985, I agreed with Solomon and officials of Drexel that the High Yield Department would recoup the commission for Drexel. To attempt to do so, we charged Solomon a fraction of a point more on certain purchases he made for his clients or a fraction of a point less on certain sales he made for his clients to help recoup the 1 percent commission paid to Drexel salesmen.

All adjustments were to be within the bid/ask range for the particular security at the time of the transaction. To the best of my information, this was done on a number of trades and the adjustments totaled several hundred thousand dollars.

These adjustments were not disclosed by Drexel or me to the shareholders of Finsbury or to Solomon's other clients. The confirmations for Solomon's purchase of securities were mailed by Drexel and did not disclose the adjustments or that they were made to reimburse Drexel for the selling expenses of the Finsbury Fund. This failure to disclose was wrong and is the basis of Count 5.

In December 1985, Mr. Solomon asked whether Drexel could engage in securities transactions with him on which he could generate short-term losses for his personal income tax purposes.

In light of the customer relationship between Mr. Solomon and Drexel, I assisted him in purchasing from Drexel certain securities, set forth in the information, which traded at a significant spread between the bid and the ask price. Drexel thereafter repurchased these securities at a substantially lower price, thus generating a loss for him and a profit for Drexel.

I either told him that we would provide him with an investment opportunity or opportunities in the following year to make up his loss to him, or that was implicit in the conversation. In fact, in the following year, we did provide him an investment opportunity which turned out to be profitable and ultimately more than made up the losses he suffered. I thus assisted Mr. Solomon in taking a tax loss to which he was not entitled, and this is the basis of Count 6 and the fifth overt act.

So there it was: Milken admitted that he had broken the law and knew it at the time. The felony counts involved conspiracy, stock parking, fraud, and the filing of a false document. Two of the five specific transactions cited—Fischbach (false filing) and MCA (stock parking) were part of the original indictment; the following three—Helmerich & Payne (stock parking), Finsbury Fund (fraud), and David Solomon (stock parking)—would have been part of the superseding indictment that had been threatened.

"Because of the tremendous amount of publicity that has surrounded this case," Milken said summing up his statement. "I wish to make clear that my plea is an acceptance of personal responsibility for my own failings and actions, and not a reflection on the underlying soundness and integrity of the segment of the capital markets in which we specialized and which provided capital that enabled hundreds of companies to survive, expand and flourish.

"Our business was in no way dependent on these practices. Nor did they comprise a fundamental part of our business and I regret them very much."

The most dramatic, and human, moments came within seconds of the end. "This investigation and proceeding are now in their fourth year," Milken concluded. "This long period has been extremely painful and difficult for my family and friends as well as myself.

"I realize that by my acts I have hurt those who are closest to me . . ." He broke down. It was as if the magnitude of what he was admitting, of what had been suffered and what would be suffered, had sunk in.

He struggled to complete his statement, fighting back the tears, as Liman offered emotional support by placing his arm on Milken's back: "I am truly sorry. I thank the court for permitting me to add this apology and for its fairness in handling this complex case."

Judge Wood responded immediately: "Thank you, Mr. Milken." In time, she asked him another question. His voice cracked as he began to answer.

Within half an hour, Milken would leave the courthouse, again in control—his wife with him—nodding and then smiling to his supporters. It would be that smile, and not the earlier pain, that the photographers would capture and the newspapers would print the next day.

If most people have a smile that reassures, Milken does not. His comes across more that of the cat who got the canary or of the fellow who beat the system. It wouldn't be surprising if people, looking into that smile over breakfast or on their commute to work, said to themselves, "That bastard thinks he bought himself a great deal, doesn't he?"

But he didn't. The smile was meant to tell the world that he hadn't been beaten, at least not completely. It was a show of bravado.

"As the wolves of Wall Street go, he wasn't too bad," proclaimed one syndicated columnist on the courthouse steps. Later, I realized what Drexel had no doubt already learned for itself: Milken was now an easy target for the backhanded compliments and clever criticisms of the serenely self-righteous, as well as for the justifiable skepticism and anger of the average person on the street.

Someone who has known Milken for years drew a crude but effective analogy, one that he associated with Drexel's decision to settle, but which he recognized applied to Milken's decision as well. This analogy, which I've cleaned up considerably, involves a fellow "with a gun to his head, maybe a real gun, maybe a water pistol," forced to strip naked and run through the streets. "And the picture is shown throughout the country.

"This guy can say, 'I never [did this] before; I thought it was a real gun. But the reality is that you're a [fool], and your kids will know."

Then why settle? If Milken genuinely believed in his innocence, why would he, of all people, put himself in that picture? Because it was the lesser of two "terrible, terrible choices," argued his friend: To fight the charges—the ones we considered in the last chapter *and* those in the superseding indictment that the prosecutors were ready to file—to fight all these charges would involve another year before a trial even began and at least six months of sitting in court each day, both Milken and his wife. And then, when all that was done, Milken would still face the possibility of a RICO conviction. On the other hand, to settle the case would make Milken an admitted felon and would place him at the prosecutors' beck and call in their ongoing investigation.

In trying to explain Milken's decision, this friend mentioned the story of two professors who were captured in the jungle by natives and put in a cage. The chief gives the first professor a choice: death or ru-ru. "I'll take ru-ru," the professor says. The natives drag him out of the cage, beat him, then toss him into a pit with tigers, and then throw the bloody carcass on the ground in front of the cage.

"Death or ru-ru!" says the native chief to the second professor.

"I think I'll take death," the professor replies.

"Okay," says the chief. "But first, a little ru-ru."

CHAPTER FOURTEEN

FORTUNE AND MEN'S EYES

The history of Drexel Burnham was one of surprises—surprises that in retrospect seem to have had a malicious inevitability about them. If you thought up this story yourself, no one would believe it—like a badly contrived tragedy, the mighty are brought down by a chain of tragic flaws and unlikely events. An honorable second-tier firm rises to the top on the back of an extraordinary individual, but in the process, the seeds are sown for the destruction of both the individual and the firm.

The unconventional success of Drexel Burnham was, oddly enough, the result of its desire to achieve conventional success. In 1973, Burnham & Co., a retail-oriented broker, acquired Drexel Firestone, an old-line investment banking firm, with the hope of improving its position in the syndicates that dominated Wall Street's clubby atmosphere.

In the bargain, Burnham & Co. also picked up a "nuclear power-cell," a twenty-six-year-old trader who would propell the firm to the first rank not by joining the club, but by beating it. He would focus on a market that Wall Street had ignored and ignore the etiquette that the Street had relied on. He would make a fortune for himself and an absurd amount of money for his associates. Primarily because of him, his firm would become the most profitable on Wall Street, but also one of the riskiest.

In 1986, at the absolute height of Milken's power and that of his firm, both would be forced onto a slow, improbable path to disgrace and ruin. Dennis Levine, a successful investment banker, would be implicated for insider trading, the victim of naked greed and of an anonymous letter from Venezuela that put the authorities on his trail. His arrest and cooperation, although not a threat to Drexel, would scare Ivan Boesky into cutting a deal with the government, his chief bargaining chip being the allegations against the most influential man on Wall Street.

The SEC had already initiated four investigations "in which Michael Milken was named as a witness, officer and/or principal between 1981 and 1985.

Name	Open	Closed
Leasco Corp.	08-14-79	10-21-81
Certain Issuers	01-26-82	03-29-84
Drexel Burnham Lambert, Inc.	03-19-84	09-30-86
Centrust Savings Bank	04-19-85	pending"

By late 1986, none of these investigations had turned up sufficient evidence for prosecution. But now the government had a witness. And with that witness, came a weapon: the ability to force others at Boesky's firm to cooperate rather than face prosecution. This cooperation meant that certain allegations could be corroborated and that other people—members of Milken's department—could be implicated. In a widening web around the main target, these people would themselves choose to cooperate in return for leniency or immunity.

As the walls around Milken were slowly being chipped apart, his firm, which had chosen to support him completely, became aware of another weapon—this one unexpected—that was being rolled onto the battlefield: RICO. The U.S. attorney on Drexel's case, Rudolf Giuliani, happened to be the man who had pioneered the use of this powerful statute against individuals—mobsters mainly—and was now extending its sights to financial firms.

Princeton/Newport was hit first, and was destroyed before it ever went to trial. Drexel Burnham, as a corporation rather than a partnership, stood a better chance of surviving, but no one knew how much better. Under the weight of both the RICO threat and the evidence, within an hour of indictment the firm acquiesed to a draconian guilty plea after twenty-five months of arguing its innocence.

Six felonies and a $650-million fine, inconceivable only a year earlier, were devastating but not fatal. It was the decisions and events of the following year that drove a weakened firm into bankruptcy.

The loss of Milken did not destroy the firm's belief that it could continue to dominate and prosper in the junk-bond market—*his* market. Because of this belief, bridge loans were offered and new offerings were accepted, loans and deals that he might not have done or that he might have gotten done.

Along with this focus on its previous strengths, Drexel also "restructured" its areas of weakness. Retail was the primary casualty; its elimination saved the firm tens of millions in annual losses, but cost the firm its direct contact with the average person on the street.

Events spiraled out of Drexel's control in the second half of 1989 with the passage of the S&L bill, the collapse of the junk-bond market, and the mini stock market crash. These unpleasant surprises led directly to a shocking one: The firm's commercial paper was downgraded, thereby rendering it too risky for money-market funds, its chief customers. Drexel's risky financial structure—the most highly leveraged among the major firms—which had seemed acceptable only five months earlier, was now in danger of collapse.

The last and worst of the surprises came in February 1990 when management realized that the firm would not be able to survive without outside help and that nobody—not the regulators, the banks, the foreigners, or the Street—was going to provide that help.

Of course, the real surprise here was that Drexel put itself in a position to need such support. Throughout its glory days, the firm had managed to alienate the powers that be among competitors, regulators, and corporate America. Hostile takeovers and hardball tactics invited retaliation, whether or not these takeovers and tactics were justified.

"We understood the implications of getting into the financing of large acquisitions before we did it," Fred Joseph noted in a May 1986 interview for *Manhattan, inc.* "And we succeeded beyond our expectations, and the heat was greater than we expected." But, in retrospect, hostile takeovers probably generated more heat than the firm ever anticipated. "They didn't think about it or about the concerted effort against them," one West Coast officer said about his colleagues. "There was a certain naïveté."

But there was also a tremendous arrogance among the rainmakers. "A crummy neighbor" was how one East Coaster described the firm's image. "If it ain't illegal, we can do it."

When it came to Drexel, the other neighbors got mad. And eventually they were given a chance to get even—the top people at Drexel, in trying to change the comfortable status quo, left their firm vulnerable to the establishment that despised them.

Bear in mind, however, that if the firm's unpopularity was due to the actions of hundreds, its vulnerability was due to the actions of a dozen. Four people were investigated and cut deals, four are still under investigation, and four were indicted. The net result: three convictions and ten thousand people out of their jobs.

When one thinks about such a mismatch, or that a firm with $800 million in equity went down the tubes seemingly overnight, one knows that some serious mistakes were made. Now that I've stated the obvious, let's consider some specifics, naturally with the benefit of twenty/twenty hindsight.

1. The Partners vs. the Shareholders. The partnerships—numbering in the hundreds—that Michael Milken created beginning in the late 1970s caused a series of problems for the firm. Even though these partnerships were ripe for abuse, Drexel's top management allowed them. "I thought it was sensible," one senior executive said of the idea. "It would keep people from being distracted," spending time worrying about their personal investments.

But the partnerships also gave selected officers a terrific alternative to investing their money in the shares of their firm. More, this alternative investment was in competition with their firm. Although in theory the partnerships were only entitled to those bonds, stocks, and warrants that Drexel refused for its stockholders, in practice the lines could not have been so clearly drawn.

The members of the partnerships—representing only some 2 percent of the firm's employees—were the rainmakers, the big boys. And management wanted to keep them happy. If not, it wouldn't have allowed the partnerships in the first place. If not, why would the partners end up with four times as many warrants in Harris Graphics, purchased at $1 each and sold three years later at $22 each, as did their firm? If not, why would the partners end up with the lion's share of Beatrice warrants, bought for twenty-five cents each which four years later would be worth *fifty* times that much?

While the partnerships generated huge profits for their participants, they also created a poor image for a firm that found itself very much in the public eye. This image of favoritism, and even self-dealing, particularly affected two important constituencies close to home: the employees and the clients.

Most important, the partnerships encouraged a level of risk taking that endangered the survival of the firm. The partners, with little of their own money in Drexel's stock, didn't need to worry about the bottom line. They were paid based on the *revenues* they generated, *not* the profits. They had a personal incentive to bring in deals, however risky, deals that created huge fees. And they had stood to benefit by encouraging their firm to own large amounts of junk bonds, bonds that kept the high-yield market active and liquid, and profitable.

They made their enormous bonuses, and invested parts of these bonuses in partnerships that had an inside track to the choicest merchandise. It was "heads I win, tails you lose," and it led to a situation in which those who were most important to the firm's future had, proportionally, a minuscule stake in that future.

The final chapter on the Drexel partnerships has yet to be written. The House Oversight and Investigations Subcommittee, which grilled Fred Joseph in April 1988, will be conducting further hearings, perhaps as early as October 1990. The featured witness will be Michael Milken, although his memory may very well become cloudy when answering questions about the abuses and possible illegalities committed by these partnerships.

Meanwhile, the Securities and Exchange Commission is said to be investigating the partnerships, probably with a particular eye on those clients of Milken's who were limited partners. It seems logical that the SEC will want to address the question: To what extent did individual clients benefit personally as a reward for the decisions they made as junk-bond portfolio managers? My guess is that at least a few face a long and discontented winter.

Further in the future, the firm, whose board of directors agreed to use shareholders' money to indemnify the partnerships against loss, may have to make good on that promise. Perhaps those on the board who voted for this proposal—which allegedly includes just about every member of the board—would consider taking the money out of their own pockets instead of out of their employees'. But I wouldn't bet on it.

2. The Boesky Allegations. "One of my theories is Don't try to figure out what you will do next when you are in a free-fall," said Fred Joseph over the hoot and holler on November 26, 1986—twelve days after Boesky's arrest. "We ought to take it easy. I have several rules for things like this. The top rule is don't die; and another top one is don't panic."

Actually, panicking would've been a terrific idea. There were several reasons for thinking settlement, fast. "I always want to know my downside," is one smart trader's view of life. But Drexel was flying blind. The firm's response to the subpoenas delivered from the SEC and the allegations leaked to the press was that it knew of no wrong-doing by anyone at the firm. The problem was that it had no way of knowing whether or not laws had been broken—Michael Milken would only address these concerns through his battery of lawyers.

So what, in retrospect, should the firm have done? Milken was under investigation, not indictment. Perhaps if he had been arrested, the firm would have insisted on speaking with him directly, as happened three months later at Goldman Sachs with Robert Freeman (who reportedly also agreed to take a lie detector test). Actually, it's doubtful that Milken would have ever spoken to Drexel's lawyers directly, or that the firm would have demanded it—let's face it, this was no ordinary employee.

But management had other factors to consider. It had almost two thousand shareholders and a legal responsibility to protect their best interests. It also operated in the most regulated industry in the world. As a securities firm, Drexel enjoyed many privileges, the chief one being the protection of the Glass-Steagal Act, a Depression-era law that kept the banks out of the brokerage business. But along with the privileges came the regulations of the SEC. And, as a general rule, you don't take on the folks who interpret and enforce the rules.

This is particularly true when those folks had already conducted four investigations involving Michael Milken, a fact that Drexel's management was aware of, even if the employees and the rest of the world weren't. Under these conditions, fighting "the war," as the government's investigation was known among the firm's top officials, was a high-risk strategy.

On the other hand, settling with the government and effectively cutting off Milken at the knees was a potentially dangerous strategy, as well. He was the reason for the firm's phenomenal success in the 1980s, and he had a nearly fanatical following (by Wall Street standards) among his people and his clients. Nobody on the Street is tied to his job, and a bad deal for Milken might have led to devastating defections in the junk-bond department and in corporate finance.

Another concern: Drexel held nearly $4 billion in high-yield bonds in its inventory, a result of its excessive willingness to back Milken's vision with its own money. At this point, the loss of Milken might have caused a panic in that market, which could have wiped out a major chunk of the firm's equity. In effect, the firm, by its own choices, had made itself a hostage to Milken's future.

Of course, an immediate settlement with the government might have allowed Milken to remain at the firm, but I would guess the odds of that were a thousand to one against. Which raises another question: *Would* the government have settled with Drexel in late 1986, at the beginning of the investigation? One board member offered the opinion that the firm could have settled for $5 million with a three-month suspension for Milken, a ludicrously optimistic hope on his part. Still, as an officer at the firm argued to me in 1987, there is always a settlement offer if you want it.

If Drexel had settled with the government early on, there would have been an uproar within the firm, an anger that I would have shared at the time. Fred Joseph might have been driven out in a popular uprising. Important employees in corporate finance might have moved down the street to Salomon Brothers or uptown to First Boston. These firms might have opened up satellite offices in Beverly Hills to entice the dissatisfied away from Drexel's high-yield bond department. The junk-bond market would certainly have plummeted, at least temporarily, causing huge losses on the bonds that Drexel held.

It would have been a mess, but a decision to settle the case in late 1986 would have been the correct one. Without strong reason to believe that the allegations were false, the firm was forced to recognize the fact that a brokerage firm is too dependent on the rules of regulators and the confidence of lenders, employees, and customers to fight a protracted battle with the SEC and the U.S. attorney's office. Nobody could have fought that battle better than Drexel did—a tribute to the loyalty of its people and its clients—but it was a fight, even without the threat of RICO, that was destined for defeat.

3. COOPERATION Instead of "Cooperation." Once Drexel had decided that it would fight the allegations rather than settle with the government, it should have cooperated fully with the investigation. According to the firm, that's what it did; according to the government, it did not. The government's point of view is more believable on this one.

Part of the problem was that the dominant attitude at Drexel in 1986 was confrontational, because the dominant person at Drexel was confrontational; more than that, he was the focus of the investigation. Another part of the problem was that the firm might have thought that delay would work to its advantage, as it often does in civil and criminal cases.

If the firm thought this, however, it was being naive. This was no ordinary case, and the government prosecutors weren't about to get bored or frustrated and leave for private practice before the investigation was complete. On the contrary, a strategy of delay was more likely to inflame the other side than to wear it down.

This wasn't the Battle of Britain, a total war between the good guys and the bad guys, fighting on the beaches if necessary. This was supposed to be a cooperative effort between a brokerage firm and its regulators, with a common goal: to find out if any laws had been broken.

Initially, Drexel did seem to approach the SEC with that attitude in mind, but was rejected. Following that, I suspect that the firm's management slid into a siege mentality—I know I did—and cooperation became more rhetoric than reality. As a result, Drexel found itself in a war of attrition, without fully understanding or accepting the firepower on the other side.

4. Don't Mess with RICO. The attorneys for Drexel Burnham consistently underestimated the chances that the racketeering law would be used against the firm. "Lawyers are mortal," said Fred Joseph in their defense. "This is beyond their ken of what could happen." But was it?

In late 1986, it is true that RICO was generally unknown. Still, top criminal lawyers—and those are the ones we hired—should have been more conscious of the risk. Rudolf Giuliani had a reputation for aggressiveness, and he had shown his willingness to use RICO against defendants as diverse as Carmine Persico, head of the Colombo crime family, and Stanley Friedman, head of the Bronx Democratic party.

He had also extended RICO's grasp to the financial community in the case of Marc Rich, a commodities trader, whose companies had pleaded guilty to tax fraud and had paid a fine approaching $200 million. And if anyone needed any reminder about RICO's presence or power, there was the twelve-year sentence given Stanley Friedman in November 1986, the same month that Drexel fell under investigation.

There were two conclusions that one feels the lawyers should have reached: RICO could be used against a financial firm such as Drexel and, in the hands of Giuliani, that use was quite possible. Indeed, the indictment of Princeton/Newport in August 1988 made the possibility a near certainty.

By the time Drexel realized it would be indicted under RICO—an indictment it didn't believe it could survive—the firm's bargaining position was almost nonexistent. Except for the argument that RICO would be fatal, an argument the prosecutors didn't accept, Drexel had nothing. The result was an eleventh-hour shotgun settlement.

Of course, the firm wasn't required to settle, RICO or not. Perhaps RICO was a bluff and would have disappeared if Drexel hadn't buckled—after all, there were those three hundred and fifty thousand retail accounts that the firm still had. It's a logical argument, but not necessarily the relevant one, because the government didn't believe that RICO would annihilate the firm. "We asked around," said Assistant U.S. Attorney Bruce Baird, "It was more or less unanimous that it would not cause Drexel's downfall in the short run." Maybe he was right, maybe not—personally, I think RICO would've buried the firm. The problem was that by the time everyone learned the impact of RICO, it would be too late to reverse.

The corollary to the "call the bluff" strategy was the "so what?" strategy. Here again, the firm would refuse to settle, and if RICO kicked Drexel into bankruptcy, so be it. Liquidate the firm—sell off the assets, pay off the debts—and give the remainder to the stockholders. At least there would be no doubt of the cause. Unfortunately, martyrdom makes more sense for revolutionaries than for ten thousand employees with bills to pay. As for the two thousand stockholders among those employees, the fire sale of assets that would occur might wipe out their stake by wiping out the firm's equity. Not much of a strategy there.

There was also the "thanks, but no thanks" approach: Take the settlement and then refuse it after Rudy Giuliani's resignation in late January 1990. The firm had a valid excuse to renounce the settlement—as of February, it still hadn't come to terms with the SEC, which was one of the requirements of a final settlement.

The logic behind the strategy of tearing up the deal was that although Benito Romano, who had succeeded Giuliani as U.S. attorney for the Southern District of New York, would have indicted Drexel, he might have not RICO'd the firm. And even had he supported the idea of dropping the bomb, Richard Thornburgh, the new U.S. attorney general and the man who had the final say on the use of RICO, might have just said no. Indict Drexel under the securities laws if you want, but not under a racketeering statute.

As clever as this idea sounds, however, I doubt it would have worked for one simple reason: It's too clever. The new prosecutors would have realized Drexel's game and, because of that, would have refused to give the firm what it wanted even if they felt in their heart of hearts that RICO was unfair.

5. *Life without Mike:* Everybody knew that Milken was the best, but very few realized just how much better he was. "You're playing on the Lakers," was the analogy drawn by one West Coast officer, "and you think you're hot shit, but if you don't have Magic Johnson feeding you the ball . . . you're [just] shit." According to an East Coast investment banker: "A couple of guys thought they were the smartest that ever walked the hallowed halls of Wall Street." "They surrounded Milken with the best and brightest," said another banker, "but they couldn't clone him."

With the loss of Mike Milken, who had faded from the day-to-day scene by April 1988 and had officially left the firm a year later, Drexel pretty much became just another firm. In high-yield bonds, it had a tremendous head start, but it had lost its edge. "We were as much at risk from a bad street crossing as we were from the SEC," noted one officer in explaining the importance of Milken to his firm and his market.

Drexel, however, chose to focus on the strengths it had enjoyed under Milken, even though it no longer had his analytical skills, his salesmanship, and his influence. The firm had depended on his knowledge and insight, on his ability to understand what the stuff was really worth. Drexel had also relied on his ability to move the junk-bond merchandise—one West Coast officer recalled that it had never been easy to sell the junk-bond deals, even in the glory days of the mid-1980s. Milken had made all the difference.

Without him, the confidence that had helped this market grow to $200 billion in a decade was replaced with doubt. The clients weren't as eager to buy, the bonds weren't as carefully tailored to what these clients wanted, and the deals weren't as successful. It was a very different ball game.

What hadn't changed was that a young, volatile market like the high-yield bond market offered both tremendous profits and extraordinary risks. When Milken ran the show, he was able to find the profits and, if not avoid, at least defer the dangers. When he left, the risk-to-reward ratio shifted.

Rather than catering to the implicit threats of the rainmakers, the firm would have been better served if Fred Joseph had told them, in the words of one officer, "Look, guys, there's a three-part enemy. One part is our past. One part is public opinion. And one part is you."

Rather than offering the so-called superstars guaranteed incomes, Fred could have leveraged the one piece of good fortune that had come his way: the financing of the RJR/Nabisco buyout. The RJR deal, which mitigated the impact of Milken's departure, provided $227 million in fees, and many of the big boys in corporate finance and on the Coast had a claim to a slice of the largest pie in Wall Street's history. Fred, as chief exec, had the major say in the allocation of the slices, which would be part of the 1989 bonuses. These bonuses were almost a year away, and it is not likely that the folks with a claim were going to leave the firm and give up *their* leverage—out of sight, out of luck.

Most important, rather than holding to a strategy that had been made obsolete by events, Drexel should have steered clear of those deals that couldn't be sold. "We didn't need to portray ourselves as

the junk-bond powers that we had been under Michael," said a two-
decade veteran of the firm. Some fees would have been sacrificed,
some clients would have been angered, and some investment bankers
would have screamed bloody murder, but the firm wouldn't have
stuck itself with the unwanted debt of West Point-Pepperell, Paramount Petroleum, WPS Textile, and others.

Our competitors may have ended up with *relatively* more bridge
loans and unwanted bonds than we did, as one senior exec argued,
but they were in better financial shape. The other major firms on Wall
Street had wealthy parents and deep pockets that could absorb this
illiquid junk debt. What for them were expensive learning experiences
was for us a banzai charge.

6. The Face of the Firm. If the decision to focus on the high-yield
bond market was half of Drexel's 1989 strategy, the decision to eliminate the retail system was the other. The first decision was easy—
nobody lost, until almost everybody lost; the second decision was
extremely difficult and still controversial over a year later.

Perhaps the firm couldn't have afforded to subsidize the retail
operation, or perhaps it couldn't have afforded *not* to. The retail sales
department might have continued to shrink, eventually bleeding the
firm dry. But it would have provided the firm with an army of retail
customers—a million investors and their families, easily panicked,
God bless them—to man the front lines if Drexel needed government
help.

"The only way to make money in a highly cyclical business is to be
highly diversified," argued one board member in defense of retail. "If
you do away with it all that remained would be a high-yield shell that
the government didn't like much."

The securities business—so dependent on the confidence of its
lenders and its clients—is a risky business under the best of circumstances. For a firm that has pleaded guilty to six felonies and agreed
to pay $650 million, the risk of collapse are that much greater.

Drexel would have been better served to keep its retail department
and its customer accounts—its insurance policy, its widows and orphans. Should the firm find itself facing the abyss, these customers
would have projected just the image—the ghosts of financial crises
past and future—that might have forced the government's hand.
Loans might have been reluctantly offered from the Fed or from its

member banks, or a merger partner might have been arranged at the last minute.

On a less cynical level, a decision to retain retail would have saved the jobs of thousands of employees, which is a pretty good reason all by itself.

7. The Dance of Debt. One bitter irony of Drexel's fall is that the firm that came to represent the leveraging of American business put itself out of business when it couldn't pay its own debts. In effect, the experts on leverage building did a poor job on their own house.

On Wall Street, firms employ *double leverage,* with both their holding companies and their subsidiaries borrowing money. Drexel was reportedly the most aggressive, using more double leverage than its seven major competitors. Viewed from another perspective, again according to Standard & Poor's, Drexel had the most short-term debt relative to its equity as of September 30, 1989.

Without a secure fallback position, this is a formula for disaster. And Drexel had no strong back-up plan. It didn't have an American Express or a Credit Suisse to write a check if worst came to worst. It didn't even have written commitments from its banks to provide it a line of credit in a pinch. (Even written commitments would have been suspect; however, Integrated Resources had such commitments, but it still didn't get its money when needed.)

Drexel was in a cash business and found itself running out of that cash, with fewer sources as time went on. One possible source was the payment of bonuses in December 1989 and in the following month. Of the $260 million paid, $196 million was paid in cash, the rest in preferred stock. If the firm had decided to pay all bonuses above $100,000 in stock, it probably would have saved over $100 million in cash.

Another source was the excess net regulatory capital, which the firm did tap into until the SEC closed down the pipeline in early February 1990. The SEC, however, cannot require a firm to put up excess capital, it can only require a firm to leave that money there. Accordingly, Drexel should have tried to remove the excess before its crisis occurred. By August 1989, when the S&L Bill passed and the Ohio Mattress deal failed, the firm should have realized that serious problems were possible.

By December, with the downgrading of its commercial paper,

those problems were inevitable; by mid-February, its problems were terminal. Drexel Burnham made the one mistake it could not afford to make: It gave up control of its own destiny.

The demise of Drexel raised serious questions about the junk-bond market. Was this market more speculative than investors ever realized? Was it in fact a pseudomarket levitated by Milken the Magician, a confidence game based on smoke and mirrors?

"Drexel junk was never anything but a boiler-room scam," Benjamin Stein wrote in *Barron's* April 1990. "The junk-bond effort was probably the single biggest private financial scandal of the century." Buyout specialist Theodore Forstmann offered a less overheated, but still negative, point of view to *The New York Times* in June 1990: "Now that there is no more of that phony money around, we're getting back to the real money people." Money manager David Schultz, in putting together a fund to invest in companies devastated by too much debt, told *The Wall Street Journal,* "It's the flip side of the Milken Revolution."

Not surprisingly, there were other interpretations of the revolution. "All that stuff about financing America—it really was true," said one Drexel officer, who argued that his firm did not "simply follow the gaggle of investment banking firms trying to chase the *Fortune* 100. . . . The things we were doing made a difference—they certainly made a difference to the clients." "All firms said they were interested in small- to medium-sized companies," said a manager on my trading floor, "but very few of them did much about it." In the words of another officer: "I'm hard pressed to find negative results on the economy from funding high-yield companies." These companies ranged from American Motors to Cablevision to Fox Television to Hasbro to MCI Communications to Pier One to Zayre.

What were the facts? First and most important, junk bonds are not inherently evil—they're just bonds that pay a higher yield and involve greater risk. Second, junk bonds are not a new creation. These bonds "existed most of the century, just in different forms at different times," said a high-yield specialist at First Boston.

As for the statistics, 95 percent of U.S. companies with sales *above* $35 million a year would be junk-bond companies if they tried to raise money. Of these twenty thousand companies, some eight hundred have sold bonds, raising $200 billion in the public market and an additional $100 to 150 billion in private placements. Less than 5 percent of this money was used to finance hostile takeovers.

How risky are junk bonds? The answer to this one would resolve a great deal of the controversy; unfortunately, the answer is we don't know. Historically, these bonds have been good investments. Over the decades, the return from junk bonds, including the impact of all defaults, was better than the return from U.S. Treasury bonds.

The junk bonds that floated around during most of the twentieth century, however, were very different from the junk bonds sold in the last decade or so. The first group were primarily those of companies that were once considered high quality, and that later fell on hard times. The more recent group were the bonds of companies that were too young or small to receive an investment-grade rating at *any* time. One group wasn't necessarily a better investment than the other— they were just apples and oranges, not comparable.

Nevertheless, you might say, the new group of junk bonds—the original-issue high-yield bonds—have now been around for more than a decade. Shouldn't we be able to judge their risk from their performance?

Not quite, and here's why: The junk-bond market has grown so rapidly that the popular measure of risk, the default rate, is irrelevant. The default rate is the number of bonds that miss an interest payment in a given year relative to the total number of bonds outstanding. For example, if $3 billion worth of junk bonds default and there are $100 billion worth in the market, the default rate is 3 percent.

The problem is that newly issued bonds tend not to default for at least a few years for the simple reason that their companies have plenty of cash on hand for a while; after all, these companies raised a ton of cash when the bonds were sold to the public. In a growing market, where the supply of newer bonds dwarfs the supply of older ones, results get confused. Which means that the default rates for junk bonds were fairly meaningless, because the high-yield bond market was unquestionably a growing market. (According to First Boston, junk bonds grew from $8 billion to $200 billion in a decade.)

Another approach to gauge the risk of junk bonds is to look at *cumulative* default rates—the percentage of bonds that miss an interest payment at some point in their lives. The Asquith study, mentioned in the previous chapter, concluded that 34 percent of all junk bonds issued in 1977 and 1978 defaulted by the end of 1988—more than one out of three. Compare this figure with the current wisdom at the time that the *annual* default rate was only about 3 percent. What's interesting is that these two figures are the same—an annual default rate of about 3 percent will result in a cumulative default rate over eleven or twelve years of 34 percent.

Still, neither of these figures tells us what we need to know: How risky are the junk bonds issued more recently, the $100 billion worth sold in the last three years alone? It's difficult to be optimistic. Success leads to excess, and the safety that was built into the earlier junk bonds, the margin of error that made them salable to skeptical investors, faded with that skepticism. "We created such a demand for our product that, over time, the quality dropped," said one East Coast investment banker. According to a West Coast officer, "The market was killed due to truth."

Perhaps the greater truth was that the high-yield bond market served—and continues to serve—a valid purpose. Junk bonds give thousands of companies an alternative that they didn't have fifteen years ago. And while they are currently viewed as the financial equivalent of asbestos, it's good to remember that you can't judge a market simply by its players or by the short-run impact of fear and greed, ignorance and hubris.

The impact of 1989's junk-bond debacle was felt in varying degrees by Drexel's competitors. In March 1990, First Boston sold the majority of its $450 million Ohio Mattress loan to its Swiss-based parent company, leaving it with $700 million in bridge loans, almost 40 percent of those to the bankrupt Campeau Corporation. The following month, Kidder Peabody announced that it would sell all its high-yield, illiquid inventory to its parent, General Electric, taking a $25 million loss.

Also in April, Shearson Lehman Hutton decided to sell its $480 million junk-bond portfolio, only accumulated in the previous fifteen months, at an expected loss of $115 million. Merrill Lynch, reportedly with $540 million in bridge loans and $350 million in junk bonds, replaced its top high-yield specialists, Ray Minella and Jeffrey Berenson, in June 1990.

The mess in the high-yield market was the most visible disaster on Wall Street in recent years, but it certainly wasn't the only one. In response to bad markets and bad decisions, retrenchment has now become the major strategy on the Street, replacing the expansionist visions of the early 1980s, which were heralded by the acquisitions of Bache by Prudential Insurance, Shearson by American Express, and Dean Witter by Sears.

Although the brokers needed—and in time, many could not survive without—the deep pockets of their new owners, there was little in common between these firms and their parents. This cultural clash was highlighted by a dignified advertisement that appeared in a parody of *The Wall Street Journal:* "The Investment Banking Firm of Dean Witter Reynolds is Proud to Announce a Sale on Socks at Sears."

The price tag for this ill-advised expansion was highest at American Express, which had followed its acquisition of Shearson in 1981 with those of Lehman Brothers in 1984 and E. F. Hutton in 1988. In the first quarter of 1990, these firms reported a staggering loss of $917 million, leading to the infusion of $1.35 billion by American Express into its brokerage subsidiary.

The chairman of the parent company, James Robinson, announced that "Howard Clark [the head of the subsidiary] and his team have our full support as they move to reduce Shearson's risk profile and get back to basics by focusing on the things they do best." What made this statement striking was that the shareholders of American Express would have been better served if Robinson had taken his own advice when he took the helm in 1978. By my estimates, the market value of American Express would have risen to almost $20 billion if it hadn't diversified into the brokerage business; with that diversification, the market value rose to $10.4 billion. The difference: roughly $9 billion.

The shareholders who suffered because of the bad times in the financial markets, however, deserve a great deal less sympathy than the investors who suffered during the "good" times that preceded them. From the penny-stock bucket shops that cheated people out of an estimated $2 billion a year to the august Wall Street firms that sold unattractive deals through an army of often unqualified, unprincipled retail brokers, the average investor was abused by those who were supposed to protect his financial security.

Yet, no firm on Wall Street was ever meaningfully held to account for giving ill-conceived, self-serving advice to an unsophisticated family man investing for his kid's education or to an elderly woman concerned about the quality of her retirement. And that is a crime as great as anything that any firm was convicted of in the 1980s.

The SEC, Congress, and Wall Street should require every retail broker, from the boiler room to the private office, to provide a complete account of his or her advice to every prospective customer. It's possible in this age of computerized trading—all purchases and sales are recorded. The aggregate results for the clients of every broker can be tabulated and provided. To pay for the costs involved, the brokerage firms could charge the customers one cent more on each share they buy or sell, which would raise over $100 million a year. This approach would give both the brokers and their customers the same goals—that's what this business is all about, isn't it?

If the judgment and tactics of Wall Street deserve to be questioned on some points, so also do those of its prosecutors. And I think it's fair to say that certain aspects of the Drexel investigation reflected bad judgment and perhaps even bad faith.

The use of the RICO statute against a financial firm is a weapon that threatens the basic principle of our jurisprudence that one is innocent until proven guilty. And this principle is surely more important than victory in any given case. Giuliani may not have realized the potential impact of RICO—his prosecutors evidently didn't believe that a racketeering indictment would wipe out the firm—but he didn't need it. He could have indicted Drexel under the Securities Act of 1934, the source of all prosecutions of securities fraud.

That's not to say that using RICO against the firm would have been the incorrect use of the law—it would have been the use of an incorrect law. The passage of RICO reflected the frustration of a country in which the criminals were thought to hold the legal cards; with the approval of one section of one act, the balance of power was shifted.

The problem was that RICO was vaguely written, shifting the responsibility and discretion from elected officials to appointed prosecutors. The breadth and reach of our racketeering statute at the time of the Drexel case was unnervingly similar to that of the Soviet "antislander" law, reminding us as Charleton Heston did in the film *Touch of Evil* that "It's only easy to be a policeman in a police state."

"The sorry history of this law and its abuse by ambitious prosecutors is a testament to the indivisibility of rights," wrote Ira Glasser of the ACLU in early 1988. "RICO was passed because a lot of good people were willing to blink at unconstitutional provisions if the intended target was 'organized crime.' "

"Drexel may have broken rules calling for indictments under normal statutes," wrote *New York Times* columnist William Safire almost a year later, "but its junk-bond dealings did not include the knee-capping, kidnapping, murder and pimping that Senator John McClellan had in mind when he put forward what the called "a major new tool in extirpating the baneful influence of organized crime in our economic life."

Still, according to G. Robert Blakey, who as a young lawyer on McClellan's committee wrote the RICO bill, this statute was designed for more than mobsters. "Organized crime was the occasion," he said, "but it didn't define its scope." The Supreme Court agreed, he noted, referring to the June 1989 Northwestern Bell decision.

By a slim five to four majority the Court held: "Neither RICO's language nor its legislative history supports a rule that a defendant's racketeering activities form a pattern only if they are characteristic of organized crime." The minority opinion, however, raised a crucial point: RICO may be unconstitutional. "No constitutional challenge to this law has been raised in the present case, and so that issue is not before us," wrote Justice Antonin Scalia. "That the highest Court in the land has been unable to derive from this statute anything more than today's meager guidance bodes ill for the day when that challenge is presented."

Which is to say that RICO may not be with us for much longer. More important to the Drexel case is whether or not RICO should have been part of the case. Giuliani had the authority under law to use it, but did he have the responsibility according to fairness *not* to use it?

"The high-yield bond department was a criminal organization," said Bruce Baird. But the alleged crimes, even if true, constituted an insignificant part of Drexel's business, or of its revenues and profits.

At the time of the negotiations with the government, Milken's department was accused of some twenty illegal transactions over the course of three years. The firm as a whole, however, had completed about ten *million* transactions during that same time period.

If every transaction alleged to be illegal was illegal, Drexel earned roughly $73 million in illicit revenues based on the SEC complaint; if one more than doubles that figure to allow for a superseding indictment, one reaches $150 million. During the three years in question, Drexel's total revenues were sixty times as much, exceeding $10 *billion*.

As for profits, $150 million on the top line would have produced about $45 million after bonuses, expenses, and taxes. In the 1984–1986 period, the firm as a whole earned nearly $1 billion.

There is another consideration in the threatened use of RICO against Drexel: If Rudolf Giuliani's decision was intended to coerce the firm into a settlement, this was a violation not just of fairness, but of Justice Department policy. According to L. Gordon Crovitz of *The Wall Street Journal,* there is a 398-page set of guidelines for the use of the racketeering statute; among these guidelines: "Inclusion of a RICO count in an indictment solely or even primarily to create a bargaining tool for later plea negotiations on lesser counts would not be appropriate and would violate the *Principles of Federal Prosecution.* "

Perhaps the most compelling argument against the use of RICO can be made by simply looking at the rewards and the risks from Giuliani's point of view. RICOing the firm doesn't give him much more firepower if he wins the case in court. The onerous twenty-year jail term obviously doesn't apply to a company, and the triple damages provision is for civil cases, not criminal ones.

Of course, a victory in a criminal RICO case would make it easier for aggrieved investors to win a large sum in their civil RICO cases, noted attorney Neil Getnick, who specializes in this area of the law. Still, a victory in a criminal *non-*RICO case would certainly help the plaintiffs in the inevitable civil RICO cases that would follow.

The key point is that, if Giuliani really believed in the concept of innocent until proven guilty, in the absolute right to a trial, why not indict Drexel under the Securities Act of 1934? Even under the worst of assumptions, the firm was not a boiler-room operation based on fraud, or a business infiltrated by organized crime. Drexel may have survived under a RICO indictment, however unlikely, or it may have collapsed with a normal indictment—"Even in the absence of criminal RICO, the Milken matters were life-threatening matters," said Gary Lynch of the SEC—but at least without RICO the firm would have had the chance it felt was necessary for a trial.

Of course, the folks at Princeton/Newport would have liked the same chance, and they certainly didn't get it. In fact, the Princeton/Newport case raised some disturbing questions about prosecutorial tactics. That firm, the first financial one ever RICO'd, was shut down before a trial. The reason, as you might remember, was the superseding indictment that wasn't filed until after the firm had closed its doors.

According to Jack Arseneault, a defense attorney for Paul Berkman of Princeton/Newport, "The superseding indictment did very little to change the earlier indictment," adding that the tactics with the superseder were "vindictive, spiteful, unnecessary." Paul Grand, the attorney for Charles Zarzecki, argued that the new charges had been presented to the grand jury at the time that the old charges had been raised. In his opinion, the prosecutors withheld charges from the original indictment so that they would have the (ultimately fatal) threat of the superseder. In response to a clarifying question on whether there were any new charges that had not been presented to the original grand jury, he replied sharply, "Take it from me, nothing!"

There was also the alleged "roll right over you" threat, mentioned in the previous chapter, and the use of RICO for what was primarily a tax case. Think of that for a moment: If you had cheated on your taxes twice in a ten-year period, you could have faced a RICO indictment and perhaps twenty years in jail—that's no joke.

The threat of RICO in cases that, until the 1980s, had been handled as civil matters gave Giuliani and his prosecutors an incredible weapon to encourage cooperation. Which raises an odd question: Do prosecutors have a responsibility to tell people when they're going to change their methods? Legally no. But what about fairness? How would you feel if speeding on the highway was suddenly prosecuted as reckless endangerment? It's not as absurd or farfetched as it sounds.

On Wall Street, RICO can make all the difference. A person facing the possibility of an indictment, the possibility of a trial before a jury that probably views the Street as a pit of greed, and the possibility of a sentence exceeding twenty years in jail—a person facing these possibilities is a person who is a great deal more likely to plea bargain and cooperate. In the Drexel Burnham case, this category included Dennis Levine, Ivan Boesky, Michael Davidoff, Setrag Mooradian, Gary Maultasch, Jim Dahl, and Michael Milken.

The list of those in the Drexel case who fought RICO in court is not only shorter, it's nonexistent. In a related case, Princeton/Newport, all five defendants including Drexel's Bruce Newburg, went to trial in mid-1989. At that trial, Assistant U.S. Attorney Mark Hansen told the jury, "You don't need a fancy tax law expert because common sense tells you it's fraudulent, it's phony. . . . Doesn't it feel wrong? Doesn't it sound sleazy? If it sounds sleazy it's because it is sleazy. Your common sense tells you that." The jury agreed, finding them guilty on sixty-three out of sixty-four counts.

Their potential sentences exceeded one hundred years each. The judge, obviously unimpressed by the use of RICO in a tax case, sentenced them to terms ranging from three to six *months*. (The defendants are appealing their cases, which may eventually provide the Supreme Court with the opportunity to rule on RICO's constitutionality.)

It may seem bizarre to say, particularly in view of the guilty verdicts, that the Princeton/Newport defendants showed an unusual sense of honor, in refusing to plea-bargain with the prosecutors. They could have almost certainly received a light sentence, perhaps even complete immunity, in return for testimony against Drexel Burnham and others. Instead, at the risk of spending the rest of their lives in prison, they argued that they were innocent and they demanded a fair trial, rather than use their colleagues and friends as bargaining chips.

In a sad case related to the Princeton/Newport prosecution, a young Drexel employee named Lisa Ann Jones was convicted of perjury. A runaway at fourteen, she had eventually joined Drexel's West Coast office at an initial salary of some $18,000 a year; by the time of the investigation, she was earning $100,000 as an assistant to Bruce Newberg. She was offered immunity in exchange for cooperation, but she refused.

Before the grand jury, Lisa lied on three occasions, motivated by a misguided sense of loyalty to her boss. Among the incriminating evidence was a tape recording from the Princeton/Newport raid that indicates a parking arrangement:

LISA: We bought 295,800—is that an unusual figure?

P/N: We bought them. Bruce wanted us to own them for him for awhile.

The cross-examination of Lisa Jones by Assistant U.S. Attorney Mark Hansen, who also prosecuted the Princeton/Newport case, was said to be brutal. Listening to Hansen's side of the story on television, one person watching with me blurted out, "I'd like to stick a harpoon in his head."

As for Lisa Jones, she was sentenced to eighteen months, later reduced to ten months, and is currently in prison.

The primary reason the prosecutors wanted cooperation from Lisa Jones and from those involved in the Princeton/Newport case was the Drexel case—but there was another investigation that needed help. Robert Freeman, an arbitrageur at Goldman Sachs, had been arrested in February 1987, along with Richard Wigton of Kidder Peabody and Timothy Tabor of Merrill Lynch.

Within three months, the charges were dropped, although a new indictment was promised "in record time." The new charges never materialized.

The Princeton/Newport case gave prosecutors another opportunity to implicate Freeman, because Jay Regan, a partner at Princeton/Newport, was a friend from college days, and their two firms traded together. Regan, however, argued that his dealings with Goldman Sachs (and with Drexel Burnham) had been legal.

In time, according to allegations reported by *The Wall Street Journal*, the prosecutors did find some evidence of possible illegalities involving Robert Freeman among the Princeton/Newport files, also securing corroboration of some of the original charges against Freeman from one of his employees in Goldman Sachs's arbitrage department. On August 17, 1989, Freeman announced that he would plead guilty to one count of mail fraud; on April 17, 1990, he was sentenced to four months in jail and fined $1 million.

As for Richard Wigton and Timothy Tabor, the investigation against them was dropped in August 1989, two and a half years after Wigton had been handcuffed on his trading floor and Tabor had been forced to spend a night in a holding cell.

In commenting on the tactics against Wall Street defendants, Bruce Baird told *The New York Times*, "Every poor kid who goes through the Manhattan criminal courts in an average day gets a fraction of the due process given to the average white-collar defendant with the best of defense counsel." And he's probably right.

A poor kid from the street has an advantage over a defendant from Wall Street in at least one regard—his vulnerability to leaks of confidential information to the media. Drexel Burnham and other defendants, so dependent on public respect, were particularly vulnerable to trial by media. "Constant, unbelievable leaks," was the comment of Gerald Lefcourt, Bruce Newberg's attorney; "I've never worked on a case where I've seen so many leaks," said another attorney.

It appears the sources of these disclosures included unknown officials within the government. If true, these officials, who are responsible for upholding our standards and our laws, used unethical *and* illegal tactics.

"This constant stream of innuendo, for almost two years before the filing of a civil complaint, created public antagonism against Drexel and cost Drexel valuable reputation and business," wrote Dean Henry Manne and Professor Larry Ribstein, both of George Mason Law School. "All of this made the SEC's case seem stronger than it was, and may have undermined Drexel's right to a fair trial."

The staff of the SEC's enforcement division, for its part, denied in a May 1988 memorandum that it had disclosed confidential information; this memo, which was leaked to *The Washington Post* in August 1989, stated, "The staff has not been the source of any information which has appeared in the press and has strong suspicions that Drexel itself or persons representing their interests have been providing information to the press for the purpose of being able to make accusations against and discredit the [SEC] staff as well as to isolate and discredit cooperating witnesses."

This discussion of leaks raises another issue: accountability. Consider the situation at the SEC, one of several government offices which handled confidential and damaging information. Even if some of the alleged leaks did originate there, it's important to recognize that the head of the SEC's enforcement division, Gary Lynch, was never accused, publicly or privately, of leaking information or of condoning those leaks. ("Gary's a straight guy," was Fred Joseph's comment.) But Lynch had 21 attorneys working on the Drexel Burnham case, any one of whom could have walked to a pay phone and called *The Washington Post* or *The Wall Street Journal*.

Could the SEC have prevented anonymous leaks? Should it have been held liable for the actions of those employees who were allegedly breaking the law? Criminally liable? Should it have been prosecuted by the Justice Department?

Of course not, and it never was. But Drexel Burnham *was* prosecuted because a dozen of its ten thousand employees were accused of breaking the law. It was faced with a RICO indictment that it genuinely believed would destroy the firm, and it agreed to a harsh settlement to avoid that possibility.

Which raises two crucial questions. First, did the board of directors or anyone in senior management know about these allegedly illegal transactions? The answer, I believe, is no.

Second, could they have known? In most cases, no. How do you prevent someone from making secret deals with a client? How do you discover a scheme by a small group operating within a huge firm and involving the exchange of unwritten favors?

Review the allegations in the Milken indictment. Of the eighteen, I doubt that any internal compliance system could have caught thirteen of those: MGM/UA, Fischbach, Harris Graphics, Phillips Petroleum, Diamond Shamrock, Storer Broadcasting, Maxxam, MCA, Mattel, C.O.M.B., U.S. Home, the tax loss trades in 1985 and 1986, and the $5.3 million payment.

The allegedly bogus trades between Boesky and Drexel in the first half of 1985 and on March 21, 1986 could have been flagged by an ideal system, one that could detect discrepancies in prices on trades with different customers on the same day, and on trades with the same customer on different days. The Stone Container and Wickes transactions could have been identified only by a system programmed to notice unusual volume in the shares of a corporate client—a long shot at that time.

As for the final two allegations, the Lorimar merger and the Viacom buyout, at least one of these was said to be questioned by Drexel's compliance people, who evidently were satisfied with the answers they got, rightly or wrongly.

In effect, there was little opportunity for Drexel, or for the government, to suspect most of these transactions until Ivan Boesky became a cooperating witness. The prosecutors indirectly acknowledged the difficulty of identifying the secret schemes of a few employees: They never even raised the threat of indicting or sanctioning Drexel's senior management. Yet, the firm itself was forced to plead guilty to six felonies and pay $650 million.

As this unfortunate story becomes just a bad memory for most, it's natural to wonder what's happened to the key players. Among the prosecutors in the U.S. attorney's office, John Carroll and Jeff Fridella, the two assistant U.S. attorneys on the Drexel case since its inception, have remained. Mark Hansen, who tried the Princeton/ Newport and Lisa Jones cases was hired by the law firm of Weil, Gotshal & Manges.

Charles Carberry, the head of the securities fraud unit at the time of Boesky's arrest, joined the private sector on October 1, 1987. Bruce Baird, who succeeded Carberry and who provoked extraordinary criticism from various combatants, was hired by the Washington-based law firm of Covington & Burling in the summer of 1989.

Rudolf Giuliani resigned as U.S. attorney for the Southern District on January 31, 1989, and became a partner at White & Case and later at Anderson Kill, both New York law firms. To no one's surprise, he ran for mayor of New York, easily winning the Republican primary against Ronald Lauder. In the general election, Giuliani lost to David Dinkins, but his showing was better than expected, boding well for his political future.

Currently, the smart money is betting that Giuliani will run for the U.S. Senate in 1992 against Alphonse D'Amato, the Republican incumbent who has boosted the concept of "politics as usual." But if, as some claim, he is an easy target for Giuliani, he won't be an easy opponent—D'Amato has a reputation as a tough fighter and there is little love lost between the two.

John Shad, the head of the SEC, became the head of Drexel Burnham in April 1989, a post that he resigned in August 1990. Gary Lynch, the head of the enforcement division, joined the New York law firm of Davis, Polk & Wardwell.

On Wall Street, Dennis Levine received a two-year sentence and currently heads a New York–based advisory firm called Adasar. As for the two men he implicated, his friend Robert Wilkis was sentenced to a year and a day in jail, while Ivan Boesky served approximately two years of his three-year term.

Among the major figures that Boesky fingered, Marty Siegel bought a multi–million–dollar house in Florida after pleading guilty to two insider trading charges and was eventually sentenced to two months in prison. Siegel, as part of his cooperation with prosecutors, implicated Robert Freeman, Richard Wigton, and Timothy Tabor of trading on inside information provided by him.

Freeman left Goldman Sachs in August 1989, at the time of his decision to plead guilty; his firm has not been penalized by either the

U.S. attorney's office or the SEC. Wigton has remained on Kidder Peabody's payroll since May 1987 when the prosecutors dropped the original charges against him, while Tabor left Merrill Lynch following his arrest.

Boyd Jeffries, also fingered by Boesky, pleaded guilty to two felonies and was sentenced to five years probation—he is teaching golf to kids in Aspen, Colorado (seriously). Jeffries, in turn, implicated Salim Lewis and James Sherwin. Lewis, an arbitrageur pleaded guilty to three felonies for manipulating the stock price of American Express in May 1986, and was sentenced to three years of community service. Sherwin, vice-chairman of GAF Corporation, was convicted of stock manipulation after two mistrials. Sherwin's boss, Sam Heyman, was identified as an unindicted co-conspirator, which is theoretically self-explanatory.

Ivan Boesky also implicated John Mulheren, the head of Jaime Securities and the godfather of one of his children. Mulheren, the only person accused by the former arbitrageur who chose to face trial, was convicted on one count of conspiracy and three counts of parking; the jury deadlocked on the remaining twenty-six charges. At the time of this writing, he is awaiting sentencing.

As is Michael Milken. After three and a half years of arguing his innocence, Milken pleaded guilty to six felonies and paid $600 million, a settlement very similar to that of his firm. And he faces up to twenty-eight years in prison.

What if Milken had instead fought his case in court, and won? He could "probably create the most powerful bank in the world," one investment banker speculated a few weeks before the plea bargain. "He could raise $10 billion in equity in a week." I don't doubt it. And with $10 billion in equity, "The Bank of Milken" would control $200 billion in assets. Just imagine.

But when the imagining is done, there is the reality that Michael Milken's chances in court would have been slim. To begin with, this is the wrong time to be a Wall Street defendant, especially if you're the defendant who, in many people's eyes, represents everything that went wrong with Wall Street. Especially if you're the defendant who made $550 million in one year.

The average panel of jurors, each of whom earns less in a year than Milken earned in an hour, would find it hard to comprehend that anyone could earn that much legally. And whether they're right or wrong, they're still the jury.

Then there is the evidence. The prosecution would have played to the jury's suspicions of greed by highlighting the partnerships, particularly MacPherson Partners. It was a partnership with all the elements—a prosecutor's dream, and for good reason. MacPherson was a phantom, allegedly created without the firm's knowledge, and used to hold the lucrative warrants from the Storer Communications buyout.

According to a senior executive at Drexel, a chunk of these warrants was sold to one client, who soon after resold them to Milken's department. The high-yield bond department then sold these warrants to MacPherson Partners, without offering them to the firm as required. The profit to the partners, by my guesstimate, was $55 million, based on figures provided both in the MacPherson partnership agreement and in the ammended SCI Equity Associates agreement, and on the alleged profit mentioned in an August 25, 1989 article in *The New York Times*.

There are two other allegations: (1) MacPherson's limited partners included key players at important client companies who were allowed to benefit *personally* from the Storer warrants; (2) Milken set aside some 40 percent of these warrants for the benefit of his three children, as suggested by a *Wall Street Journal* article on August 28, 1989.

Once the prosecutors had finished with MacPherson, and the other several hundred partnerships, they would have moved on to the charges in the first indictment, which were considered in an earlier chapter. The lead witness would have been Ivan Boesky who would have repeated the allegations he had made in 1986.

Michael Davidoff, Boesky's chief trader, would have been called to the stand to discuss the 1985 trades he conducted, allegedly on Milken's instructions.

Setrag Mooradian would have testified about the ledgers he kept that recorded the profits and losses on transactions said to be related to Drexel. He would have explained to the jury what the various categories and figures signified, what he meant by cryptic entries such as: "they owe us (4627000-)," implying a loss of $4,627,000.

Charles Thurnher, Milken's administrative head, and Cary Maultasch, who handled equity trades for Milken, would have been asked to corroborate details of the various allegations.

For color, the prosecutor could have entered into evidence such documents as a December 18, 1984 memorandum from Lance Lessman to his boss, Ivan Boesky. It reads in part:

I received a call from a guy named Alan B—— at the relevant firm. He refused to discuss face value numbers with me indicating that he felt that these things were better discussed by his king and my king.

The jury would also have been asked to consider charges that were not in the original indictment, including Milken's involvement with David Solomon. The key witnesses here would have been Solomon himself and Drexel's Terren Peizer, who reportedly alerted investigators in late 1988 to alleged schemes that supposedly would help Solomon avoid taxes and that allowed Milken's department to take advantage of some of Solomon's clients. Evidently, Peizer also provided the government with a spreadsheet that included figures on the suspect tax trades.

The prosecutors might also have accused Milken of an alleged tax evasion scheme with Columbia Savings & Loan, by far the largest junk-bond owner among the nation's three thousand thrifts. This allegation was made by Drexel's Jim Dahl, who received immunity.

Milken's defense attorneys, some of the best in the country, would naturally have attempted to discredit the witnesses, virtually all of whom had plea-bargained their testimony for favorable treatment by the prosecutors. As for the written evidence, they would try to dismiss it as irrelevant or inconclusive.

And they almost certainly would have lost, buried under the tremendous wealth of their client, the apparent logic underlying the allegations against him, the testimony of customers and key employees, the ledger sheets regarding transactions with Boesky and Solomon, and the weight of more than one hundred charges.

So Milken settled. But his agreement with the government, reached after forty-one months, raised several questions: At what point does the public have the right to learn the truth, to hear both sides of a story that had dominated the financial world? At what point do the prosecutors have a *responsibility* to take their case to court?

And where is the line that separates a settlement from an injustice? At least in one aspect of Michael Milken's case, that line was crossed: The seventeen-count indictment against his brother was dropped as part of the settlement.

The government should never allow a man's brother to be a bargaining chip, a hostage to a deceptive higher purpose. If the prosecutors truly believed the allegations against Lowell Milken, they should have pursued those allegations; if not, they should never have brought the charges in the first place. This is a simple standard of justice.

Here's another question that may seem absurd in view of Michael Milken's settlement: Was he guilty? There are those who no doubt believe that Milken never broke the law, that he was forced to plead guilty with a gun at his head, a shotgun with a RICO indictment in one barrel and a poisoned public opinion in the other.

Once his sentence—unknown at this writing—is served, his public relations people will probably intensify their image-building campaign. Mike Milken will be presented as the gifted entrepreneur who shook up the status quo, and was, in effect, railroaded into jail. The accusations against him will be dismissed as overblown or untrue, as petty allegations that in any event were irrelevant to his extraordinary success or as schemes that he was too intelligent to risk his career for.

Some of these arguments may well be valid, but as brilliant and as motivated as Milken is, as unnecessary as these alleged crimes were, the evidence seems convincing.

The bitter irony is that, of all the powerful enemies in the wings, perhaps the only one who could have destroyed Milken was Milken himself. If the prosecutors did indeed hold a gun to his head, the bullets were provided by him. When the SEC investigated him during the early 1980s, he didn't recognize the implications. He didn't raise his department above suspicion; instead, the record says, he took part in illegal schemes.

"Am I a good man or a bad man?" is a question asked by Anthony Hopkins in the film *The Elephant Man*—it is a question that people try to apply to Mike Milken even though they couldn't answer it about themselves. Milken is as complex as the average person, and then some. He is brilliant, naive, ruthless, compassionate, selfish, and generous. He is a man who appears to be motivated by extraordinary greed who spent almost nothing on himself and who contributed almost $200 million to charity in 1987 alone.

He was, in the words of a friend, "a great screamer, a great belittler," but he was also a boss who was concerned about his people as people. He worked eighteen hours a day, yet he cared deeply about his family. "He was one of those guys who focused on different parts of the financial services industry, and became the absolute best at them—trader, salesman, corporate finance, M&A," said a West Coast investment banker, who added, "He's probably the best lawyer in the country today." But when it came to his own case, he refused to accept the inevitable.

"Mike Milken was a decent man," said one of his traders, "but the world and history will view him as the plague." "He was always fair, always challenging, always asked about your family," said another member of the fourth floor. "He had it right."

But, of course, in some important respects he did not. His obsession with success colored his judgment, and his sense of invincibility colored it further. He took great risks, and when those risks threatened to ruin him, he invoked the loyalty of ten thousand employees. He learned from history how much one man can accomplish, but he ignored or was oblivious of the antagonism one man can provoke and the damage one man can cause his followers.

Milken began the process that ended with the firm's collapse, but it was senior management, particularly Fred Joseph, that must accept the responsibility for the decisions of the final years. Perhaps the top executives could not have known of illegalities in Milken's department. Certainly, they should have known enough about the dark side of Milken's tactics to be concerned in the wake of Boesky's arrest, and to be eager to settle with the government. But they also didn't want to lose the golden goose, and when it was lost, they didn't want to adjust to a new reality. Their mistakes were honest ones, but those employees who lost their jobs and their savings might not care about that distinction.

It's easy to question decisions after the fact, but one thing that few people would question was whether Fred Joseph cared about his firm. He may have had, in the words of one corporate finance officer, "a magical belief that he could charm, talk, work his way out of anything, a feeling of manifest destiny that he could prevail." Or perhaps in his dealings with the rainmakers, he was, as one salesman argued, "never able to say no—he couldn't see through a good line of bullshit."

But he also represented Drexel with tremendous grace under pressure and his priorities were clear. And although he was wrong about the firm's chances in January 1990, he wasn't deceitful: he took his entire bonus in preferred stock, and exercised options to buy common stock as did four other members on the board of directors. One month later, the value of that stock was decimated by Drexel's bankruptcy.

For all the criticism that Fred Joseph has received over the last year and a half, if Mike Milken had Fred's stricter view of the law, Drexel Burnham would currently be the premier firm on Wall Street. There would have been no investigation, no *reason* for an investigation. By the end of this year, the firm's profits might have reached $1 billion, and its influence would have been immeasurable. Rather than fighting the Establishment, the firm probably would have reconfigured it, and joined it.

Instead Drexel Burnham is out of business and Michael Milken is facing sentencing on six felonies. And even now, it's hard to believe, and hard not to believe in him. We all realized that Milken was a once-in-a-lifetime phenomenon, an aggressive visionary who we felt would never be so self-destructive as to do what he evidently did.

As one Drexel executive noted, if every allegation against Michael Milken were true, he still *legally* earned $530 million of his $550 million bonus for 1986.

The firm I joined in June 1981 was very different from the firm I left in September 1989, but one thing hadn't changed: it was a good place to work. More than that, it was a *better* place to work, better than any other on Wall Street.

And when Drexel collapsed, the Street was quick to hire the majority of our investment bankers and traders and salesmen and analysts. But the world wasn't such a friendly place for those in the back office, the men and women who key-punched the trades or sent out the dividend checks or delivered the securities or made sure that each trade balanced at the end of the day. Such administrative jobs were already filled throughout the Street.

And worse, the investments that all the employees had in their firm, the shares of stock that they had earned in Drexel's profit-sharing plan or bought each year with their savings, were destroyed. "There were rapacious people who just raped the place," said one salesman, "but there were also secretaries and clerks and other folks whose nest eggs went up in smoke." And while The Great Acquisitor received more in his January 1990 bonus than the average family will earn in one hundred years, thousands of regular people took overnight losses that totaled in the hundreds of millions. Said one trader to his colleague, "I will never have the financial security that I had two years ago."

The final words belong to I. W. Burnham, who founded the firm on April 1, 1935. "The securities business has always been people and capital," he wrote in September 1988. "This firm has always had both, and today we have more wonderful people and more capital than ever before in the past. We will certainly be able to withstand the storm and come out with flying colors."

And so we should have.

INDEX

accountability, 231
Ackerman, Peter, 192
Advertising, 127
A.E. Staley, 60–61
American Brands, 29
American Can, 33
American Express, 221, 234
American Natural Resources, 65
American Stock Exchange, 108
AM International, 136
annual default rate, 223
anti-Semitism, 9, 36
Apache Petroleum, 37–38
Arseneault, Jack, 144, 228
Asquith, Paul, 189

Bachelor, Herb, 155
Baird, Bruce, 141, 144, 145, 158,
    216, 226, 230

Baker, James, 105
banks, 34–35
BCI Holdings, 132
Bear Stearns, 38
Beatrice Companies, 29, 33, 58,
    132
Berenson, Jeffrey, 223
Bergerac, Michel, 47
Bernstein, Richard, 83
Bidermann Group, 191
Bilirakis, Michael, 131
Birsch, Phil, 46
Black, Leon, 155
Blacks, 77
Blakey, G. Robert, 226
block trading, 75
Boesky, Ivan, 1, 33, 65–68,
    118–121, 123–126, 139, 141,
    148–150, 157, 161–174,

179–180, 202, 203, 209, 213–215, 228, 232–235

bonds, 117, 190
  Chinese paper, 22
  convertible, 25
  fallen angels, 22
  high-grade, 39, 57
  high-grade corporate, 117
  high-yield, 21–26, 34, 39–40, 117, 186–189, 194
  junk, 7, 22, 23, 25–26, 29, 34, 57, 60, 116, 123, 126, 133, 186, 188–189, 194, 196, 210, 221–223, 236
  municipal and government, 117
  Treasury, 22, 222
The Boston Globe, 196
Boyum, Paul, 25
Brady, Nicholas, 37
Brenner, Howard, 155
bridge loans, 191
Briloff, Abraham, 58
Brooks, John, 115
Bruck, Connie, 47, 63
Buffalo News, 84
Buffett, Warren, 84
Burnham, Isaac Wolfe (I.W.), 11, 63, 77, 139, 239
Burnham and Co., 12, 13, 208
buyouts *see* takeovers

cable television, 16, 83
Cahill, Gordon & Reindel, 120, 131
Campbell Soup, 12
Campeau, Robert, 196
Campeau Corp., 37, 196, 223
Carberry, Charles, 141, 233
Carroll, John, 142, 154, 164, 171, 201, 232
Cathcart, Silas, 125
Causey, Charlie, 23

Chemical Bank, 31, 82
Chevron, 32
Chiat/Day, 127
Chicago Board of Trade, 111
Chicago Mercantile Exchange, 110
Churchill, Winston, 5
Citibank, 196
Citicorp, 111
Cities Service, 31
Clark, Howard L., 83, 224
Cluett Peabody, 191–192
coercion, 60
Cohen, Saul, 182
Columbia Savings & Loan, 236
C.O.M.B., 157, 175, 176, 232
Comcast Corp., 167
commissions, 80, 84, 86, 184
computerized trading, 86, 225
Conable, Barber, 79
ConAgra, 29
confidence, 145–147, 188
Conoco, 30
Corrigan, Gerald, 200
Crovitz, L. Gordon, 227
Crown Zellerbach, 65
cumulative default rate, 222–223
Curnin, tom, 154

Dahl, Jim, 26, 60, 149, 186, 228, 236
D'Amato, Alphonse, 233
Davidoff, Michael, 164, 228, 235
default rate, 222–223
Delaware, 36
Diamond Shamrock, 137, 162–163, 232
Dingell, John, 130–131, 134, 157
Disney Co., 32
Dorrance family, 12
double leverage, 220
Drexel Burnham Lambert
  and anti-Semitism, 9, 36

bankruptcy, 200
chronology of events, xiii-xv
client confidence, 145–147
commercial paper, 196–197, 199, 200, 210
corporate finance department, 2, 186
downfall, 198–200
equity department, 69–80, 184–186
ethics, 53–57
fictional dialogue with client, 88–101
government charges, 136–154
government investigation, 116–135, 215
history, 11–13, 208
institutional equity department, 2
institutional fixed income department, 2
layoffs, 1–9, 183
limited partnerships, 130
lobbying, 127
loss of Milken, 217–219
mistakes, 211–221
as most profitable Wall Street firm, 39, 41
municipal bond department, 3
in 1989, 181–197, 210
and October 1987 crash, 106–107, 112, 116
partnerships, 130, 211–213
relations with press, 120
relations with Salomon Brothers, 38–39
relations with Wall Street, 34–38
risk arbitrage department, 2
settlement terms, 154–157, 181–183, 195
stock offerings, 81–82

superclass within, 58
trading floor, 77, 184
West Coast office, 17–19, 48–49, 64
see also specific employees
Drexel Burnham Lambert Group, 198–199
Drexel Burnham Lambert Trading Corp., 199
Drexel Firestone, 12, 208
Du Pont, 30

Eckart, Dennis, 131
Edgcomb Metals, 193
E.F. Hutton, 224
entertainment, 78–79
equity kickers, 25
Esmark, 29
Executive's Guide to Business Law, 122

Farley, Bill, 82, 190–191
Federal Reserve, 9, 103, 108–110
Federated Department Stores, 37, 196
felonies, 3
Finsbury Fund, 204, 205
Firestone Tire, 12
First Boston, 37, 192, 196, 223
Fischbach Corp., 118, 156, 157, 161 162, 163 165, 202, 205, 232
Fleming, Peter, 148
Flight Transportation, 83
Flynn, John T., 114
foreign stocks, 3, 185
Forstmann, Theodore, 9, 221
Fortune, 109
free enterprise system, 11
Freeman, Robert, 124, 125, 213, 230, 233
freezing of assets, 145

Fridella, Jeff, 142, 232–233
Fruit of the Loom, 82

GAF Corp., 33, 111, 234
General Electric, 125, 223
General Motors, 111
Getnick, Neil, 227
Getty Oil, 37
Gibson Greetings, 28
Gillette Co., 118
Giuliani, Rudolf, 5, 140–144, 148, 151, 155, 185, 209, 216, 217, 225–228, 233
Glasser, Ira, 225
Glass-Steagal Act, 213
Golden Books, 83
Golden Nugget, 136, 162, 203
Goldman Sachs, 111, 124, 125, 193, 213, 230, 233
Goldsmith, Sir James, 31, 65
Goodbye, Darkness, 140
Graham, Benjamin, 86
Grand, Paul, 144, 228
Great Depression, 114, 116
Greater Fool Theory, 104, 112
Greenspan, Alan, 108–110
Green Tree Acceptance Inc., 24–25
Groupe Bruxelles Lambert, 14, 154, 197
Gulf Oil, 31–32
Gutfreund, John, 99–100

Hancock, William, 122
Hansen, Mark, 228–229, 233
Harriman, Edward, 12
Harris Graphics, 136, 156, 157, 168–169, 232
Hartley, Keith, 25, 33
Healy, David, 71
hedge funds, 73
Helmerich & Payne, 203, 205

Heymann, Sam, 33, 234
High-Yield Bond Conference, 40
Hills, Roderick, 182
Hoffman, Robert, 60
holding company, 198
Hollander, Nancy, 161

Icahn, Carl, 31, 33, 65, 67, 118, 126
ideas, 10–11
illegal profits, repayment of, 170–173
immunity from prosecution, 149
inflation, 27
Ingersoll, Ralph, 24
insider trading, 7, 65, 132, 136, 166–170, 178
institutional investors, 85–86
insurance, 107–108, 183
Integrated Resources, 193
investment banking, 35–37, 85

Jacobs, Irv (the Liquidator), 31
Japan, 43
Jeffries, Boyd, 118, 234
Jews, 9, 13, 22, 36
Johnston, Moira, 67
Jones, Lisa Ann, 229–230
Joseph, Fred, 1–4, 13–14, 16, 38, 46–47, 52, 57, 61, 77, 119–120, 123, 128–134, 138, 139, 143, 150–152, 155, 156, 181, 182, 186, 188, 190, 195, 198, 200, 210–213, 215, 218, 231, 238, 239
Joseph, Steve, 47, 55, 117, 154
J.P. Stevens, 192
JPS Textile, 192
junk bonds see bonds
Justice Department, 7, 148, 154, 227

Kane, Arthur, 112
Kellogg Co., 111
Kelly, Donald, 29
Kerkorian, Kirk, 169
Kidder Peabody, 61, 124, 125, 223, 234
Kirsch, Arthur, 71, 195
Kissick, John, 155
Koerner, Gerald, 25
Kohlberg Kravis Roberts and Co., 29, 33, 58, 137, 166–167, 187–188
Kravis, Henry, 188

Lazard Freres, 65
leaks, 231
Lear Petroleum, 177
LeBow, Ben, 192
Lefcourt, Gerald, 231
Lehman Brothers, 23–24
Lenin, Vladimir, 11
Lent, Norman, 131
Lessman, Lance, 235
leveraged buyouts, 28–29, 61–62, 178–179
Levine, Dennis, 64–65, 123, 124, 141, 150, 171, 173, 179, 209, 228, 233
Lewis, Salim, 234
Liman, Arthur, 201, 205
Lindner, Carl, 82
Linton, Robert, 119, 139, 182
loans, 34–35, 191
Lodestar Group, 191
Lorenzo, Frank, 82
Lorimar, 136, 139, 156, 178, 232
Lutheran Life, 132
Lynch, Gary, 128, 138, 158, 181, 227, 231, 233

MacPherson Partners, 153, 235
Macy's, 37, 42

Malamed, Leo, 110
Manchester, William, 140
Manne, Henry, 231
Markey, Ed, 137
Mattel, 176–177, 232
Maultasch, Cary, 138, 149, 159, 170, 178, 228, 235
Maxxam Group, 136, 156, 167–168, 232
MCA, 136, 156, 157, 162, 163–165, 203, 205, 232
McCarthy, Allan, 11
McCaw Cellular Communications, 83
McClellan, John, 226
MCI Communications, 57
Memorex, 193
Merger Mania, 67
mergers, 66
Merrill Lynch, 65, 112, 117, 187, 223, 234
Mesa Petroleum, 31
Metromedia, 57, 82
Mexico, 103
Meyer, Tony, 13–14, 47, 52
MGM, 137, 156, 169–170, 232
Milken, Lowell, 138, 150, 164, 177, 236
Milken, Michael, 21–29
  and bank loans, 35
  credibility, 154
  deals, 52–57, 62
  and Drexel partnerships, 212
  driving forces, 45
  ethics, 53–57, 64, 119
  firing of, 5, 152, 158, 186, 217–219
  government charges, 136–140, 159–180
  government investigation of, 118, 119, 120, 129, 213, 214

guilty plea, 200–207, 228,
    234–237
heavy side, 40–43
at High-Yield Bond Conference,
    40
income, 44
indictment, 5, 6, 159–180, 232
market share ambitions, 51
as most influential financier in
    free world, 44
personal characteristics, 45–47,
    237–238
physical appearance, 22
push-to-wall pattern, 60
and Salomon Brothers, 38–39
stamina, 46
stock offerings, 81–82
subordinates, 49–51
and takeovers, 32–33
as top man at Drexel, 39
trading favors, 63
typical day, 48–49
on West Coast, 24, 64
when thwarted, 59–60
Minella, Ray, 223
Minerals & Resources, 99–100
Monzert, Pamela, 138
Moody's, 21, 24
Mooradian, Setrag, 150–151,
    170–172, 228, 235
Morgan, J.P., 12, 192
mortgage-backed securities, 117
Muhammed Ali Arcades, 81
Mulheren, John, 234
Murdoch, Rupert, 57, 82
Music Television (MTV), 83
mutual funds, 108

Nasar, Sylvia, 109
National Can, 33
National Gypsum, 137
Navistar, 37

Newberg, Bruce, 54, 144,
    149–150, 159, 175, 176, 177,
    228, 229, 231
Newscorp, 57
New York Stock Exchange, 75,
    108, 110, 113
New York Times, 126
Nixon, Richard, 31
Nixon administration, 12
Northwestern Bell, 226
Northwest Industries, 191

Occidental Petroleum, 54–55, 137,
    156, 162–163
Odyssey Partners, 193
Ohio Mattress, 192, 196, 223
Once in Golconda, 115
organized crime, 226
overfunding, 63
over-the-counter trading, 76

Pacific Lumber, 156, 167–168
Paradyne, 72
Paramount Petroleum, 192
Parker, Diane, 145
parking see stock parking
Peizer, Terren, 149, 159, 186, 236
Peltz, Nelson, 31, 33
Penn Central, 193
Pennsylvania Engineering, 136,
    161
Pennzoil, 37
Perelman, Ron, 31, 33, 65,
    99–100
Phelan, Richard, 106
Phelps Dodge, 71
Philip Morris, 71
Phillips Petroleum, 32–33, 65,
    137, 156, 157, 165–166, 232
Pickens, Boone, 31–32, 36
Piper Jaffrey, 37
Pittman, Bob, 83

Podell, Bertram, 141
Pollack, Milton, 153, 156, 195
portfolio insurance, 107–108
position trading, 76
Posner, Victor, 118, 161, 202
Prime Computer, 192
Princeton/Newport, 144–145,
    149, 175, 176, 177, 210,
    216, 227–230
Professional Investor Group, 2
Proxmire, William, 127

Racketeer Influenced Corrupt
    Organizations (RICO), 5, 7,
    142–148, 151, 154, 155, 160,
    185, 206, 209–210, 215–217,
    225–229, 231, 237
RCA, 28
Read, Dillon, 36
Reagan, Ronald, 27, 108
Reagan administration, 105
real estate investment trusts
    (REITs), 23
reconciling books, 166
Regan, Jay, 230
Reidy, John, 83
REITs see real estate investment
    trusts
Reliance Co., 82
repayment trades, 163–165
Resorts International, 193
retail sales, 3–4, 183–184, 210,
    219–220
Revlon, 33, 65
Ribstein, Larry, 231
Rich, Marc, 216
Richie, Lionel, 130
RICO see Racketeer Influenced
    Corrupt Organizations
risk arbitrage, 66–67
RJR Nabisco, 187–188, 192, 218
Robinson, James, 224

Rogers, Jimmy, 109
Rogers, Will, 8
Romano, Benito, 159
Ryder, Chris, 46

Safire, William, 226
St. Joe Mineral case, 153
salesmanship, 42–43
salespeople, 3–4, 72–80, 83–86
Salomon Brothers, 38–39,
    99–101, 111
Saul, Ralph, 182
savings and loans, 194–195, 210
Scalia, Antonin, 226
Schneiderman, Irwin, 131
Schultz, David, 221
SCI Equity Associates, 235
Seagram's, 30
SEC see Securities and Exchange
    Commission
Securities and Exchange Acts, 114,
    121–122, 131, 147, 225, 227
Securities and Exchange
    Commission (SEC), 3, 9, 19,
    114, 116, 118, 122, 125,
    126, 128–131, 133, 136–140,
    149, 155, 168, 170, 173,
    178, 181, 182, 198–199, 209,
    212, 213, 220, 225, 231, 237
Securities Investor Protection
    Corporation, 155
self-dealing in after market, 133
sell-side analysts, 71–74
Shad, John, 13, 182, 233
shareholders, 5
Shearson Lehman Hutton, 37,
    111, 223, 224
Sheehy, Gail, 140
Sher, Alan, 155
Sherwin, James, 234
Shields, Mark, 79
short stocks, 73

Siegel, Burt, 45, 148, 149, 152, 154, 155, 197
Siegel, Marty, 61, 124, 233
Sikorski, Gerry, 131
Simon, William, 28
Slattery, Jim, 131, 132
small technology stocks, 81
Smoot-Hawley Tariff Bill, 114
Solomon, David, 204, 205, 236
Solomon Asset Management Co., 204
Soros, George, 112
Standard & Poor's, 21, 24, 220
Stein, Benjamin, 221
Steinberg, Saul, 31, 32, 82
stock market *see* Wall Street
stock parking, 122, 161–162, 165–166, 168–169, 176–177, 229
Stone Container, 137, 156, 157, 174–175, 232
Storer Broadcasting, 153, 156, 166–167, 232, 235

Tabor, Timothy, 124, 230, 233–234
takeovers, 26–33, 36, 61–62, 66–67, 127, 166–168, 189, 210–211
see also specific companies
Tax Act of 1981, 27
Tax loss trades, 156, 165, 177, 232
Telepictures, 136, 139, 178
Telex, 83
Texaco, 37
Texas Air, 42
Texstyrene, 132, 133
Third World, 43, 103
Thurnher, Charles, 128, 170, 172, 173, 235
Tome, Guisseppe, 153

trading favors, 62–63
travel, 78–79
Trepp, Warren, 188
Turner, Ted, 83
Turner Broadcasting, 137, 169–170
TWA, 33

United Airlines, 196
United Artists, 137, 156, 169–170, 232
Unocal, 36–37
U.S. Attorney's Office, 3, 116, 140
U.S. Home, 176, 232
U.S. Steel, 111

Vanguard Mutual Fund, 132
Viacom, 137, 156, 178–179, 232

Wall Street
  deals, 83–87
  ideas as product of, 10–11
  money-making process, 70
  October 1987 crash, 102–115
  relations with Drexel, 34–38
  retrenchment, 224
  trading favors, 62–63
Wall Street Journal, 41, 119–120, 125, 138, 230
Warner Communications, 42
warrants, 25, 57–59, 153–154, 235
Washington Post, 137, 231
WASPs (white Anglo-Saxon Protestants), 13, 22
Wasserstein, Bruce, 37
Welch, Jack, 125
Wesray, 28
Western Capital, 132
West Germany, 105

West Point-Pepperel, 190–192, 219
Wickes Companies, 137, 156, 173–174, 232
Wigton, Richard, 124, 230, 233–234
Wilkis, Robert, 65, 233
Will, George, 11
William D. Witter, 14

Wolfe, Tom, 109
women, 78
Wood, Kimba, 200–201, 205
Wyatt, Oscar, 65
Wyden, Ron, 131
Wynn, Steve, 130

Zarzecki, Charles, 144, 149, 175, 228